Praise for *PLAY HIM PLAY HER*

"The author expertly weaves together the worlds of fame,
deceit, affairs, family, and the dark side of the entertainment
industry in a way that will keep readers on the edge of their seats.
…a captivating and thrilling read."
– Hayley Hammersley, Amazon Reviewer

"Claire Stibbe's latest psychological thriller is the work of a
brilliant novelist at the top of her game. The literary device of the
unreliable narrator is groundbreaking… it would make great TV."
– Mark Stibbe, bestselling author of *The House of Dreams*

"This is my first book by this author,
and it most certainly won't be my last…fast-paced,
gripping…keeps you on the edge of your seat."
– Cosykindler, Amazon Reviewer

"…just brilliant…one of those stories that's so deep and rich…
I absolutely would never have guessed the ending."
– Amorina.carlton, Goodreads Reviewer

"This was such a fantastic book, one of my favourite reads this
year…it's intense, dark and unnerving, I didn't want it to end."
– Ericas_bookreviews

"I love this author. I've read a few of her books
now and she is a top favourite for me."
– Afelton6212

"If you're looking for the perfect thriller, this is exactly
what you need to read…the ending, wow."
– Reading.runes

"…I couldn't put it down. It's so atmospheric and tense
and left me breathless and desperately wanting more."
– Fiction_vixen18

"What a clever, intricate, sophisticated thriller.
The premise was unlike any other thriller I've read.
I never saw that plot twist coming either."
– Betweenkirstyscovers

PLAY
HIM
PLAY
HER

CLAIRE STIBBE

Berkely Square Books

Library of Congress Control Number: 2 0 2 4 9 3 6 9 7 8

979-8-9904871-2-3 (hardcover)
979-8-9904871-1-6 (paperback)
979-8-9904871-0-9 (eBook)

Cover illustration by Jane Dixon-Smith.
Script © Claire Stibbe.
Editing by David Imrie and Sandra Mangan

To receive special offers, bonus content, and
info on new releases and other great reads,
sign up for our newsletter
www.claire-stibbe.com

An artist's only concern is to shoot for some kind of perfection,
and on his own terms, not anyone else's.

J. D. Salinger.

PROLOGUE

Two teenagers cross the footbridge at the railway station and follow the sea wall path to Langstone Rock. Oystercatchers and waders feed at the water's edge, hunkering down against the biting winds, and seagulls scream overhead. As daylight bleeds into evening, they walk beneath the wave-eroded arch, hoping to go deeper into the caves where they can smoke and drink unseen. The sound of flies and a persistent smell causes them to cover their mouths.

Before they abandon their plan, the beam from their torch shudders and comes to life. A flash of butter yellow clothing, shredded at the bodice reveals greenish-black skin. The back of her head is a gnarled mess of blood and hair, and a crab nestles in her upturned hand. One boy backs away while the other stares at the shiny watch on her wrist, its face strangely intact. A drowning. Perhaps a fall from a boat.

The flow and ebb of the tide may have jostled her this far. Now she rests under Aeolian sandstone, hidden within sea stacks and caves. When a breeze ruffles the rock pool, strands of her hair roll and swell. She is as much part of the putrefying effluvia as the surrounding algae.

Instantly, they run from the stench towards the gaping mouth of the cave. Outside, they shake and retch, two shapes hunkering on the beach. They sit under a muddy sky, time warping and stretching, and one boy kicks and scuffs the sand as shock takes hold. The other fixes his gaze on the distant horizon, trying not to think about what he has seen.

By the time the police arrive, they can't speak. Forensics enter wearing waders, torches disturbing the cave's murk. Trucks and tape and lights spoil a secret hideaway. There's nothing to explain why she lies in the waters of Dawlish Bay.

For months to come, they will dream of her out there alone. They will wonder who she was and how she died. What she once looked like. They will lose sleep imagining if they ever passed her in the street or knew someone she knew. Despite the shock, they will search for her on the internet when they think about her.

When they finally know her name, she will become personal to them. She will live again in those few seconds, as if she is a long-lost friend.

PART I

THE CHARACTER

1

LILJA

Six months earlier.

There's something different about my husband.

It must have happened after the script for Season 2 arrived for Zane's Netflix series. It was the chirp of a text message on his phone, his hand shielding its illuminated face from me. He insisted it was his agent requesting a meeting the following day. When I spoke with her, she didn't know what the appointment was about and said how sorry she was for the misunderstanding. These discrepancies are like an ominous whisper in the back of my mind, an advertising jingle you can't shut off.

Sometimes the thought dissolves by the time I'm making breakfast or arranging flowers on the hall table, but it soon comes flooding back. The truth is, I have a bone-deep sense of unease that only Zane can bring.

Yesterday, I overheard him telling his therapist on the phone that there was a hole inside of him and he was afraid he'd never find the missing piece. It was a comment I found hard to take seriously. Yet there's a part of her that clings to this house like a shadow you pass on the stairs.

I squint at the TV, a neon square in the darkness, the high-end speakers whispering true crime. Zane lies half on the sofa and half on the ottoman, and the shadows on his naked back appear like two dunes separated by a tidal inlet. But with one notable feature; a faint scratch that stretches to the waistband of his shorts, like a scent marker left by another cat. He's on the wrong side of a fifth of Johnny Walker and I take his hand, the one not holding the bottle of whisky, and settle him on the couch.

'Let me take that,' I say.

He makes a sound, a cross between a firm no and a moan, and grips the bottle tighter.

'I'll put it on the floor. Right here next to you.'

This he accepts with a feeble nod and the bottle slips out of his hand and firmly into mine. As I watch him sleeping, it's no good pining for the past when the present will be so much better. My life has moved forward. Not his.

It's past 1.00 am and I wish I hadn't talked myself into binge watching twenty-year-old cold cases with their cliff-hanger endings while Zane posted pictures of himself on Twitter all evening. For someone who has many friends online, he has surprisingly few in real life.

He's also been sending emails from his computer to his therapist, Meggy Russell. Yet none of these sync to his phone. Let's say her therapy is unconventional. Zane has given her the code to our front gate as his dependence on her has intensified. When I ask him about her, he tells me she's simply his psychoanalyst – someone who taps into his subconscious and helps him return from the character he plays. It's a deep form of therapy, something I wouldn't understand.

Tap, ratta-tap-tap. Staccato, like a knuckle on glass.

I move towards the window. The house is set back from a country lane and half a mile from the nearest main road. A narrow drive running through an avenue of beach trees connects it to an electronic gate and I doubt anyone vaulted over it, not without the shriek of alarms.

Barton Manor is a grade two listed Georgian house, sitting on a ten-acre plot. There is a large circular window on the landing, looking out over green lawns and Italian cypress trees. On the south side, is a large duck pond with weeping willows and apple trees, and a ha-ha — a sunken wall, which provides a boundary from grazing deer.

My sister and I spent our childhood here, skilfully steering our tricycles between the box hedges and sailing grandpa's homemade model yacht on the pond. I feel a surge of determination, like a marine defending his homeland. *The house is a part of me. I will protect it.*

The cameras pick up every movement — one hundred feet of illumination equal to the camera's field of vision — and I check notifications for the front of the house.

Motion. Front Gate 12.43 PM.

Motion. Front Gate 1.05 AM.

Watching the video, I realise the settings for the perimeters are too wide. Have passing cars in the lane triggered the sensors? I sort through the sounds, dripping gutter, gurgling drain, husband snorting in the throes of a dream.

I'm thirty-nine, he's forty-five and reminds me of a classic movie you have to re-watch, a comforting slice of nostalgia. He styles his salt and pepper hair in a crew cut and buys expensive colognes. These signs have tripped my alarm. If I point it out, he tells me to get a life and to stop finding things to stoke my jealousy.

He stops breathing for a second before exhaling, plunging into a slow-wave sleep. There is something liberating about it, the depth of it, like a sinkhole in the sand pulling him out to sea. Part of me wishes he'd float to Orcombe point and along the Jurassic coast, never to be seen again. The next time I talk about starting a restaurant at a dinner party and he whispers in my ear 'Fat chance,' I'll laugh.

There's a loud thud. I look up at the ceiling and it sickens me that someone could be in my daughter's bedroom. As I run upstairs, my finger is poised on the emergency number. Her door is ajar and it's dark inside.

'Bizzy?' I whisper.

Every room has lofty ceilings and marble fireplaces, and my gaze slides to the open window where a stretch of moonlight angles over the bed. A pixie cut dyed blue at the ends frames her oval face and she has stronger bones than I do. She is an only child and so are her two best friends.

The book she was reading is now on the floor, the most obvious culprit. I remove her glasses and set them on the bedside table. She can sleep through anything.

Moonglow lends a bluish tinge to the drive which is puddle-strewn and deserted. But beyond the gate is a big-eyed Porsche crouching in the shadows. I check the live video on my phone. We get reporters even in sleet and snow, the worst kind of weather for that sort of palaver, but mostly at a Godly hour. Zane says all celebrities need privacy and security, both of which this house affords.

I take a note of the licence plate and return to the sitting room. 'Zane. There's a car outside.'

I await his usual dismissive tone; *It's just another sodding reporter. Ignore it.* But his snoring tells me he's too out of it to care.

His phone lights up again like an invitation. A number without a name. I slide the phone from between his fingers, convinced he'll grab my wrist, but there's not a flicker. The first text is from an undisclosed number which simply has an emoji — a yellow face with a monocle. It's a thinking face, but what is it thinking about?

The second from Meggy says: *Check your email.*

Her email message, which arrived early this morning, requests a meeting today. There's a brief paragraph about her wanting Zane to stop thinking he's alone and under attack. He is not the victim and Holloway is not the villain. She suggests he's giving another excellent performance and disowning all responsibility.

I replace the phone an inch shy of his fingers and go downstairs. When the door is closed, I'm not allowed in his study. That's the rule. He's either rehearsing lines or burying himself deep inside the character he plays. Since I keep spare keys, I have access to every lock.

An antique desk dominates the room, and first editions line many of the shelves, separated by ornaments and Victorian jewellery boxes. As I gaze at my grandfather's empty chair, a lump forms in my throat. He died over ten years ago, and yet I expect him to walk into the room with his familiar limp, his arms outstretched.

Lily! My Lily!

Zane's computer light blinks, stirring me to type in the login we've used for the past two years. When it doesn't work, prickles of doubt creep in, but not enough to distract me from unlocking the top drawer. There I find a small leather notebook with the words *Shit I Can't Remember* embossed across the front. It lists his most recent passwords.

The document open on his screen is marked PHPH SCRIPT. Perhaps it will shed light on where his mind is. There's no mistaking a handful of comments he's typed in the reviewing pane.

What is intravenous propofol?

Is it fast acting?

How long does it last?

High strength, water-proof gaffer tape.

Vacuum storage bag, 110 x 90 cm, airtight.

Somehow, I feel winded by it, a jab to the stomach I didn't expect. Keeping up to date with any revisions is vital to managing my small world, keeping me sane, one day at a time.

Zane tells me they're filming a new season of *Play Him, Play Her* on Bodmin Moor where he will camp out before filming to get a "feel" for the place. The scenes he is currently reading bring me a mix of fear and disgust.


```
FADE IN:


INT - A FLAT IN THE HEART OF LONDON'S
WEST END - DAY


AMAYA'S MEMORY: Amaya sits in a garret
room, writing a letter to Mr Holloway's
wife.


          AMAYA (V.O.)

     Dear Maura. I'm not asking for
     forgiveness. I'm asking for
```

<pre>
            help. You won't care that he's
            been threatening me or that
            I'm afraid for my life. If
            anything should happen to me,
            I want you to tell the police
            who did it.
</pre>

I didn't understand what method acting entailed or what it would mean for us. Zane dedicates hours, drawing on childhood memories to develop Holloway; a cosmetic surgeon who treats individuals with various disfigurements. Sounds good until you get to the serial killer part.

He speaks with an accent sometimes. No, not an accent, more an intonation to his words, as if reciting a line from Euripides' *Medea*. I remember hearing my first Greek play when I was fourteen, where the actors' voices struck me as otherworldly.

I read on.

<pre>
            FLASHCUT of dark sky and rain pelting
            the streets. Holloway stamps on a ciga-
            rette outside his house and climbs into
            a taxi bound for London's West End.

            EXT. IN A PARK OPPOSITE AMAYA'S FLAT
            - NIGHT

            Holloway looks up at her window, trying
            unsuccessfully to hide his rage. Her
            letter addressed to his wife is in his
            hand.

            NEW ANGLE - REVEALS AMAYA INSIDE, PACING

            She wears a trouser suit, hair neatly
            coiled. Anxious, she checks her phone
            and makes a call.
</pre>

```
         CLOSE ON

         Holloway's face, resisting the urge to
         answer his phone, walks towards the
         house at a fast clip. He presses the
         buzzer, and the door opens. Amaya, back-
         lit, stands motionless.

                    HOLLOWAY

              (holding up the letter)

         Now then, what's all this
         about?
```

When Zane smiles, it's always in his eyes, an imperceptible flicker of ruthlessness as if he enjoys seeing me flinch. Complaints about my "moods" are part of the game, only I don't have moods, merely quiet times where I process everything he says. I don't react and I don't look away and I ignore the sick feeling in the pit of my stomach.

Restoring everything to unread, I close the laptop, angling the mouse slightly to the right and level with the corner of his keypad. It's an important detail. There must be no evidence of tampering, not even an indentation in the chair cushion. His phone should receive no new login notifications since I've accessed everything from his devices.

The outside floodlights cut through the darkness and the terrace is lit like a stadium. I study a stand of trees at the south side of our property and beyond it a narrow country lane cutting into hills, typically speckled with sheep. There is no sign of anyone skulking behind the ornamental evergreens or the boxwoods along the path.

I follow every window to the front of the house. Nothing moves outside, except for a chalky vapour behind the front gate — exhaust from a departing car.

Replaying the outside CCTV footage from my phone reveals a

time stamp of two minutes ago and the grainy image of a woman.

Pause. Rewind. Play.

I look closer at the angle of her face, the curve of her cheek. I know she has light ash-brown hair, the type that goes blonde in the sun and I know she's tall — birdlike — pacing on slender legs. My gut always knows things before my mind does.

Meggy Russell is twenty-nine and has a degree in psychology from Exeter. Been a celebrity psychoanalyst for five years, preferred, if her credentials do her credit. I'm trying to make sense of this over the noise of my internal screaming. How many grainy frames must I go through to find more of her? The second thought is, what is so urgent it cannot wait until morning?

I hover between two choices. Call the police or find her number and confront her. But what's the point? She's long gone now, and the police will want a full-blown statement about how we know her. I can't risk the publicity.

A thin blade of dread passes through me at a thought that has niggled these past two weeks. Zane has a presence about him, a mood that I find unsettling. Is this slow metamorphosis acting? Or is he seduced by Holloway's predatory nature?

If it's the latter, it would make him dangerous.

2

ZANE

Why does it have to rain today? Big fat drops pounding against the windows. Last night, thunder and lightning kept me wake. Duvet on. Duvet off. Too bloody hot. That, and my restless wife, wandering about the house looking for intruders, as if one could get the better of our alarms.

Her text: *Could you ask Meggy to refrain from parking outside the house at night. It's creepy!* goes unanswered. I'm willing to forgive this serious lapse in judgement. She knows better than to interrupt my day with trivial domestic issues.

Thankfully, we're sitting in a rehearsal room and not sequestered in trailers that leak and smell of mould. It's the end of pre-production and we're doing the table read for season two's first episode of *Play Him, Play Her.* I play Holloway, where the respectable side of him is a renowned surgeon who treats burn victims. The seedy side is he's sleeping with a patient and putting his reputation at risk.

Quiana Thompson, my co-star, sits next to me. She is wearing stylish jeans, white trainers, and a navy blazer over a T-shirt. She plays Holloway's young love interest.

The director, Simon Berne, welcomes us. Short, tanned and with eyes glittering beneath soft, angled brows. He explores how intimate scenes can add meaning to the narrative and a lack of them interrupts the emotional flow.

'Who doesn't like sex?' he says, wiping a hand down a pair of cargo trousers that look like rejects from the *Indiana Jones* prop department. 'That doesn't mean viewers want to watch two people smash. It's about making the abstract tangible. Holloway must portray to the audience what he experiences.'

I think of the film *Don't Look Now*. Two grieving parents who have not been together romantically for a while resign from their guilt and make love. Beginning with a light touch, a little conversation, the scene cuts back and forth from passion to aftermath. It may not be as risqué as more recent films, which are awkward and sometimes badly done, but it's one of the most memorable scenes of its kind.

Nic sits opposite me with a bright red phone on her lap. I suspect, as protocol demands, the volume is off. She's nineteen, a would-be actor who is now working as an actor's assistant. She looks different today. Smaller. More fragile.

You like her, don't you?

I enjoy her face, the shape of it, and the way her mouth turns up when she smiles. She has shiny black hair and eyes darker than a mineshaft, and a dimple, just *one*. I suspect the muscles behave differently on the other side of her face.

There you go, thinking like a doctor.

The voice again. Not inside my head, but a few feet away. My eyes spiral upwards as if I can see the shape of a man emerging from a cluster of dust motes. I must be having a "greyout" – dots at the edge of my vision brought on by acute stress.

Nic grins at me. I'm embarrassed she may have heard my not-so internal monologue. Although we are doing a straight read today, my mind is out to lunch.

Getting into my head excites you, doesn't it? You want to live and breathe me. You want to be me.

I look around the table for a radio or an open mic and brush it aside in favour of Simon rousing Nic from staring at me and suggesting she read the scene headings.

"PLAY HIM, PLAY HER"

By

James English

FADE IN:

INT: HOSPITAL - DAY (DIMLY LIT)

PUSH IN.

A man sits on a leather chair. He is studying a room from his laptop. This is MR ETHAN HOLLOWAY, a world-renowned plastic surgeon, mid-forties trim, very attractive. He wears grey trousers, a navy shirt and tie.

CLOSE ON

On the laptop screen, a young woman lies in a hospital bed, admitted for second degree burns. The file reveals that her ex-boyfriend doused her legs in kerosene and set them alight. This is Holloway's patient. He records everything she does.

WITH HOLLOWAY - MOVING SHOT

HOLLOWAY'S POV - He walks down a corridor, entering the first door to his right and sits on the edge of an elevated bed.

A patient sleeps. This is AMAYA STONE, late teens, attractive. She wears a gown, her hair spilling down her shoulders.

                    She is hooked to fluids and her thighs
                    are covered with dressings.

I rest a hand on Quiana's arm and allow the lust I feel for Nic to seep into the scene.

                              HOLLOWAY

                    I didn't mean to startle you.
                    How are you feeling?

                               AMAYA

                    Not great.

                              HOLLOWAY

                    You look great. In fact, you
                    look amazing.

                               AMAYA

                    Do you flatter all your pa-
                    tients, doctor?

                              HOLLOWAY

                    Ethan. And no.

Quiana looks at me, an imperceptible twitch at the corner of her mouth. She's enjoying this as much as I am.

                              HOLLOWAY

                    Promise you won't agree to what
                    I'm proposing unless you want
                    to. After you leave, I'd like

                to see you again. There'll be
                no expectations. I don't want
                you to feel pressured. I'd
                hate myself if you did.

Quiana hesitates a beat and glances at me, a glance that lingers longer than it needs to.

                        AMAYA

                I thought you'd seen enough of
                me.

                        HOLLOWAY

                If I'm honest, it's your com-
                pany I crave. Do you trust me?

                        AMAYA

                        (softly)

                If a woman can't trust the man
                who healed her, who can she
                trust?

The scene veers to Marschōne Robinson, who plays Deandre Bryant, another surgeon in the practice. He appears lost, as if the lines he delivers are from another scene. Simon looks up and studies him for a moment and then everyone's looking at Marschōne as if he's grown two heads. He says, sorry, and flips several pages until he finds his place.

His exaggerated acting last season was laughably absurd. The scene where he threw himself onto a gurney in the last episode and started howling had no logical reason or context. He's known for doing too many takes, trying out different approaches as he goes.

Every time we hear the director's words "rolling" and "sound," we all flinch. More shots mean bigger budget and creates tension on set.

Let's not forget talking negatively about co-stars helps no one. The voice is stern now. *Some nail it the first time, others need twenty-eight takes. I know you think little of M. But he provides the right amount of fluff to an otherwise chilling series. They love him, the man with over two million followers on TikTok. Did you know there's a drool piece about him in the* Daily Mail *this morning, likening him to the statue of pharaoh Akhenaten? They said his beauty is the kind that stops you from focusing on what he's saying because you're fixating on his cheekbones.*

This time, the voice clamours for attention and I'm wiping a film of sweat from my upper lip.

Consider this as an internship. Lesson number one, I'll talk, and you'll learn. You have great potential, my friend. Which is why I chose you. That's right. I chose you. *Lesson number two, remember where you met Nic? Last season's wrap party. The same party your lovely wife boycotted because she was sneezing and snuffling from some kind of disgusting virus.*

My mind tracks back to that night. When I left the house, Lilja was wrapped up in a scarf, her hair greasy with sweat. I'm ashamed to say, the dinner party provided the excuse I needed to remove myself. Marschōne struck me as self-satisfied and smug, and he ridiculed Nic mercilessly. I get she is baffling, but it was excessive and made me even more competitive. They had been sleeping and working together for months.

She kept doing that thing with her eyes and sending me signals. Marschōne wouldn't have liked us getting to know each other, but he was absorbed in the striking, grey-haired woman to his left to notice us leaving the room. It was then I realised Nic didn't like him much and had struggled on, pretending everything was fine. She thought he could help her, but he was only helping himself.

I followed her to the swimming pool, hoping I could prise her away from him and offer her something more meaningful. She took off her clothes and dived in. It took a few seconds before she came up for air, her hair slicked back.

'It's the perfect temperature,' she said. 'You should come in.'

'I'll pass thanks.'

'Chicken.'

I smiled. There she was naked in the water, floodlit by the pool lights. I didn't want to appear too eager.

'You've a natural flair to put people at ease,' I said. 'It's a real skill. Marschōne is a lucky man.'

'Not for much longer. We're parting ways.'

I raised my brows. 'I'm surprised.'

'Really? This is where your acting fails you. You're not surprised at all.'

'So where will you go?'

'Back to the agency to find another job. Unless you're looking.'

I was looking, and still am, but my wife employs our staff and that's where I prefer to leave things.

Guilt brings me to a saying that a man must love his wife as he loves himself. Lilja is the light in my dark world, but she has become withdrawn after losing her job. Whenever I talk about the series, she seems eager to change the subject. Nic has an infectious enthusiasm about everything I do, and I'm propelled by the sudden lightness that follows an unburdening.

It feels good to be wanted again. To be a little reckless.

Her eyes meet mine. I'm always struck by her the way she moves, sinuously, like a ballet dancer. We've never talked about feelings, about what it would do to either of us, but the possibility of me leaving my wife seems to fascinate her.

A jolt of laughter brings me back to the present. Marschōne slides a look in Nic's direction and then at me in the split second my eyes follow Simon. Such a small thing, a look. Merely a friendly thing people do to one another. Or a threat. If he doesn't know I'm already screwing his soon to be ex-girlfriend, he certainly suspects.

In between breaks, I study my phone. *CNN Entertainment* has kept tabs on Holloway and states, "*Play Him, Play Her* will return for a further season." They're comparing my performance with *Grey's Anatomy*'s Patrick Dempsey. It's a tremendous compliment and completely over the top, but I'll take it.

The ghostly voice interrupts me.

You couldn't quite get to the meat of Holloway in the first season until you drove to a cottage hospital and talked to three patients. They were confident in your scrubs and cap. You had a purpose, and that was to care for them. They believed you were part of the medical team.

Sense memory and affective memory are important tools; recalling an event from the past and reaching deep down inside for that emotion to bring the character alive. I used to think Method actors were a pretentious bunch of egomaniacs. Too much dedication, replacing actual skill. But what is pretentious is believing one approach is better than another, because some of the best actors have used The Method.

The minor characters you played in your early thirties were uninspiring. Twenty per cent on Rotten Tomatoes *made your first film the second worst-rated that year. I expect you were sick of investing energy into roles people were likely to forget. You need a greater range, and it means finding the right skill to craft each role.*

He's right. These minor roles were ones I could bounce back from. Characters I could compartmentalise and turn off. When I saw the script for *Play Him, Play Her*, it was an opportunity to establish myself as a serious actor.

Holloway was unreservedly me.

At the end of the read, Simon tells us we're all the best he's ever worked with. But he says that at every table read. We stretch and yawn and drink more coffee. Simon wants to hear my ideas.

'Holloway manifests in everything I feel,' I say. 'I find it hard not to think like him, dress like him, shag like him, and I've started drinking his brand of whisky.'

Simon taps his chin thoughtfully. 'I trust your method and you do glorious work. Don't go overboard, that's all.'

Before I leave, I check comments on *BarbedWire*, where a group of people I call the Grave Diggers (a la Hamlet) can't keep their noses out of my business. Today, they are predictably negative about my acting and a sickening brew of emotions begs the question; how much deeper can I immerse myself into the life of a serial killer without becoming one?

BarbedWire - Trending #InZane

@CirceAtNight: Holloway first endears himself to patients in *PLAY HIM, PLAY HER*, but then encourages them to sleep with him. What a disgusting person.

@Titmouse: @CirceAtNight You're the disgusting person. Spouting off things you know nothing about. Crawl back under your stone.

@SherylAdams: Pity he continues administering overdoses of the patients' prescribed drugs. He may never be caught.

@HeyWhatsUP: @SherylAdams Oh. Right. You think no one's going to notice the similarities in all these deaths? C'mon. Get real.

3

LILJA

Today, Zane is shuttered in his study downstairs. I imagine he is sifting through layers of unresolved emotions, summoned by a voice only he can hear. Shooting has been postponed for two months. Marschōne, who is finishing up a film in Italy, has been called back to do retakes. Nobody is in the least bit surprised.

It's breakfast when I receive his text: *Tell Burgess to stop mowing the lawn outside my window, the noise is drilling a hole in my brain.*

I suspect Zane is sitting in the dark, curtains drawn, the air dank with the smell of rotting food. Whenever he leaves the house, I creep downstairs and stumble over dirty socks and overflowing bins and fling the windows open to air the house out. It suggests his world has become more chaotic. Last week, I found shopping bags hidden behind the door, designer dresses and jewellery, none of which were in my size.

I decided to get it over with – no more dancing around. 'Whose clothes are these?'

He studied me with a faint look of contempt. 'When did you become so nosy?'

'Maybe it's just me being thorough.'

'I see. When you're being *thorough*, what else do you look through?'

'Why? Does it bother you?'

He didn't respond to that, but I could see it unsettled him.

I lie in the dark sometimes, watching him while he sleeps, wanting to reach out and tell him, 'I'm here. Talk to me.' But the person I've promised to love until death has gone, and I'm left with a stranger.

As I head for the kitchen garden, I see a lapwing with a wonky leg, dragging a wing and hopping about. I read somewhere they are associated with deception and drama, hence a group of them is a "deceit." Is it feigning the injury to keep a predator from its nest?

Thousands of wading birds come to Dawlish Warren for the winter, including the town emblem, the black swan. Longshore currents formed flats and bars at the point where the Exe enters the sea, but the spit has gradually eroded and despite efforts to preserve it, sea breaches continue to happen. I wonder how long it will be until the coastline changes completely.

The clock tower on the old stables looms ahead and I notice the lavender barrels need a coat of varnish. It's only May, one more month and the blooms will be a riot of deep blue. I harvest a little mint, sage, and lemon balm, and take the stairs to the kitchen balcony.

I notice a flash of movement skimming across the deer park. A man dabs his sweaty forehead with the corner of his sleeve and a wink of glass alerts me to his camera. Another prying journalist. I close the sliding doors against a light patter of rain.

The kitchen counters are speckled with breadcrumbs and a large dollop of ketchup. I don't allow readymade meals, but my daughter brought this unhealthy offering from school yesterday and has reheated it in the microwave for breakfast.

My home cooking channel on TikTok has yet another great recipe for Kladdkaka; sticky chocolate cake decorated with raspberries and paired with a creamy cup of cappuccino. The comments about my fabulous kitchen with its sun-fired windows are flattering and I'm racking up the likes and follows.

All this keeps me from feeling raw about losing my job at the hotel a month ago. Chef de Partie at the Magdalen Hotel in Exeter's city centre was nothing to sniff at. My position was the second stage in the kitchen, overseeing the commis chef. With a 1:30 am finish, there was barely enough time to sleep before the day started all over again.

The publicity began after my promotion from fish station to meat entremets – the second highest position on the line before sous chef. My mind keeps scrolling back to that morning when Chef called me into his office.

'I want you to look at this tape,' he said, rolling CCTV video from Saturday night.

I watched the media storm collecting in the car park, and particularly a camera man shoving a guest out of the way of a reporter. There was another leaning against the bonnet of my grey Audi. There was no way I could drive home.

'The video ends with you being escorted under a blanket to your brother-in-law's car. I'm sure you see the problem.'

'I do,' I said.

'It won't just be last week; it'll be next week and the week after that.'

I looked at the man who had been my mentor for years, and I realised why he was meeting with me and not the Food and Beverage Manager. It was personal.

'Chef, none of this is my fault.'

'I'm not saying it is. I think it's very unfair you must suffer on account of your husband. But the hotel isn't equipped to handle this type of publicity.' He pointed to the screen again. 'These guests are being muscled out of the way by camera crews. Vans are blocking the street.'

I knew what was coming next. 'You know how hard I've worked.'

'I do, and I couldn't wish for a better chef.' He looked down at his clasped hands. 'But I've been told by management to let you go.'

He handed me my P45 – the official certificate of termination. I remember crying at the unfairness of it all. I miss our family of culinary sculptors, fanning, shingling, and moulding, the perfect blend of artistry and science. The grief stabs as much as Zane's love scene in the last episode of *Play Him, Play Her*. They looked so in love.

Even socialising is an ordeal. I can't walk fast enough through the supermarket in case anyone wants the skinny on Zane with barely a "How are *you*, Lilja? Being married to such a hot celebrity must be *ghastly*." It's all the digging and prodding, mouths set in wide Os. I'm beginning to wonder if my friends knew Zane better than they were letting on. It's why they all drifted away.

The security system chimes for the front gate and my phone rings. I check the video. In this desirable neighbourhood you'll find high-end cars, but outside is a white Honda with a dent on the rear bumper. Of course, it could be someone hand-delivering Zane's scripts, but they usually come in the post. Not everything gets communicated.

I press the call button. 'Hello?'

Her voice sounds high-pitched through the intercom. 'It's Nicola Gatlin. I'm here for the assistant position?'

The call button at the gate rings a list of numbers in order; Zane's first, then mine, then Bizzy's. As usual, I'm the only one answering. I push a key on my phone and the metal gates open.

As scruffy as this car is, its occupant couldn't be more polished. Baby blue dress, navy jacket. I'd guess late teens, early twenties – brunette, no-nonsense, using her newspaper to ward off the rain. I rush downstairs to open the front door. Her jaw drops, arm raised for the doorbell.

She offers me a shaky hand and looks behind me. Stella, the cleaner, must have heard the buzzer and has decided the bronze statue of Dionysus on the hall table needs a good dusting.

'You must be Mrs Osborne. Nice to meet you.'

I size up a busty, petite woman in ruffle sleeves and a shirred bodice. A beautiful woman with beach waves and slutty make-up. Okay, that was unkind. But she could do with less eyeliner.

I open the door a little wider. 'This is Ted.' I point to the cat. 'You do like cats?'

'Yes, I love them.'

She doesn't appear too sure, but what else can those pouty lips say with a tabby twining between her ankles?

I escort her to the sitting room. 'Coffee?'

'Thanks. Black. No sugar.'

I go into the kitchen and text Zane. *Your new assistant is here.* I'm not about to run around a large house shouting his name.

I take the coffee into the sitting-room. She's studying our

photos on the mantelpiece; family posing in front of fossilised dunes and Permian sands, and I feel a pang of possessiveness. Dawlish Warren has always been *our* special place, not one to be shared with outsiders.

My mind drifts back to the early days. Zane and I met over twenty-five years ago when I was younger and plumper with curled hair like hers. There were other couples around a bonfire, some lying on blankets, some drinking. I remember the girls — particularly the girls — looking up at him with a wide-eyed stare. It was Zane's charisma, his ability to make me laugh until my belly hurt. He was beguiling, and I allowed myself to be swept away.

Our wedding photo seems to have caught her eye. That's when she looks at me, her eyes running up and down my drainpipe jeans and resting somewhere between my breasts and my waist. I'm thinner by a dress size and taller by five or six inches. But she is what Zane calls doll-like. Exactly his type.

'Zane will be here shortly.' I hand her the mug, resisting the urge to stare.

She takes a sip and leans forward a little. 'You have a lovely home.'

'Thanks. My grandfather left the wine business to my sister and the house to me.'

I half expect her to say I have a lovely husband too. Everybody does. But she notices Stella in the hall and lowers her eyes. When Zane neither appears nor responds to my text, I excuse myself.

He has taken over the territory of the house's lower ground floor. His headshots line the corridor and mark the acts of our marriage, as I like to think of them.

By Act One, Zane was twenty-two. He landed a few commercials, namely The John Lewis Christmas commercial, Jaffa Cakes – Deliciously Self-Centred, and Budweiser Wassup. He then filmed his own backpacking trip to Thailand, which was a runner-up for Best Documentary Feature in the New York International Film Awards.

By Act Two, he'd submitted a resume of his survival expertise to *SOLO* casting, and he was picked for Season 6. He was amongst a team of twelve people dropped by helicopter in Labrador to survive on the land. His burst of fame came when he won.

It was his television debut in *Loving Alice*, where he played Harry Price, husband and caregiver to a dying wife that everyone loved. He followed this with a minor role in *Sidelined* as troubled student protestor Harry Kallisti. His feature film debut came a year later when he starred as Edward Hancock in the popular drama *Lady Doddridge*. That same year, Zane wanted to do something for Bizzy so he lent his voice to the Netflix animated version of *The Bone Horse* as Prince Osvald.

His breakout bow came in Act Three with a supporting role in *The Eidolon* where he played Will Innes-Kerr. Lydia Whitman of *The Hollywood Reporter* described his act as "compelling and startling" and his character's speech upon meeting the ghost of John Brown, Queen Victoria's personal favourite, the best she'd ever seen.

Two years after this initial burst of fame, things ebbed. He was worried he was getting typecast and his career drifted. Six months ago, the part of Holloway was his chance. The pilot was a sensation and his ratings soured. The latest photograph on the wall is the one when he landed the pilot for Holloway.

There was no proof he was cheating, just a feeling. I was convinced Zane was having an affair with his co-star, Quiana Thompson. When I gave him the ultimatum to show me his phone's GPS data, he explained stalking her, the friendly kind, was all for Holloway; the surgeon-cum-murderer he currently plays.

It's hard being married to a man who isolates himself and seldom comes up for air. He lives and breathes his characters and demands my understanding. All this groundwork is what our daughter calls a bunch of pretentious bollocks. But it's not Zane who demands believable realism, he insists Holloway demands it of him.

I knock louder this time. 'Zane? Miss Gatlin is here to see you.'

I hear the word *shit!* Followed by the rustling of papers and a few thumps. I open the door a crack. The study floor is littered with camping equipment and rolls of clothing, which he stuffs into a backpack. In Season 2, Holloway is running from the police and hiding out on the land, so, of course, Zane must live it and feel it too.

'Did you hear me?' I shout.

'Yes, Lilja. Hold on.'

I open the door a little wider. My elegantly dressed husband has draped himself across the couch and is marinating in freshly applied cologne.

'She's upstairs,' I say with the tone of disgust I use when he keeps me waiting.

He stares at me like I'm an imbecile. 'What are you waiting for?'

4

ZANE

My study occupies almost half of the lower ground floor, a forty-inch TV fixed to the wall between the bookshelves, and an expansive seating arrangement of couches and chairs.

Nicola Gatlin enters, carrying her phone. I absorb the dress she wears; the way it hugs the swell of her breasts and catches on her thighs every time she moves.

'Thank you,' I say to my golden-brown wife. I mouth, *I'll take it from here.*

Lilja's eyes seem to roam from Nic's to mine, as if she hopes to catch a spark of attraction. It's a constant juggling act of pretending to appear detached when all I want to do is drool. When she closes the door behind her, I offer Nic a seat.

'She has a habit of listening at doors. If you look underneath, you can see her feet,' I say, in a moment of facetiousness.

'So, I can't sit on your lap?'

'No. Ask me another question, a serious one this time.'

'Okay.' She raises her voice. 'Were you about to advertise?'

'I was. But you've saved me the trouble.'

She's like a butterfly, can't sit still, her hands circling the air whenever she speaks. She smiles at me, as if to say, *Relax, this'll be fun.*

I turn off both my phones, a spare is a precaution I have found necessary. I don't want my wife seeing spicy texts to my girlfriend or confidential ones to my therapist.

Unlike my blonde wife with her Viking heritage, Nic is fair skinned, with a tendency to redden in the sun. When I look at her, I think of the house in London three weeks ago, where we sat on the patio, drinking Chateau Lafite. She gave me a look, a sly look, and something about it excited me. She ran upstairs and I ran after her, mostly because of that smile. I know her body and how perfect it is, how strong her legs are, how her fingernails feel on the back of my neck. I could go on and on and never get tired. I can't get enough of her, and she knows it.

Under her spell…

The voice snaps me out of the memory and catapults me back into the study. I ask Nic to describe her work experience with Marschōne, as if I'm acting the part of a stern military commander.

'I'd never met him prior to my interview,' she says. 'But I'd heard he was looking and applied. My agency pointed out there were over five hundred applicants, and I was one of three he wanted to see.' She grins, and I notice how small her teeth are. 'Then came the hard part. Getting to know one another, settling into the swing of things. You know how it is.'

I keep nodding. It's the emotional equivalent of playing blasé; the less admiration I show for Marschōne's staggering work ethic, the less resentful I'll be.

'He's charming in a self-effacing way. I guess you could say we hit it off. Later, when I asked him why he chose me, he said, *intuition.*'

Intuition, my arse. I turn a page and pretend to be riveted by her previous responsibilities. 'How long were you with him?'

'A year, until the week you asked me to call you.'

I clear my throat. 'What have you been doing since?'

'This and that. I was temping for a law firm in the city and doing odd jobs for my brother.'

'So, a little more of *that.*'

'Exactly.'

It coaxes a smile out of her that doesn't make me feel as if she's doing it out of politeness or obligation.

'Did Marschōne compensate you in any way? I mean, bonuses. Clearly, he paid you.'

She pulls up a flouncy sleeve. 'I don't know if you would consider this a bonus.'

I study the Sole Blu Italian masterpiece on her wrist. 'Is that a Panerai?'

'It is.'

'What a lovely gift.'

I try to take the sarcasm out of my voice. But why would Marschöne have parted with something worth well over twenty grand? *Obviously, for services rendered.*

This time, I don't look around the room like an idiot. The voice is sharp and distinctively Holloway's. He's intuitive. It's something we share.

'Somehow he juggles everything and still makes you feel you're the most important addition to his team.' She lowers her eyes and swivels a thumb ring. 'Except for the tantrums.'

My back straightens. 'Not bad ones, I hope?'

'More on the scale of intermittent explosive disorder.'

'I'm sorry to hear that.'

You're not sorry at all. I try batting the voice away, afraid it might be about to spoon a good helping of fire and brimstone upon me. *Ask her if Marschöne's outburst was justified. Maybe she did something bad.*

'Perhaps I shouldn't have said anything.' She tucks a strand of hair behind one ear with a long fingernail. 'I'm being disloyal.'

'Hardly. You don't work for him anymore.'

'I thought you should know.'

She smooths the hem of her dress over plump knees, and I think about the pleasure of touching them. Why does she disturb me? Is it her body? Or the way she looks at me? For some men, it's the face or the breasts or the legs. For me, it's always been the waist. Nic's is pinched and narrow, you'd think she was wearing a corset.

I describe her duties, which include managing my expenses, three bank accounts, and overseeing the Hellman's Trust, a fundraiser to support victims of domestic violence. 'Then there's taking Bizzy to school.'

'What's she like?'

'Bizz? Imagine a queer bull terrier with blue hair.'

'Sounds like we'll be friends.'

Nic's legs have become a distraction. They're not crossed anymore, and I can see the line that goes through the top of her thigh. I'm rooted in the moment and my mind can't go anywhere else, and that's a bad thing because she's waiting for me to speak.

'Do you have questions for me?' I ask.

'Have you always lived here?'

'I'm a Dawlish lifer. Who doesn't love the Red County? Did you know the town appears in a Jane Austen novel? It's where Robert Ferras and Lucy Steele honeymooned in *Sense and Sensibility*.'

We spend a few moments talking about the Charles Dickens' character Nicholas Nickleby the elder, who inherited a farm in Dawlish. When she asks me what it was like to film *SOLO*, all the old emotions start welling.

'Documenting myself was the hardest part. Especially towards the end. I struggled with hunger and thirst and freezing temperatures. I had to be alert to predator movement patterns, bears in particular. As you know, the sodding rain never stopped and some days it would snow. When I caught something, those were the best days. A mouse, a fish, anything. When you don't have food, you move your traps, keep your lines in the water. Keep watching more game. Mostly, I was accurate with my bow. Less so when I was hungry. If you're cold, you build a fire, change your shelter. You deal with it.'

'That's why I've been fan-girling you ever since.'

'I doubt it's justified.'

'Do you have any favourite fans?'

'Apart from you, there's a thirteen-year-old boy called Milo. So that makes two.'

She grins and then her eyes shift to the picture on the mantlepiece. 'Was your father an actor?'

I stare at it too. Dad wearing waders and holding a catfish. 'Hell, no. He was a doctor. Médecins Sans Frontières. He went missing back in the nineties.'

'How awful.'

'It's not something I tell everyone. The facts, such as they were, was that Dad went camping in Canada and disappeared. Some speculated he'd broken a leg while trapping in the woods, some said he simply starved. Another theory was suicide.'

She nods, but her smile has disappeared. 'What do you think?'

'I thought he might have gone abroad. He spoke French. Why not Monaco, Switzerland? The Ivory Coast?'

'Surely, someone would have recognised him.'

I wanted to say not if he'd had plastic surgery. But that would open a whole new discussion about Dad, and I didn't want to think of him living out there with a new family, a new son. A new life without me. I would have disappointed him in my teens; a boy who spent hours playing sax in a jazz band with best-friend Rick, whose life is now squared away in Wakefield Prison, living nice 'n' orderly. You can see my point.

'I've accepted he might have suffered from some type of mental illness.'

Which is bullshit. I mean, of course he could have but it made little sense. His desire to help people went way beyond any selfish motivation. But there was a part of him he kept secret, a dark side buried deep in his psyche.

'In the first season, where Holloway had been restructuring facial tissue, scars, and burns, he's now having a relationship with his patient. In the second season, I will have to portray a killer.'

'Amaya Stone is delusional. Holloway's not in love with her.'

'No, but it's how he deals with transference that matters.'

'For instance?'

'He should have referred her to Dr Deandre Bryant — Marschōne's character — and not allowed her to be obsessed with him. It seems unfair.' Nic's quizzical expression tells me my statement needs more explanation. 'She wants him to marry her. It's understandable.'

'But he refuses because she threatens to tell his wife.'

'He kills her because he knows she will.'

The ticking clock seems like a faint heartbeat, insistent and persuasive, and I feel my skin itch. Our eyes meet for a fleeting second as she takes a sip of her coffee, which by now must be tepid.

'You don't like where this is going, do you?'

'The script? No.' I pause for a moment. 'A brilliant doctor healing burn victims is now a serial killer. Don't you think it cheapens the whole thing?'

'Not at all. Everyone's loving it. *IndieWire* listed your performance as stylishly elegant and multi-nuanced. They also said it featured a diverse cast where one key new performer made his breakout bow.'

She has an excellent memory and she certainly knows how to flatter.

'But not like this,' I say, hoping to drown out Holloway's voice. 'This freak show. This sordid dismantling of a brilliant career.'

She tilts her head and frowns. 'Why take it so personally? This is Holloway's disgrace, not yours. Are you nervous about playing him? About getting into his character?'

'*Getting into* is a rough description. Absorbing the building blocks of his DNA might be more accurate. It's weeks of talking, breathing, and shitting like Holloway, with no interruption from crew or co-stars. I interviewed surgeons to get the gist of him. He had to be firmly tucked inside me, so I could align with him completely.'

'Those are some dark places.'

'I suppose.'

'You use a therapist, don't you?' she asks. 'Does it work?'

'The therapist or the process?'

'Both.'

'Yes. I believe it does.'

Nic pulls out a newspaper cutting from her handbag and reads the article. 'Listen to this. "Zane Osborne is well on his way to becoming a household name. From the moment he's introduced as Ethan Holloway, he dominates the screen. Osborne has an intimidating presence, but with a deep well of emotion tapped into his character arc. One of the more atmospheric parts of the series is how Holloway treats his patients. His bedside manner and his empathy are electric. When Osborne commits to a role, he is com-mit-ted."'

'I've not seen that article.'

'Amanda Yeboah, the face of *Celebrity UK* no less. It's not every actor who can step into a role and deliver a truly original character.' There's a pause, which she fills expertly. 'It's easy for you, isn't it? The way you turn it on and off. Marschōne is intimidated by you because you never petitioned for the role of Holloway. Nor did you audition.'

'Marschōne should feel intimidated. He had two lines in the last scene we did and spent the entire day trying to remember them.'

It's no use telling her the casting agent saw me in a few minor roles and sold me the part. It was Simon who did the honours.

'There's no escaping who the streaming audiences think is the draw. You and I will go through the script together so there's more of an emphasis on performance instead of merely reading.' I shrug to give the next statement a little less brio. 'The writers want the second season to be more fun — and sensual. Instead of Holloway doing his job, he's doing his patients.'

Nic laughs. She will be the perfect person to prepare me for these sequences which, before now, have been mundane. I choose a short scene set in Holloway's house and ask Nic to read the slug lines and pick up Amaya Stone.


```
INT. HOLLOWAY'S HOUSE, LONDON - EVENING


Holloway sits in an armchair with a book
in his lap. Amaya reclines opposite him
on the couch. Between them, we sense a
subtle tug of desire.


                    HOLLOWAY

            (reading from the book)

        "Love    doesn't   look   closely
        at   the   scars.   Even   the ones
        you can trace with a finger. I
        remember her eyes, green turn-
        ing  gold  at  the  centre,  the
```

prettiest I'd ever seen. It
finally dawned on me I'd made
a fundamental mistake. I'd let
her get to me."

AMAYA

She's a little cornered, don't
you think?

HOLLOWAY

No. She craves the attention.
That's the draw.

AMAYA

It's not love. Not in the way
she recognises as love.

HOLLOWAY

Have you ever been in love?

AMAYA

I thought I was once. Now I'm
not sure.

HOLLOWAY

But you think about it?

AMAYA

(looks intently at Holloway)

All the time.

Looking at Nic is the worst sexual tension of my entire life – as if a garden hose has been turned off but the tap is running. Her face glows and it's hard not to get caught up in her beauty. I want to believe that the next few weeks will take away my doubts, loosen my body and give my audience the performance of a lifetime.

'Let me show you around.'

Instead of tugging the hem of her dress, which has ridden dangerously high, she rises to her dainty sandaled feet.

She's around fifty kilos and easy to lift.

We start at the foot of the servant's stairs and my study door. I show her the pantry where we have our own coffee station which opens into the laundry room. From there, a person has access to the back door. Outside my study and down a narrow corridor is the wine cellar. I key in the code and tell her to watch the steps.

She tilts her head to the vaulted ceiling, her gaze dropping to the wine displays and metal wall mounts my wife has filled with old wine jugs. Behind the hidden wine rack door is a game larder and a butchery station with a solid oak table.

'Lilja has been known to divide carcases down here. Hence the leak-proof containers which she takes to the rendering plant.'

Nic shivers. 'Does she hang pheasants?'

Now it's my turn to shiver. 'We don't eat pheasant. Long story.'

At the far end of the cellar, there are steps that take us back up to ground level, where a central aisle of wine barrels leads to two wooden arched doors.

'It's modelled on a winery entrance in Crimea,' I say, throwing them open to the drive.

She runs a finger along the hand-forged hinges and admires the stone façade. Inside the niches are carriage lanterns with wine barrels mortared beneath them. We end our tour outside the front door.

'Lilja will make us homemade muffins and croissants every morning. If she mentions our house in London, you know nothing about it.'

Nic grins, daring me to grin back. Instead of a fade to black in my mental movie, I imagine some kind of hodgepodge sequence, where we're in the Holland Park house in London, warming ourselves in front of the fireplace. Then dining on the balcony, which takes in a view of the private garden below. There was a part of me – a small part – that loved her then, but now… now it's merely a need.

I snap out of it and walk Nic to her car. She moves her fingers around in a scraggly wave and drives off.

I realise the parallels with Holloway having a consensual relationship with his patient and me having an affair with my assistant are too striking to ignore. In my mind, I'd crafted a new narrative, in which Holloway's affair will somehow excuse me from mine, giving me creative licence to play the part convincingly.

Somehow, I feel as if I'm being tested. As soon as I climb out of one ordeal, I'm plunged into another, where the flame is even hotter.

Trending #InZane

@HeyWhatsUP: Hello BarbedWire chums. Amazing scene of Amaya Stone getting her skin grafts. All that Z-plasty and skin flaps.

@CirceAtNight: Must be agony. You wonder how long she will be in hospital for. Do you think Holloway is prolonging her stay because he likes her?

@BantaBadger: @CirceAtNight: If he is, he's a dumbass.

@HeyWhatsUP: @BantaBadger Holloway's qualifications are modelled on Dr Swango, apparently. Valedictorian at school, honours in college and MD from Southern Illinois Uni. Fatally poisoned sixty patients. Not so dumb.

5

LILJA

Nic and Bizzy have struck up a thick-as-thieves friendship, talking everything Billie Eilish to football star Keira Walsh. Whenever Nic returns from dropping Bizzy at school, she parks under the weeping willow, lowers the sun visor, and applies her lipstick. A thick smear which doesn't come off even after eating. She walks to the front door, occasionally glancing at the sitting room window to wave and I wave back.

Upon entering, she always says good morning and bounces slightly on her toes. These few short minutes break the ice for me, and I wonder how much of a friend Nic would make. Today, instead of rushing downstairs to start work, she lingers.

'Would you like me to help you with anything?'

Her smile is wide and I can't help smiling back. 'Our cellar steps are crumbling. I'd appreciate it if you could call a local builder before one of us breaks our necks.'

She opens her laptop and settles herself at the kitchen table. While I dictate a list of to-dos, I study her blouse, buttoned to her chin, and the milkmaid sleeves. She has a style which is hard to replicate. Her jeans fit perfectly on her tiny frame, not too tight, not too loose, and her perfume – some kind of cloying grapefruit – has begun to attach itself to the fabric of the house.

'I've ordered the centrepieces for Zane's birthday party in June,' she says. 'You've chosen a great theme.'

I picked Agatha Christie's *Evil Under the Sun*, although the plot of a man having an affair and flaunting it in his wife's face is a little inappropriate. But Zane isn't to know.

'You're an excellent cook,' she says, glancing at my table of baked items. 'I can barely boil an egg.'

'I'm sure that's not true.'

'They say if you can read you can cook, but there's more to it than that, isn't there?'

'My Swedish grandmother taught me. We'd pick berries for Smulpaj – a sweet and sour crumble – and eat in the orchard a la Pop Larkin.' I see she's frowning. '*Darling Buds of May*?'

'I loved that series, if only for the beguiling Mariette.'

She seems taken by the glossy white Aga, tucked under a disused fireplace and backed by an exposed brick wall, before studying a vase of blue lupins. Then her eyes seek mine again, as if she senses me watching.

'Zane said you used to work at the Hotel Magdalene in Exeter. You must miss it.'

'In the weeks after I lost my job, days merged into each other with no shape or structure. It felt unnatural not to be working, as if I had become part of the landscape and somehow forgotten. I don't feel bitter for him bringing the press into our lives. It's not just him living this paralysing hell. It's all of us.' I see her yawn behind a hand and change the subject. 'How's the reading going?'

'They're never straight reads. We've moved past that now. I find myself forgetting it's him and believing it's Holloway. You see every detail, every emotion in a subtle glance.'

'Must be fascinating.'

'Being Holloway makes him do things he wouldn't normally do.'

'What things?'

'Impulsive things. Sensual things. He does it so convincingly.'

I nod, hoping to dispel a sudden lurch of nausea. 'And you? How do you feel?'

'I'm all about aligning myself with him and taking his direction. He says he's thrilled to have me. But that's why I'm here, isn't it?'

I nod, feeling the adrenaline dump into my body. There was a time when Zane was thrilled to have me as his wife — someone he could take to an assortment of parties, introduce to all his friends, show off in restaurants. It made him feel valued. Now I'm dodging the tripwires of his ever-changing moods, most of which lead to a collection of high explosives.

She leans forward, her voice a whisper. 'It's hard not to fall in love with him.'

Panic creeps over me, as if I've done something that can't be undone. 'Who? Zane or Holloway?'

She's about to say something and then turns her face towards the hall as if she senses someone listening. 'I'd better get back.' She closes her laptop and hurries downstairs.

If it weren't for the open kitchen window, I wouldn't be able to hear Zane and Nic's conversations on the terrace below. Their daily routine starts with drinking coffee and going through his schedule. Each day, he clips a cluster of hydrangeas and puts them in a vase on her desk, seeks her opinion from tapping into his emotions to recounting his backstory. Her duties include making him coffee, reading lines, and taking dictation on her laptop. She types well over 120 words per minute. Phenomenal. She picks up his dry cleaning, runs errands and texts him even after hours. They go out in his car and walk on the beach. I know because I use a spy app to track him. On those days she wears drainpipe jeans and sweaters, and my daughter always remarks on her cool combat boots.

It's a relief Zane has someone else to read scripts with him. Since he took the role of Holloway, they have turned more violent and unpleasant, and worst of all, they seem to delve into the growing cracks of our relationship. When Nic reads with him, there's a passion there that isn't anywhere in our marriage. I can't help feeling a burning jealousy.

Zane knows I have a website, but he doesn't know about my *ChefDePartaay* profile on TikTok. From there I can monitor Nic's. She has posted a photo of Ozzy Osbourne with the comment, *Three guesses — Not quite, but almost.* Different spelling, no relation. Comments are flooding in, which she has cleverly evaded.

It could mean anything from not working for Ozzy Osbourne

but for an actor of the same name. Or it could mean *Not quite, but almost* in a relationship with a celebrity. What makes my stomach churn is Zane's flattering tone, which has the potential to be loving and is anything but. Nicola Gatlin is out of her league.

I go upstairs to make beds, opening sleep misted windows to an expanse of freshly mown lawns. I think of the years my grandparents listened to the whistling crescendo of the nightingale, or more rarely, the dunnock, trilling like a squeaky wheel. All the afternoons they played croquet on the lawn and drank peach schnaps in front of a crackling fire. I want to continue the traditions, yet all I see are ghosts.

As the morning slowly extends to the afternoon. I make soup for lunch with leftover lamb and chickpeas. After sending a *lunch is ready* text to Zane, which elicits no response, Stella and I sit down at two of the four place settings. Bracing and eccentric with a halo of white hair, I marvel at her delightfully posh accent and larger-than-life personality. Nothing spooks her, not at seventy-two.

'It's awfully quiet downstairs,' she says. 'What do they do all day?'

'Reading, I expect. They're always reading.'

'Do you ever go down there and listen?'

'Huh? No. I mean, sometimes I do, but not really.'

'It's filthy. Wine spatter against the cupboards, cushions thrown on the floor, papers scattered about the study. He walks barefoot in the garden, traipsing all manner of dirt into the carpets. I keep telling myself he's an actor and not subject to the same rules as everyone else.'

'Which means what?'

'It means he's different, that's all.'

'Don't you think it's all part of the process?'

'Possibly.' Then she stares towards the garden. 'This *thing* with Nic. Is it permanent?'

'For as long as Zane needs an assistant.'

'I ask because it's more than rehearsing. Before you say it's acting, it's not *acting*.'

I get an uncomfortable feeling in my stomach and I'm not sure how to phrase my next question. 'You mean…'

She nods.

I swipe angrily at a fly hovering over Zane's soup. There's no notification that he's responded to my text or even read it. On any normal day, I would discuss my worries with him and we'd work out what to do. But normal is now a distant memory and bringing it up will only make him angry.

'What would you do if you were me?' Butterflies are gathering in my stomach.

She utters a long, uneasy sigh. 'I'm probably the wrong person to ask, but I wouldn't have allowed her to work here in the first place.'

She helps me put the lunch away. Everything is, 'That's nice, dear' or 'how about another cuppa?' She puts her arms around my shoulders and tells me she loves me.

After she goes upstairs to finish polishing, I stare at two cold bowls of soup on the table. Rather than text Zane again, I creep downstairs to call them for lunch.

His study door is open a crack and I inch forward to listen. Her accent isn't posh like Stella's but smooth and pretty like a talk show host. They're sitting on the carpet, reading lines, her hand moving up and down his back with long, deliberate strokes. They seem too comfortable together, too open. I find it disturbing that he would find any satisfaction in betraying me.

Then their faces are too close, and my brain doesn't want to process what I'm seeing, another woman's lips pressed against my husband's, her arms around his neck. For a moment I can't move, can't breathe, and I do the only thing I can to stop him from lying, and from me thinking it never happened.

I take a photo.

Creeping backwards, I grapple for the cloakroom door. The walls start to close in on me, and I brace my hands on the edge of the sink. I'm startled to hear laughter. How can they be laughing after what I've just seen?

I let myself imagine, for a moment, grabbing the paper knife from the desk and plunging it into the back of his neck, yanking it out and ramming it in a kidney or a lung and listening to him screaming for mercy. I half expect to hear the swish of a belt and the rustle of clothes falling to the floor, but there's an eerie silence.

Then footsteps.

Beyond the pantry, a lamp blazes in the short hallway at the foot of the stairs. Zane is standing halfway between the study door and the bannister, listening for something, as if he senses a presence. I keep perfectly still or he'll spot the slightest movement from the corner of his eye. The floors are carpeted, but after decades of use, they creak underfoot. I listen to his retreating footsteps and the click of his study door.

Moving swiftly out into the hall and keeping close to the skirting board, I launch myself at the stairs. Another thought gains momentum. He hasn't kissed me like that in a long time and the image of them blurs through my tears.

This isn't a representation of Holloway's affair, it's something far deeper and scandalous. Something premeditated. I brace myself for another emotional pang, but my heart is already splitting in two.

6

LILJA

I fumble my way into the sitting room, feeling homesick for a marriage we no longer have.

I used to love how we escaped to new worlds driven by the scripts he loved to share and the characters he played. He taught me about screenplays and wrote a few of his own. In between commercials and minor roles, he taught me how to speak with different accents. His were convincing, mine were mediocre.

I loved the way he dressed, whether it was shredded jeans or an Armani suit and tie. Half the fun was the tantalising way he removed those same clothes, draping them over the couch in his study. We nestled on the Persian rug; our bodies squeezed into each other. Flickers of pleasure sparking in unexpected places, a force that pushed us along, savagely, and out of control.

We rehearsed together, laughed together, fought together, cried together. Precious hours where we could pretend to be anything other than ourselves. Because *ourselves* was where the novelty had worn off.

We settled into a relationship that veered between mind-numbing discussions about who got what part and long stretches of complete silence. It was an exhausting pattern. After Bizzy was born, everything changed. He competed for my attention when Bizzy needed me more and treated me like a stranger at parties so he could flirt with everyone else.

If I trace the blame backwards to the beginning of this year, Zane and I had got past the period where he was using his newfound fame to drink and party, and I got a feeling he was sleeping around. We decided to do couple's therapy. Trust, or at least a covenant, had been established and I had put all suspicion behind me.

Until today.

I've wrestled with the idea of divorce, wondering why the prospect scares me. Rather than force myself to survive without his love, it might be better to acknowledge that I no longer depend on it. Cheaters are weak and cruel. They don't deserve to be happy.

I lie on the couch, clutching a cushion, trying to process when all the snapping and nipping began and last-minute deadlines and late nights eroded our routine. He would appear in the early hours with a wine-blurred voice, affronted that I had laid a guilt trip on him for not calling or texting. All the resentment came out when he was drunk.

'Life isn't hard for you, Lily,' he'd said. 'It's never been *hard*. That job you do in the hotel, that chef stuff, it's just a hobby.'

'That's a shitty thing to say.'

'You don't get it, do you? I was mowing lawns at fifteen, mopping pub toilets, delivering food while you were swimming in a friend's pool and doing sleepovers and shit knows what else.'

For months, we've been hiding behind deliberate silences and heavy sighs, neither of us admitting how lonely we are.

There's no point calling Mum or my sister, Elin. I can't expect any sympathy when they think I'm nuts to have allowed Zane all this freedom. I'd like to put the past behind me, including Zane, but the adage of setting your beloved free so that fate might bring them back – hopefully a more humble, repentant version – hasn't worked.

It's nothing the spy cams in our Holland Park house can't solve. I check the recording and find both views have been blocked by a vase of lupins. Blue, like the ones in the kitchen. One camera is in the bedroom installed inside the spine of a book; the other is in the sitting room planted within the metal loop of a small ship's bell. It's not like I can drive up to London and do something about it and I can't help feeling beaten.

Keep busy, I tell myself. The time goes faster when you're *busy*.

I overheard Zane on the phone asking his agent for Episode 2. Mostly he gets one Epi at a time like the audience — so he's on the ride with the viewers. But good old resourceful me has managed to track one down and I leave it in an envelope on the stairs outside his study.

I rearrange the kitchen drawers, cupboards, and shelves, and wash every gadget I own. Hours passing in slow motion, until I'm jolted by the slam of the front door.

Bizzy charges through the sitting-room, home from school. 'Hi Mumzy.'

I smile at her and see a young version of myself, something in the way she speaks, the corner of her mouth as it turns up and the quirk of an eyebrow. I'm also conscious of Nic's shadow standing awkwardly behind her. The frown that has burned into her forehead is slowly becoming a deep crevice and she hesitates before going downstairs. No hello, no questions about my day. I begin to reconsider what I've allowed in my house.

I turn to Bizzy. 'How was it?'

'Algebra – yawn. Science – full out nap. Art – progress on Hamlet poster. Eng Lit – Why won't Marianne look at Colonel Brandon? He's the *sense* in *Sense and Sensibility*.'

'From Marianne's point of view, he's too old.'

'Thirty-five?'

'The wrong side of, yes.' I follow her into the kitchen. 'Homework?'

'Loads.' She takes two mango yoghurts from the fridge and bolts upstairs.

I encourage myself to keep things normal for Bizzy and go through the motions of what needs to be done. My mind loops and tangles, and I can't sit still. I decide to make coffee marinated mutton chops with a balsamic reduction for dinner, then I change my mind and settle on chicken followed by left-over chocolate mousse.

I rarely use poultry shears to spatchcock a bird. My block of Japanese knives has one I favour, which slices through meat and bone in one satisfying snap. I remove the backbone and make a half inch slit in the cartilage before the keel bone, splaying the chicken on the board. It looks oddly grotesque. Headless and naked, like something you'd find dead on a road. Before I know it, the bird is roasting in the oven.

I hear talking and then the snick of the front door latch. Nic has left for the day without saying goodbye. I pour the wine and raise the glass to my lips while casually leafing through a magazine. Zane comes trotting in, arms out front and cracking his knuckles.

'Amaaazing day.'

'You missed lunch. Missed my text, too.'

He makes a show of looking at his phone. 'I'm sorry. I didn't even check.'

'How's Nic?'

'Fine.'

'Just wondered why she didn't say goodbye, that's all.' I hand him a glass. 'She looked upset.'

'Nic? Nah. She's always chirpy.'

I get the general gist that he's cracked two episodes in a single day and his agent has landed him an interview with Gary O'Malley. All pluses. Although kissing his assistant is strangely absent from the list.

I grip the carving knife and stab the bird harder than I intended, juices oozing from the crease between the breast and the drumstick. Zane gives a palpable shudder, his eyes widening a little and the colour draining from his face.

'Hungry?' I use the tone I reserve for guests, and I can tell it confuses him.

He nods and holds out his plate.

Everything is so weird I want to pinch myself. He doesn't seem real. *This* doesn't seem real. It's like one of those thriller movies, *Flightplan*, where the six-year-old daughter of a recently widowed woman vanishes on a plane, only the flight attendant tells her there was no record of her daughter on that plane in the first place.

Did I imagine them kissing downstairs? Was Nic here today?

I'm anxious – really anxious. I don't want to suffer a load of unreliable narrator angst. The fork trembles in my hand and so does the chicken and when I load his plate with vegetables, I can see he's frowning at me.

Bizzy appears with the imprint of a cushion on her cheek.

'Homework done?' Zane asks.

'Almost.' She yawns and rubs sleep from her eyes.

'It works best if you do it all at once and preferably awake.'

'It's better for me if I take regular breaks.'

'Okay.' He steeples his fingers and studies her carefully. 'Are you sure you're spending enough time reading and not staying up late, posting irrelevant stuff on TikTok?'

'I don't get why you're uptight about it. You post irrelevant stuff on TikTok.'

Zane holds her gaze. 'Sorry. Am I missing something?'

Bizzy's face is red, not from embarrassment but because she's baking in an oversized sweatshirt, her blue-tipped hair poking out from under a baseball cap.

'Who were you talking to last night?' She waves her fork. '*Does, Shit, I can't stop thinking about you. You're driving me nuts,* jog your memory?'

Zane leans back in his chair, his eyes darting to my face. 'She doesn't miss a thing, does she?'

Bizzy shrugs and goes back to eating as if pushing the incident behind her. I'm reluctant to let it go. To a fourteen-year-old, it would have sounded off, certainly enough to bring it up. But to me, it's a chasm of insecurity.

'Was there someone here last night?' I ask.

'No.' He laughs. 'It's a line from my script.'

It occurs to me, in the ensuing silence, that it could be a mistake. Bizzy misheard him. It was all a big nothing. I want to hold on to his words that it was something he was reciting.

Bizzy stares at Zane as if she's not fully comprehending. 'You were on the phone.'

The moment is shattered. It's no use pretending my hands aren't suddenly shaking in my lap.

'Rather than running your mouth off about what I might or might not have been doing, get your facts straight.' He turns to me. 'I can't do anything without it being turned into a shit show.'

'Honey, I think she was just—'

'Eavesdropping? That's exactly what she was doing.' He turns to Bizzy. 'What can you find so fascinating in a one-sided telephone conversation? What is that? Some kind of delusion? Or some kind of primal thing? Because we're not living in prehistoric times when people had wattle houses and no privacy. How embarrassing that must have been. Neighbours tantalised by you taking a shit.'

Bizzy's what's-eaten-Dad expression tells me she's not convinced. We both know wattle houses have nothing to do with rehearsing a scene. His voice drones on about Holloway walking the wards at night, while on the phone to former patient, Amaya Stone. The tension melts away, but I'm sceptical. He's desperately tired and I know he'll be pacing the corridors tonight.

By the time we all go to bed, I'm exhausted again. I sit in front of the mirror and brush my hair. 'You said this was a four-part TV?'

'Yep.' He throws his extra pillows on the floor and lies in bed, facing me.

Despite the growing emotional and physical distance between us, and at the risk of inviting resentment, I tell him I saw him kissing Nic. 'Okay, you were rehearsing. Why not simply bypass that part?'

He reaches out and takes my hand. 'Lily, you knew how explicit the script was before I signed.'

'You didn't mention how explicit—'

'It's an artistic illustration and has nothing to do with sex. Holloway has control over a delusional patient who is simply repeating the emotional patterns she experienced as a child.'

I stare at his face, searching for a clue that he's trying to mislead me. 'Yet in this vulnerable state, Holloway exploits her.'

He throws up his hands and turns over on his back. 'It's an infusion of beauty and horror and redefines the concept of exploitation. Amaya willingly having a relationship with Holloway is hardly abuse. When she takes matters into her own hands, the viewers have more empathy towards Holloway for the distress he's going through. They understand *why* he must protect his family, even if they don't like *how*.'

He lies back against his pillow, eyes closed, while I keep brushing my hair. I don't need a lecture to tell me what's going on with Nic. I haven't forgotten what I saw or how gutted it made me feel. If I stopped enabling him to live in blissful ignorance and steered him closer to reality, would things go back to how they were? Could we recapture a tiny piece of that old magic?

I turn to ask him, but he's out like a light. His face is smooth, without the frown that follows him around during the day. The trouble with being an actor's wife is that you can watch your husband age. But not on screen. There, he is forever young and memorialised in full colour.

I'm woken in the dark of early morning by his lips running along my shoulder. The thought of having sex with him doesn't rouse me and I tell him I'm too tired.

He can say I'm beautiful a thousand times, but it's meaningless. Because the person I want to hear those things from is no longer the man I married.

7

ZANE

Newsflash. Lilja rejected me again. She even turned her face away when I tried to kiss her.

Is there's another man in her life? Someone who has stolen and corrupted your most precious possession?

I doubt it. Maybe I don't care.

Which is why you deleted that lovely photo of you and Nic kissing from her phone. That's how much you care.

When I was reading lines with Nic, I heard the floorboards creaking outside my study door, matching the soundtrack of Lilya's frantic breathing. I suspected she was out there, spying, and now I know she was. Her phone was on the bedside table, so I helped myself.

While my wife snores through the early hours – I shouldn't say *snores*, more like purrs – I've been up for the past two hours drinking double shots of espresso.

I suppose bumping her off would be too much like hard work.

Are you serious? I slam the French doors and lock them. Holloway is hardly going to wheeze his way through a keyhole, sneaky buzzard.

I imagine a camera rig above our bed, monitoring every twitch.

INT. OUR BEDROOM - NIGHT

The evening light casts shadows across
the floor. We are in bed, and I'm propped
up on an elbow, staring at her.

                    ME

          Is something wrong?

                    LILJA

          I'm tired that's all.

                    ME

          You'd tell me if there was?

                    LILJA

          There's nothing wrong.

                    ME

          Something's different. I feel
          like I'm an imposter and this
          isn't my bedroom. I feel like…
          you don't love me the way you
          used to.

CUT BACK WIDE to show Lilja swinging her
legs out of the bed.

                    LILJA

          (pulling on her dressing gown)

          You're right. I don't.

The tiny scene makes for a strangely unsettling image and I keep spooling it out, hoping for a different ending. Before this humiliation, there have been high hazard flags I should have paid attention to.

The last time I took Lilja to dinner, she wore a form-grazing dress, its racer-back top dividing two well-defined shoulder blades. I wouldn't be recalling this if it weren't torture when I slipped my hand under the table and up her thigh, and she flinched.

Not a subtle *your hands are cold* flinch, but a palpable shudder. It was no use me calculating how easy that dress would be to remove in the bedroom later, not when she froze me out on the way home.

I hear the voice at my shoulder, like a sudden gust of warm air.

Well, guess what, Zaney-boy, would it knock you off your stride if I tell you my wife has been freezing me out since the series began?

I check the windows this time. All locked. The more I try to rework Holloway, the deeper I travel into his brain, along neuron networks and circuits, until I see a hairline crack in the frontal lobe. How can a damaged brain hold that much ingenuity?

Now I can't tell which thoughts are mine and which are his. I worry that it's not me who has an insatiable desire to be like Holloway, but that he has taken possession of me.

Acting is a way for me go beyond myself, getting out of my own head and into my character's. It's multisensory. I can dig away at all those emotions and get lost in the moment, profound moments that can only be shared with someone else. You can become a lifetime of hurt and loss, pleasure, and pain. There's nothing more exhilarating and nothing else matters.

My phone buzzes on the coffee table and I accept the call. 'Marschöne. What a surprise.'

'I couldn't sleep.'

'That makes two of us.'

'Don't hang up. I understand Nic's working for you now.'

'Correct.'

A pause. 'Before you think I have some ulterior motive…'

'Which you do.'

'Did she tell you I fired her?'

I sink into the nearest chair, wishing this wasn't the conversation that got us talking again. 'Look, what is this? Some kind of revenge kick?'

'Word of advice. She's trouble.'

'Thanks for the warning, M. I'll keep it in mind.'

I hang up. Who does he think he is, alerting me to a crisis that isn't happening?

Nic made the first move and told me she'd never met anyone like me before. It's weird because I felt the same way. There was something exciting about stealing moments in the cathedral grounds, hand in hand at night, a beanie pulled low over my head. We used my car for intimate meetings and afterwards, my house in London. I told her anything more would be too big of a risk, and she said she understood.

I even wrote her lines from a poem. *Love* by Samuel Taylor Coleridge.

> *She listened with a flitting blush,*
> *With downcast eyes, and modest grace;*
> *And she forgave me, that I gazed*
> *Too fondly on her face!*

She kept it in her handbag and swore she'd never tell anyone. I doubt she even told her flatmate. Nic is not trouble.

Lilja, however, wears her bitterness like a badge and she's become the type of person to leave scathing reviews on Netflix. There's a side of her that no one else sees. She may have fooled everyone else, but I know my lovely wife, and nothing is more unlovely than her secrets.

After a long shower in the downstairs bathroom, I pick a classic white shirt and chinos from the clean laundry and unwrap a new Ferragamo tie from a selection in my desk drawer. A growling stomach propels me to the kitchen, where to my surprise, I find my wife, fully dressed, sitting at the kitchen table nursing a coffee.

I take my seat at the table and say, 'Good morning. How did you sleep?'

All I hear in return is the crisp rustle of leaves in the early morning wind. My wife's chin points downwards, her eyes on mine. Not meek, but fox-like, as if the pole up her arse is getting bigger by the day.

'By the way,' I say, ignoring the icy stare. 'Cotterell's have submitted the best RFP for the cellar steps. Nic says the soonest they can come is the beginning of July.'

My wife mutters something between 'Yes' and 'Nic told me' and saunters to the Aga.

My daughter walks into the kitchen, studying her phone, her thumbs racing across the screen at a million miles an hour. Why is she pretending I'm not here? Am I that difficult to talk to? Or is she simply not a morning person?

You know how it is, you're suddenly invisible until they want something.

I try to cancel the thought and can't quite manage it. Lilja is pretending the frying pan needs fiddling with. She breaks two eggs and drops them into hot oil. I like the yokes runny but today, she leaves them sizzling for well over a minute before she teases them onto a plate. All this while studying the garden for "Lappy" (so bloody original).

If Lilja hadn't stopped reading scripts with me, Nic wouldn't have happened. Now this staring at phones, which has become a meal-time ritual, is anything to avoid being a family, or what remains of it.

After Bizzy got into one of the best schools in the area, Lilja got her life back. Yes, she's a brilliant chef, but her initial breaks were based on my celebrity. I admit I was a little resentful until my fame destroyed everything she'd built. *Food & Wine, bon appétit, Cook's Illustrated Magazine* and *BBC Good Food* have all featured her dishes. There are photos of her with Delia Smith, Mary Berry, Nigella Lawson and Levi Roots. It's who you know.

I follow her gaze to the garden and all I can see is topless Burgess mowing the lawn, the belt of his jeans barely covering his pubis.

'Walking hard on,' I mumble.

A strange expression crosses Lilja's face, as if she finds the topic vulgar, and Bizzy rolls her eyes in typical teenage disgust. While an uncomfortable silence falls between us, I admire Burgess' flat top haircut, where the side stubble shows some kind of zigzag design. Or is it lightning? Anyway, he makes a sizeable dent in the lawn and barely breaks a sweat.

'Wasn't he here yesterday?' I ask.

'Yes, and he'll be here tomorrow.'

'Right.' I tried to sound chipper, but I hate the way she gawps at him. 'Quite young to be owning a gardening business, isn't he?'

'He's thirty-six. So, no.'

I entice her with a smile to make her believe I'm okay with it. But my stomach contracts with the notion that Burgess might function as a bodyguard, and I don't like that either. Our staff eats lunch in the kitchen as my wife prefers a full table, and I've got to know him over the last few months. He is a nice enough guy, talks *Homes & Gardens* with my wife and sometimes plays Monopoly with Bizz. He looks bored when I talk to him about my hydrangeas. It's bad manners to look bored.

His girlfriend dumped him recently, so all of us must be understanding. But he's not the type of man I'd want to leave my wife alone with. He's encouraging her to turn the patio into some kind of bistro. Imagine the village idiots that would attract.

She looks up abruptly, as if sensing my stare. 'Your eyes.' She makes circles with her finger. 'You look like Peter Dinklage on Valium.'

'Thanks.' I try to sound upbeat, but my mind is stuck on sex. Or the lack of it.

'It's time you stopped running yourself ragged and start getting some sleep.'

The past few days have been a daze of weird moods and blackouts and I refrain from telling her. Lilja reaches into the drawer for the tablets, her fingers grazing over the Valium the dentist prescribed for a root canal she had a month ago. She studies an out-of-date bottle of oxycodone but shakes a bottle of ibuprofen instead. I slug them back with my coffee and make a show of looking at my watch.

I move to kiss her, but she turns away. 'No kiss? Not a good sign. Important decision, a kiss.' I touch her cheek. 'I have a meeting with Emma Harkness, *publicist* Emma... about my interview with Amanda Yeboah. What are you doing today?'

The girls look at me and then look at each other, trying to decide which one of them I'm talking to.

Lilja speaks first. 'I'm arranging our cooking demo in Bruges next weekend. Remember?'

Bizzy tucks her phone in her pocket. 'Surprise! I've got school and Granny's taking me.'

'Granny? What about Nic?' Lilja asks.

Bizzy gives her a wink. 'Hot date, apparently.'

Lilja's eyes slide to mine, and I shrug.

If only Bizzy didn't see everything I say and do as a tackle. Just because she has a range of football tricks doesn't mean she can leave me mentally knot-legged and twisted.

I must be getting hard in my old age because I disagree with everyone else driving my daughter to school rather than letting her take the bus. I don't believe in spoiling Biz, even with this recent wave of child abductions. I know she can protect herself with all the weightlifting she does for football. Despite her sarcasm and the need to rib me any chance she gets; she has a good heart.

At least she's wearing a tie that reaches the tip of her waistband, and her pleated skirt isn't riding up her thighs. Why must she always have her hands in her pockets, or her sleeves pulled down to her bitten-down fingernails? It's slovenly.

I check my face in the hall mirror. My eyes look like two wet pebbles and wearing a flat cap and glasses isn't helping. But when you've got a date in Exeter's west-quarter, any disguise will do.

I pat Dionysus' bronze bottom for luck, after all, he is the god of wine, theatre, and ecstasy. Sliding my car keys from his extended finger, I make a dash for it.

The only vacant parking space is next to Nic's car. If that's not synchronicity, I don't know what is. I proceed under a bubbling canopy of clouds to the Glorious Art House, glad to exchange the gloomy greys for the vibrant colours of Mexico. It's a safe enough distance from home to avoid any gossip.

The coffee shop is unusually empty, except for a textile workshop upstairs. I order an Exmoor Herbal Tea for Nic and an Americano for me. There's a stuffed squirrel with googly eyes in a basket near the cash register. I buy that too.

Nic sits in the corner near an ornate clock, wearing an unusually thin sweater which hangs provocatively off one shoulder. I meet her eyes from under the peak of my cap and shoot her a smile. She scowls at my disguise – full rim glasses and a workman's jacket.

I sidle in beside her. 'What? You know I can't go out in public unless I wrap my head in a blanket like ET on a fly-by.'

'You need to get a life.'

'Thanks for worrying about me.'

'I don't know why you bother. Nobody's looking.'

'Correction. Two people very much are.'

The owner is huddling and whispering with her son and they're angling their phones to take a photo. Not only of me, but also of Nic as we huddle brazenly in a dark corner. That's the part I hadn't expected, my not-so-private life with a mystery woman shared on social media. I hope I'm not slavering like a dog.

I turn my back to them and place the squirrel on the table. 'Say hello to your new desk buddy.'

She brushes it against her cheek. 'I'll love it until the day I die.'

Placing a friendly hand on her knee under the table, I tell her to keep her face down, describing the surveillance team as Pinky and Perky. She removes my hand, either to divert our onlookers or a subtle way of saying "later." Nic doesn't play the passive role, she drives the relationship in any way she wants.

'Why did you tell Bizzy you had a hot date?'

She lifts two perfectly sculpted eyebrows. 'Because it's true and because she asked me if I had a boyfriend.'

'What did you say?'

'I said yes. I also said he's a little older than me.' She lets out a long-suffering sigh. 'Come on, you think I'd tell her I was shagging her dad?'

For a second, I'm hit by an intense wave of suspicion. 'Would you?'

'No.' She ruffles my hair and lays her head on my shoulder. 'That would be a horrible thing to do.'

We both watch the rain, globules pearling the windows and Devon mud swirling on the street like gravy. Since the bulk of the conversation has for the past few weeks centred on me, it might be helpful to get to know her better.

She has mentioned a mother and brother but is hesitant to talk about her childhood. This time, the words seem to tumble from her mouth, which means I can drink my coffee while it's still hot.

'We lived in Cornwall with my grandmother,' she says with a tone of weariness she uses for everything in her past. 'She owned a brewery. Hogstones. You've probably heard of it.'

I nod.

'During term-time, there was no TV except on Saturday night and that depended on grades. During the school holidays, Mum and Dad were away on business, which meant they left Tim and me to an almost riotous abandon. We had hardly any routine.'

'Then you were freer than I ever was.'

'We'd go out and meet friends after Gran went to bed. That's how I met my first boyfriend. Ricky Delaney.'

'Cool name,' I say, trying to sound trendy and failing. 'What was he like?'

'Kind of psycho, tangled with my head and made me believe I was nothing. The whole thing felt forced, like I had to pretend he was the biggest and the best, and bow to his vanity.' She stares past me at the window. 'I was too young, too gullible, and he knew it. Now, it's about sealing up those dark spaces and working my way through it.'

I put my arm around her and pull her close. I want her to feel as if there's an understanding between us, and that we both know how it feels to be broken.

I notice her handbag on the seat between us, zipper open, key-ring hooked to the handle – a silver guitar charm and a tiny pink pig. It's the packet of birth control pills peeking out of an inside pocket that interests me. As she turns her head away to study a picture, I pull them out far enough to see they're half empty.

'It's stopped raining,' she says. 'Might be time to make a run for it.'

On the way back to her car, I keep swerving into her and apologising. There's something magnetic about walking side by side, no matter how I try to correct it. It's nice being close to her and watching her excitement over the smallest things. A seagull deposits a shower of acid rain on someone's car and a child sprays his mother's face with a sneeze. Nic grabs my arm when a man on a bike narrowly avoids us.

We stop two feet from her little white Honda. She looks up at me, light pouring on her cheekbones. 'This was fun.'

Was. I don't like the tense. 'We'll do it again, if you like.'

Since nobody is meandering casually between the cars with a camera slung over their shoulder… I'd start as you mean to go on.

I want to say I can't, but Holloway dares me to do it and who can resist a dare? I slip a hand around the back of her neck and kiss her on the mouth.

She gives a slight shake of her head, almost undetectable. 'Not here.'

I lean forward and kiss her again. This time she returns that kiss, and I can feel her fingers in my hair and my heart gallops. The damage I've inflicted on her seems unfair, but the slide down that slope began at Marschōne's party. It's hard not to let my mind wander when she looks at me, and harder still not to think of the nights we've already spent together. It doesn't matter how she feels. It matters how she makes me feel.

It's troughs of time like this when Holloway and I are two natures sharing the same body, two minds precariously connected by a script. He follows me home from the studio, refusing to be left there, and doesn't wait for me to climb into him like I used to. He envelops me. There's a fetid whiff about him, a robust, metallic odour, as if a wild animal has died under the floorboards. I awake to nightmares that are darker and denser and smell of blood.

She tilts her head, her lips touching my neck. I breathe in her hair and skin, my eyes occasionally opening to scan the street. I decide my car is more luxurious, plus there's room on the back seat.

We lock ourselves in and hunker down into leather and darkness. Here we are, skin to skin, and she's gripping onto me like a mantrap, but when you're at your lowest ebb, there's no undoing what you've done. Rather than drift on in a miserable marriage, sod it. Life is too short.

Sweat runs down between my shoulder blades and I'm almost gasping for breath. I feel like a twenty-year-old again, zipping through life like a racing greyhound. She pours everything out, every minute detail of what she's feeling, and I could have burst open, right there and then. We manage one round and then another, and then she's begging me to stop, and I do.

She slumps forward, her chin on my shoulder. I hate myself for setting a chain of events in motion that will inevitably lead to a mental and moral breakdown, not to mention tabloid hell. Yet I continue to take the risk.

'I love you,' she says, her heart thumping.

'I adore you.'

Adore is a safe word, like I adore a summer breeze or a glass of single malt. It doesn't tangle you up and hold you prisoner, and it doesn't make promises like the word *love* does.

On the drive home, I can't help thinking about Stan Marriott, senior reporter for *DevonLive*. A solid, bald, sallow-skinned man about my age, his confidence is evident the moment he speaks. We've swapped emails, so he doesn't have to go through my PR Company, and I wonder if he could help to shake off any rumours.

When we get home, Nic goes to her desk while I inspect my naked body in the bathroom mirror. A red scratch, etched across my back, brings an extra dimension to the deceit I'd never even considered. Concealing evidence is only part of a larger and darker issue. I still lie to Lilja about where I've been, why I'm always late, and why I can't take my daughter to school. Any excuse to exclude me from the marital routine, tasks for which I'm normally responsible.

In the shower, I try to rise above the deluge of guilt, but Holloway's voice pierces the surface like a longsword.

You're killing it!

Trending #InZane

@CirceAtNight: Hey guys! Was that Shelby from Peaky Blinders I saw running out of The Glorious Art House? Or ZaneO in a flat cap?

@Titmouse: Was he singing a sea shanty?

@HeyWhatsUP: Come out of the wardrobe @CliveAtNight. Next, you'll be seeing a snowy forest and men dressed as goats.

8

ZANE

My stomach cramps in the silence and I slump onto the sofa, dropping my head in my hands. The gravediggers creep over me like a frigid mist, their comments obscuring my peace of mind.

If it weren't for young Milo Morales jumping in to offer some encouraging anecdote, I'd be toast. I've never been a religious man myself, but I'll take today's message: *…so be wise as serpents, and innocent as doves.* Whatever that means.

A knock on the door. Nic leaves a steaming mug of coffee on my desk, unpins her hair, and shakes out a thicket of curls.

'Door open or closed?' she asks.

I refuse to be aroused. 'Closed, preferably with you on the other side of it.'

She gives a pink-lipped pout and shuts the door behind her.

I spend the rest of the morning studying Holloway's DNA, taken from memories and incidents ransacked from the past. The death of my first pet, for instance, or the bullying I suffered at school. Sometimes I hear Dad's voice, the perfect pitch and depth for a character like Holloway. But the more I research him, the more I sense what will happen next. It looms over me, the threat of violence, as if the danger has been drilled into me since childhood.

I return to a time where I felt the same sensations, to understand why it affected me. It means locking myself away so I can understand how Holloway's body moves. His passions, his drive. I hear the thud of Dad's axe and my ten-year-old voice, begging him not to hurt the pheasants. I imagine blood and feathers and I cry actual tears.

There's no value in taking Holloway home with me and treating my wife and daughter as if they're someone else's. Or jumping up in the middle of a dinner party when someone asks, 'Is there a doctor in the house?'

That's why I must become a part of you.

The voice shocks me. It knows things about me, intimate things that no one must ever know. I answer back, like a defiant child.

'Don't ask me to wear a sling like Ted Bundy and commit obscene acts. Don't bring up that clown killer, John Wayne Gacy, or expect me to keep trophies.'

I wouldn't dream of discussing either of these cowardly degenerates. You, my boy, wear the mask of Holloway. I'm a first-class act.

'My performance won't suffer if I don't dig a grave in a wood or find an unsuspecting cyclist to bump off. All that effort sounds exhausting, if not illegal, and infringes on the production. None of this makes me a better actor. It would make me a psychopath.'

No, but your scenes with Thompson suffer from a severe lack of chemistry.

'At least I'm not gluing my eyelids shut, or getting staph infections, no matter how dedicated that might be.'

You slept with Nicola Gatlin. Amid all that pleasure and guilt, you stored every meeting in your head. You had to feel it until it became a part of you.

With numb fingers, I read through a portion of Marschone's lines before I hit mine.

```
INT. HOSPITAL - DAY

Dr Deandre Bryant helps Amaya into to a
waiting taxi.
```

DEANDRE

You have no idea what you're
dealing with. Don't listen to
him and don't turn your back
on him. I mean it.

AMAYA

He's been nothing but kind.

DEANDRE

Is he, though? No disrespect.
But you don't know him.

AMAYA

Even so, you can't get around
the fact that he's an excellent doctor. He's talented and
he's sought after. Look what
he's done for me.

DEANDRE

Doesn't make it right, does
it? All that insecurity and
impulsiveness. Although   he
tries hard to hide it, Holloway
doesn't manage rejection well.
In fact, he doesn't manage it
at all.

Along with everything else, I'm learning about Holloway, the dark
mysteries that tempt him and the horrors he commits. Whenever
I try to pull away or suggest changes to the script, I feel as if I'm
disappointing him.

```
INT.   HOLLOWAY'S   CADOGAN   PLACE   HOUSE
- NIGHT


Holloway lounges on the couch, reading
a book about Castor and Pollux in an-
cient Rome. He rises smoothly when Amaya
enters the room, smelling of perfume
after a shower. He offers her a drink,
then sits in the chair opposite.
```

I feel the terrible weight of what comes next, realising that this is the sign to her that something is wrong. Her eyes narrow at him in horrified anticipation. *It won't happen. It can't…*

```
                    AMAYA


          (looks at him, surprised)

     Won't you sit with me?


                  HOLLOWAY

     I can watch you better from
     here.


                    AMAYA


          (takes a long sip of wine)

     Do you love me?


                  HOLLOWAY

     Heavens, no. Clearly you misun-
     derstand my intentions. You've
     asked me twice if I will leave
```

my wife. The answer is still
no. I'm sorry you feel as if
you're living in her shadow,
but there it is.

AMAYA

I thought this was something
special. I trusted you.

HOLLOWAY

Yet you came here anyway, even
when every instinct screamed
at you to stay away.

AMAYA

You're not suggesting we end
this?

HOLLOWAY

Now you're being melodramatic and delusional. Tomorrow,
you'll be convinced I'm seeing
someone else.

AMAYA

Where is your wife? Surely,
she doesn't stay in in Oxford
all the time.

HOLLOWAY

Please don't make the mistake
of asking about her.

I sit like a ghost through the end of the scene, listening to the sound of his voice. I can almost see the bow of his lips stretching in a curve and the dark intellect behind his eyes. Can I blame his coldness if he was rejected too?

IN FLASHBACK

a window in a dilapidated Victorian house, and a 9-year-old boy - the young Holloway - watching -

MOVING ANGLE - THE BOY'S POV

a man, Holloway's father, standing on the porch, shouldering a backpack. The boy runs outside and begs him not to leave, but his father pushes him aside. The CAMERA captures the boy's tear-stained face, before we abruptly return to -

THE ADULT HOLLOWAY.

                    HOLLOWAY

        If you think you're breaking
        up a family, you're not. Mine
        was broken a long time ago.
        My father didn't love me. Un-
        fortunately, he left before he
        could show me any.

                    AMAYA

Why? Why did he leave?

<pre>
                    HOLLOWAY

        He couldn't handle the shame
        of me knowing everything about
        him.

                    AMAYA

        Same as you.

                    HOLLOWAY

        What is?

                    AMAYA

        You don't want me knowing ev-
        erything about you. Are you
        really married?

                    HOLLOWAY

        I'm not married tonight.
</pre>

Holloway wants to see how far she is prepared to trust him and he knows she'll take the risk.

I abandon the script and stretch my legs. There's no sign of the lapwing, but the cat glides around the garden, licking his lips, his silhouette visible between blinks of sunlight.

The TV remote sits on the coffee table and I pick it up mechanically. The TV hums in the background, Mikaela O'Leary's voice from this morning's *Grain of Truth*. She starts by showing unused footage from the first season of *Play Him, Play Her* and reads the strapline from the IMDb Episode Guide. Then plunges into a recap.

'Previous episodes have focused on the lead's journey over the course of the first season. To underscore how popular this drama is, here is one of many five-star reviews: "Lush is the word I would use to describe the Netflix series, *Play Him, Play Her*. Berne Brothers have hit a home run, balancing the professional and private life of a doctor to create something captivating and satisfying." Another review states: "Love the series! Plenty of plot twists and sultry scenes. Lots of characters to love and hate." But Holloway's brilliant work with burn victims juxtaposed with his scandalous private life has left some viewers angry. Serena from Solihull says, "Holloway said some nasty things to his wife while dumping her for Amaya Stone. He should apologise for demeaning her." Brandon from Chester says, "Shouldn't he promise to be a better man?" I would agree if Holloway intended to stay in his marriage. The most interesting portion of this first season are his mental debates delivered as voice overs.

'But let's not linger in the past. The narrative expands in Season 2 to include more of the delectable Dr Deandre Bryant and the backstory of Maura Holloway. If you're keeping track, what do we learn from a police investigation into the disappearance of a patient?'

Mikaela turns to Marschōne Robinson (he was there!) and asks him about the most brilliant moments from the season. She ends the segment by asking about his upcoming movie, which he evades as skilfully as an MP. Then she signs off with her signature 'Keep in touch!'

I'm bummed they invited M on the show and not me. Last season, when Simon released me from the set for three days in a row, I should have seen this coming.

You're badly mistaken in believing he has the slightest shred of respect for you. Glorious work… *He's so full of shit.*

Same as my lunatic wife, who will no doubt be down here to ask me how the meeting with my "publicist" went. There's no way I'm going to be able to squirm my way out of that one, not if she calls Emma to check.

Better shake her off the subject.

I creep upstairs to the kitchen where her laptop is open on the table and already logged in. The cranking of the toilet roll holder from the cloakroom tells me where she is, and I can't help uttering a silent bark of laughter.

Trending #InZane

@CirceAtNight: ZaneO has hired Marschone's former assistant who is smoking hot!

@Titmouse: @CirceAtNight I don't get why people are so obsessed with her.

@SherylAdams Wasn't she Miss Torquay?

@HeyWhatsUP: @SherylAdams She's wants to get a degree in Business and Communications. Not just a pretty face.

9

LILJA

If someone is trying to scare me, it's working.

An estate agent called about an email, requesting her services over the sale of our house. I told her our house wasn't for sale and I'd never sent an email. Since she was responding on the back of mine, I must admit it looks authentic. Hackers are getting better by the day.

It leaves me feeling cold along the base of my spine. In the same way the cellar is inexplicably cold, a silvery glare emanating from the game larder. When I turn the corner, the chest freezer lid is open, its internal light struggling to illuminate that part of the room. Since no one is bending over the contents, their face a pale circle, I'm at a loss. With over fifty cuts of meat at risk, which are fortunately still frozen, I shut the lid. This, on top of finding my photo of Zane kissing Nic deleted, has almost paralyzed my ability to think. The time of sharing passwords with Zane is gone.

I glance up at the wall mounted rails where meat mallets and cleavers hang, including the utensils in my barbeque drawer. I can't blame it on an intruder if the outer doors are locked.

In the silence of the morning, I find Nic at her desk, her eyes fixed on her laptop. She doesn't look up, but she knows I'm here.

'Do you know anything about the cellar freezer?' I ask.

She shrugs and shakes her head.

'It was left open,' I say. 'Not good.'

'Might have been Stella.' She carries on typing. 'She was sweeping the steps earlier.'

How would Nic know Stella was sweeping the steps if she wasn't down there herself? They rarely speak.

'Did Zane mention anything… props for a scene, that kind of thing?'

'He didn't mention it to me.'

'I assume he's in his study?' It's eerily silent.

'Yep.' *Tap, tap, tap.*

'Just reminding you we'll be in Bruges this weekend. Help yourself to anything you need.'

'Righto.' She licks a finger and turns over a page of Zane's handwriting.

'There's a cooking demonstration tonight at Hotel De Tuile-rieën. It's a 15th century house that sits on one of the oldest canals in Bruges.'

'Sounds nice.' Her eyes flit from me to her screen.

The sound of her fingernails clicking against the keys is giving me a headache. Although I long to know what's really going on, any further conversation would be pointless.

Even Bizzy is quiet in the car, monosyllabic and sighing all the time. I see the anger in her eyes. Zane is her *father*, not a distant celebrity whose life is being shredded on social media. I tell her no marriage is easy.

She responds with, 'Uh huh. Yep. Okay,' while staring at her phone.

She's heard the story of my parents a thousand times. My father was a racing driver; Mum was a model. They rubbed shoulders with the Hemingway sisters and Mum did runway appearances for Givenchy and Chanel. When Dad died in a tragic car accident, her life changed irreparably. She couldn't eat, couldn't sleep, and wandered around in a daze. My grandparents took Elin and me to live with them with the reassurance that things would return to normal. It was almost three years before Mum could be a mum again and it was hard to let her hug me after she'd withheld her love for so long.

I know how Bizzy feels because I've been carrying around my own anger ever since.

We park outside a quaint Victorian house my sister and I once called home. A white fronted cottage near the train tracks and overlooking the sea. A plaque on the front door reads *Verbeke &* *Frank Goody* and pink dog roses curl around the porch. I remember the garden was a haven of butterflies which Elin and I caught in our nets. Yet as a girl, I'd sat on those same steps, dreaming of becoming wife and mother, not realising the consequence of such a wish.

We find Mum tearing along the beach, her bun unravelling in the wind, and Frank's floppy hat is about to make a mad dash across the English Channel. Their cockapoo has run off again and it feels like a massive search that's going nowhere.

'They do horrible things to dogs,' Mum says, running towards me. 'Cruel things. What if he's locked in a van with fifty others?'

'He's not locked in a van.' I wrap her in a hug and reassure her we'll find him.

I study the coastline for a teddy bear dog paddling in the surf or nosing through a wash of mermaid's purses. Somewhere near the groynes, a man lingers, camera panning the houses behind us as if recording a video.

I feel a mix of panic and terror and I don't want him taking pictures of Bizzy. I march towards him, my arms waving wildly. For an awful second, I think he's not going to leave. To my relief, he runs up the beach and scurries between the cars.

Bizzy catches up and grabs me by the arm. 'That was seriously badass.'

'Did he take a photo of you?'

'Shit knows.'

My heart is beating too fast and there's a prickling in the back of my neck. I scan the beach, feeling a little melodramatic for thinking he's still here.

'When you get a chance, I need you to try on those boots I got you for the trip.'

'What boots?' She gives a snort of disgust. 'Oh, God, they're not those black quilted ones from M&S.'

'Stop making a face. They're the same as Nic's.'

She pumps the air and rattles off two texts to George and Saneh, and I agree to let them come for the short autumn break. We link arms and begin our usual humorous patter in the worst Southern drawls we can muster, while Frank finds the dog behind a neighbour's bin, eating something hideous in a plastic bag.

'I don't think…' Bizzy ventures, 'I don't think we'll make the train now.'

I check my phone and we're already half an hour late. I try to change our tickets, but every Eurostar seat is booked until Sunday.

'It's not like Bruges is that great, anyway,' she says. 'All those canals and lace. Bor-ing.'

'You love it. You know you do.'

Zane hates it when I change plans. He says we need to stick to things and stop improvising, it spoils his day. But the possibility that Nic could be with him in an empty house causes a cold claw of panic to surge inside my chest.

Frank takes Bizzy into the kitchen to play Scrabble. I can hear her laughing, a familiar huff of a sound, which makes me laugh too.

'You're cheating,' she says with her usual sass. 'There's no such word as *exjinx*, whatever that is.'

'It's a former jinx, as in ex-girlfriend.'

'That's two words not one.'

'Which is allowed, provided the words are not independent of one another. So… twenty-seven points, or thereabouts. Write it down.'

This makes me laugh from my belly, a sound I haven't made in a long time. Frank is a notorious tease and I've loved him from the moment he came into our lives.

Mum pulls me outside to sit on the doorstep and we drink wine and hunch against the sea wind. The view across the beach lifts my spirits.

'Don't be hard on yourself,' she says. 'We both know what a car crash Zane's father was, forcing him to clean pheasant brain and giblets in the kitchen sink. He must have been sick in the head to expose a child to all of that.'

'He's had it much harder than I have.'

'Yes, but look who's paying for it? You've spent your whole life taking care of him. It's time he started taking care of you.'

'That's not entirely true. He's supported me financially since I stopped work.'

'I mean, emotionally. Ever since you had Bizzy, he's been irresponsible. Don't forget Irena.'

Irena, the Swedish au pair we had for Bizzy, left us abruptly after six glorious months. I found her throwing dirty clothes from her hamper into an open suitcase. Her face was blotchy and red as she rushed past me for the stairs. Zane was standing in the hall, shaking his head.

'Your wife doesn't deserve this!' Irena stopped short and glared at him. 'You're a monster!'

Suddenly, something came apart inside me, and I focused on the look that passed between them, a silent communication.

'What's going on?' I stepped forward and put a hand on her arm.

'Ask him.' She trundled her suitcase to the waiting taxi and was gone.

Zane kept his back to the front door, his face glued to mine. He said one word to me, 'What?' as if my questioning expression was too much to bear.

My mouth spurted the words. 'You slept with her?'

'Well done, Lily. Au pair leaves in a huff, must be the husband's fault. She asked for a pay increase. I said no.'

He was full of plausible excuses and resentment, and I began questioning myself. Mum doesn't do prodigals, there was no forgiveness for a cheating, lying, utter prick of a son-in-law. Now I begin questioning Nic. Her visits to the kitchen in the mornings are brief and she winces at my questions as if there's something sour in her mouth. She's always on her phone, swiping through photos, her demeanour guarded as if she doesn't want me to see.

It's hard not to convey a sense of desperation without worrying Mum, but she understands where I'm coming from. We fall silent for a while, listening to the drum of waves.

'Come on.' She pulls me to my feet. 'I'll run you a hot bath.'

I take my wine upstairs and soak in the hottest water I can stand. While Mum's TV hums in the background, I open my spy app and see Zane is at home. Instead of sending him the customary, *is this a good moment* text, I call him instead.

'How's it going?' I ask when he finally picks up.

'It's going. How's V and F?'

'Very well. They send their love.'

'I'd like to believe that.'

'You don't?'

'Afraid not.'

'Okay,' I say. 'I bought Bizzy those boots.'

'Nic will be flattered.' His voice quietens, as if he turned his head when he said her name.

'You okay?'

'Yep. Just finished memorising the murder scene at the end of Act 2. Way too intense.'

'Why don't you go for a run? Get some fresh air.'

'Maybe I will.'

Neither of us speaks and my head swims with things to say. I don't mention the reporter on the beach this morning or our cancelled trip. I don't say anything about the deleted photo or the open freezer. Before my mind starts racing down blind alleys, I tell him to have a good night and hang up.

A memory wedges its way into my mind. About three months ago, Zane asked me to go over the plot points relating to his script. It flattered me he wanted my opinion. We sat in his study, drinking wine and watching snow flurries settling on the grass. I watched him go into character; an exciting transformation, even when the character was creepy. The murder he described was from this very scene and later, the aftermath. Skull bashed in; body too decomposed to identify. He said the air was thick with the stench of death, as if recalling parallels with his father's abattoir of a kitchen. But his sense of reality had shifted and I'd hoped it was a mildly disruptive stretch to be endured until the season ended. When he snapped back, he was in a different place. A questioning place.

'If you were Holloway and killed someone, where would you hide the body? Hypothetically, of course?'

I didn't know how to answer. It's not something a normal person thinks about. 'A graveyard? A disused well?'

I watched the set of his jaw, the curl of his fingers and the fleeting change in his expression. 'What if the killer rowed the victim out to sea? A body washed up on the beach would appear as an accident, a drunken skinny dip gone bad.'

'Depends on the wounds,' I said.

'Head wounds, the type you get from a fall. There wouldn't be much forensic evidence for police to trace it back to the killer.'

'There's always forensic evidence.'

He tilted his head, taking in my answer. 'Not if the body had been in the sea for a couple of weeks.'

It hits me as I lie in the bath that the exchange was far uglier and more disturbing than I'd realised. Zane's always been an emotionally expressive man, but that night, he graphically described a murder, while I sat in silent horror.

Drowsiness rolls over me in a smooth, black wave and I'm yanked awake by the sound of a man's laugh. Briefly disoriented, I almost swipe my wine glass off the side of the bath. The room flickers with blue light from the television screen, and then I see him. A replay of an interview Zane did in March with Holly and Will on *This Morning*.

It doesn't matter where I am or where I go. Every time I pick up a magazine, see a billboard or watch TV, Zane's face stares back at me. Happy. Completely on top of things.

Yet, deep down, he is weaker and frailer than he's ever been.

10

ZANE

Through the French doors, the pond glints like a mirror, everything softened by moonlight. I flinch at the sharp, wailing call of the lapwing. He's left a sleek black feather on the terrace, iridescent with tones of green and purple. His calling card.

I know toying with Lilya's mental state is childish; the cellar freezer for one, *and* an email to Savills about the sale of Barton Manor. She'll experience the earth-shattering epiphany that she needs therapy – who doesn't? – only it would take a better man than me to suggest it to her.

I head back into the study and uncork a bottle of Moët. Nic knows to park at the church and walk along the lane to a narrow gap between our wall and the hedge to the deer park. The only thing bothering me is that interfering knob of a reporter, Stan Marriott from *DevonLive*, glasses like dinner plates – a full windscreen. He's been climbing the hundred-year-old tree in the park and watching me through his binoculars. I know because I've been watching him through mine.

I should have gone to the police for a restraining order, stating an invasion of privacy. But the park is public land. It would be his word against mine. Since I saw Marriott's bespectacled and charismatic smoulder on the news earlier, this is the best opportunity to invite a guest.

My phone app shows the cameras trained on the south side of the house and the rolling lawn. There's no sign of parked cars between the rungs of the gate or a young woman climbing over the ha-ha.

Lying back against the cushions, my eyes slide briefly to a photograph of Dad on the bookshelf. There is a likeness in the front teeth and the steep curve of the chin, although I have Mum's thick brown hair.

The house has an indefinable quality other than the whispers I hear when I'm alone. I don't believe in the paranormal, not to the extent of capering spirits with their eerie glow, but as an actor with deep intuition. My brain shuffles through scenes like a pack of cards, keeping Holloway fluid in my head. In terms of the division of labour, he is the driver and I'm the passenger. We're a team. That's not to say I don't clamour for control occasionally.

An acrid smell wafts through the study, unfamiliar like a different brand of cigarettes. Holloway is in the house, hiding or trying to psych me out, and the room is suddenly full of moonlight.

A voice worms its way into my head: *There's something different about your wife. Something about her manner that augurs secrecy.*

'I doubt she's a threat, if that's what you mean.'

Just because you've both fallen into a silent standoff doesn't mean she's not plotting.

'Then I should gaslight her a little more.'

What will you do next? Stick a nappy on the statue of Dionysus?

'Now that's really childish.'

Childish or not, we have someone else to consider. Before Nic arrives, it might pay to go back to the scene where I tell Amaya exactly where she stands. There'll be no misunderstanding then.

'Nic understands your relationship with Amaya mirrors ours.'

Yes, but does she?

For the first time since Holloway arrived, I consider the question seriously. What if Nic sees this as an opportunity for stardom, a leg up the celebrity ladder and I'm simply the catalyst? I adjust the cushions behind my head and close my eyes, falling immediately into a long thinking silence.

Nic's hand on my arm jolts me awake, and she takes the script, which is tented over my face. She has a messy bun at the base of her neck and wears a shirt with a shirred waistband. It's white with blue seashells that complement her washed out jeans. Exactly how Amaya would dress.

Before I offer her a drink, she takes my whisky and drains it. I match her hungry stare and pull her down beside me, tracing the line of her spine with my fingers. I can't stop touching her, it's a throbbing, persistent craving beyond my control, and the more I do this – the hiding, the running around – the more I want her.

'Here, let me show you something.' I flip to the scene where Amaya leaves the hospital. 'Why don't you read it?'

She takes the script and reads.

```
INT. HOSPITAL - NIGHT (DIMLY LIT)


Amaya Stone sits in a chair beside a
hospital bed. There is a suitcase by her
feet, and she is dozing.


ANGLE ON HOLLOWAY


Holloway approaches. He studies the clip
chart at the end of the bed and hooks
it back in place. He studies his patient
before kissing her on the lips.
```

Voices roar in my ears – and the more they speak, the further away they sound. I lean towards her and brush her lip with my thumb and kiss her. In another lifetime, I would have smoothed back her hair and stared at her face, wondering how it would feel to love her. I take a deep, shuddering breath because I can never love her. This isn't love. She is simply an indispensable prop.

Again, Nic reads.

Amaya wakes and smiles up at him.

                    AMAYA

          You haven't told me how you
          feel.

                    HOLLOWAY

          What do you want me to say?
          Other than I'll continue to
          treat you for as long as you
          want.

                    AMAYA

          We're more than doctor and pa-
          tient, aren't we?

                    HOLLOWAY

          It's something we should dis-
          cuss. When you feel up to it,
          of course.

                    AMAYA

          I feel up to it now.

                    HOLLOWAY

          You fell in love with a doctor,
          only to discover he can't love
          you back. You'll resent him
          because he will never leave
          his wife.

                    AMAYA

         Now you're playing me.

    He takes hold of her wrist and a shadow
    passes over his face.

                    HOLLOWAY

         I'm not playing you any more
         than you want to be played.

The scene in my head shrinks to a pinhead. I see Holloway and his mischievous smile and I'm struck by how unflappable he is, how he coaxes and soothes in all the right places. He traps me in a question.

Our devious doc is quite the lothario. What is it that excites him? Tormenting her or the power he has over her?

My thoughts ping-pong from him to Nic, lying on the couch with a mind full of secrets. I realise how the role can break the stereotype for me and make me one of the most bankable actors in the industry.

She looks at me with those smoky eyes. 'How many people did you really interview for my job?'

'Four or five.' It's a lie. She was the only one.

'What made me stand out?'

Which is unfair, considering my eyes have taken their natural downward plunge. 'You were nervous, for one. Too much confidence can be offensive.'

'Is this offensive?'

She wriggles out of her clothes and my body responds in its predictable way. 'We shouldn't be doing this.'

'Says one devil to another.'

I don't want to leap into the pages of Screwtape and Wormwood. There's enough of the demonic in Holloway. Sensing my hesitation, she presses against me, insistent and playful, with layers of impatience beneath the lust. Afterwards, she holds me in a tight embrace, each limb locking me in place. Her eyes flit from me to the Moët idling in the bucket. It seems a like petty power play, but I make her wait for that drink.

Holloway's voice intrudes again.

She's undeniably beautiful. Further study tells me her lips could be plumper and genioplasty will correct a receding chin. But at least she has Mila Kunis eyes.

'I hope nobody saw me coming here this weekend,' she says.

'You did park where I told you to?'

'I'm not a complete idiot.'

'Then we're fine.'

She's careful not to say anything but I realise it's what she isn't saying. Nothing big, just the minutest frisson that something isn't right. She'd parked her car outside the church and walked through the field that borders the south side of our house. Nobody would have seen her.

While she swings her legs off the couch and reaches for her underwear, I take my phone and switch to the front-facing camera. My neck is a deep, angry red, a bruise flared out like a bird's wing, and an autograph my wife will see.

'We'd agreed no love bites, Nic. No scratches.'

'But somehow they happen.' She affects a look of concern. 'Poor baby. Want a little concealer?'

I don't delude myself into thinking the Zane side of me would have done this. This is how Holloway plays his part, no guilt, no remorse.

She reties her bun. 'Got anything to eat?'

'There's food upstairs.'

I fully expected her to stay the weekend but knowing her insatiable appetite for sex, all I want to do is absent myself from her. She leans over my desk to get something out of her handbag and then smiles back at me as if I'm looking at something I shouldn't.

We go upstairs, her in her undies, me in mine. When I find calamari with lemon aioli in the fridge *and* chocolate orange mousse, bile rises in my throat. I hadn't considered Lilja had lovingly put it together, knowing it was one of my favourites. I share it with Nic, gripped with an overwhelming guilt.

We eat in silence, and I want to choose my words kindly, but she speaks first.

'Would you ever leave your wife?'

I give her a full three seconds before I answer. 'The thought hadn't occurred to me.'

'I'm sure it's occurred to her.' There's a thread of sarcasm in her voice. 'She knows you're sleeping with me.'

'This is all very fascinating. But she doesn't.' I suspect Nic is jealous. Not that I care. My feelings for her are complicated. 'You should be wary of my wife. It's not what she says, it's what she doesn't say.'

Even though the thought of Lilja knowing is abhorrent, I downplay the warning. She can't know. She's two hundred and sixty odd miles away. That's well over five hours.

Nic toys with her food. 'You've thought about it, haven't you?'

I'm looking at her as if I'm calculating why she's asking me versus how utterly ridiculous it sounds. 'I won't leave my wife, for the same reasons Holloway won't leave his.'

'You mean love, money, property and reputation.'

'That's putting it bluntly.' I'm glad she understands.

My eyes water and I'm seeing an accumulation of colours and shadows, and a smudge where her face should be. My mind scrabbles at the right words to explain how I feel, but the fact is, I'm blindsided by Holloway's constant mental infiltration. I force myself to take deep breaths, but a lightness zips through me, one voice urging me to run, the other winding me too tight I want to scream.

'Are you okay?' Nic's eyes glow like a cat's in headlights.

'I'm feeling a little weird, that's all.'

'Let me un-weird you.' She begins kneading my shoulders.

My heart rate drops and I'm no longer sweating. I soon lose myself in the deep compression provided by her strong fingers, tension ebbing.

'Better?' she says.

'Much better.'

As I leave the plates in the sink, I see her watching me in the window's reflection, her face set in a deep frown. She looks upset – and upsetting her is the last thing I want.

'Let's get you home,' I say, drying my hands.

'You don't want me to stay?'

'Seriously, Nic?' I tap the red mark on my neck and see her flinch. 'How am I going to explain this?'

Her voice is steady and cold. 'Maybe you should just tell her the truth.'

'Truth about what?'

'Us.'

'There is no us.'

Layered within that statement is a threat, Zane. If you won't tell Lilja, she will.

I turn and raise my hand. 'If you tell anyone about us, anyone at all, I swear I'll—'

'What? What will you do?'

I'm levelled by the frightening idea that I wanted to say *kill you*, but a few terrifying words out of my mouth and she'll tell everyone on social media that I'm someone to be hated. I storm downstairs, frustration consuming me and rage creeping alongside.

'I didn't mean it,' she says, trailing after me.

'Then why say it? Obviously, you can see how ridiculous that is?'

'It's just a love bite.'

'It's *evidence!*'

Her voice cracks. 'This is wrong. It's so wrong.'

Why the hell is she crying? I should be the one crying. It's like watching a horror movie, the unravelling of someone in a part they never agreed to.

I move towards the couch on slack legs. She slumps down next to me, her head leaning against my shoulder. She tries to speak, hiccupping through words I can't make out. *I've been feeling sick… and frightened… I don't know what to do.*

I stare at her, stunned. I don't trust her emotional instability, coupled with my anger that came from a simple comment, *Maybe you should just tell her the truth.* More than that, it's Holloway's anger I'm feeling, his vile thoughts pulling me apart.

The relationship is too risky and her heart already knows it. I wrap my arm around her waist and her gaze meets mine for a split second before sliding away.

'I'm sorry. I know this isn't what you want to hear, but I can't do this anymore.'

She shakes her head as if trying to rationalise what I've just ended. Us, having sex everywhere, sometimes two or three times a day. She made me feel like the most desirable man in the world, and I got excited by the way she looked at me, the way she wanted me.

I hear the desperation in her voice. 'Zane, this isn't just about you.'

'You're right about that. It's about my wife and my daughter and what it'll do to them.' I pull away and she tries to reach for me, her hand sliding down my arm as the distance gets wider. 'Can't you hear what I'm saying? It's over.'

She's unable to take her eyes from me, her body racked with sobs. When she finally pulls herself together, she puts on her clothes and gathers her things.

'You can keep everything,' I say, handing her the laptop. 'If you tell people we parted ways amicably, I'll give you a reference.'

She takes the laptop but leaves the stuffed squirrel with the googly eyes. I watch her walk through the French doors with her overnight bag, pity grinding away at my conscience.

Holloway has beaten me into madness. I was dangerously close to hurting her.

Trending #InZane

@CirceAtNight: I can't believe we're all watching Epi 9 and completely OBLIVIOUS to the grooming! Oh, Holloway, the sicko you are.

@SherylAdams: Great write-up in *The Guardian* and *Huff Post*. The King of Sublime. Love me some ZaneO.

@BantaBadger: He owns it. Everyone goes nuts for his style and calls him a role model.

@HeyWhatsUP: @BantaBadger Role model, my arse.

11

LILJA

I sip my coffee as the sun rises, my unease from last night morphing into panic. While Mum and Frank chatter about the remains of a woolly mammoth found near Plymouth, a horrible twisting sensation starts in my gut and worms its way up my throat. I suddenly feel caught in a beach holiday time-warp, while precious minutes are slipping away.

I scroll through TikTok. Someone called HeyWhatsUP is running a film title thread, *Becoming Holloway… Slumdog Holloway… No Country for old Holloways… 12 Angry Holloways… Has Zane Osborne gone too far?* Which isn't a film but a comment about his state of mind.

I jump between the open tabs to catch up on all the Zanish comments. One says, *Is Zane Osborne shagging his assistant?* accompanied by a shot of them walking on Warren beach. Then there's another of them in a coffee shop and one of Zane's parked car, thankfully without the license plate. Why would anyone take a photo of his car? There's a lingering feeling of whether the photographer has taken the whole thing out of context.

I know what Zane would say if I asked him. That there's nothing going on with Nic, it's simply the Method. Thing is "actor" is close to "clever liar."

When Zane's phone goes through to voicemail, every inch of me wants to scream. I text: *How are you?* It's a full minute of silence before three dots flicker across the screen. *Oil change xo.*

I tilt my head back in relief and breathe again. It explains his GPS proximity to Sainsbury's, which is near JD's Auto. Then there's another silence that rivals the first, and he's suspicious why I asked him.

He texts: *Where are you?*

I tell him: *Bruges w/e cancelled.*

He's caught between dread and suspicion, thinking *maybe, just maybe…* she knows. When my phone buzzes, Zane's name bannered across the screen, I reject the call.

'I need to go home,' I say to Frank, pouring the rest of my coffee in the sink.

'Is everything okay?' He presses a large hand against my back. 'Can we help?'

A cramp of anxiety goes through me. 'Is it okay if Bizzy stays here. I won't be long.'

He nods. 'Let her stay the weekend. We'll take her to school on Monday.'

I look up at a great wall of a man with merry eyes. 'Thanks… for everything.'

He gathers my hands in his and whispers, 'You don't know this, but every year I leave flowers and other things on your father's grave on his birthday, and every year I promise to take care of his girls. I've never broken that promise and I'm not about to start now. If that husband of yours *ever* lays a hand on you, I swear I'll wring his scrawny little neck.'

I throw my arms around him, crushing him to me, this soft padding of a man who has done more for me than my father ever could.

The drive home seems long in the silence and there's a ball of grief in my heart. It's not just flowers Frank leaves on Dad's grave – Elin and I go there together sometimes – but a small collection of vintage Formula 1 Dinky Cars lined up on the headstone. We often wondered who left them there. Now we know.

By the time I tap in our code at the front gate, dread swirls in my stomach. The GPS shows Zane somewhere along Warren Road and before I call him and ram an accusation down his throat, I check the house.

His side of the bed has been slept in and there's only one damp towel tossed over the shower door. The cushions are fluffed up in the sitting room and the calamari I'd made for him yesterday is half-eaten. There's only one bottle of champagne in the fridge where there should be two. Then I notice the plates in the sink. Mousse pots. Empty champagne glasses. Two of everything. I go from drawer to drawer, cupboard to cupboard, room to room. Digging, rifling, probing. On the coffee table in his study is the missing champagne bottle, still sitting in an ice bucket.

I feel as if I'm becoming untethered from any rational thought. A floorboard creaks and I'm suddenly gripped by a nightmarish vision. Nic in a trench coat, clutching a metal poker and following me around in the darkness. I swing around, my hand in a fist.

Stop! Just… STOP!

First the open freezer, then the missing photos. Now this.

I throw open the French doors and step out into a breezeless morning. Potted yews are bright from the rain and yoke-yellow daffodils peep through the long grass. Somewhere above, a pigeon coos. Everything is peaceful, yet my body is buzzing, and not in a good way.

On the terrace is a half-drunk cup of coffee, cold to the touch, and a plate caked with dried egg. God knows Zane's no genius with a pan, but he's a two eggs man. Has been for years. Recently, he's been getting fussier about his diet, cutting back on carbs and grumbling about how he must keep in physical shape. Now he's eating like a horse.

It's possible he invited Nic for a spur-of-the-moment reading last night. Of course, that's what he will tell me. He's had hours to plan his side of the story.

Oh, Lily, don't be silly. We went over my shooting schedule and all that pre-production stuff you hate, and completely forgot the time. Oh, I didn't tell you she was here? Sorry, must have slipped my mind.

Then the blood starts rushing in my ears. Nic's desk is unusually clear, no yellow sticky notes on her writing pad and no sign of her laptop. The only thing remaining is that stupid stuffed squirrel, sitting like a begging dog in a paperclip holder.

Zane may have allowed her to take the laptop home for the

weekend, but I'd rather nothing of my husband's schedule or personal correspondence leaves this house.

Grabbing her employment file, I add her address to my contacts and decide to take a drive.

12

LILJA

On the way, my mind refuses to settle on the important things, like Zane's upcoming interview with Amanda Yeboah. When I stop at traffic lights, I pull up a YouTube video of Amanda. The audacity of her talking about my husband as if he's one of her best friends makes me itch.

He's the story of the week in the *Sun*, the *Daily Mail*, and the *Mirror* — *Where there's muck, there's Osborne*. The worst is *in flagrante delicto: Ozzie unzipped*. Everyone watching will judge him, but what's the point of the interview if he doesn't present the unvarnished Zane?

I follow directions to a house in Springfield Gardens. Several thoughts go through my head, none of them savoury: first, that Nic will come flying down the steps and wonder why I'm here or that a neighbour sees me climbing through an open window and calls the police. It's the third thought that tops the others. *I've no right to be here.*

It's twenty minutes of trying to talk myself into leaving when the front door opens and a dog drags Nic's exotic flatmate down the steps. As her car reverses into the street, I raise my head over the dashboard.

The house doesn't appear to have CCTV, at least not at the front. That doesn't mean they don't have a doorbell camera with a full view of the street. I ring the buzzer twice, but no one answers. I glance over my shoulder at the street and at the neighbouring houses, confident no one is watching, and slip around the back of the house.

The only entrance available is through an open gate and I find myself in a garden of scrubland and weeds. There are no security decals on the windows or garden signs and the house doesn't appear to have an intricate alarm system.

Along the foot of the house is a transom window, where the top sash is tilted outwards. Since a stand of trees between the properties obscures any view the neighbours might have, I crouch and unhook the catch. No pulsing siren shatters the silence.

I lower myself onto the gravel path and stare into a small scullery, estimating a five-foot drop to a farmhouse sink. As thoughts of breaking into someone's house swirl around my head, something hits me: It might be silent down there, but Nic could be upstairs, reading or ironing her clothes. Or she could be with Zane.

The gap is big enough to crawl through, even though a nagging voice in the back of my mind keeps telling me this is a *bad* idea, I lower myself feet first, the frame of the window bobbing against my back. When my feet touch the sink, I resist the urge to look over my shoulder to see if anyone is here, like a police officer waiting patiently for me to drop to the floor or a drooling Saint Bernard ravaged by rabies.

Thankfully, I'm met with silence, and I find myself in a neat little kitchen with a table and chairs. I take the stairs to the first floor and make a mental note of hiding places should either of them come home. Silky yellow light streams through the sitting-room window, revealing a coating of dust on every surface. My gaze sweeps over the coffee table, the couch, and under every chair, until I feel a flash of anger. The laptop must be here somewhere.

Think, Lilja, think. For a minute, I feel frozen inside, but as I move into the hall, I start to thaw. Opposite the cloakroom is a small study with a desk and chair, and then in a sudden, hopeful rush, I see a flash drive blinking between the bookcase and the wall.

Taking the laptop from its hiding place, I type in the agreed passcode, pulling up emails, photos, and documents, all of which appear professional. Every few seconds, I stop and listen.

When I open the backup drive, everything nosedives like a drop ride. Photos of my husband shamelessly naked and in all of them his eyes are closed. The trembling in my stomach turns into cramps.

Had Nic taken them without him knowing? If so, why had he been so careless?

I pop out the flash drive and slip it into my pocket. Nic may take photos to feed her insecurities, but she may be tempted to cultivate her contacts with the press. I can't allow these photos to be published on social media. I have my daughter to think of first.

A car door slams, followed by the familiar beep of a remote. My heart is jackhammering in my chest and I'm wondering if I have time to run to the back door. I get as far as the sitting-room window to see Nic walking across the street with a shopping bag, keys jangling in her hand.

I could stand my ground and confront her – the thief, the blackmailer, the slut – but as the front door opens, I duck behind the couch.

Her shoes clatter across the hall and then downstairs to the kitchen. All this noise drowns out the snick of the front door, as I charge down the steps to the pavement, barging past a woman with a complaining infant in her arms.

My body sags with relief as I stare through the car windscreen at the house two hundred yards away. In that instant, reality strings out like an elastic band and snaps.

I left the laptop open on the desk. If it weren't for the manic breathing echoing in my ears, I might have thought it was a nightmare.

On the way home, I connect my phone to Blue-tooth and the screen yawns to life. *One step at a time. Call Zane, figure out how to get rid of Nic and then worry about getting rid of him.*

'Are you home?' He must hear I'm breathless.

'Yep.'

'Any reporters skulking around in the lane?' I'm simply making conversation.

'There was someone taking pictures from a satellite van. It's all clear now.'

'I'm no legal expert, Zane, but that's got to be trespass.'

'It's the price we pay.'

The price we pay... I'm trying to dissect how a reporter with any iota of respect would believe surveillance on their "targets" isn't stalking.

Then I remind myself that what I'd done to Nic is ten times worse.

13

ZANE

I'm sitting at my desk when my wife opens the study door. 'We need to talk.'

The curtness of her statement surprises me, and I force myself to stay calm. 'About Bruges?'

'About Nic. When were you going to tell me?'

I feel a jolt in my chest. Tell her what?

'We both know she was here last night. I'd like to know why.'

I lower my voice a notch. 'She had an unhealthy interest in my cash flow. I'm not an accountant, but "how much are you worth" is a question for a gold-digger. Then there was the indelicate subject of her photoshopping celebs faces on TikTok. Mine included. So, I asked her to leave.'

'I find it hard to believe you got rid of her.'

'It's a little more complicated than that.' I feel the familiar tug of regret and the guilt I'd been pretending never existed. 'There're a few legal things I need to sort out.'

By the look on her face, anyone would think I'd stuck a knife between her ribs. I realise she's weighing the pros and cons of Nic's dismissal. Favourably, I hope.

'Look, I've got a zoom call with the lawyer in less than a minute. Can we talk about this later?'

She leans over my desk and places a flash drive on the blotter. 'These definitely aren't photo-shopped.'

My stomach has drawn itself into an aching, throbbing knot.

After she leaves, I slot it in my laptop and start breathing rapidly. There are too many photos of me and Nic to deny it and worse, I don't remember her taking them.

How many more incriminating backups has the bitch made?

After deleting the photos, I put my face in my hands for a moment, not sure what to do next. What the hell was I thinking?

Then Holloway's restless voice. *Be grateful your wife has just saved you from becoming the next centre spread in a smutty magazine.*

I decide to nuke the flash drive in the microwave, but in doing so, tiny little sparks arc behind the glass which means not only is the data destroyed, but the oven too. Now the pantry smells like a burnt light socket.

Half of me wants to run after Lilja, the other part decides I'd be running in the wrong direction. It's Nic I need to confront. Here I am, against my better judgement, wanting to take a good hard look at Nic's phone. The thought that she might do considerable damage to my reputation is burning a hole in my head.

I dictate a text. *Can't eat. Can't sleep.*

After a minute she responds: *Arseholes never do.*

I call and tell her this arsehole is shitting himself big time and if there's a teeny tiny chance she's willing to talk, he would truly appreciate it.

After telling her I'll pick her up and take her to the beach, which, of all places, only reacquaints me with her lethal sexuality, she agrees.

I turn off the alarm and lock my study door, beating a retreat through the French doors. On the way over, the clouds fill up the sky, turning everything a dull grey. My mind becomes more entangled over how the affair began. I was perpetually side swiped by a fierce shot of yearning that niggled beneath my skin like an itch I shouldn't scratch. The more I resisted, the more distracting it became. Even before she worked for me, I'd taken her to Holland Park where we could be free and uninterrupted. Each disguise she'd curated out of a long scarf, wrapped up to my nose, and a flat cap enabled us to walk together in Covent Garden. We'd kiss under craft stall canopies, enjoy the theatre, and dine at upscale restaurants. I bought her gifts, name brands I knew she loved.

Her timing and sense of drama was intoxicating. Whether she was in love with a mix of Will Innes-Kerr and me, plus a dash of Holloway, didn't matter. I'd made love to her in every alley, every shop fitting room, and every empty hotel conference room. The most daring of which was less than sixty seconds on the upper deck of a London bus.

We'd walked every stretch of the beach, all the way to the Exe Estuary in one direction and Dawlish town the other. Skinny-dipping under a full moon and brazenly holding hands as we walked around the cathedral. It felt real. More real than any part I'd ever played.

Deep down, we knew it couldn't last. Neither of us said anything because it was part of the fictitious relationship we maintained.

Holloway always has an opinion. *Better hope you'll get away with this ugly matter and no one will be any the wiser.*

I realise I don't need the script to entice Holloway. He's suddenly beside me; a living thing I can't get rid of.

It's time to rehearse. Here's a good line: "We owe it to ourselves not to mess things up. Look at you? You're amazing. I'll give you a fantastic reference."

But as soon as I park outside her house, I lose my nerve. A lone figure sits on the steps, dabbing her eyes with a tissue. She wears a black cap, long hair spilling down her back, and only one side of her face is visible. On the way to the beach, she tells me something weird happened and not to get mad.

'My flash drive's missing. My flatmate hasn't seen it. I already asked her.'

Since I was stupidly oblivious when she took the photos, I should act stupidly oblivious now. 'Anything personal?'

'Photos of us.' She lets out a long breath. 'Intimate ones.'

'How the hell did that happen?'

'I don't know, okay? It was in a secret hiding place and then it wasn't. Everything's been so… stressful lately.'

'I'm not talking about how you lost it. I'm talking about why you took those photos in the first place.'

She goes horribly quiet and the minutes stretch. Without looking at her, I can tell her face has gone a rare shade of pale.

'When you say intimate, Nic, do you mean in bed?'

'Uh huh.'

'As in naked?'

She nods.

Horror bursts out of my mouth and I mash the steering wheel with both hands. 'Un-sodding-believable!'

For a moment or two, she sounds afraid. 'I'm sorry… I didn't… I didn't expect this to happen.'

I'm sure she can see how ridiculous it is, someone taking a flash drive and not the laptop, someone who knew exactly what they wanted. It's how Lilja got it that interests me more.

I park the car at the beach and open my window. A strong north-westerly breeze scrambles along the dunes and catches in her hair, gusting a few strands across her face.

'Please don't tell me I've ruined everything,' she says. 'I don't need a lecture.'

'How about I say nothing and just listen?'

'That's how it feels, anyway – like it's all my fault.' She stares at me with tear-logged eyes, utterly defeated.

'I hope it wasn't a reporter. What an article that would make.'

Her gaze searches the dunes as if there's someone watching us. Panic worms in my gut for she could have taken pictures of us everywhere.

'So, what do we do now?' I ask.

'I'll keep looking. I'm sure it'll show up.'

There's silence for about a minute as we both think through the improbability of anything as juicy as a flash drive full of incriminating photos showing up at all. Suddenly her taking them without my permission is the central issue and I can't let it slide.

'What I can't figure out is how or when you took them? Was it some crazy game. Some kind of dare?'

'Please don't say it's over. Not because of this.' She leans towards me. 'Do you know what it's like to sleep alone? Without you curved around me, your breath on my shoulder. You're in everything I do. Everything I see.'

'I can imagine.'

'I'm not giving you up, Zane.'

The muscles in my stomach shudder with a sensation of seasickness, and I keep looking over my shoulder for witnesses. I also keep looking down at her phone. If I could just snatch it and restore everything to factory settings…

'We both knew what it was from the start, Nic.'

'An unspoken contract?' She leans back against the car door.

'If you like. We both agreed this was about the craft, not a relationship.'

'It wasn't though, was it?' The wind picks up again and she tethers her hair in one hand. 'You pulled me in. You… you captured me. Now I've fallen in love with you. Is that my fault?'

I don't answer. For the past few weeks, Nic and I have been living in the moment, no responsibilities, nothing to feel guilty about. But now when I look at her, I'm reminded of how I've been easily deceived.

It was your idea to shape your role into something spectacular. Not hers.

'Nic, look at me. There can't be anything that links us. That means texts and photos.'

She throws her arms wide, her expression a mix of horror and hurt. 'Do you think I did this on purpose?'

No kidding, my lips twitch. 'I want you to understand what's at stake, that's all.'

Every affair must have its ending. Tell me, how will you end this one?

Holloway's right. I can't let Nic continue to outplay me. Rules are rules and I get upset when she breaks them. I'm feeling both anxious and hopeless, or just overwhelmed. What started as exploration into Holloway territory has turned into something far more sinister.

'Lilja said something strange the other day.' She looks off into the distance. 'She asked me what I'd do if I suspected my partner was having an affair.'

'What did you say?'

Her eyes drill into mine. 'I told her I'd kill him.'

Holloway's voice rattles up from inside. *You can cope with bad write-ups from the gutter press but not this. If you don't end it, I will.*

Nic opens the car door and walks towards the dunes. I run after her and pull her back, allowing myself to look at her, to really study her. No makeup. The natural, mesmeric Nic I adore. She stands too close, her arms around my neck, pulling my face towards hers. Her kiss is gentle and I'm lost in it, sinking beneath its delicious weight. All I can hear is the roar of the wind streaking through sand and grass. I can't kick her out of my life in the same way I can't evict Holloway. I'm a prisoner to both.

Prisoner? That's funny. It's apparent to me and your rampant little girlfriend that you're hardly a prisoner. You don't need a second opinion for that.

Holloway is right. Despite her beauty, she is reckless and deadly, and I flinch as if she's on fire.

I can't remember the last time I'd been so tired and now I've the nastiest humdinger of a headache. I'm getting too old for this.

Her voice is steady, but the tears are coming. 'I can't stop loving you, don't you understand? There's nothing else I want more than you.' She catches her breath. 'I told myself not to love you, that you'd hate me if I did.'

'I don't hate you. I've never hated you.' My headache flares.

I'm hoping this isn't some kind of *Candid Camera* bullshit and the whole of the British Isles hasn't suddenly tuned in live. It scares me… the look on her face. I see resignation and something else, something that scares me and conflicts with the one in my head: the one I have kissed and loved.

Her voice carries a deeper timbre as if she's reading lines. 'You're all I think about. What you're doing, who you're with. If you're okay. Now I'm sorry I ever took those damn photos and I'm sorry I ever met you.'

Holloway steps into my head and uses my mouth as a speaker. 'No shit! You've stage-managed this whole thing from the start.'

Her eyes go wide as if I've been injected with some kind of demon vaccine. 'What is wrong with you?'

Apart from a pulsing headache. 'There's nothing wrong with me.

It's you. It's this… this shit you've put me in. I've spent the last twenty-four hours wondering how much of it is my fault and how much is yours. Because it's beginning to look very one sided from over here.'

'Put a cork in it, Zane. If you want something to kick around, get a dog!'

My mind tries to slip away from the subject of photos and affairs and the last thing I want to do is tear into her. She could retaliate.

'Look, I'm sorry. I just feel…'

… a vague disquiet, and the worried part of your mind keeps asking if she's sold those photos to the press.

Suddenly, Nic's face is swollen, a type of mumps bloat, which is strange – she looked normal a moment ago. The yapping of panic is louder now and that sense – the Holloway sensory which sees through skin and bone – knows something I don't. Then the vision breaks up, and I can see again.

'You don't look well.' Nic takes my arm and pulls me to the car. 'You haven't looked well for days.'

She drives me to her flat in the approaching dusk, windows down, fresh air blowing into my face. The rational part of my mind clamours in the voice of Holloway.

Pull yourself together, boy. Deep breaths.

Instead of going inside for a drink, I insist on driving home. She watches me leave, the distance between us swimming with unspoken words.

When I arrive at the house, the motion detector lights creep through the trees, silence dropping like a curtain. My first clue that something is amiss is the squeak of an alarm at the back door. The second clue is my study door is unlocked and the chair, which was tucked under the desk is now turned sideways, as if someone had vacated it only moments ago.

In those few seconds, my suspicion of Lilja turns to anger. There is one element I've been able to keep out of enemy hands and that's my spare phone. I keep it switched off and only answer it if I'm alone.

Would you want to hurt your wife? It's perfectly natural to consider it. She has been going through your things.

'I wouldn't dream of hurting her.'

No. Right. Forget I mentioned it.

Damn Holloway. I creep upstairs to find Lilja curled under a blanket on the couch, the TV on in the background. There was a time when I'd slip in beside her and pinch the tender spot around her waist and she'd yelp and kick free. She has always been the strong one, guiding me through the baffling process of marriage. I would never have managed it without her. As I study her eyelashes flickering in a dream, I'm reminded how bittersweet love can be.

Wives are like little terriers, sniffing out lies and chasing them into the open. We mustn't forget that.

Her phone is within easy reach. I snatch a look behind me, to my right and to my left, for Bizzy could be behind any door. My fingers intuitively type in the passcode she uses, but it doesn't work. My heart races as I try again, hoping to change the outcome.

You're being demoted. How do you feel about that?

Excluded. Vulnerable. Alone. If I hadn't dismissed her suspicion of me as idle snooping, I would have known she was serious.

It makes no difference if I lock her out of the study computer and hide my passcodes, she still manages to hack them. She won't confront me, that's not how Lilja works. She'll wait until I lower my guard and begin trusting her again, and then she'll take me by surprise.

If she finds out about my previous sexual encounters, she'll be more than disappointed. I can already see her hurling my clothes out of a window, high end jackets and suits all torn to shreds. Or she'll show me the sharpest knife she owns.

Don't fall asleep on me, Zane. You know what I'll cut next.

I decide to sleep downstairs.

Trending #InZane

@CirceAtNight: ZaneO is trending again. Here's a reminder from Loving Alice of just how good his acting was.

@Titmouse: @CirceAtNight. Nice vid. Who can forget his screen chemistry with Alice made that nude scene the highlight of the whole movie. Everyone thought they really did it.

@HeyWhatsUP: In a rare twist, I agree with @Titmouse. No acting there.

14

ZANE

A pinch of purple light comes through the blinds and a sea breeze wafts through the French doors. It has taken me twenty minutes to recognise I've been robbed. My stash of weed is not in its usual hiding place and now there's a buzz of crickets in my head.

I don't know if Lilja took it, but it's entirely possible because she knows more about me than I know about myself. Best to escape to the house in Holland Park until the whole thing blows over.

Wearing my favourite linen shirt with chinos — laid-back cool — the aroma of espresso lures me to the kitchen. No doubt my wife will want to know why I fired Nic, including the sordid matter of how I arrived at the decision. She will also ask when shooting starts, but she doesn't understand that acting involves resting, so you could say this is another rest after the last rest.

I hear a sound. A window twitching in the wind or a squeaky door. I've tasted a mood like this in childhood; Dad crouching behind a shrub in our garden, watching his snares. It frightened me then, and it frightens me now. Then familiar footsteps, efficient and unhurried. Drainpipe jeans nip her ankles, narrowing from a shapely calf to a slender foot. I study her pointed chin and her pale blue eyes, and I wonder why we're both lost in our own thoughts.

There are no more *Love you, Studdo* notes on my computer. This version of my wife doesn't jibe with the girl I fell in love with nor is she the predictable, malleable one I married.

'Why are you sitting in the dark?' she asks.

She's got a point. I could have shifted my preoccupied arse of the bar stool and opened the blinds. 'Good morning to you too.'

She takes eggs, bell peppers, courgettes, chickpeas, onions, and harissa from the fridge and lays them out on the counter. Some kind of Moroccan thing she's pulled out of her head.

'Coffee?' I ask.

'Thank you.' She takes a mug from the cupboard and nudges it in my direction.

It's usually Lilja who makes the coffee and serves it, but I get the reluctance. Anything for my lovely wife. I place two steaming mugs on the counter, hoping my face doesn't betray my nerves.

'I have a question. For the past three months you've been listening in on my phone calls, checking my texts and emails, and snooping around my office. Why not just ask?'

She gives me an unapologetic look, a strand of hair dangling over one eye. 'You would have denied it like all the others.'

'You know I was faithful to you before Nic.'

'Oh, no question. You're faithful to every woman you sleep with. Remember, you're not popular in the media for this topic alone – and you ought to take that as an attack on your dignity. I know I would.'

This will be the last time she smirks at me, her sarcasm putting a dent in my day. I'm almost longing for a knock-down, drag-out fight over my missing weed, but since Bizzy will be down soon, a brief ceasefire would be prudent.

'As you know, Nic no longer works for us. I admit that I asked her here on Friday night, at least in part, because of how she might help me. But I didn't realise she misunderstood the agreement and thought the scenes we played were real.' There is one more subject I must broach. 'How did you get the flash drive?'

'Does it matter? You screwed your assistant and she took photos while you were doing it. What were you both thinking?'

'Things went too far. Now I'm trying to repair it.'

'Repair what, Zane? Our marriage or your reputation? Because I wouldn't bother with the first.' She looks towards the sitting room and lowers her voice. 'What did the lawyer say?'

The fact that I never spoke to one about Nic's contract is a moot point. 'I left a message.'

'Great. Bloody great.' She presses one hand against her forehead. 'How many more are there?'

'Photos?'

'Women.'

'Just Nic.'

I barely hear the "Look what you've done to us" lecture and the horrible fact that my daughter could have seen the photos. Somewhere in that wild outburst is the predictable summons to get packing. Yet here I am clinging on to every vestige of hope that she might forgive me. Poor sod that I am.

Now it's my turn to point an incriminating finger. 'How do I know Nic wasn't conspiring with Marschōne? How do I know they weren't trying to ruin me?'

'Don't be ridiculous. No one could have pulled that one off.'

'I employed a woman who came to me with excellent references, a woman I thought I could trust. Now, she's selling photo-shopped shit about me to the gutter press.'

'Whose fault is that?'

'I'm sorry, okay? It was a stupid mistake.'

'And that's it? You admit you made a mistake and everything goes back to normal?'

'No. Nothing will ever go back to normal.'

If I agree to a divorce, Lilja's life will proceed the same as before, whereas mine will be exposed to the worst kind of media attention. If I have any hope of reconciliation, I should at least show her remorse.

Thinking of the last day I saw my father – determination and sadness grooved into his face and his hand pressed lightly against my shoulder – I allow grief to build inside me, slow and relentless. Then it engulfs me. I sob, great bellowing sobs that makes my nose run. The ache inside me is like homesickness, and I tell her I love her, despite everything, and I am as terrified of losing her as I am of losing my daughter.

I notice how tense her face is with the effort of trying not to cry too. I want to tell myself when all this is over, it'll be Lilja and me and Bizzy, just like it always used to be. But her decision has already been made.

'You'll leave after the party.'

For a second, I'm too startled to hear her words, and then the penny drops. 'As in for good?'

She stares at me, her eyebrows drawn together. I sense the faintest trace of contempt in her expression at how pathetic I'm being. 'Divorce would be a better option.'

Everything feels upside down and I need air, preferably a long drive to the cliffs to think it through. 'Are you sure this is what you want?'

'I think it's right for both of us.'

She carries on dicing and chopping, occasionally sipping her coffee like it's any normal morning. A bead of sweat rolls down the side of my face and the room sways. Her voice sounds far away, yet she's suddenly next to me, one hand on my back and the other on my arm.

'Zane, look at me. Are you okay?'

I shake my head.

'Did you take anything besides ibuprofen?'

I shake my head again and pull my arm away. Getting to my feet, I steady myself against the counter. 'I haven't taken anything.'

'Where are you going?'

'Downstairs.'

She tries following me but gives up when I lift both hands to ward her off. The stairs seem to swim but I make it to my study in one piece.

Holloway always has such impeccable timing.

We can discuss who the bigger threat is. But I'll save you the trouble. Your ex-girlfriend. I suppose the idea of your reputation being washed out to sea doesn't bother you. It would bother me.

Trending #InZane

@CirceAtNight: Did anyone else see those weird photos on Nicola Gatlin's Insta? Close-ups of hands and lips and someone's leg. It's all over the news now.

@SherylAdams: @CirceAtNight British media fawning over ZaneO and saturating the news with more rumours is utter batshit.

@HeyWhatsUp: @SherylAdams. Not batshit. Stroke of genius. Naughty Nic is trying to tell us something.

15

LILJA

Zane is acting distressed and wounded in a way that feels suspicious to me. I want to believe him, but… I don't really.

The following day, Bizzy is silent on the way to school, plugged into her phone and mouthing her favourite songs. I don't care to bring up her dad's affairs or get into what an arsehole he is. I brave a few questions about bullying. I expect her to pretend it's better, like no one is talking about her dirty dad, even though it's a blatant lie.

'Everything's good.' She crosses her arms and avoids my gaze.

'You'd let me know if that senior… what's his name?'

'Simon Galbraith.'

'Makes inappropriate comments?'

'It's not like anyone can stop it and if you tell a teacher, it only makes things worse, so, you know.'

I do know. But I'm concerned my daughter is being bullied with no one to champion her. And then…

'They're legit awful people, especially Simon,' she says. 'But I don't let him get to me.'

'Has he done something?'

'If you call sending embarrassing photos of me bending over in front of my locker and calling me a lard arse, then, yes.'

'Did you tell someone?'

'No. I returned the favour. I took dad's weed and put it in Simon's maths folder. And yes, I wore gloves. Those latex ones you keep in the kitchen. It only took an anonymous call to Mrs Willis to search his locker, and now he's been suspended.'

I can't believe she just said that. My daughter is a genius *and* quite capable of looking after herself as she has done countless times.

'Nicely done.' I realise my voice holds a hint of laughter. 'Incidentally, where did you find Dad's weed?'

'The middle cushion of his couch.' She gives me a sideways smile.

'No wonder he's a little ticked off. I doubt he'll use that same hiding place twice.'

I try to examine when her father's late nights became more frequent, together with his temper. I assumed it was the strain of his work and the frustrating burdens he had to bear, and I simply wrote it off. He'd stagger into the bedroom full of apologies and tell me, *It was a boring arts and entertainment party, Lily, top floor of the BBC.* I'd rub his back while he threw up the alcohol he'd drunk and by morning, he'd have forgotten it all.

Now I feel him watching me, his face twisted in disgust, as if he hates me for wanting him gone. Bizzy and I have each other and we can make a life for ourselves if we try.

After dropping her off, I return home. Stella's upstairs vacuuming and there's no sign of Zane. My spy app confirms he's driving along Wellington Street which gives me a good hour to go through his things.

As I walk into his study, I can't help feeling Holloway's presence, as if he's not only the product of my husband's twisted brain but mine too. His one flaw is that he exists only between the pages. I sit at Zane's desk and study the scene he's been reading.


```
FADE IN:


INT - AMAYA'S FLAT - AFTERNOON

CLOSE ON: Holloway sits next to Amaya on
```

the couch. There's a bottle of whisky on the coffee table and two half empty glasses. He hands her a bag from a high-end boutique.

Amaya pulls out a dress and studies the material, red, silky. She pauses at the slit. It will reveal the scars on her thigh.

                    HOLLOWAY

          Beautiful, isn't it?

                    AMAYA

          It's delicate.

                    HOLLOWAY

          I happen to like delicate.
          More whisky?

                    AMAYA

          Yes. Thanks.

                    Holloway

               (pours two glass)

          The colour… would you say it's
          blood-red?

                    AMAYA

          I think they call it claret.

HOLLOWAY

Ah. There's always a proper
name for everything.

AMAYA

It would suit your wife's co-
louring better. Incidentally,
she knows you're having an
affair.

HOLLOWAY

That's all very fascinating,
but she doesn't.

AMAYA

I overheard her talking to a
friend in Harmon's Grill. She
said it wasn't for the first
time.

HOLLOWAY

Pretty coincidental you happen
to be in Harmon's the exact
moment that my wife was there.
Were you following her?

AMAYA

I know it sounds crazy...

HOLLOWAY

So, you were.

                    AMAYA

     What? No... it was a coinci-
     dence. I thought you should
     know.

                    HOLLOWAY

     Very thoughtful. Now tell me,
     can you stand to look at a mu-
     tilated corpse?

                    AMAYA

     I'm sorry?

                    HOLLOWAY

     That's what you'll become if
     you continue to stalk my wife.

They sit in silence for a few uncomfortable moments. Even though he leans over and kisses her, Amaya knows her situation has become more threatening. When his hands are on her thighs and under her shirt, she can't blame it on the whisky. I don't know whether to be disgusted with her or horrified. Hard to say. But no one can say she wasn't warned.

Moving the mouse on the blotter, brings up Zane's screensaver and login, but the password doesn't work. The one thing I've learned about my husband is that he sees things in patterns, even when he's hiding something. He tucks half-smoked joints inside the cushion he sits on and new clothes under old jackets on a hangar. It makes perfect sense for him to hide his notebook on the bookshelf and preferably between books of the same size.

Ten minutes later, I find it slotted between Robert Louis Stevenson's *Kidnapped* and *Lamb to the Slaughter* by Roald Dahl.

I hack deeper into Zane's search history and find lists of *How to*

Have an Affair and Not Get Caught, How to Keep Your Private Life Private, How Not to Leave a Paper Trail. Hide The Evidence, Use a Condom, Foolproof Your Phone. I wonder if I'm being paranoid. These searches mean nothing if he's using them to explore Holloway.

Which brings me to another file marked *Second quarter goals.* Since when has Zane been interested in financials?

The first page is a mind-numbingly boring corporate report, but scrolling to the second page reveals the file's true intent. Screenshots of steamy texts between him and Nic, ones he'd intentionally saved from an app called GETLOST, where messages disappear only seconds after the recipient has read them. Even more disturbing is Zane's cloud service, HIDEPRO, which is locked by a PIN.

I take a photo of his computer, showing the texts, and since I've changed my password, Zane can't hack into my phone to delete them.

I'm dreading the talk I know we will have to have, but there are two hundred guests coming on Saturday for his birthday. As the shadows lengthen and the stairwell swallows the light, I glance across the terrace with its teak furniture and potted maples. I half expect him to be sitting outside like he used to, typing his lines in the silvery glow of his laptop.

The grinding of the garage door tells me he's back. I close all the files and turn off the computer. At the far end of the terrace, cigarette smoke rises into the air, and I hear talking long before I see him.

'What do you mean, it's not an issue? Because of the photo you just posted, I don't *have* a private life.' Muffled words followed by a long silence. 'Fine. You've dug your own grave.'

I back up into the room and slam into the side of the desk. The antique gimbal compass wobbles, but my hip takes the full force. The word *shit* flies out of my mouth, causing Zane to twist his neck around. He lowers the phone and walks towards his study.

I'm in the hall before I hear the click of the French doors, my shoes skidding on the floors. It's no good trying to replicate the noise I've made. Nothing comes close to *shit.* I rush upstairs, followed by an excited cat, and hide behind the bedroom door. I'm looking down at Ted, willing him not to start meeping.

Minutes later, I hear a thudding on the stairs and then silence. I can sense Zane's confusion by the way he pauses on the landing, and then shuffles down the corridor towards the spare room. He interrupts Stella's polishing with a threat.

'If I catch you snooping in my study one more time, you'll be fired.'

I never considered he'd attack Stella. It was me he heard, and he knows it. I slip out from my hiding place and creep downstairs, glancing up at the landing balustrade to see if he's leaning over. Not yet. But he will.

He'll be hanging around outside the kitchen soon, listening to me videoing a recipe or simply staring through the crack in the door. If I look up, he'll hurry off and pretend he wasn't looking, keeping his distance, watching me as I watch him.

I could spend the entire day agonising over why he was talking to Nic. Why the words "You've dug your own grave" make me uneasy. I can't be too sure, but I think he's watching her too.

The front gate buzzer pulls me out of my trance. It's Mum and Frank, followed by the florist and a van carrying tables and chairs.

Thank God! Company.

I spare a moment to look at TikTok. It's peppered with new posts, but none more flagrant than Nic's. The words — *The new us* — and a blurry image of two people in low light, a selfie held out by a long arm. One head is lowered to accommodate the other, mouths touching.

Pressure fills my head like I'm being pushed underwater. Everyone has seen this, including my daughter. Nic has betrayed us all.

All I want to do is grab her hair, throw her to the floor and beat her with a meat mallet until there's nothing left. But there's a timing element to all of this and I need to be cautious.

16

ZANE

I try to prepare for my interview with Gary O'Malley tomorrow, but Lilja's meddling is getting to me.

My mouse and keyboard have moved a fraction of an inch beyond the tiny nicks I've scratched in the blotter and the script is open at the wrong page. How I manage to keep away from my wife for the rest of the day, I've no idea. It must be as much of a relief for her as it is for me.

There's a shit-ton of noise today since preparations for the *Evil Under the Sun* party are underway. Our house will become an isolated hotel in Devon, with everyone dressed up in evening gowns of the 1930s. There will be picture hats and shoulder pads and long flowing scarves.

I check my social media for a little encouragement from Milo. Today, he's left a comment on *BarbedWire*. *God, grant me the serenity to accept the morons I cannot smack. The courage to smack the morons I can. And the wisdom to know when to stop smacking the morons.* No one shreds him for it and there's a ton of smiley faces and likes, and I wonder how someone underage can access the website in the first place.

The knock on the study door makes me flinch. Stella examines me with troubled eyes. 'You should open a window and get some fresh air.'

For the first time I detect a note of concern in her voice, borne out of my threat to fire her, I expect. 'The French doors are open. Isn't that enough?'

'Nothing is ever enough for you, is it?'

'Listen, I'm sorry. I didn't mean what I said. I don't know what we'd do without you.'

I'd miss Stella and that old banger of hers with spider web cracks on the dashboard and a colony of fungus in the air vents. I'd have nothing to laugh at.

She gives me a silent, knowing look, and for a moment I think she's about to break into a smile, crack a joke, tell me the local gossip. But her eyes roam over the stack of dirty plates on my desk, which have been joined by the fly population of Dawlish.

'We've talked about this before,' she says.

'About me living like a pig?'

'About you betraying your wife. It's disgusting, a man of your age, pretending to be a stud.'

Pretending? There's no pretending about it.

'Do you even know what you're doing?'

Startled, I can only gulp and nod.

She lowers her voice, but the venom is deafening. 'You've no idea how much evidence I've got rid of to save your despicable arse. I won't do it any longer. Do you hear?'

'Evidence?'

'Underwear under the spare bed.'

'Could have been mine.'

She holds up a lacy thong. Not mine.

'That sneaky arrangement where the poor young girl parks at the pub and you drive out on the pretext of getting another bottle of whisky. Only you're not. You're having a quickie in the back of your car and steaming up the windows like the lovers in *Titanic*. Better than Nic approaching the house on foot from the fields. Far too risky, given all the press outside and your wife's diligence over the CCTV.'

I fall into resentful silence, my mouth open to say, *what the hell*, but she interrupts me.

'And don't try pulling the wool over my eyes. I thought I'd heard and seen everything. But this… this is abuse.' She grabs the dirty plates off my desk and marches out of the room.

I slump onto the nearest chair and let out a shaky breath. Stella reprimanding me is a hell of a character shift and something I need to rectify. Of all the people to piss off, our gossipy cleaner isn't one of them.

The pain of feeling worthless and unlovable is like a hollow ache I've been carrying around for years. I know what Dad would say. 'You're a man now and you have a choice. Stop repeating the past.' But the past is stitched into my skin and it would take years to unpick the threads.

I snatch my phone off the desk and check Nic's TikTok feed, which shows photos of timbered buildings and rain-soaked streets, and the 19th century gable of Mol's Coffee House. It's a photo of hands entwined, hers and mine, and where a large diamond ring is prominent.

HeyWhatsUP: *Married man alert.*

Every part of my body goes rigid. I try to remember if I'd seen anyone glancing around at Nic and me. But there were only three other people sitting outside. One couple was kissing, her legs entwined in his, and the other was reading a book. These posts are making me stir crazy.

I am not responsible for Nic nor do I have any relationship with her beyond what we've agreed upon. Continuing the affair will set off a bigger shitstorm than I can manage.

While my wife is organising caterers and selecting wines, and servers are traipsing up and downstairs with clanking wine bottles and glasses, I text Nic again.

This absolutely has to end.

She responds. *You said that last time.*

I roll my eyes: *I mean the photos.*

I slip on a light summer jacket and run outside, all this while dodging a swooping lapwing, filling the skies with its pee-wit calls.

I text Nic and tell her I'm on my way. Her suggestion that we go to the beach is in poor taste, but I don't bother pointing it out. We find a spot beneath a canopy of trees and sit on the bonnet of my car, watching a wind-ruffled sea.

'I know you're hurting,' I say. 'I will help you.'

'Why don't you help yourself?' She hands me her phone. 'This is what you came for, isn't it?'

Am I that obvious? Only I can't deny what I'm looking at, videos of her and Tom Hiddleston, talking about who is the hottest actor, selfies with celebrities and their partners, and dinners to which I wasn't invited. Everything other than us. A few months ago, I would have been livid. Now, I'm relieved.

Tom Hiddleston? Is he her next conquest?

Should I warn him as Marschōne had done for me? I push the idea out of my mind and hand the phone back.

She caresses her necklace, knowing where my eyes will go and smiling when she catches me looking. 'You don't trust me, do you?'

'Not entirely, no. You could have duplicates.' The flash drive proves it.

'Why would I keep copies?'

'I don't know. You tell me.'

I rake through my memory to retrieve one time I'd seen her without a phone. Whether there was anything she said that I should have picked up on.

Every breath she takes conveys amusement at your expense. That, and the reporter she knows is hiding in the bushes.

I scan the surrounding area. The seagulls seem to have quietened, and unless there's someone flattened in the marram grass like a sniper, I see nothing suspicious. Then I spot the walker on the beach, zigzagging after a dog which is running towards us.

'I bet he wants a photo,' she says, waving her arms. 'Over here!'

Slapping one hand behind Nic's head and the other across her mouth, I tell her to be quiet. I'm struck by how wide her eyes are, how her gaze wanders and doesn't settle. Her body is rigid, and I suspect she's dizzy and numb.

You're thinking of your father. His fingers reaching for the pheasant's throat, gripping and twisting. You don't remember how it stopped, only that it had.

I wish Holloway would stop littering my head with obnoxious memories. I've almost forgotten how it feels to be normal.

A shout and a high-pitched whistle restores the dog to its owner and I release my grip on her, realising how violent this might look.

'Shit! He could have taken a photo.'

'Seriously? That's what you're worried about?'

'He could have been a reporter. Have either of us thought of that? No, of course we hadn't. Us. Here. Right now, will be in the papers tomorrow. Is that what you want?'

Her face hardens, her lips pressed together. 'You think this is all about you? People are far more interested in Gary Lineker presenting *Match of The Day* than a bit-actor in a car park. You weren't worried when we had sex in the dunes, and on your sofa, and in the car. How many times was it? I bet you can't even count?'

She's right, I can't. We've had a pattern of risky sex where anyone could have taken a video. Wait… what did she call me?

'Twenty minutes ago, we were having a friendly conversation.' Her face flashes with an emotion I can't track and the tears fall.

'Until one of us went against the rules. I don't want you intruding on my life. Is that understood?'

'It doesn't suit you to be such a shit.'

'It's the sort of person I've become. Particularly if you thrive on pissing me off.'

The tilt of her head and the light in her eyes do something to me. I pull her off the car and behind a tree. The dog walker is scanning the car park and the surrounding dunes. He cannot see us.

For all you know, you're being filmed right now. That's why she brought you here, isn't it?

I keep looking around for the glint of a lens peeking through a hedge, and I can see my vigilance has caught her off guard. I feel a niggling anxiety as the wind picks up, a bracing inshore breeze that ruffles her hair.

'This is a violation of the contract.' I stand over her like one of those vintage Sod Off posters. 'We both agreed this relationship was temporary and now it's over.'

It hurts to see her crying. Almost as much as it hurts her to see me again. I want to tell her that it will okay. That I loved her in my own way. That it wasn't her fault. It was mine. That I'd found the best part Holloway because of her. That somehow, if things hadn't been this way, if I hadn't been married, it would have been about us.

Her and me.

Here right now.

But I can't tell her any of this. I'm here for one reason and one reason only, and that is to end it.

She teeters around as if she's trying to find somewhere to sit and reaches out for me, but I shrink away. I expect she's finally allowed the words *now it's over* to sink in.

You think the bitch isn't playing you? Come on! She's directing this whole thing. Look how she's prepared the scene? Your face is recognisable to anyone who cares to be watching. Hers is too. Including those tears.

Frankly, it disturbs me, and I can't help thinking Holloway has got the upper hand, turning the once robust me into something so utterly un-me.

On the strength of Nic's character and state of mind, I must be cautious. I've assumed, wrongly, that she wanted something brief and exciting like I did, living day to day, seeing where the tide took us. I can't tell her why I've put myself through this pleasurable ordeal with a woman ravishingly gorgeous and impossibly brilliant. But to me, she has always been, quite simply, Amaya.

I open the car door for her and while she puts on her seat belt, the glint of silver on the ground catches my eye. It's not simply a guitar charm which has snapped off her keyring, but a thumb drive where the diamond between the frets is a built-in microphone. We bought Bizzy something similar for school. I quickly slip it into my pocket.

On the way back, we don't look at each other. We don't talk. I map the fastest route in my head. 60, 70, 80 mph – and her voice is a sharp needle in my brain, pleading for me to slow down. But everything mists in a sea of anger, accompanied by a darker, more dangerous sensation.

Hate.

Dizziness ebbs and flows and pain gathers behind my eyes. As the wind rushes through a slit in the window, I know I'll have to slow down at the corner ahead. But I wait until the last moment, that final exhilarating second before my foot slams on the brake. It's wild how the car responds – no fishtailing, just a perfect, slowing arc – and I realise I've revealed my messy side, the cat toying with a vole side, departing from the better me.

Her face contorts with the struggle not to cry, voice wavering and cracked. 'You honestly think scaring me half out of my wits is as bad as me taking photos of us together?'

'There's speaks someone with integrity.'

My insides loosen as she cries again. I couldn't have underestimated her more. A young woman who told me she was professionally discreet, but has failed to keep her side of the bargain – and why would she? I've worked too hard to become a household name, I won't let her screw it up.

I park near a large red-brick Victorian house set back from the street. We sit for a while, not knowing what to say. A knot twists in my gut when she talks.

'I thought this was it,' she says. 'That you'd protect me and love me until I was old and grey. I thought you were someone I could trust. But it's not true, is it?'

'It's not possible.'

'I'm not talking about what's possible or what isn't possible. I'm talking about trust. You abused that trust.'

Trust must be earned; don't you agree? Her games must annoy you. She's a terrible liar.

I'd often thought about how she would react when I ended it, versus how she's acting now. Not with dignity but lacing the air with accusations.

Anger merges on her face and then fritters to disgust. 'It's not over.'

Trending #InZane

@CirceAtNight: Been bird-spotting lately? My grand-pa reckoned he saw ZaneO with his pretty assistant on the beach earlier, that pinch me moment, with his hand over her mouth.

@BantaBadger: Total violation. I can't believe there are men out there like this. Just because he's a celeb doesn't mean he can treat women like that.

@Titmouse: @BantaBadger Agreed. How's he gonna explain that shit to his wife?

@HeyWhatsUP: He'll do what he always does. Lie. I'm already singing *Sympathy for the Devil*.

17

LILJA

Our guests anticipate a flamboyant birthday celebration with a garden party, fireworks, and fine wine. It's already 6.30 pm and kick-off is in one hour.

Zane has not returned from his interview with Gary O'Malley from BBC One. I've texted him not to go on a bender with Gary afterwards, but I've received no response.

I stayed up all night making mini-New York cheesecakes with wild blueberry compote for dessert. Sleep was impossible. I kept hearing noises outside, snapping twigs and rustling, but when I checked the security cam, it was nothing but a deer too close to the ha-ha.

Our gardener has garlanded the terrace and trees with fairy lights and my amazing mother is adding the finishing touches to the floral arrangements. I pour tumblers of iced water for the servers and tell them to keep hydrated. The temperatures this summer are soaring to record highs, and a steamy kitchen in this heat is unbearable.

Elin makes smoked salmon citrus with creamed spinach, and Paul, my brother-in-law, sears lamb with sauteed mushroom and vermicelli rice. I'd rather cook, but I can hardly expect the party to host itself.

I coordinate the security firm and check my phone for any more guest cancellations. I rush upstairs to take a shower. Nic's TikTok has become a daily obsession for me, something tangible I can dig my nails into. I keep refreshing the feed and suddenly there's something.

The triptych presents tantalising silhouettes where two faces are pixelated. I want to slice Zane's throat and watch him bleed. I want to kick his limp body until I've exhausted all the anger and hurt and can breathe again.

While hot water lashes against my forehead, burning away my tears, I make a decision. Somehow, I'll bury all this until the party is over. Somehow, as my fingers work up a lather in my hair, I'll pretend I'm single.

Drying myself, I open the door to let out the steam and there's Mum sitting on the bed with a concerned look on her face. I hope she hadn't heard me thumping the shower cubical with a fist. She wears a monochrome Ascot suit and hat, with a bright red corsage on her lapel.

'You look beautiful,' I say.

When is Mum not beautiful? She could be gardening or cleaning up dog poo, and she'd still be in full makeup with perfect hair. She helps me into a hand-beaded blue dress with Hepburnesque bows on the straps and stands back to admire me.

'French knot, I think.' She gets my brush and dries my hair.

Afterwards, Mum gives me, and the room, a good dousing of hair spray. The gate buzzer tells me two reporters have arrived to take photos. Guests are trickling in; agents, publicists, talk-show hosts, and Simon and Alizha Berne.

Flashes burst along the drive while Mum and I stand at the front door shaking hands. I allow one photo and then tell my favourite reporters not to photograph my daughter and not to follow me back inside the house. There is a round of laughter and teasing.

I use the same joyful mask to get me through the alfresco dinner. During the dessert, I don't have to turn to see if Zane has arrived. It's a sense, like the spread of foul air. I feel his light kiss on my cheek and smell the stench of whisky.

'You look amazing, as always,' he whispers.

I feel nauseous and my head is throbbing, and I wonder if my anxiety filters through. He does his rounds, followed by bursts of laughter and clapping. There are too many wide-brimmed hats, you can barely see a face. Someone congratulates him and another commends him on his performance as Holloway.

As each guest smiles, I can hear the cogs turning, Harley Street surgeon, cheater, killer. How entrenched is Zane in a man who abuses his position as a doctor?

They're all about to find out.

18

ZANE

Lilja is stunning tonight. The most beautiful I have ever seen her. My daughter has chosen to go her own way as usual and has glammed it up in a chequered pyjama set and slippers à la Billie Eilish at the Met Gala. They're both chatting with Isabella de Bruin, one of the hottest models in London, who is dressed in a beach kaftan.

The lights snap out as the first rocket flares in the night sky, expanding like an umbrella and dispersing into stars. The phone in my pocket buzzes out a rallying cry.

The text is three words. *Meet me downstairs.*

I have a weird feeling the guests will soon be singing *Happy Birthday* to a man who isn't there.

The French doors are open and I can't figure out why Nic's sitting on my couch. I thought we'd already parted ways and now I struggle between the crying act she's promoting and a thorny sulk. She is becoming a nuisance.

'Are you stalking me?'

'I wanted to see you.'

She's sobbing a little and I pass her a tissue. 'So you thought you could just turn up at my birthday party?'

'It's not like I climbed over the wall. A bodyguard let me in and—'

'Offered you wine and canapés? Unlikely.'

I'm thinking a less invasive alternative would have benefitted her and chastise myself for not including her name on the barred list.

I take off my jacket and hang it over a chair. 'There are guests in my house, and you're not supposed to be here.'

'I have a question,' she says.

'Fire away.'

'Did you ever love me?' Grief bruises her face and her voice is getting louder. 'Did you?'

The question twines its tentacles about me and I'm on the knife-edge of losing my mind. 'In my own way, yes.'

'We were happy and then you ended it… You ended something special. You really shouldn't have done that. The truth is, your wife hates you. It's not just your life she's destroyed, it's mine too.'

My head aches and I try to think if there are any painkillers in the cloakroom.

Holloway strikes up his usual banter.

She takes no responsibility for following you around the house like a horny cat and flashing you every chance she got. Now there are photos of you in every post. Blurred photos, granted. But someone will recognise you.

The clatter of plates in the pantry makes me flinch. I grab her hand and drag her to the back door. A server appears from the terrace, and I nod and smile at him, as if Nic has had too much to drink. I'm about to tell him to give us some privacy when the wine cellar seems like a better solution. I chaperone Nic down the corridor, key in the code and lock the door behind us.

'Careful,' I say, pointing at a dimple of crumbling brick on the steps.

She lurches towards me, throwing her arms around my waist and resting her head on my chest.

'We need to make a decision,' I say, my arms limp at my sides. 'The right one, okay? For both of us.'

I know what she's thinking. Why won't he walk away from this life and make a new one with me?

She looks up at me. 'Marry me?'

I stare at her blankly, bewildered at the question. 'You're not making sense.'

She pushes me away and begins circling the room. 'You can't get rid of me and delete everything we did. I know you love me. You do.'

'This has gone far enough. You need to leave.'

'I won't leave. I'll never leave!' Her faces creases into a grimace, fists pummelling her thighs. 'I did everything for you. *Everything*! I won't let you take it all away.'

She screeches at me through clenched teeth, but I don't hear the words over the punches she throws. My chest takes the full brunt of it and I back up as far as I can go. She picks at my tie and my shirt, pulling and scratching, and I hear the ping of a button as it tumbles to the floor.

I fend her off, but she comes at me again, forcing me back against the wine racks. I'm shocked by how strong she is, but a punch to the chin could dislocate her jaw. She could bite her tongue.

Pay attention, Zane. Who's in charge here?

I raise my fist, a warning that I won't hesitate.

That won't do it, I'm afraid. Think again.

Her fingers thread through my hair in a vice-like tug and her face is sharp like a bird's. I pin her against the wall, my hand against her throat. The veins in her neck are like sprawling worms and my ears ring.

Her knee collides with my groin and brings me down. A blinding, throbbing flash, as if someone's pressing on an open cut, and I curl up into a ball and surrender to the nausea. Somewhere within that maelstrom of sounds, everything goes black, my thoughts barely keeping pace with my pulse.

Smashing glass brings me back, and fearing she might use a broken bottle as a weapon, I make a run for the stairs. Her hands claw at my arm, dragging me back. She shouts, her words muffled, as if bubbling underwater. Any illusions of a resolution vanish, and the edges of my vision begin their greyout, a frothing of tiny bubbles moving in toward the centre.

When she rams me again, I give her forceful shove. Instead of slamming into the wall, her back arches. This is where the action slows. I see the expression of surprise on her face, her eyes tilted to the ceiling as she falls, the sound of her head as it snaps against the jagged stone steps. She gasps for a breath that isn't there and my arms are shaking too much to have caught her. A dark shadow seeps out from under her head.

'Nic.'

I search frantically for a pulse. Curling my hand in hers, my voice sounds as if it comes from someone else.

'Nic. NIC!'

I try to rouse her, telling her if we hadn't fought, none of this would have happened. We could have talked about it. We could have resolved everything.

I press my hands against her chest and count, but there's no warm breath against my ear.

'Nic. Wake up.' I'm begging with everything I've got because her eyes don't flutter and there is nothing left. No one inside.

'Nic. Stop it!'

I pull her shoulders off the ground and shake her. She's being hateful, and the silence is killing me. Heat dashes up my spine, expanding into a white-hot panic.

What have I done? Is she dead? She can't be dead. It was only a fall.

But it wasn't just a fall, it was a snapping of bone on stone, a horrible, unavoidable accident. The more I look at her, the more I realise there's no way it looks like one.

I'm paralysed by the thought that I was the last person to see her or the first to find her. Both look suspicious. Calling the police will reveal someone pushed her. Why else is she lying at an angle to the bottom step and not parallel to the handrail as if she'd simply fallen?

A wave of nausea wells up. The server... he saw us together briefly or at least he saw me with someone. Could he give a detailed description?

My shoes crunch through glass as I approach the butcher's station. Taking a carcass bag from the shelf, I slide it over her head, while part of me yearns for her breath to mist against the plastic, anything to tell me she isn't dead.

There's a rush of noise in my head and it feels as if I'm standing on the side-lines looking in. This isn't an animal to be incinerated, this is a woman who used to be a lover, an employee, a friend.

I lay her out on the butcher's table and see the glint of diamonds on her finger. There will be a jeweller's hallmark inside the ring, something to lead the police to me. I prise it off and pocket everything, including her car keys and phone.

But not Marschōne's watch. That beautiful Panerei might be your saving grace.

There's a scrubbing brush under the sink, a tub of lemon scented wipes and a bucket. I pull the hand towel off the iron ring. That's when I notice the missing button and spots of blood on the sleeve of my shirt. I can't change it now.

I clean up the glass and scrub the floor and walls until the water turns brown. The smell makes me gag.

Don't forget to scrape under her fingernails. Thoroughly.

Touching her hands makes me queasy, and I scrunch my eyes closed and then open them again, there's no way to avoid it.

Zane, focus! Sluice the water down the drain, post the bloody wipes through the grating and leave the bucket under the table. Got it?

My mind buzzes with all the things I must do. The butcher's station door has a slide lock on the inside. I don't expect the servers will need access but keeping it locked is an extra precaution.

I tuck my shirt into my trousers, at least the jacket hides the blood on my cuffs. I leave the house via the outer cellar door and see Nic's white Honda, obscured by the boughs of our weeping willow. That's not to say a guest wouldn't have noticed it on the way in or read the license plate, and I know I'll have to get rid of it later.

I enter through the front door, hoping I don't look as dreadful as I feel. The hall mirror tells me another story. Through the gap in my shirt are two deep trenches, undeniably scored by fingernails. A list of excuses rallies. *A fan jumped me outside the studio this afternoon. Police report? Forget it. I didn't get a good look at my attacker. It all happened too fast.* No matter how I recount it, there is one minor problem. Why hadn't I mentioned it to Lilja when I first arrived? Would she remember my shirt being intact then?

The sound of my wife's voice, shouting my name, makes me

flinch. Better she finds me having a sneaky fag downstairs rather than covering those scratches with concealer. I run to my study and stuff Nic's things into a padded envelope, leaving it in an antique jewellery box on the bookshelf.

I light a cigarette and let it hang from my mouth. Trust Lilja to burst in while I'm shrugging on my jacket.

'What the hell are you doing?'

'What does it look like I'm doing?'

She squints at me, and for a moment I think she's going to accuse me of something. 'Everyone's wondering where you are. It's time to cut the cake.'

My hands are shaking as I mash the cigarette in the ashtray. Shoving my hands deep in my pockets, I follow my wife to the terrace. A large chocolate cake and a crowd awaits me, and there are cheers and raucous rounds of *Happy Birthday*, mostly out of tune.

Bizzy helps me blow out forty-six candles. I try to keep a smile on my face as I slice through half an inch of icing. It's all I can do to stop myself screaming while twenty people pat me on the back and tell me what a great evening this is.

It's gone midnight before Lilja gives our last guest his coat. Bizzy gives me a birthday hug, eager to get upstairs.

'So, how was it?' Lilja corners me in the kitchen while I'm pouring a large whisky. I must be giving her a funny look because she says, 'Gary O'Malley,' to ground me.

'It was fun. Studioworks kept me waiting for over an hour and there was heavy traffic all the way back from West London. Sorry I was late.'

She gives a weak smile. 'Has Nic called?'

Part of me is burning with disgust and terror, and I'm seized with the irresistible urge to drain my whisky and pour another. 'Why would she call?'

The car, you fool. She must have seen the car.

No… Not if she was too busy to notice.

'She did organise your party. It seems harsh not to have invited her.'

'She's probably packing.' I can see my wife is confused. 'She mentioned a job through an agency called Celebrity PAs in New York. The last thing we discussed was a reference. I said I would provide one.'

Holloway has nudged me to the brink and left me teetering on the edge. I don't know if it's the drink or I'm simply desperate to talk. Desperate to get it all out.

I lead her to the couch and take her hand. I want her to know how lost I am. How the script has filled my head with inane banter and ruined my life. It must tickle Holloway that I'm sitting here, dribbling out my pathetic tale. But if I can stop her from filing for divorce, I will.

She hangs on to every word, while I spare her nothing about how things went too far, shamelessly unloading how cold I've been, how heartless. That none of it mattered to me. Nic meant nothing. Lilja's cheeks glisten with tears. I hate seeing her like that. Suffering because of my sick and unforgivable mistakes.

She gives me a look of undeniable sadness. 'We had something special.'

'This isn't about us. It was never about us.'

'What is it about, then?'

'It's about what I did to Nic. She didn't deserve it.'

'*I* don't deserve it!' She gulps back sobs. 'You made me think it was my fault that I'd done something wrong. But I hadn't.'

'I'm sorry…'

'Don't you dare. You're not sorry. You're never… *sorry!*'

'Lily, this is separate. It's not us or you, or what we have. It's outside of that. I can't explain it.'

Suddenly my beautiful Lilja is crying again, her pain becoming mine. She has been a part of me for so long and somewhere inside there's an invisible ache, the throb of a crushed heart. I am sobbing too because I've broken everything inside her. She has been the kind of love I've always wanted, the unselfish love that I'd dreamed of. I've betrayed her and now I'm afraid.

'Please, I'm begging you, Lily. Don't leave me. Please.'

She pulls back her hand, tears clinging to her lashes. Just for a moment she looks at me – and her face is blank and unreadable, like a drunk person's.

She pushes her chair back and leaves the kitchen. I hear her feet tapping against the stair carpet all the way to the landing. When the bedroom door closes, I'm left with Holloway's voice.

You have work to do.

Trending #InZane

@HeyWhatsUP: ZaneO is worse than any horror story Stephen King's ever written. What a loser.

@BantaBadger: The fact that @ZaneO screwed his assistant, all the time pretending he was the world's most faithful husband seriously bugs me.

@SherylAdams: @HeyWhatsUP. Give me hard core facts.

@HeyWhatsUP: @SherylAdams If you think those blurred photos of them together on TikTok aren't enough, then fine. But consider Nicola Gatlin's sacrifice. Reading scripts with him and rehearsing sex scenes. He used her!

@SherylAdams: @HeyWhatsUP How do you know all this?

19

ZANE

It's 1.35 am when the pain hits me, and I suck down a couple of oxycodone.

I look in on Lilja. Her breathing stops for two seconds then resumes, an internal antenna sensing my presence. She's lying on her side, facing the door, the curve of her shoulders and waist defined as shadow. I watch her in the darkness with a burning sense of shame and heartache.

It seems cruel to leave her in ignorance any longer and I kneel beside her and whisper every tiny detail from the first time I met Nic until the last. Although tonight's *Brainbox Challenge* mystery question has also occurred to me: is she pretending to be asleep?

'It's over, I promise. We're safe. She can't hurt us anymore.'

She's unresponsive, her eyes flickering in a dream. After a minute of watching her, I plug my phone into the charger on the bedside table. The GPS will appear as if I were here all night, keeping my toxic secrets intact.

Stuff a small backpack with joggers and a hoodie.

I take the mini backpack from the ottoman box, grab what I need and scurry downstairs.

Wrap her in a sleeping bag and drop her in the sea. Nobody seeing. Nobody knowing.

I creep downstairs to my study and unhook the sleeping bag and tarp from my backpack and take them to the wine cellar. I look down at Nic, wrapped in a transparent bag on the butcher's table, her top lip puckered by the wrapping and her skin pulled back like a ghastly face lift. I feel horribly sick.

There's no way for me to access her iCloud and even if I could delete everything, the police will have some obnoxious way of reinstating it. I'm not about to use her corpse for fingerprint and facial access.

Digging around under the table, I find the latex gloves Lilja uses for handling raw meat and slip them on. I cut up Nic's SIM card, while Holloway goads me with correct procedures and tells me low tide is at 3.00 am today.

I swear one of my ribs is bruised and I try to ignore the pain, and it takes all my strength to wrap the body inside the sleeping bag. Using cord to make a homemade deer drag, I truss it like a pork tenderloin.

Peeling the clothes from my reddened skin, I ball them up, shove them under the study couch, and change into a light-weight hoodie and khakis. Taking the tarpaulin, I open the side door to the garage and check the drive.

It suddenly dawns on me that it would be better to use Nic's car than mine, leaving it at the beach as if she'd simply driven herself there.

Holloway's voice prods me. *Before you leave, shut off the power supply to the alarms, motion sensors and outside CCTV.*

I unlock the boot, the automatic light almost blinding me as I lay the tarp out as a liner. I'm shaking all over. Either I'm having a manic episode, or this is normal after such a traumatic event.

Moonlight streaks through the trees and I know seeing things in the dark is normal. Things that aren't there, like the shadow streaking across the lawn. But it's only a fox. If I thought carrying Nic from the cellar to the drive would be straightforward, lifting the sleeping bag into her car is the worst.

From now on, you will refer to her as it. *Or simply; the remains. For she is a carcass, Zane. Let's not forget about that.*

I find a bottle of barbeque firelighter and a box of matches to burn the sleeping bag and tarp. Somewhere between the heart-thumping drive to the main road, I wonder when a body begins to liquefy or when it gets to the point of skeletonisation. Sure enough, Holloway comes to my rescue.

By the time they find her, she will be unrecognisable. The first stage of decay is taphonomic alteration, causing the stiffening of muscles and joints. Then the autolysis stage, where the skin is wrinkled and grey, followed by putrefaction – the malodorous stench of rotting eggs. Hence a burial at sea… if you get my drift.

Up ahead, a car lurches into my lane and I drive towards it, eyeing the grey-faced driver whose forehead is dipping dangerously towards the steering wheel.

Has she fallen asleep?

She doesn't slow down and neither do I, and for a hairy second, I almost turn the wheel towards the verge, but at the last moment decide to stay where I am. My front bumper clips hers and there's a brief screech of metal, sparks scattering in a dark sky. In my rearview mirror, I watch her rear lights disappearing into the black.

Close call. Too bloody close.

The road slices through the hillside to a barren chunk of cliffs and I drive along the beach road to a small car park. After killing the ignition, everything sinks into silence.

I close my eyes, my heart pounding. I don't want to think about Nic in the boot, and I'm sitting here pretending nothing's happened and then realising it most certainly has.

I shrug on my backpack and carry my burden across a foot-bridge to the coastal path, my ribs protesting all the way. The sea wall leads to a sandstone outcrop at the western extremity of the estuary, waves lapping against the rocks that protect the railway from the sea.

The air carries a hint of rotting fish – at least I hope it's rotting fish – and I breathe through my mouth. In the distance, I can see an arch in the sandstone rock and the yawning mouth of a cave. Laying the sleeping bag down on the beach, I take a rest. Nic was a 50-55 kg woman and easy to lift. Not so much now.

I didn't know I had it in me to kill. Except I hadn't killed her. She fell and hit her head.

Holloway shatters the moment and whispers, *All this spur-of-the-moment planning does you no good.*

He's right. Here I am, trying to hide the evidence rather badly. Then I summon the image of a bloodstained shirt under my couch and I'm thinking *Shit! Shit! Shit!* I should have brought it tonight.

Like I said, bad planning.

I look up at the stars and think I hear the evocative whistle of a widgeon but it's the oxycodone rafting through my veins. Drowsiness pulses through me like the murmur of wind and there's a stillness in my heart, as if somewhere in my subconscious I know all will be well.

2.55 am. The waves turn a fraction.

2.57 am. Change of wind.

3.09 am. The distance between the rocks and the water's edge is widening and I can see pebbles.

Part of me dreads unwrapping her, but it must be done, and the latex gloves feel cumbersome as I fumble with the zipper. I roll her onto the sand and stare down, unblinking, not daring to move. Her face is grey in the moonlight, as if she is as drained as I feel. The story is she was swimming, the current sucked her down and she hit her head on a rock. I try to blink the sea into focus.

Don't give up now. You've made it this far.

Unlacing my boots, I use them to anchor the bags from the wind. Carrying her against my body doesn't repulse me, her doll-like features are still intact, save for her blood-matted hair. All I want to do is to set her adrift, knowing that my secret is buried at last.

Manoeuvring through compacted sand takes all my strength, my feet stubbornly catching on pebbles and seaweed. Once the water is up to my chest, she slides off my arm and I close my eyes, trying to summon the words to a prayer through my chattering teeth.

Something brushes against my bare legs. Hair or hand?

Trying to separate myself from the horror, I take a tumble, seawater racing over me as the tide nudges me along the seabed. I'm aware of the cold and the darkness and the irrefutable pain. My heel brushes against a rock and I push off, my face bursting through a layer of seaweed and salt water into the chilly night air.

Gasping for breath, I'm surprised to see the beach further away than I'd expected, choppy water growing between me and the shore. Even though I'm a strong swimmer, the sea pulls me out; the wind joining forces with the waves.

Am I making progress? I can't tell. But I am panicking.

Stay calm. Keep your eyes on the beach.

Is this the sea's way of getting retribution? I push my muscles harder and all I can feel is my lungs, billowing, burgeoning, and gasping for breath.

Swim, boy. You can do it.

Snatches of exhaustion threaten to pull me down and I have the sudden urge to call out to God, but my request will simply go unheard. He doesn't know me.

He does, you imbecile. He formed you in your mother's womb. More's the pity.

Suddenly I'm treading sand, my knees striking against rock. The wind chafes my eyes and cheeks as I stagger towards my backpack, shaking the water from my hair. Despite dry clothes, my feet refuse to un-numb, and I can barely think over my chattering teeth. I bundle the sleeping bag and wet clothes into a roll and make my way to the caves.

The sandstone arch towers over me, my feet splashing through the pools left by the receding tide. Occasionally I lose my footing on slippery seaweed before the ground levels out to a crunch of sea-shells and sand. I drop my roll on the only dry shelf I can find and saturate everything with fuel. It catches with a flicker, illuminating the outline of the rocks above.

Misshapen faces seem to come to life, whimsical figures gyrating within layers of red sandstone. Nylon curls as it burns, darkening and smouldering, duck down swallowed by the crackling flames. As I listen to the distant thump of waves, my mind wakes up with the warmth and I stay until the last spark dies.

I bury my chin in my hoodie and walk back along the coastal path. The sky is free of clouds and the moon hangs full above the sea. I turn, occasionally, to see if there's a dying flicker near the mouth of the cave, but it's dark and burnt out. All I can hope is that no one finds a body, battered by rocks and bloated with seawater.

I open the car door, making a mental note of the driving seat position and the wing mirrors and leave everything as I found it. On the long walk home, I realise there will be fibres of mine under the seats or a tiny strand of hair caught in an air vent. If the police ask, I'll tell them she often picked me up in her car. It was less conspicuous than mine.

Passing houses with their sleeping occupants and a dog howling in the distance makes me see the bleakness of my future more clearly now. I should have set the example, not fallen for Nic's open blouse invitations.

Outcast. Murderer. Misfit. Any self defence argument will look a little thin, given how deep the gash was in the back of her head.

It seems like hours before I open the back door. After a second's pause, I slip into my study and lock myself in. It's just me now and several shots of whisky and I drink until I'm warm again.

Thankfully, my dress clothes are still under the couch. It's no use taking them to the dry cleaners in case blood spatter arouses suspicion. I notice a shopping bag behind the door and swallow the lump in my throat. Inside is a red backless dress I'd bought for Nic. As I decant it on my desk, a visceral shudder goes through me.

Don't get distracted. We're in this together.

Using the bag for my bloodstained clothes, the boot of my car is the best hiding place for now. Running back and forth from the house to the garage makes me feel like a headless pheasant. Now my arms and neck prickle with goosebumps.

Right then. Let's see what we're dealing with, shall we?

The police will come here, no matter how well I pretend they won't. Even though the thought chills me, I can already imagine them roaring up the drive, their sirens echoing across the deer park. They'll cuff me in front of my wife and daughter and drag me away.

I can't let that happen.

20

LILJA

My eyes are still stinging from last night's tears and I suspect they're bloodshot. Having spent a restless night, clutching the duvet and crying out in my sleep, I had images of Zane pushing me towards the landing bannisters outside our room, teasing and laughing at my panic. Then his face stiffened and with one final heave, my body arched over, my arms flailing all the way down.

I had to keep reminding myself: *It was just a dream and I'm okay.*

It doesn't stop me feeling dazed and afraid. A terrible thought begins to surface, rising like a pale corpse through a layer of algae.

Would he hurt me?

It's possible. But how come he hasn't done it before now?

I take out my phone. According to Twitter, Zane is currently facing a crisis in his acting career – #HollyWeird – a once promising actor the public had pinned their hopes on. His affair is becoming too public and something I prefer to cope with in private.

Celebrity UK online.

Thursday 2 June 2022. Last updated at 07:15.

BREAKING:

Sham marriage and midnight meetings. In-Zane Osborne takes us on a wild ride as news of his serial cheating becomes public.

By Amanda Yeboah

Most of you are familiar with *PLAY HIM, PLAY HER*, a crime drama series starring Zane Osborne as Dr Ethan Holloway and Quiana Thompson as Amaya Stone. To better understand the mind of a predatory heartbreaker, Osborne adopted the disturbing practice of stalking his lead to her home in St Leonards.

He stated: "*I followed her at a distance, my lights on dim… she turned off a few side streets and I almost lost her. It was touch and go as she stopped outside her front gate to access the keypad. I doused my lights, and she didn't see me parked along the kerb. I counted to ten and climbed over the wall. There was a shit-load of solar lights in her garden and I was worried she'd see me crossing the lawn. But I watched her window from the terrace. It felt kind of kinky and weird. Not something I'd normally do.*"

You might want to ask yourselves what other creepy practices Osborne has adopted to ready himself for his role. How Ms Thompson is feeling now the cat's out of the bag. How you, his loyal fans, are feeling. Have the excesses of Mr Holloway gone to his head?

The photo attached to the article shows my husband straddling a wall, the second photo shows his hands fanned against his car windscreen to cover his face. I'm prickling with embarrassment. I keep praying it wasn't Zane in that car and the papers will rescind the article and publish an apology. But fans insist he is the secret man in Nicola Gatlin's TikTok posts.

Sweat trickles down my cheeks and my T-shirt sticks to my back. I creep to the lower ground floor, my bare feet crunching through a fresh layer of sand. It's silent, except for the soft drone of snores coming from the spare bedroom. Through the crack in the door, his face is turned to one side, revealing a cheek pitted with sores.

I swallow rapidly, trying to dispel a thick ache in my throat. Is this the beginning of an incurable disease? Will I have to nurse him back to health?

I'm struck by a story from childhood. Elin and I were raised by Anglican parents who observed the Sabbath, and as many holy feasts that warranted a party. The story I remembered most at church was the plagues visited on a stubborn pharaoh who refused to let the Hebrews go. A pharaoh like Zane, sold out to worldly pleasures and addicted to a lifestyle he refused to change. Had the same angel of death passed over our house last night because of something he'd done? Would our taps run with bloody water? Would our firstborn perish?

I walk closer to the bed and realise those aren't sores on his face, but the reflection of raindrops on the window, cast there by an outside floodlight. I close my eyes and quietly exhale, dismissing such creepy thoughts in favour of breakfast.

Half an hour later, I'm ladling a small quantity of hollandaise sauce on a poached egg and searing leftover steak, when I hear a distant yawn. Not Bizzy, it's too deep for one of hers. Then he trips over her backpack, and a string of vulgarities lace the silence.

He wears a slim-fit Montagio suit and a tie, although none of this detracts from the dark circles under his eyes. My guess is he went clubbing last night. It was his birthday. I'm about to suggest he lies down, but there's only so much lying down Zane can do.

'Morning,' he says.

I shrug and look away.

'I know I'm a shitty husband and I've hurt you terribly, but is there any way I can make it up to you?'

'Seriously?' I plate the meat and hand it to him.

Only there's steak and there's burning at the stake. He may need reminding.

His voice is more refined, as if he has done away with the metallic rasp that often follows a bout of drinking. He holds out a bag. 'I thought maybe this might cheer you up.'

I know the gift must be expensive by the mound of tissue spilling from the opening. Anything to ease his conscience, assuming he feels anything at all. My belly knots and I cringe at the sound of his coaxing.

'Open it.'

I lift the red satin dress out of the bag. The slits are too high and the material is too flimsy, an unstructured style that can't seem to make up its mind.

'I saw it in a boutique in London a while ago and had this dumb idea you might like it.'

'I don't,' I say, dodging a kiss.

'Why don't you try it on.'

'It's backless. I hate backless.'

It's the same hellish little dress Holloway bought for Amaya. I walk towards the door, but he catches me by the arm and twists me around to face him, his eyes lighting up like a slot machine. In the past, it would have been intoxicating. Now I can't stand the sight of him.

'You won't even try it on?'

'You didn't buy it for me. You bought it for her.'

He leans forward intently as if he hadn't heard me. 'It's yours now.'

I don't want to think about Nic wearing it, her scent on it, her sweat. While I'm saying no, he grabs my wrists and unbuttons my shirt and I'm trying to understand why he's so insistent, why the look on his face scares me. He stretches the dress over my head and pulls it over my jeans.

'There. That's better,' he says.

It's repulsive, I want to respond, but we're staring at each other in silence, seconds ticking by.

'We'll celebrate on Saturday night,' he says, his fingers tracing the fabric between my breasts. 'I want people to see us together. I want them to see us happy.'

So far, I have been spared from being his social prop, but now I'm being fashion-managed and told what to wear. He knows how I hate publicity interviews and tabloid parties, all because he wants a united front. But this… this is torture.

What's got into him... This isn't the Zane of the past. This a different Zane. A dangerous Zane. I walk unsteadily towards the Aga rail, glancing up at a set of knives hanging from magnetic steel runners and thinking if I could slit his throat, how quickly would he die?

'It won't make any difference.' I turn to him. 'You're in the news again today, and not in a good way.'

Maybe I put a little too much emphasis on "not in a good way" because he gives me a sour look I'm not completely comfortable with.

He punches out a short laugh. 'I don't know what you're thinking or what you believe. But all this *stuff* people keep spewing about me is a bunch of crap. You know how it works. Celebrity gets a speeding ticket and suddenly he's a dangerous driver. Can't you see what I'm going through?'

'Saturdays are our cooking nights. I promised Bizzy.'

'Then un-promise Bizzy. She can stay with your mother.'

My mother. Never Vibeke, happy to rush him to the hospital when he got blind drunk and fell and hit his head two years ago. It was because they had rejected him for the role of a human computer in a big film. Mum was a calm voice who stayed with us for four days, happy to help and swap shifts so we could watch him around the clock. He looked lost and inexplicably childlike, even I reached out a maternal hand.

I move aside and pull off the dress, leaving it in a heap on the floor. I'm standing there in my jeans and bra, and his voice changes pitch again.

'You don't want to give us one last try, do you?' He searches my face for tell-tale tics. 'I can always tell when you don't want to do something.'

'It's over.'

'Maybe I don't want it to be over.'

There's something in the subtext of his tone, the set of his shoulders, which screams at me to be careful. Over the roar of my anger, my brain is kicking into high gear, calculating the perfect time to run past him to the stairs. He sees the direction of my gaze and blocks me, only this time I'm not afraid.

Tapping his chest with a finger, I say, 'What you're saying is, we go as a happy couple, hiding the fact that we're living separate lives?'

'That's great, Lily. You can't put on a friendly face for my sake? This is about my career which, by the look of it, you're trying to ruin. For a wife, that's a jerk move.'

'You expect me to pretend everything's okay? Everyone knows what you've done. Including your own daughter!'

He repeats what I've just said in a high-pitched voice. I know exactly what he's trying to do but belittling me has little impact now.

My eyes slide from his face to the kitchen window, where our gardener is shaping one of our topiaries into a rabbit. Zane's gaze follows mine and then snaps back to me, his lips curling into a sneer.

'He won't help you. He's been talking to reporters through the gate and accepting bribes.'

It's not true and I'm not falling for it. He goes on and on about my tiny brain and how I'll never manage a restaurant without a degree. How he's supported me for years.

What stops me from yelling at him that this is all his fault and not mine, is Stella's cheery voice as she opens the front door. She hangs her coat in her usual place, her bright eyes surveying us.

I could tell her our marriage had been spinning in different directions. How we are no longer one, but two separate entities, bouncing off one another like sumo wrestlers.

As Zane stamps a path to the lower ground floor and I stand in the kitchen half-undressed, I suspect she already knows.

PART II

The Client

21

ZANE

It's been four days since it happened – the thing I can't talk or think about. I take a deep breath, count to five, and let it out slowly.

It's no use thinking hours of scrubbing the cellar floor will remove the finer traces, but I've done my best. I even appealed to Cotterell Builders to repair the dodgy steps immediately, alluding to the obvious dangers. The supervisor was adamant the flooring beyond the bottom step didn't need replacing, but I was unrelenting. They thought I was insane.

I've had time to study Nic's phone. There was nothing superficial about her feelings for me, as evidenced by her listing my name in her contacts rather than Ethan Holloway's. I'd allowed myself to simply enjoy her, taking pleasure from her pleasure without giving anything in return.

I'm disturbed by a sharp vibration from my phone, the insistent sound of someone who won't go away. My heart beats with slow, heavy thuds and my hands are shaking. It's a call from my therapist.

'Meet me outside.'

'Outside where?' I ask.

'Your house.'

There are psychological side effects to method acting or, as I prefer to call it, "deeper" acting. Anxiety, personality changes, the emotional need to stay in character. I have all three. Berne Bros. Entertainment provides actors with psychoanalysts, and that's how

I met Meggy. To think we could have a psychic connection makes me uneasy. Has she come to hear my confession?

I check the drive through the sitting-room window. Sunlight tinges the trees and beyond them, a Porsche idles outside the front gate, its headlights flashing on and off. I run to meet her and look over my shoulder before pivoting into the passenger seat.

'Seriously, Megs, what are you doing here?'

'It's urgent. And no, we're not crossing the line of therapist-patient. You know traditional therapy won't work for you.'

'So this unorthodox approach of you driving over to my house at all hours is part of the twenty-four-seven agreement I signed?'

'You need to check your voicemail. I called twice this morning.' She hands me her phone.

Missing woman's car found near Langston Cliffs

By Stan Marriott
Senior Reporter

18:22, 2 JULY 2022

Police have launched an urgent appeal to find a missing woman from Dawlish Warren, after her car was found near a local beauty spot this afternoon.

Nicola Ann Gatlin, 22, was reported missing by her flatmate earlier this week. A white Honda belonging to Ms Gatlin was found near Langstone Cliffs this afternoon. She is described as white, of slim build, with long, dark hair and is 5ft 4in tall.

The car was said to have been seriously damaged. Scrapes along the driving side door indicate a recent accident, which may be linked to a hit and run on Warren Road.

Her brother describes Nicola as very sociable and loves hiking. He said she had landed her dream job around the middle of May but had not heard from her recently.

Members of Exmoor Search & Rescue Team alongside Devon and Cornwall Police have been deployed to Langstone Cliffs.

Dread swamps me and everything seems to fall into a low spin. For whatever reason, Meggy is concerned enough to show me this in person.

'Do you think your wife has seen it?' she asks.

'She hasn't said anything.'

I glance at a camera on the back seat and something about it unnerves me. Is it me Meggy is disturbed by or Holloway, the provocateur I reveal through my sessions?

Would she want to counsel you if she knew you'd committed murder? The man you once were and the man you've become are two different people. It's like trying to wrap your head around Luke Skywalker and Norman Bates.

She taps my arm. 'Zane. Focus.'

Another greyout. That's what I call the brief interludes where Holloway intrudes and I can't find my way back. I don't want to repeat the episode, especially not a few hundred feet from my own front door.

She shows me two posts on *BarbedWire* hosted by Andrie Vander-Meulen. The accompanying photo depicts a couple standing under a tree with the comment: *He picked the wrong b*tch*. It's a long shot. Hazy. Could be anyone.

'Sex scandals always eclipse everything else.' Her tone is deadpan. 'Will you have to give a statement or something?'

'Shit, no. I'm not giving them anything.'

I shouldn't be so confident. *BarbedWire* is not where you want your secrets aired, not now Nic has been reported missing. The comments are sympathetic: *My heart goes out to you, Nic. Wherever you are!*

Meggy continues with a grimace. 'Andrie explains statistics in her latest post: *One in four women experience violence by an intimate partner.*'

'Is this Andrie woman legit?'

'No one knows. Imperial College did a study on deep fake tech, combining profile photos with audio files to generate talking portraits. She could be anyone using someone else's voice. But you can guarantee whatever videos she and her gang have found will go viral.'

'What exactly does this have to do with me?' I ask.

'Nic's TikTok mentions her recent experience with domestic violence, supported by blurry photos. If you've ever thought of getting your PR team to manage your social media, now would be a good time.' She puts her phone away. 'Did Nic mention having a boyfriend, someone who might have had a temper?'

My heart is thudding in my chest. She must be able to feel the vibration through the seat. 'Everyone knows she dated Marschōne and everyone knows how that ended.'

I want to stop thinking about it, stop talking about it, but the nightmare I'm going through is the one I will continue to drown in every day. I keep thinking I'll wake up from all this. Maybe I have. Maybe I haven't. Maybe I never will. I bite my lip, as if to stop the wretchedness coming off me in painful waves.

Meggy takes two shaky breaths. 'You look terrible.'

'You're a bag of bad news.'

'And so are your ratings.'

'You're not selling shit about me to the *Daily Mail, are you?*'

'And risk tarnishing my reputation? Hell, no.'

The rumours about me are a setback, yes, and maybe this *Barbed-Wire* thing is concerning. I want to ask Andrie Vander-Meulen why she's linking violence towards women with Nic, but I don't want to reason through a hundred different answers because every one would be a horror.

We decide to go for a drive. Rather than silence, we unpack and study Ethan Holloway, we relate to him, and we feel his emotions. I wonder if the enigmatic charm of a doctor who makes women beautiful for a living fascinates her more than the waning appeal of Zane Osborne.

'I'm feeling strait-jacketed by Holloway,' I say. 'I know too much about him, the brogues he wears, the black, silky stout he drinks. He's a *Mad Men* aficionado, a lady-killer like Don Draper. These are only some of the rooms in Holloway's corridor of nightmares.'

Her smile is unguarded, then sympathy creeps over her face. 'Yet if you opened his skull, it would be full of sentences written on twists of paper, scripted words he can't possibly form himself.'

'Then why does he talk to me? Why does everything have to be what he wants?'

She frowns, no doubt trying to tell me I'm going too deep. 'Whose voice do you hear when he speaks?'

'Dad's.'

I tell her how I hated Dad for abandoning me. I tell her all the things I wanted to do to him. The axe and the tree stump. How it should have been his head, not the pheasant's. How the police should have made an arrest, not only based on medical malpractice, but abandoning me, his only son. But they couldn't find him.

'His disappearance wasn't necessarily meant as an escape route,' she says.

'How do you know? You don't know what he was thinking. What he was planning.' I suddenly feel a need to throw up. 'He could have remarried.'

'That scares you?'

'No. He'd be committing bigamy if he had.'

She parks the car beside a stubble field and reaches between the seats for a Thermos. 'You look pale. How about a drink.'

She pours two cups of cocoa and hands me one. 'I think what scares you is if he'd had another child and treated them better than you.'

'Or worse.' I take a sip, disappointed it's not spiked with whisky. 'Dad is like Holloway, trashing the things he's broken because he doesn't know how to fix them. Yeah, so Holloway's a plastic surgeon. He knows how to enhance a person on the outside, but it's the inside that's gutted and trashed. That's what he's done. Destroyed the good and trusting parts, the pieces that really matter.'

I want to scream at Holloway's quiet and unrelenting whispers in my head. But he keeps reminding me I should ask Meggy about her background, to understand who she really is.

I imagine a camera rig overhead, lights flaring through the car's interior and the crew, dark and silent nearby. While she talks and I listen.

'My full name is Margot Saas-Grund. My mother, a Swiss actor, married hotelier David Russell, quintessentially American and a Forbes lister. The fascinating part is how minimalist they were. You'd expect a collection of Fabergé eggs and gilt bidets in every bathroom. Instead, our house displayed Georgian elegance and organic food, everything in line with an eco-friendly ethos.'

'Sounds like a dream.'

'The house, yes. My education, not so much. It was a Swiss convent school, which could have caused sexual repression and a keenness to get wild but turned me into a religious fanatic. That's why Holloway is a case of demon possession.'

I smile. It's the first time I've felt this buoyant in weeks. Meggy has refused to tell me about herself since it's unethical, and yet here she is sharing a tiny portion with the promise of more.

She looks closely at my face. 'You ought to go home and lie down. You really don't look well.'

We head back to my house in silence and she pulls up outside the front gate.

'I don't want anything bad to happen to you or your family. Positive thoughts, okay?'

'Promise.'

Walking down the drive, reminds me of Mum dropping me off at boarding school on a Sunday night, on the rare occasion I was lucky enough to go home. She'd wave until she couldn't see me anymore and when her car pulled away, my heart snapped.

Holloway reminds me of what I'm overlooking. *Inviting Meggy here gives her the same access you gave Nic. I know this must be hard to accept, but your contract isn't random. It was curated so Meggy could monitor you. By the way, that's some gorgeous cologne you're wearing.*

I doubt Meggy watches me in the way Holloway thinks. She's not omniscient.

No. But she suspects. Why do you think she was here?

There's no proof. Besides, I've buried Nic's phone and other belongings in the new foundations of a care home near Sainsbury's, over which they plan to pour concrete. Although there was something I'd forgotten and that was Nic's guitar charm, which I found in the jacket I wore at the beach.

On returning to my study, I take it out of my drawer and plug it into my computer. There are photos of us in full colour, lying asleep on a tartan rug, her head on my shoulder. Later, opening a bottle of champagne, and again, the blur of me behind a spray of seawater, droplets caught in mid-air. Sometimes we're kissing, lost in our own exquisite space, until I realise these are more selfies she'd taken without my permission.

Then I see a sound file and reluctantly I press PLAY. Nic's moans, my murmurs — prolonged one minute and animalistic the next — and after a full minute, her voice asking me if I would leave my wife.

The occasion floods back to the weekend I'd asked her to stay. She must have plugged it into my computer while I was sleeping on the couch and then removed it before we went upstairs to eat. The vision of her leaning over my desk makes sense to me now. Not an invitation for more sex, but an opportunity to record everything we said before ejecting the drive.

Why? Why would she need to record all this? Marschōne's voice pounds in my head. *Word of advice. She's trouble.*

My mind won't stop replaying Nic's last moments, her arms flailing, her body falling. I hadn't realised how close she was to the steps, and I flinched when I heard the sickening crack.

Pulling the thumb drive from my computer, I mash it with the blunt handle of my paper knife. Staring at jagged pieces of that tiny little guitar, I begin sweating. Am I coming down with something?

Apocrine sweat glands, my boy, the ones in the armpits and groin. Might explain that oily, fatty whiff.

I take a shower, scouring my head with extra soap as if I can scrub away the memory. Tying a towel around my waist, I cuff the condensation off the mirror and shave.

I prefer sleeping on the lower ground floor. It's cooler down here and I don't have to wear T-shirts to bed in 38°C July weather to hide the fading scratches on my chest. The worst part of this is trying to act normal around my wife.

I keep thinking everyone's watching me. There could be a camera behind the bathroom mirror and strands of wires within the walls, there could be hundreds of them all over the house. Worse, my remote for the front gate doesn't work and limited security means I'm at risk. Lilja oversees maintenance, why hasn't she called the alarm company?

'I'm assuming you've heard Nic's missing?'

'Shit! You scared me.'

My wife's reflection appears in the mirror next to mine. I'm wondering how to answer this. Should my tone be perplexed or composed? I imagine someone shouting, 'First positions,' and a makeup brush dabbing the sweat from my forehead. I pin the edges of my mouth in a smile.

Sound. Speed. Camera. Rolling. And Action…

'She's not missing. Obviously, she got that job in New York.'

'Why wouldn't she tell her family? Her flatmate?'

'I haven't the foggiest.'

'Did she mention this America idea during her interview?'

'I might not have offered her the job if she had.'

I retreat to the bedroom, and as I close the door, I shout, 'She was quite smitten with the place. Had a *thing* for Frank Sinatra.' There will be no retakes on this one. So Frank it is.

I'm briefly side-tracked by the sound of whistling from the garden and the theme from *New York, New York*. Sunlight diffracting through the open window distracts me, but not as much as the slope of Burgess' head as he passes.

Is the bastard eavesdropping?

I slam the window and quickly dress in a shirt and jeans and walk out to the pantry barefoot. Lilja's eyes track the scratches at the base of my neck and I'm starting to feel dizzy. I tell her the story about an aggressive reporter outside Gary O'Malley's and no, I can't make a case out of it when I didn't catch his name.

'Something's not right.' Hostility drains from her eyes, curiosity taking its place. 'Nic would have texted Bizzy.'

'Perhaps she thought it best to make a clean break. More professional.' I can see it bothers her. 'That's what I would do.'

Why is she worried? I'm starting to lose hope. *They'll arrest me*, I think. It's worse than *Play Him, Play Her*, it's Holloway in a prison yard.

I can't stop thinking about Nic. Nic at the bottom of the stairs. Nic in the water. Nic washed out to sea. Now I'm really dizzy.

I feel my wife's hand on my arm, her voice asking me if I'm okay. Then the screen fades to black. Show's over.

Trending: #InZane

@Titmouse: How did *DevonLive* not spot the missing girl was ZaneO's assistant?

@CirceAtNight: @Titmouse Dude that IS totally fishy. I guess ZaneO's fans won't be fans over this tidbit.

@SherylAdams: Haters will be haters. I think he's taken enough of their sanctimonious abuse. He needs better fans.

@BantaBadger: I have to say it's rich coming from 45% of people who cheat on their spouses. But… if he wants to play the Ding-a-ling.

@HeyWhatsUP: Why are we talking about #InZane when Nicola Gatlin's still missing? You wait. He'll drop out of sight and then the NCA will complain they never saw it coming. #FindNicola

22

LILJA

I'm sick with terror. What if Zane had fallen and hit his head against a cupboard?

Fortunately, Stella was polishing the back door handles when it happened. We took him to the bedroom to lie down and gave him a tumbler of water.

She was struck with a fleeting compassion. 'He looks miserable, staring out the window and sighing all the time. I reckon he's got no one to talk to.'

'You make it sound like he's been abandoned. He has friends.'

'People liking him because he's a celebrity doesn't make them friends.'

I'd never seen him like this. Flinching every time his telephone rings and dragging his feet to answer it. He knows the consequences of having an affair, especially with a woman the police are desperate to find. Now I'm begging for a way through Zane-Gate, starting with deleting his access to our front gate. It's the first step to moving him out.

While he's still asleep, I find myself wanting to read his script. Walking to his study on shaky legs, I find it on the corner of the desk, a postcard marking the last page he read.

AMAYA

Another patient died.

                    HOLLOWAY

          Yes. At least she was in a good
          place for it.

                    AMAYA

          Is that supposed to be funny?

                    HOLLOWAY

          I'm sorry, it was in poor
          taste.

                    AMAYA

          She's the third one this month.

                    HOLLOWAY

          You're very observant.

                    AMAYA

          It's not like you'd miss some-
          thing like that. The gurneys.
          The fuss. It's strange, I only
          spoke to her yesterday.

                    HOLLOWAY

          If it makes you feel better,
          sepsis is often the culprit. It
          can lead to nosocomial infec-
          tions. The other two patients
          had acute respiratory failure
          and died within four days of
          admission.

AMAYA

But they were walking around
the ward.

HOLLOWAY

Look... I know it bothers you.
There's always a high risk of
shock, fluid loss, and cardi-
ac arrest. But you... You have
nothing to worry about.

But does she? Amaya was a witness to what Holloway did and that puts her at risk. Even the commenters on BarbedWire weigh in.

@SherylAdams: So, she saw a doctor injecting a patient. That's what doctors do.

@BantaBadger: @SherylAdams Yeah, but Holloway rewinding his spy cam and realising she was watching him. That's some scary shit.

@CirceAtNight: Why date her after she leaves? Seems pointless to me.

@HeyWhatsUP @CirceAtNight: Because it's much harder to accuse the man you're sleeping with of murder.

Nic is missing, had an accident or even… No, that's irrational, *unless* a police statement confirms it. But the script, the commentary – and the inevitable fact that satellite vans and press will be outside our house soon – all factor in Zane's deteriorating state of mind.

I try to block out the past week, but there's nowhere else for my mind to go. It's no use torturing myself or feeling somehow responsible. Now I'm having to deal with a disgruntled daughter who misses Nic driving her to the local coffee shop for frothy lattes and croissants before school.

Zane has his gloomy moods, which stem from his beloved father disappearing when he was young. His mother was a strong woman, but raising a grieving son wasn't easy when she was a widow herself.

My phone rings. 'I'm not intruding, am I?'

A male voice. 'Who is this?'

'Stan Marriott, *DevonLive*.'

'How did you get my number? Oh, wait, my website.'

'Actually, it was your newsletter.'

I'm flattered he'd signed up. 'Is it about your article?'

'It is.'

Stan Marriott is not an investigative journalist. But Nic, being a celebrity PA, might well be part of his brief.

'There's been a lot of support over Ms Gatlin,' he says. 'The police are interviewing friends and family. I'd like to ask... was there anything she said, anything at all, which might help us find her?'

The word *find* stretches and contracts, and I can't focus. I shouldn't be talking to him, but the words fly out. 'No. Although Zane mentioned something about America.'

'I think UK border control would have a record of her leaving the country.' Stan gives a sigh that seems to come from deep inside, the sigh of a man haunted by what he has to say. 'The police might want to talk to Zane.'

My heart jolts – a sharp physical pain. There's no *might* about it. I want to tell him she simply left, but comments like that require legal counsel, and I don't believe it myself.

Stan drops his voice a notch. 'I should advise that the press will become more intrusive.'

'I've nothing to hide.'

'No. But does he?'

It's an unspoken thing between us, and I'm suddenly aware of a looming threat. After he hangs up, it feels like more has happened in the past twenty-four hours than in the entire span or our marriage.

Zane's voice shatters my train of thought. He's thundering upstairs with a phone pressed to his ear and jabbing his finger at something outside.

'Are those reporters?'

Bizzy stands beside him at the sitting-room window. 'Hideous, isn't it? Like the march on Versailles.'

'Shouldn't you be in bed?' I ask.

'No. I'm sick of being in bed.' The half-formed grimace slides off Zane's face. 'I bet this is Marriott's doing. You know I'd written it off as morbid curiosity, a reporter looking for reassurance that we're made of the same stuff. I've downplayed my success, knowing it's what he wants to hear. But this? This is just plain shitty!'

'Stan Marriott isn't a mob-stirrer,' I say, moving closer to the window. 'You always blame him.'

'Seen his latest article? #lady-killer. What a role to cast me in.' He searches my face, like a man realising he is teetering on a knife-edge. 'It would be nice to believe I have your support.'

'I've given you sixteen years of it.'

His eyes drill into mine, a suspicious stare that nips at my skin. We stand side by side, an unhappy couple faking the illusion of intimacy.

'Does this have anything to do with today's headlines?' Bizzy asks. 'They're saying Nic was kidnapped.'

Zane looks at her as if someone's spray painted the cat. 'Who said that?'

'George.'

'Has your best friend ever heard of fake news?'

So the rebellion begins. Zane is unaware that his daughter's world is filled with more pressing problems like bullying at school because her father is famous. Not to mention the usual things from which a teenager suffers: heavy periods, boys, and I shudder at what else he doesn't know.

Thoughts race through my mind, and I say a silent prayer. *Be nice, Zane. Can't you just leave without arguing for once?* Before I resolve to make those words reality, he opens his mouth.

'We've received another dress code complaint from school, Bizz. *Derry Girl* style doesn't cut it. Not when I'm up for a major award.'

'For what?' She squints behind her glasses. 'Having affairs so you can "dedicate" yourself to the role? Can't you just act for a change? It's called *talent*, Dad.'

His fury no longer erupts with the swear words he uses on-screen. Since becoming a "father" he has mostly put them away. She's upset about Nic, and Zane hasn't provided one word of comfort or explanation. I'm desperate to keep Bizzy away from all this and to carry the brunt of it myself.

A muscle twitches under his left eye. He unhooks his jacket from the back of a chair and grabs a small holdall. 'I'm going to the gym.'

'You can't go out there,' I say.

'Watch me.'

We hear the rattle of keys and the front door slamming. Pressing our faces to the window, we watch his car fishtail up the drive, blinding flashes blinking on and off. He barely has enough room to exit the gate before a horde of photographers rushes his car. A stream suddenly released.

They'll follow him as far as the corner, the majority giving up, while stragglers with the energy to dart through the church will follow him as far as the Swan Inn.

'Can Gran take me to the park?' Bizzy asks. 'It's not that I don't want you to. It's just…'

'I think that's a great idea.'

I send Mum a text asking her to come over, knowing she'll drop everything for her only granddaughter.

Bizzy shakes her head like a dashboard ornament. 'I'm tired of things getting weird around here. Everyone at school says my dad's turning creepy. They said that. To *me!*'

My nerves loosen and I try not to panic as she gives me a hard frown. Her friends have always loved the fact that her dad's an actor. Even she was hugely proud of him, until a brief nude scene he did in *Loving Alice* grossed her out. Her words were "Why does Dad have to do all that sex stuff? It's so cringe."

It takes me a moment to speak. 'Bizz, I need to tell you something. Dad and I… we've decided to take a break.'

'You mean, you're getting divorced?'

'No. At least, not yet.'

'Oh, Mum.'

I pull her into my arms and she hangs there at the tipping point of talking and sobbing. I can't apologise for the fights I didn't start or the pitying stares Bizzy gets at school, and I wish I could make it all go away.

We break apart, her hands in mine. 'Nothing will change. We'll be okay.'

She nods, her eyes flitting from me to the window. 'Nic's not coming back, is she?'

'No. She isn't.'

She blinks rapidly as if looking for subtext, subtle omissions in my words, as if I'm leaving anything out. I don't elaborate over the details and I don't make any excuses. She has already seen what the tabloids have published about her father. She knows why we can't stay together.

Then she goes over to the couch, reaches over the back, and pulls out a canvas. 'I painted something for you. I thought it might cheer you up.'

The painting depicts a woman with her back to the viewer. She wears swirls of peacock blues and greens in a form-fitting gown. The mystery of the subject is heightened by not seeing the face, but Bizzy has captured a tiny essence of me.

'It's wonderful.'

She rolls her eyes. 'It's okay.'

'It's a masterpiece.' I trace the image with my fingertips. 'It should be hanging in the Louvre.'

Her kindness has extended to stick-it notes on my mirror, my steering wheel, and my phone. Inspirational quotes that make me feel motivated again. I fold her in my arms, squeezing and thanking her.

'I've been thinking.' She hesitates, the way she does when she wants something. 'Wouldn't it be easier if I were a boarder? Afsaneh and George board.'

'Afsaneh lives in Iran, George lives in Dublin. You live four miles away.'

'What does it matter? George says boarding provides personal growth, and it makes you independent. You wouldn't have to drive me to school.'

'Nice try.'

'I'd be more responsible.'

'Then you'd be unrecognisable.'

The doorbell intrudes on my thoughts of Bizzy wanting her freedom and whether I should let her go. She rushes into the hall and peers through the spyhole. 'It's Gran.'

Mum offers her middle finger to a reporter left behind in the scuffle. She's slicked her hair back like Yolanda Hadid and strides in on the long legs that once made her a fortune.

'Get your cleats.' She snaps a finger at Bizzy and points upstairs.

Bizzy blows out a breath. 'Fine.'

Her cleats are already in her kit, but she obliges because she knows her grandmother has something to say.

Mum pulls me into the kitchen. 'What's he done now? Screwed half the neighbourhood?'

'Not now Mum.'

'Who are all those people outside?' Her ice-blue eyes widen.

'You've read the news.'

'The missing assistant.' She makes air quotes. 'This whole thing is bizarre. ("Bizarre," is a very Mum word.) Next, she'll be on *Cold Case Files* and so will this house.'

'Mum. Stop.'

'No plans for divorce, then?'

'Not every affair has to be about divorce.'

'What about cutting off his teeny tiny…'

'Mum!'

Okay, I admit I've fantasised about it, but I've never come close to seeking such horrific revenge. Of all the people I know, Zane causes more emotional harm to himself than others.

Bizzy saunters towards us, rapidly two-thumb typing on her phone. She barely looks up. 'Can I stay the night with Gran?'

'Can she?' Mum asks. 'I'll take her to school in the morning.'

'Fine. But don't get out of the car if there's a photographer at the park.'

Mum rubs my arm, shadows of anxiety stretching across her face. I suspect she doesn't want to risk leaving me here alone, but it takes the utmost strength and secrecy to keep a lid on the details of Zane's cheating.

When her car flickers between the trees along the drive, I feel lost in the gnawing silence. The house is under siege by the press because something has happened to Nic, something terrible, and I need to know where she is.

23

ZANE

I'm not going to the gym. I'm going to the bank, and there's also the dress shirt in the boot of my car. Getting a trowel is an impossible task when bulldog Burgess watches the garden shed.

On the way, I'm deep in the zone, foot down, squealing out of the drive when the surge happens. A flash of grey in my wing mirror and a photographer bouncing off my rear bumper.

The inkling of a question nibbles at my subconscious. What if he broke a rib?

It's hardly my fault if a bunch of snappers insist on crowding my car. I can't tell you how many times reporters try to buy call sheets from production assistants to find out when I'm shooting. If the tabloid hacks are hoping for a story, there's nothing to tell.

My phone connects to Bluetooth and I book a room in Exeter. The traffic is chaotic on the main road and every car is jockeying for space. Will I ever be in a public place without having to consider the risk of people recognising me?

I keep imagining Holloway gaping at me in the rear-view mirror, his skin puffy and threaded with crimson veins, as if he's going through a psychological collapse like Dorian Gray. Only instead of the portrait prematurely ageing, it's him.

I turn on the radio and BBC Radio *5 Live* rolls up to the news on the hour. After the day's temperatures and travel disruptions, the host reads out a review on *Play Him, Play Her* by David Hufstader at *The Guardian*.

'As long-time devotees of Zane Osborne's work will know, Play Him, Play Her *is Ozzie's most promising role so far. The first series delves into the affair between doctor and patient, where Osborne clearly carries the weight. Even more menacing are the inner workings of Dr Ethan Holloway, a depraved and narcissistic surgeon, who poisons his victims before killing them. There is violence, yes, but not the type to provide sensationalism, as Berne Brothers did in* Loving Alice. *That's a good thing: Holloway is supposed to burrow under your skin. You are caught in his gaze with each creepy close-up. Photographed in stunning, saturated colours, the film brings a grave chill to the bones — no pun intended. But it's Osborne who adds a pleasant gravitas to every scene. His psychological performance is mesmerizing and utterly convincing. Zane Osborne is… Holloway.'*

Holloway sings a round of Cliff Richard's *Congratulations* from the back seat. *There you were,* he says, *camera tight in, and your rich, languid voice like Richard Burton's in Hamlet. Utter genius.*

I wonder what Milo is thinking. Would a kid like him have access to the newspaper? He certainly has access to everything else. Unlike all the other profiles, Milo's seems legit. It's his face on his profile page and not some heavily filtered avatar.

The ping of Bizzy's text separates me from Holloway. There's no, 'Hi Dad. How are you?' simply a news link.

My eyes flick from the road to the touchscreen display. There's an achingly embarrassing clip of me parachuting at Headcorn Aerodrome in Kent, reckless publicity for Food for the Homeless. Then a photo of Nic and me drinking coffee and eating chocolate digestives in her car behind Opa Restaurant and Bar.

The comment reads: *Osborne, in the first flush of success, has had a reputation for partying hard. But this takes the biscuit.*

Bizzy's next text brings a strange note of sadness: *Were you and Nic more than friends?*

I dictate a text: *No. It was nothing like that.*

She ends with: *Just wish she would call. I miss her.*

I respond: *We all do.*

Bizzy rarely uses the words *love you* at the end of a message. There's this brittleness about her and she won't let me close. My mind juggles with complimenting her androgyny, the determination to be who she is. I should tell her that one day.

I light a cigarette and inhale deeply. The nightmare picks up again. Nic's face screams at me from petrol stations and bus stops, there are posters of her everywhere. There's not one person who ever wanted to have partner problems. It's not like I woke up and said I'm going to screw my assistant to get out of this dreary, stuffy prison you call a home. Nic made me feel strong and daring – and yes, she was a younger version of Lilja, perhaps an impatient version, winding me up and playing me until I couldn't take it anymore.

I should have been more careful.

The journey to Exeter should have taken me only half an hour, but the shortest route time is hampered with traffic. While looking for an alternate route to Lloyds Bank, I'm aware of a black SUV in my rearview mirror, its windscreen burnished with reflected sunlight. No ghostly face emerges behind high-tech optical gear, nor is the car imbued with the menace I expect. The paps will do anything to get an exclusive.

The twisted thought that my wife could have contracted a PI to video me, raises every flag in my mind. I'm starting to think this is a reality show and I'm running around with a mic pack.

I make a sharp turn and the SUV follows, pushing me well above the speed limit. I accelerate up a narrow driveway that cuts behind the houses when a wheelie bin catches on the side of the car and topples to the ground, leaving a cloud of shredded bags in my wake. There's a parked van up ahead, narrowing the gap, but my car noses through and I yank on the steering wheel and shoot out onto a main road, cutting off a motor bike.

The SUV follows, headlights burning into the early morning haze before shimmering down a side road. I pick up the pace, hurtling past shops and a small roundabout without looking back.

Carrying my empty holdall into the bank, I wait behind a stream of customers. The SUV incident is putting me on edge. There's a tipping point in any day where I escape from my present and start analysing the past, and I've reached that point.

***

I'm distracted by the child in front holding an ice cream cone, his fingers plucking at the flake. The first time I remember having a "99" was during a bank holiday weekend. I must have been ten.

Dad pulled a few bob out to take me to the beach. 'Ice cream, son?'

Since he said it in front of my mother, I assumed it was code for the local pub, so I shook my head. Pub toilets stank of pee and bleach, and I was bound to want to use one.

'C'mon. It'll be fun. You can go for a paddle in your undies.'

It was the hottest day of the year, sea water cold enough to snatch your breath, the kind that makes you shriek at the shock of it. My small toes dawdled in the froth, ice cream running down my wrist. When I turned to show Dad, he was lying on a beach towel with a woman in a red dress called Tina. He'd grunted it often enough. She was young and freckly, and there they were, limbs entangled. Right then, I decided it would never happen again… this strange, frenzied thing he was doing to a girl.

The sun was warm on the top of my head, wind gusting over the water, hatred mounting with the advancement of the waves. I dropped the ice cream and let it slide in and out with the current. It would look like I'd drowned. I paddled out a little further, fully clothed, wading hip deep.

Now. Do it now.

Ducking under the water, I hooked my fingers into the seabed, and pretended to be drowning. My lungs gripped tighter and tighter until I couldn't hold it any longer. With one explosive burst, I pushed myself to the surface, gulping air. I did this several times until I heard a noise. Someone was coming.

I recognised the shape of him, the dip in his shoulder, and the snarl on his lips. 'Get out, you little shit!'

I couldn't move. Couldn't speak. My lips were trembling with the cold. A quiet premonition that a spanking might entirely be possible.

'Look what you've done!' he said, spray shooting upwards in his wake. 'Only gone and got the entire Devon and Cornwall Police out looking for you.'

I wasn't aware I'd been gone that long. But another man appeared behind him. A uniform and a badge. He pulled a sodden me from the sea, pushed Dad aside and carried me up the beach.

'Did you fall?' he asked.

'Yes,' I sobbed, peering over his shoulder. Dad was getting worryingly close.

'He left you alone. That what you're saying?'

I nodded, trying hard to keep the triumph from my face. The police officer read Dad the riot act, asked him why a doctor like him didn't run in after me. I remember words like *child neglect* and *abuse*, and I wondered if I'd overdone it.

A doctor. Yes. That was Dad. He had a small practice on Warren Road until he had a "thing" with a patient. Tina Solace. What a name. Anyway, it was medical malpractice, and it was all over the news.

I never realised how torn apart our lives were. How I got in everyone's way, blocking their paths with all my to-dos. The bullying, the slipping grades. Dad said I wouldn't amount to much. It was he who suggested acting since I was naturally given to exaggeration.

As I stare at the ice cream sign, I ask myself: Has Dad's profession, which I secretly admired, enticed me to Holloway's? Thinking about him makes me feel strange, like a spirit has moved past me, stirring each tiny hair on my skin.

* * *

I'd been withdrawing small amounts for months, but this time I decided to pre-order the transaction in advance. It's the final £10,000 to add to the cash I've secreted in a designer duffel I bought from Harrods – one my nosy wife will never suspect.

Pulling the car out into the road, I pick up speed and head for the park. Suddenly, I hear sirens and the glare of flashing lights in my rear-view mirror.

You've got to be kidding?

I park on the side of the road and watch a lanky police officer sauntering towards my open window. 'How are you doing today?'

She's not wanting small talk. I can tell by the scowl. 'Good, thanks.'

She places a hand on the roof of my car and looks down at me. 'Know why I stopped you?'

'I was speeding?' It's a rough guess.

She raises an eyebrow. 'You're lucky I didn't see that. No, I noticed your brake lights flickering on and off. It's unsafe. Someone will run into the back of you.'

She's seen this a thousand times and I'll simply get a Fixed Penalty Notice and then off I go. I surrender my license and insurance certificate, and she takes her time examining them.

'Barton Manor. Nice place.' Not a flicker of recognition.

She doesn't watch Netflix and thinks I'm a snob living in a gated house with a palm tree. Two, if you count the dwarf palmetto around the back. When she asks me to get out of the car, all I can think of is the balled-up shirt and a holdall filled with cash.

'Probably the connector to the light.' She nods at the keys in my hand. 'Mind opening the boot?'

Shit. Really? Her eyes are drawn to my thumb hesitating on the remote and one eyebrow flickers.

'Sir? The boot?'

She barely glances at the shopping bag and the holdall appears to be of no interest. Technically, having them there isn't a crime, so what the hell's she staring at?

'This a new car?' she asks.

My back is drenched with sweat and I'm tugging at my shirt to let in more air. 'Fairly new, yes.'

She leans forward to study the sealed panelling around the brake lights, her nose twitching. Then gestures for me to close the boot.

'Probably a good idea to take it to the garage. Can't see you doing it yourself.' She brushes her nose with her hand. 'Do you hunt?'

She can't be referring to the shirt. The blood is dry and doesn't smell. When Lilja's car was in the garage, she used mine to pick up a brace of rabbits to cook. But that was months ago.

'Pheasants.' It's the first thing that comes to mind. 'They were hanging too long. Over-gamey.'

Dad used to leave pheasants on his basement shelf for up to a week at a constant 50 degrees Fahrenheit. Ungutted and un-plucked, and no noxious gases when he cut into them. Although I can't attest to their flavour. I wouldn't eat one even if you paid me.

She suggests I return to the car, and it's the longest five minutes of my life. Her knuckle against my closed window makes me jump. She flicks a Vehicle Defect Rectification in front of my nose and tells me to get it sorted ASAP.

I've seen enough crime shows to know a flickering brake light is a warning to other drivers that there's a kidnapped girl in the boot. In my case it's faulty wiring.

She waits for me to pull back into the road and keeps a close distance behind. It's ten sweltering seconds before she overtakes, her face assessing mine as she passes.

I head to the nearest hardware store and buy a trowel. It's less conspicuous than a spade, especially if anyone were watching. Which they're not. If they were, I'd tell them I'm a gardener. Only it's not to my garden I go.

Dawlish Countryside Park is famous for woodland and wide-open spaces. I take the bag and its bloody contents from my boot and find a stand of trees about a quarter of a mile off the beaten track. The soil is damp, allowing me to dig a deep hole, and I tamp the bag down and cover it with leaves and moss. No one will ever know it's there.

I'd congratulate you if it weren't for our four-legged friends. A dog would be all over it like flies on warm shit.

Trending: #InZane

@CirceAtNight: Did you see the paparazzi chase on *Celebrity UK* online? Yeboah said they followed ZaneO all the way to Exeter.

@Mark Adams: @CirceAtNight There was another photo of Ozzie in a car with his therapist. Is he poking her now? Or is it image editing software?

@Titmouse: @SherylAdams Why so many hate posts? There's a concentrated effort to defame ZaneO when all this woman was doing was giving him therapy.

@HeyWhatsUP: @Titmouse Where are your brain cells? What do you think they were giving each other in her flashy car? An oil change? #InZane

24

LILJA

Zane has been staying in Exeter these past few days and I've slept better than ever. *Cook's Illustrated* sent an email this morning, wanting to do an article on me at the beginning of August. I'm excited, I can't sit still.

I take my coffee to the terrace and breathe in the scent of roses. Burgess is spraying the hydrangeas and mouthing a tune from whatever is playing through his earbuds. Stella sweeps the terrace, enduring his occasional light-hearted jibes that she's missed a spot.

I'm glad to see Lappy hopping along the lawn, his leg is looking a little straighter today. It's not the only thing hopping along the lawn. To my amazement a reporter with a lanyard and a camera is brazenly walking towards me. Stan Marriott. *DevonLive*.

I take my cup and attempt to rush back inside, but what he says next stops me.

'I realise how intrusive this is. But it's important. I did press the buzzer and the doorbell.'

I didn't hear either. I suspect he vaulted over the wall between here and the deer park.

'I've been following your husband.'

'That hardly news,' I say.

'To bring him weekly updates which he has requested via email. Since I was passing…'

'You thought you'd drop in.'

'Exactly.' He pulls out a chair. 'May I?'

I sit too. What with everything that's going on with my husband, forging a relationship with a reporter might be beneficial.

'What are these updates you send to my husband?'

'Mr Osborne insisted I use his private email to contact him with articles before they're published. Tip-offs, you could say. Now I get special broadcast privileges at celebrity events.'

'I see.'

'It was the day I went to the cathedral to report on Hickory Dickory Dock. You know, the earliest cat flap in existence? Well, not exactly a flap. More of a hole. Anyway, it was early afternoon when I received a call from a distressed man. He was walking his dog on Warren Beach and saw a man and a woman talking in the car park. He claims one was Nicola Gatlin. The other was wearing a cap and sunglasses. You know the drill. She was digging around in her handbag for tissues. The man she was with wasn't exactly trying to console her. At one point, he covered her mouth with his hand. Didn't look friendly.'

'Did this man take photos?'

'No, he didn't.'

'Then why are you telling me this?'

'Because now Ms Gatlin's missing and it doesn't look good for your husband.' Stan looks down at his hands. 'But then I made enquiries. On the night of your husband's birthday party, a couple of servers saw Mr Osborne with a woman that meets her description.'

'*Here*… in my house?'

'Yes.'

'Nic wasn't working for us anymore. Nor was she invited.'

'Odd.'

Not as odd as Zane disappearing that night for a good forty minutes before I found him smoking downstairs alone. The smoke dribbled from his mouth when he spoke and my right-handed husband was holding the cigarette in his left hand, the same hand he used to cut the cake with. I noticed his shirt was creased and the third button missing, and he wandered from guest to guest with one hand in his pocket.

Stan narrows his eyes, as if straining to bring up his next subject.

'I'm guessing you don't read *BarbedWire*? That's okay, it's a domestic abuse awareness site on TikTok with over 3.6 million followers. This part is crucial. A nurse was driving home after a late shift from Dawlish Community Hospital on the night of your husband's birthday party, somewhere between 2.00 am and 3.00 am. She met a white Honda coming the other way. As far as she could tell, the driver of the other car was a woman. The car swerved into her and now she's in the hospital. Head injuries and internal bleeding. Not good. Without photo and video proof of the licence plates, you must understand what the nurse saw is speculation at this point. But it gives us a timeline. It's possible Nic abandoned her car on Langstone Cliffs that same night.'

'Are you sure?'

Stan eases off his chair and nods politely. 'There's a huge chunk of time between Nic leaving your house and the accident on Warren Road. Just thought you should know.'

Stan leaves his card and encourages me to stay in touch. I'm left with a lump hardening in my throat as I rush indoors to find that shirt.

25

LILJA

There's no sign of it in the laundry, although it wouldn't be unheard of for Zane to have dropped it off at the dry cleaners.

On the night of his birthday party, his shirt looked crisp and dapper. Surely there would be noticeable creases in the box pleats if there had been an assault. While he was pouring a whisky, his jacket barely hid a tiny spatter on one of the cuffs. At the time, I assumed it was red wine.

I find myself standing on the threshold of his study, the door making the tiniest hair-split squeal. *Pull yourself together*, I tell myself. There's no one here.

For a moment I'm distracted by his computer, the black heart of this rotten marriage, and I move the mouse to wake up the screen. His screensaver shows us on the beach over fourteen years ago when my hair was longer and blonder, and my skinny jeans were more filled out. When I look at myself now, it's hard to believe I'm the same woman. The gossamer threads around my eyes are deep creases and I'm half the size I was.

I wonder why he chose this particular photo.

His emails are mostly promotions and film reviews, and one from Stan Marriott whose signature hyperlinks to his Muck Rack account — a portfolio for his work. He's said to be one of the best entertainment reporters in Devon.

Mr Osborne,

As requested, this week's updates. It's bad news, I'm afraid. A witness from the Drummond Senior Centre emailed me, claiming to have seen you and Ms Gatlin on Warren Beach. He forgets the date, but his statement is as follows:

"I was walking my dog in the afternoon when I heard Mr Osborne and Ms Gatlin arguing. Mr Osborne's hand was covering her mouth — and she was crying. I could see they needed privacy and would have gladly walked my dog in a different direction, but I was concerned for Ms Gatlin, especially when Mr Osborne snatched her phone while repeatedly shouting at her. This abuse caused her to fight back to protect herself. It was shocking and has left me with PTSD. I know who Mr Osborne is. I've seen his series on TV. According to the police, not all abusers escape the consequences of domestic violence no matter who they are. Take it from me, he would be well-served to follow their lead."

The witness, who wishes to remain anonymous, has gone to the police. His statement will be published in Devon-Live tomorrow.

Best wishes
Stan Marriott
Senior Reporter, DevonLive

Suspicion hovers like a thundercloud. Either it blows in a different direction, or I confront Zane, but it will become an interrogation rather than a conversation, and he'll simply shut down.

I open a file labelled CTC — Celebrity Therapy and Counselling. They offer performance coaching and help actors when they go into sensory. Meggy has sent an email which reads, *You can get yourself a new life, but the guilt is always there.* The attachment is a photo of a woman in underwear, taken through our French doors.

There are several things that stand out. Although the subject is backlit, her head cast in shadow, there is enough detail thrown from the solar lamps on the patio to see that it's Nic. My first sense is that a reporter has taken it, but apart from Stan Marriott, they rarely venture further than the front gate. It gives me the sensation of a hand reaching through my abdomen and pulling at my intestines.

Meggy has breached her company's code of conduct by intruding on private property. Sending an intimate photo to a client – a very public client – means her tailored therapy plan is about to go up in smoke.

To speed her job situation on its way, I notice a link below Meggy's signature that takes me to her website. I send an urgent complaint about trespassing and inappropriate content to Catherine Gurtner, senior analyst, as if it's from Zane.

While I'm waiting for a response, I study Meggy's profile picture. Something about it nags at me. Yes, we share the same mouth, the same pointed chin, and where her eyes are turquoise, mine are blue and where she has freckles, my skin is sallow. But her face is rounder, healthier, like the one of me on Zane's screensaver.

To get a closer look, I scroll frantically through her posts. The only closeups are textural; photographs of tree bark, cracks in concrete, woodgrain, and creamy cups of coffee with the hashtag #Mols. One photo shows a row of dancers at #PrideFitness. Although this tells me where she worked out earlier this morning, it doesn't tell me if she's a regular at Pride, though it wouldn't hurt to find out.

The words come to me from a faraway place as if they have no connection to my life. *This* is what I'm thinking about, not the shirt and how my husband could be implicated in Nic's disappearance, but *this*.

I jump at the ping of an incoming message. I sit forward, expectant, and the silence sifts down like a snowfall, the stillness before the pounce. Many years honed by hard experience tell me the danger of what I've set in motion, but I must trust my instincts.

Catherine Gurtner's tone is friendly and apologetic. She assures me there must be a mistake. Ms Russell is highly professional, but she will investigate the matter and be in touch.

I wipe a sheen of sweat from my forehead and remove all evidence in both SENT and DELETE folders and turn off the computer. To force myself away from thinking about what Zane could be doing in his therapy sessions, I resume my search for the shirt.

I go through the cupboards and drawers and check under the sofa. I'd already searched the spare room and pantry and there is still no sign of it. Upstairs, his wardrobe displays too much clutter; clothes rammed tight and dinner jackets in dry-cleaner bags. Suits that don't get out much.

Under all of these is a calf leather duffel bag, embossed with a signature logo. Scrunched inside is new poplin shirt with a Saint Laurent label. I don't know if it's my distaste for Zane hiding new clothes or my desperation to find what I'm looking for, but I dump the contents onto the carpet.

My lips move but my throat is too dry to make any sound. What I see isn't more clothes, but wads of £20 notes banded together in red wrappers.

Had he robbed a casino? Shoved his hand in a cashier's till?

I grip the wardrobe door, and for a moment I think I might faint. Is this the money from the Hellman's Trust, not a trust per se, but an account we opened for abused women?

We paid a monthly donation, and the balance was well over a hundred thousand. At least, that's what I thought. Only he stopped the payments last year, claiming the production hadn't reimbursed him and they were no longer offering per diem payments for travel and meals. He also claimed they hadn't sent his cheque after wrapping up the last season and promptly changed the password to the account. I never thought to question it.

Now the manure is about to hit the fan.

I run to the spare room to get an empty suitcase, slipping and sliding on the money strewn on the floor in my hurry. How unethical of him to steal money from an account that doesn't belong to him. Every penny will be returned to the bank and I'll make sure his name is removed from all other accounts as from today.

I look around the room for something to fill the duffel in its place. Under the bed are his tatty old college handbooks, Stanislavsky and Strasberg, and study guides on auditioning and memorisation. I stuff them all in the holdall, leaving the poplin shirt on top.

Lugging the suitcase downstairs, I'm about to grab my car keys when I hear the buzzer to the front gate. DC Symonds and DC Ringer, Devon and Cornwall Police, would like to talk to me.

I leave the suitcase by the hall table as their car comes to a stop in front of the house. Detective Nora Symonds has white hair, styled above her head like a dollop of ice cream. She confirms they are here to talk about Nic, while DC Ringer gives the suitcase a cursory glance.

'Is your husband here?' He looks around as if Zane might appear.

'No. He's at a meeting.'

I hope he doesn't ask me where that meeting is. I never know with Zane. It could be in London, Exeter, or sitting on a clifftop gawping at the sea. I should have been prepared for questions about Nic. I should have expected it. I don't want to hear those empty words; *when was the last time you saw her?*

Detective Symonds' eyes are on mine, her expression soft. I offer them comfy chairs in the sitting room and open the window. The heat of the day gushes in.

'The family is helping with police inquiries,' she says. 'Her brother has set up a Facebook page and they're offering a reward of up to £50,000 for information.'

Symonds won't tell me if they're questioning anyone under caution, but I wonder if there are any suspects or persons of interest. I don't tell her how Zane fired Nic. The reference I provide is general and may infer she was.

'I'd like to run you through the process,' Detective Symonds says. 'When we make a missing person's report, we get their names onto the National Crime Agency and look at all the other databases to which we have access. We check hospitals, homeless shelters, churches, and libraries. But we've found nothing.'

I can't help wondering if Nic's simply hiding out in a Cape Cod style house on Long Island, New York, with a view of rolling dunes and sea, watching her life unfold on social media.

My head swims. 'Could she be with a friend? Or somewhere with no Wi-Fi? I know it sounds stupid, but what if she wanted time alone?'

'Then we would respect her right to privacy. But in this case, her mother and brother insist Nic would never put her family through this torment. We feel her disappearance needs further investigation.'

'I hope Nic didn't go out and meet someone in a bar, someone who may have done her harm.'

The room gets darker. A cloud hangs too low. Detective Symonds mentions sightings in London and as far north as Edinburgh. Nobody mentions America.

Detective Symonds makes notes, her eyes occasionally scanning the room and pausing at Detective Ringer. He seems drawn to our wedding photo. I find myself studying it too.

'One last thing.' Her voice is calm. 'Something confidential which we have not shared with the media yet. There had been a fire in one of the caverns at Langstone Rock. The police poked through the embers and found shreds of scorched clothing, even the rocks were covered in duck down. What caught their eye was a swatch of material in a rock pool, quilted nylon, the type you find on a sleeping bag. Dark blue, they said, with a Snugpak logo.'

She waits for me to comment, but the words are stuck in my throat. Tension clamps the muscles between my shoulder blades and I'm frowning so hard my face hurts.

'How awful to be living rough,' I say. 'I thought she had a flat.'

A look passes between them, as if I'd strayed along a different track. I ramble about the way Nic dressed, how neat and expensive she looked (and smelt). Her car was a bit of an old banger and I worried about that. But she was coping. She was happy. At least that's what I thought.

'No one said anything about her living rough,' she says.

'But you said a sleeping bag caught fire?'

'We think someone was burning evidence, not that she was

homeless.' Detective Symonds places her card on the coffee table. 'Tell your husband we'd like to meet with him tomorrow.'

I watch their car clear the front gate before rain pounds the drive and thunder rumbles overhead. There's a sick feeling of dread in my stomach and my breathing is thick and heavy.

Zane lugged his backpack upstairs a few days ago to pack his clothes and every part of my body is telling me it's there. It must be.

I run to our bedroom and open the wardrobe.

A trekking backpack leans against the wall, lace-up closure facing out and pockets bulging with gear.

I'm convinced that it's a monstrous, impossible mistake. But the bottom compartment is empty, where it once held a dark blue Snugpak sleeping bag.

26

ZANE

Lilja's call about the police brings me home the following morning. The remote on my phone refuses to open the front gate and I buzz my wife to let me in.

My interview is brief.

Symonds asks how long Nicola Gatlin had worked for me and I allude to the position being temporary. My right knee won't stop bouncing under my elbow, and her eyes are fixed on that knee as if it has a mind of its own.

She says they've put a trace on Nic's phone to triangulate the signal. If I hadn't cut through the microchip of the SIM card, it might have led them to the foundations of the care home near Sainsbury's.

I suspect she takes my silence as an invitation to keep asking questions. Like most things in life, the more I pretend I haven't committed a hideous crime, the worse it gets. I feel pressed to the wall. Yes, we were close and yes, she had a crush on me like a few others I can name, but the relationship was professional. She was good at her job. The unsettling look of anxiety I'd been nurturing is replaced with a confident smile. What they don't know is that Nic lies deep in the trenches of the Atlantic Ocean where the pressure has squashed her flatter than a flounder.

After they leave, I wonder how much longer it will be without further police interference. Holloway's voice comes dripping back.

Don't think for a minute Nic didn't tell someone you and she were sleeping together. Nothing stays buried for long, Zanny-boy.

I need to send a request to my PR team to take over my social media. It would be detrimental to tackle any comments alone.

Lilja is dipping plates in a sudsy sink, which means breakfast is over. The best I can hope for is a banana. She doesn't ask how the police interview went and I don't offer any explanation.

My phone pings and Meggy's text flies in. The senior analyst at CTC almost suspended her because of a complaint I'd made. Forcing myself to detach from the whys and hows, my response is mechanical.

It makes no sense for me to report or even discuss you with the senior analyst. There must be a mistake.

There are no dots to tell me she's typing and my phone goes eerily quiet. I check my SENT folder and there's no evidence I sent anything of the sort. But there is a new email from Catherine Gurtner confirming the investigation.

Holloway's voice reverberates as if coming from a conch shell's cavity. *Want me to clarify?*

"Clarify?" – pompous knob. He knows my wife is the only person with access to my computer.

The kitchen becomes a blur of colours and I try not to stare at the back of Lilja's head, curious about what she's really thinking. But her head is the only place my eyes seem to travel to. I'm about to ask her if she's been messing around with my emails when she turns, the smile slipping from her face.

'This Nic thing. Is there anything you're not telling me?'

'Like what?'

She looks towards the sitting room in case our cleaner is listening. 'Just tell me you had nothing to do with it.'

Shit. She's not kissing any arse this morning. 'No. Of course not.'

Thankfully, a smile reattaches to her face. 'Might be best if you start packing the rest of your things. For good this time.'

I chance an interjection – 'You wouldn't agree to one more night?' – and instantly regret it.

'Not a chance.'

'Right.'

Her response is like a sucker punch and I let go of any last subconscious impulses that Lilja and I might reconcile. It leaves me with a strange melancholy I can't shake off.

My daughter taps my shoulder. I hadn't heard her galumphing down the stairs and sliding across the hall floor like she usually does. It's no good hoping her brain doesn't process much of what's happening between me and her mother. She's been eavesdropping for years.

'I thought you said you were going to the gym. Where were you? Scotland?'

'Exeter,' I say, forcing a smile.

'Is that a scratch?' She points at the gap in my open shirt which I'm trying hard to conceal.

'It was Ted.' I recognise that look; disgust almost revealed. Ted doesn't like to be held and she knows I never touch him.

Lilja waves a skillet of eggs at Bizzy and she lets out a grunt in response.

'Is it too much to make an entire sentence out of that grunt?' I say, peeved my wife didn't extend the offer to me. 'Because the way to respond to your mother would be a simple, "No, thank you, I don't want an egg." Or is that too much to ask?'

'Okay.' She pours a generous quantity of bran flakes into a bowl and douses it with too much milk.

'And Bizz? You may think you can do what you like in here, but outside… out there, gossip is off limits. I mean it. No nasty surprises.'

I get that puberty does a number on the brain, hormones triggering changes in the circuitry, but why the disdain? I don't deserve to be disparaged by my daughter, especially after the trip we did last year. She's a devout Keira Walsh fan and the England women's national midfielder is papered all over her bedroom wall. I drove her all the way to Manchester to watch Walsh practising which is a bloody long way to go to gawp at a girl.

'So, where are you going?' she asks.

I hazard a glance at Lilja, realising she hasn't told Bizzy we're separating. 'Oh, just preparing for Holloway living rough in Season 2. So, camping mostly.'

'Anywhere near where Granddad disappeared?'

Crikey. Is she talking to me in full sentences? 'No, sadly.'

'Granny said all the police found were his clothes and an empty tent.' *Munch, munch.* 'You don't think he wandered off to the nearest house?'

'Naked? Unlikely. He was fit. He could hold his breath underwater for ages and walked from John O'Groats to Land's End for charity. I think he fell and hit his head and became disorientated. A lot of hikers do.'

'Or he could have staged the whole thing and gone to live in Belize.' She waves a milky spoon in the general direction of the garden. 'Think about it?'

'I am,' I say. 'But Belize wasn't on his bucket list. British Columbia more likely.'

She raises her chin and stares down the bridge of her nose. 'That doesn't stop him from stealing a car, Dad. He could have left it in a barn with a bag of clothes and enough money, and then dumped it at the nearest airport.'

Her mother gives her an *eat your breakfast* look, but I'm not fazed. 'You've thought all this out carefully. The problem is your grandmother looked for him. So did the police.' I give a quick rendition of the opening bars to the *Twilight Zone*. 'Maybe aliens spirited him away.'

'Fifty quid he made it to British Columbia.'

'Done.' We shake on it.

When I think about my father, it's his stories, his outlandish lies to Mum that I remember. All to escape her drinking and stumbling around. She had Ménière's disease and episodes came in clusters. The doctor prescribed diuretics to restrict fluid in the inner ear. It reduced the vertigo, but not the sudden drop in hearing.

Then came the antihistamines and shots of something-a-zine for the vomiting and Betahistine to reduce the frequency. All this, according to my aunt, while Mum was pregnant with me. It's a wonder I don't have brain damage.

I snap myself out of those dark, empty memories and return to the glare of my daughter's face, recognising I've cleverly sidestepped any further questions about the scratches on my neck.

'Congratulations on the writing prize. I'm proud of you.'

She gives me a look that passes somewhere between scepticism and shock.

Lilja coughs as if there's a bubble of anxiety in her throat. 'Your phone's ringing.'

If it hadn't been for a moment of clarity, I might have pulled out a partially smoked joint instead of my phone. I make my excuses and take the call between bites of banana.

'So now I'm being investigated. Thanks a bunch, Zane.'

'Why are you blaming me, Meggs?'

She huffs out a breath. 'Who else could it have been?'

As I make my way downstairs, Holloway's shadow is faintly visible inside the study. He's stouter than me. Better fed.

You realise where she's going with this? That under my influence, you must have sent it. Don't be an ignoramus, Zane. There are better things to worry about. You don't want her thinking you're a perverted failure or a serial killer. Where's the fun in that?

I'm not about to torture myself with conversations with a phantom. But Holloway has a point. I retreat to my study before Meggy's voice bursts from the phone.

'You know exactly why I sent that email and the photo attached.'

She has a monster IQ, and little tolerance with those whose range is lesser than 130. I daren't ask her what photo she's talking about. 'Calm down, Meggy. I'll call your boss and say it was a mistake.'

'Look,' she growls. 'This isn't just *any* job. It's my dream job. Doesn't that mean anything to you?'

'A valuable job, yes. Easily restored and everything goes back to normal.'

'But it won't. If you think you can go through life destroying everyone else's, you're pathetically deluded. Let's talk about that photo.'

'What delusion are you talking about? The one where you sneak around my house at night, stealing a look through my windows?'

'You gave me the passcode to your property and invited me.'

She's right. I had. 'So, what were you hoping to find?'

'You sound a little nervous.'

I hate to admit that suddenly I am. 'Not at all.'

'I saw you with her.'

I'm hoping it wasn't in many dark corners and positions. 'Sorry, you've lost me. Who are we talking about?'

'Nicola Gatlin.'

'You are following me.'

She gives a scornful puff of laughter. 'You admit you've been secretive?'

'I'm not admitting to anything.'

'You're in too deep, Zane. You've devoted far too much time to Holloway. Do you remember the exercise we did? The one where I told you to describe the house where you grew up. You told me it had a circular driveway and an old grey fountain shingled with lichen. You described the library as floor-to-ceiling books and the chairs were worn and lumpy. Leather, you mentioned. But it wasn't your house, was it? You were giving a sensory description of Holloway's.'

She's lost me. 'Perhaps it was a nicer house.'

'I should be grateful I never asked you to describe murdering a loved one.'

Something in her tone – deliberate, significant – causes my head to pound. Had the context been different, I would have thought she was alluding to my early morning dip with a body.

Meggy must notice the change in my breathing because she asks me if I'm okay.

'I'm fine,' I say, although "*Clearly not*" is buried in my answer.

Instead of feeling shame, I feel a horrifying elation, as if a terrorist has tied explosives to my waist and I'm looking forward to the explosion. Before my skin stretches and rips from my bones, I hang up, leaving her talking into a dead line.

Trending #InZane

@CirceAtNight: Hatred over ZaneO has everything to do with covering up his affairs. Nothing to do with acting.

@SherylAdams: @CirceAtNight You're indoctrinated in celeb gossip you cannot see the attention-seeking arrogant posturing person you are.

@CirceAtNight: @SherylAdams Arrogant posturing? I'm not the one dragging Nicola Gatlin into this mess.

@HeyWhatsUP: @CirceAtNight Hello! She's missing and ZaneO keeps trending. That's not sketchy to you?

27

LILJA

It's one of those golden days that's poised between rain and shine. I breathe in the sharp fragrance of juniper through the kitchen window.

I stopped eavesdropping on the conversations between Zane and his therapist yesterday because he wasn't making any sense and babbled about Holloway as if he was a lodger. It must be clear to Meggy that Zane isn't an innocent bystander but the villain.

To escape the small matter of how mentally untethered my husband is becoming, I make beef and spinach Gözleme – a traditional Turkish meal of fried wraps and feta.

Stella walks into the kitchen with an armful of sheets. 'I see you let him stay here last night.'

'Don't look at me like that.'

'Like what?'

'Like I should have thrown him out years ago.'

She angles her head towards the door. 'He informed me that after five years of dusting his bookshelves that it's not really his preference. I'll tell you right now what my preference is. Him in a sleeping bag under a bridge on the M1 for the next forty-five.'

'I'm on the edge of my seat.'

'His behaviour… it's not normal. He left his computer on before he took a shower. Naturally, I looked. It was a science focus page about how long bodies decompose at sea. I mean, I pinched myself several times and nothing changed. Everything's turning into one of those disaster movies, all upside down with a lot of water gushing in.'

'The Poseidon Adventure?' We look at each other and for a moment we almost laugh.

'What about you? You must be feeling like a cow in a slaughterhouse, stunned from behind and hoisted mid-air.'

I put a hand over my mouth to stifle a giggle. 'I hope I don't get stunned from behind.'

She's about to say something else when she hears Zane's footsteps, followed by two quick breaths as he jumps over Bizzy's gym kit, and retreats to the terrace.

His voice is perky as he says good morning, although he looks a little off-colour.

'I'm thinking of having a barbecue later,' I say, hoping he'll leave sooner. 'I could invite Mum and Frank.'

'Shit, next, you'll be brokering a détente with the press. Look at Marriott? Nipping up a tree and spying on me. It's all part of an elaborate plan to screw me over.'

'Let's not get carried away. He's a reporter, not a voyeur.'

'He can't find a damn thing to incriminate me. Must be spitting feathers.'

I want to tell him it's not just Stan watching him. It's me, especially at night when he slips out of bed, his footsteps fading into his study. Let's not forget Meggy Russell. That makes three of us.

'I wanted to let you know the removal vans will be here in two weeks. It's the best I could do. Meanwhile, it would be easier if I stay here to box everything.'

There's a frosty silence between us, during which I grow steadily more aware of my beating pulse. Again, I feel outmanoeuvred, and I don't want to be spiteful for the sake of it. The idea of him spending more nights here is unsettling. Before I ask him if he's heard anything from Nic, he slopes off downstairs again.

#FindNicola has drummed up local and national support and the public is now actively looking for her. I try to tamp down the memories of Nic skirting around me in the hall, on the stairs, in the corridors. She was hard to miss, healthy and fit, the type to walk along the high street with a yoga mat.

What could she say to me? I'm screwing your husband and I'm sorry? Like she'd simply borrowed a pair of socks without asking.

I was relieved when she left and now, I can almost see her on the staircase, holding a plate of my homemade muffins, her face turned to me with a *thank you* smile. I feel a split second of paralysis.

'Mum! We're going to be late.' Bizzy saunters towards me with Ted under one arm.

I almost forgot she has a trip to Exeter by bus to see *Hamlet* at the Northcott Theatre.

'Got everything?' I ask. 'And don't tell me you're responsible for taking something I didn't know about.'

'Nope.'

As I pull out of the garage, Bizzy settles into her fifty questions.

'Mum, why are there three smoked joints on the terrace? Any news about Nic? What's this about Dad and removal vans?'

'Three smoked joints?' I couldn't help landing on that one.

'Mum! Reporters.'

I try to focus on the front gate rather than the press in the lane. A journalist swings a camera up on his shoulder, it's a familiar game I know how to play. Hitting the remote, I accelerate with one hand over my face as we glide through. Bizzy is lying across my lap and giggling, as she's in the habit of doing. It's not funny when a car pulls off the grass verge behind me. I'll be lucky if I lose him at the farm.

'About Nic,' I say, as Bizzy lifts her head. 'She's still missing. That's all I know.'

I expect Bizzy to say how terrifying this is. How awful to know someone who has gone missing. But she stays calm.

'Something bad happened to her. That's what they're saying at school. Aren't you curious, Mum?'

'I don't know. Should I be? Saying something bad happened sounds too specific.'

It matters to Bizzy, though, like it matters if the cat disappears for longer than a day.

I take a sharp turn down a farm track which runs parallel to the barley field. The underside of the car pings and cracks over the stubble as we head towards a narrow road, beech trees leaning across a network of steep banks, their interlocking branches blocking out the sunlight.

'Doesn't *missing* mean she's being held in a basement for nine horrible hours?'

'It's been more than nine horrible hours, Bizz. There must be some other explanation. In fact, I have a deep sense of peace about it.'

When we emerge from the canopy of beeches, I focus hard on steering myself away from thoughts of the reporter who no longer bounces around in my rear-view mirror. We pass Victorian cottages and their mossy stone walls, neat gardens competing with each other throughout the summer. Seeing Bizzy's school is a relief and I pull into the driveway.

'They're setting up ground searches around the beach and the nature reserve.' She studies her phone. 'Do you think we should volunteer to follow the teams?'

'We might attract too much publicity for all the wrong reasons. It's about Nic. Not us.'

The last time I appeared with Zane was outside the Ritz Hotel in London after his success in *Eidolon*. They described me as a "full-figured beauty" with elaborate curls and a full-length Carolina Herrera ball gown. What would they say about me now?

I drop Bizzy off at practice and talk to her coach. There are other students from prominent families and a specific drill when a reporter is spotted. On the drive home, the more time I spend replaying Zane's comment about the removal company, the more it becomes an annoying excuse he has somehow engineered. I check his GPS and he's still at home. My guess is he's used one of three removal companies.

Parking my car in the garage, I call the first company and there's no appointment listed but the second comes up trumps. In my most apologetic voice, I tell them I'd booked the wrong date and could they do it sooner. To say they couldn't be more obliging, is an understatement.

As I emerge into the kitchen, I feel amused at ruffling Zane's feathers, but I want to see what effect this sudden change of plan will have.

28

ZANE

The appointment confirmation from Busy Chaps Removals is one of the shittiest things my scheming wife has ever done. Moving me out is simply a means to an end, the end speeding closer by the day.

It's late afternoon and instead of the hard sound of plates being set out on the kitchen table, there's silence. I can't smell supper either.

I toss a couple of oxy down my throat and wait for it to take effect. It's a mistake to take it, but so was the handful that came before.

The voice is a little blurry this time, but not completely unrecognisable.

I would delete ALL the evidence from your computer and phone. Particularly those nudie pics you've saved for a rainy day. Now would be good.

I delete the shots of Nic star-fished on a bed and suddenly wish I hadn't whipped the breath out of her by pushing her against the steps. She'd still be here, and everything would go back to…

Normal? There is no normal now.

But there can be.

Let's start with your wife. Nothing normal there.

I find Lilja in the kitchen and I can't work out if her various poses are of defiance or flight. 'You cancelled my moving date.'

'Not cancelled. Rescheduled.'

'Why?'

'Because you lied.'

She looks at me as if I'm not right in the head. When Lilja gets upset, she doesn't talk and it could be days before I see her smile again. I want to end the strained silences between us, but fortunately, she speaks first.

'You've been acting weird lately. Your voice… and I don't mean accents, I mean the tone, isn't yours. You talk to yourself, or you think you're talking to someone else. I don't know. But you talk out loud.'

She doesn't need to elaborate. My study has thin walls. 'Sometimes it's good to talk through the plot. Shake it out a little. Get to the heart of it.'

We stare at each other, a silent conversation that only spouses can have. I'm half looking at her, half scanning the room as if I'm understanding it correctly. Does she believe that if I'm living in Holloway's skin, I can't expect to be accountable for everything?

'I want you to admit to something because your behaviour demands it. Do you know where Nic is?'

There's a suspended moment where we both know my conduct has thrown me into the spotlight yet again. I'm a loving husband when she loves me and an adulterer when she hates me. There's always a label for everything I do.

'You know I don't.'

Nic could be anywhere in the English Channel by now or halfway to France. I hold back a grimace, unable to separate the chaos I've created from the harmony we once lived in.

She squares the salt and pepper shakers with both hands, something she does when she's upset. 'Are you in love with her?'

'No. I'm in love with you.'

Apart from thinking Nic was seriously shaggable, it was never about love. What we had was a short fling, which satisfied her desires and fulfilled mine. Then I have a ghastly flash of Nic, trying on my wife's dresses in our London house and ordered food with her credit card.

'Affairs don't come out of thin air, Zane. They're meticulously planned. Days, months salivating over one another.'

'You seem to know a lot about it.'

'Little lies build up. White lies, grey lies, any lies. To you, it was simply the rehearsal. To Nic it was the performance.'

The words sting and I'm too shocked to find a fitting response. 'I wouldn't have done half of it if you hadn't pushed me aside.'

'I haven't pushed you aside, and you know it.'

'I'm struggling to remember the last time I enjoyed your company. The last time we had pulse-racing sex. The last time we put each other first. Our marriage has become a dirty, spidery mess with too many dark corners. You've discarded me like a hand-me-down, declined invitations to dinner and rejected every sexual advance. It's like living with a stranger.'

'What would you know?' She laughs, a sharp burst of surprise. 'You're too busy living your flashy life, holed up in that study doing God knows what. I don't give a shit about your affair. But I give a shit about Bizzy and what happens to us after you're gone.'

Gone? How *gone* does she want me? My wife knows more than she's letting on. If she does, I know little about the woman standing opposite me.

'Have you at least tried contacting her? Going to her flat?'

Bile crawls up my throat. 'You mean you haven't done a thorough investigation of your own?'

'I could, but it will save time if you just tell me the truth.'

'Then no to both. I fired her, remember? No contact seems obvious.'

Nic's death is profoundly regrettable, yes, but admitting to it would mean a major relationship shift which I can't afford at this stage in my career.

'Do you realise what all this is going to do to us?'

I do, but I don't utter it. It's the better of two options since a hard no makes me look like a fool.

'If Nic is found, hurt or worse, they could pin it on you.'

I begin *visualising* and then shake myself out of it. Noise grows inside my head and her words hit me repeatedly and I suddenly feel a boiling, toxic hate. The type that leads to violent crimes reported on *Dateline*. I try to cover it with a weak, pensive smile, a look she would normally succumb to, but the words leave my mouth before I can stop them.

'It's amazing how you do that.'

'Do what?'

'Turn everything around so it's my fault.'

'I'm not the one screwing around!'

One minute she's yelling that I'm not myself anymore. The next I'm yelling back about how un-Lilja-like she has become, creeping around outside my study, eavesdropping. Yes, I know she does it. Oh, and the email message — the one she forwarded to CTC about Meggy which Catherine Gurtner has fortunately cleared up. Back and forth, the accusations fly and the greyout begins.

I feel a deep, tarry fear seeping up from my stomach into my gullet.

You don't have a choice. She knows too much.

Before I can stop myself, things happen so quickly I'm not sure when they began. My hands are gripping her shoulders and I'm shaking her too hard, too vigorously, and her fists are pounding on my chest. I'm waiting for the director to say, 'Cut' and all I can hear is, 'Zane. ZANE!'

I snap out of the scene and release my hold on her, and she takes three steps back. I focus on my breathing and my one thought is to get away before I destroy her. Instead of her eyes brimming with tears, they're moving back and forth from the window to the door.

Then they fix on my hands. My fists. I can't feel my legs and my vision blurs.

This time, I've gone too far. It's not until I hear the words, 'Get out! Get out!' that I realise how far that is.

Trending #InZane

@SherylAdams: Look at Nicola Gatlin's photos on TikTok and tell me that isn't Ozzie? #Busted

@BantaBadger: @SherylAdams Honestly? It could be anyone. If it is, he needs a good solicitor.

@CirceAtNight: Obvs ZaneO is so wrapped up in Holloway he can't see the "wood" from the trees. Probably didn't think he was involved with her in the real *sense*.

@HeyWhatsUp: Yeah. Method made me do it. That's what they all say.

@MiloMorales: It's not the Method. It's much darker than that.

29

LILJA

It's been a couple of days since Zane left for London. I deposited the money he stole to an account I'd opened in lieu of my catering business. To protect myself, I withdrew money from a third account he might still have access to.

I haven't responded to his texts, begging for forgiveness, and apologising for what he calls his "disgusting behaviour." I have no mercy left.

I doubt he's lonely. He's used to being away, filming for seventeen hours a day, staying in hotels or sleeping under the stars if that's what his character would do. We've spent most of our marriage separated than together. Even though my heart has been smashed to pieces, fragments scattering with every unkind word that trips off his tongue, I won't carry guilt for his failures. I can imagine the abuse in a thousand different ways and still be shocked when it happens.

You can't lock me out, Lily. It's my house too. His third text in ten minutes.

Legally, he's right, but what he did was frightening and completely out of character. I tell him a police report would stir up more publicity than either of us can manage.

Our food delivery isn't until tomorrow, so a trip to Sainsbury's seems like a good idea. The aisles aren't as crowded today, but there's a line at every checkout. I pause briefly to take my car keys from my handbag when a reporter flanks me, tape recorder flashing red.

'How do you feel about Nicola Gatlin's disappearance, Mrs Osborne? Did you know she was unhappy? Did she say anything about leaving? Where do you think she's gone?'

All I want to do is swear at him. Can't a woman shop without being harassed?

I push past him and run to my car, locking myself inside. The horror of everything shrinks down to one woman, to the day she arrived, to the day she betrayed me.

'This is all your fault, Nic! If you are hiding out somewhere, it's not funny!'

I drive to Mol's, an Elizabethan fronted house at the corner of Cathedral Close to get a stiff espresso. Keeping my head down I sit in the back corner, the sun creeping against the window, the warmth stealing in. Marschōne Robinson's interview with the press has made headlines today. His relationship with Nic took a dangerous detour. He didn't know how psychologically damaged she was and described her state of mind when they split. I don't know if I should feel angry or sad – and somehow, I don't feel either.

Shrill laughter cuts through the air like a jackhammer and my phone almost slips through my fingers. A woman enters the coffee shop, crisp and lively, a silky sway of light brown hair. She slings a sports bag on the nearest chair and heads for the counter. Her cashmere crop top has thumbhole sleeves, and her yoga pants are buttery smooth. She lifts a hand to someone she knows. Two hellos. Impeccably timed. You notice women like Meggy Russell, flawless under the sheen of a Devon sky.

My eyes follow her robotically. She pays and sips her coffee, tongue dusting the froth from her upper lip. It gets the attention of the man on the next table to mine, his eyes grazing the length of her body while she continues to read her phone.

As she shrugs the sports bag over one shoulder and strides out into the sunshine, I slug the rest of my coffee and follow.

My instinct says to hang back a little, don't stare, she'll feel it if I do. I walk faster to catch up with her, knowing she'll feel the invisible tether between us, a prickle on the back of her neck. I think – this is it, the moment where she senses me looking and turns. But she doesn't.

Her phone rings and she glances at the screen, a split second of hesitation before she accepts the call. She dips into the doorway of a book shop while I pause inside a covered bus shelter, close enough to hear her mention TV outlets and Radio 4.

'Okay, okay, calm down. *BBC Breakfast*, Sky and ITN? Are you sure? It's ridiculously early for them to assume. They said there have been sightings. Nothing confirmed.'

For me, the benefits of eavesdropping outweigh the pain of it. I know the difference between stalking and coincidence, and I can't redefine them to suit my own needs. She'll turn around and see me and I'll be caught shame-faced and sweating.

I run to my car, her words banging around in my head on the drive home.

They said there have been sightings.

It's unrealistic to believe Nic is not staying connected with her family and friends, and simply gadding about in another country. For one mad moment, I imagine she's hiding out in Holland Park.

Stella greets me as I walk through the front door. 'You look tired, my love.'

'It's nothing. Shouldn't you have gone home already?'

'I was waiting for you.'

We walk to the kitchen in silence, her hand warm against my back. I'm comforted by the one person who knows me better than I know myself.

Kicking my shoes off, I put the shopping away. 'I've been making use of my time alone, reading the financial papers, keeping myself up to date with the media. I need to build my capital and set myself a target. Without Zane's income, the house and grounds are too much to keep up, unless I turn it into a restaurant. That's where you fit in. If you agree, then I have family to help with that.'

She steals a look at the bottle of Bailey's on the shelf and winks. 'I'll drink to that.'

I get two glasses from the cupboard and we tuck in. For a moment, I remember Saturday nights, how Zane and I would sit together on the couch, a bottle of Baileys on the coffee table. Sometimes we'd be wrapped in each other for hours, warm and happy.

We were happy then, weren't we? It can't have all been a lie.

'I don't want to be the bearer of bad news,' she says. 'But I'm not sure I can keep coming here—'

'Why does it always have to be about him?' I blurt out, thumbing away a tear. 'I've been cast off, exploited and patronised, while he gorges himself on champagne and oysters with a teenager.'

'Lilja, are you listening? I don't want you to think I don't care about you and Bizzy. I do. But the press, all those people outside, it's scares me.'

The tears are streaming down my face, and every nerve in body is wild and confused. 'I can't even remember the last time he asked me if I was okay or if there was anything I needed. Anything to make my world a better place. You know what I need? The old Zane. The one I fell in love with. No acting. No pretending. Just us. But every night, I wake up remembering what he's done, and it hits me again and I can't sleep.'

'I want you to be happy,' Stella says. 'Staying with him would be destructive and wrong. Deep down, you know that.'

'I don't want to fall apart and find myself alone, but losing Bizzy in a custody battle would be unbearable.'

She takes my hand in both of hers. 'You'll win through. You always have. I'll keep coming here until the press makes it impossible for me to get past the front door.'

How naïve of me not to expect her to be anxious about the press. In the same way, I never thought the press would interfere with our staff. I'm crying and telling her how sorry I am for being so selfish.

'I bought you a gift,' she says.

I watch her open her handbag, her precious head turned downwards and her wiry hair sticking out at right angles. She pulls out a small box. Inside is a black and white blown glass bird with a crest on its head.

'It's a northern lapwing,' she says. 'Speaks Geordie.'

I cup it in both hands and hold it up to the light. 'It's beautiful.'

There are flashes of blue and purple in the plumage and its crest is so delicate I'm afraid it might break. It all becomes too much,

Stella leaving and this perfect goodbye gift. The irrational stab of disappointment I feel is hard to put into words. It's the type of heartache that bites if you think about it.

She pulls on her jacket. For the first time, I see she's standing a little hunched over, like a flower that has been leaning towards the sun for too long. I try to shake the feeling that for now, if I don't do something about Zane, everyone will leave me.

30

ZANE

The weather this morning is making me feel funky, low tufted clouds threatening rain. Driving to Blundell Street Studios is scaring me shitless and the spectre in the back of my car whispers devilish things in my ear.

It's one thing being alone in a house, knowing family will come home later. It's quite another when you know they're not coming home at all.

I can almost see the dark glint behind his eyes as I search for a witty comeback. I hadn't had one when best-friend Rick picked on me at school for having a posh accent, and I don't have one now.

No need to think about Rick. He died in prison. Heart attack, apparently.

'I didn't know,' I say.

I had envisioned an abusive interaction with his cellmate, or hypothermia from the harsh conditions. Rick was always shivering in his patched-up school uniform, always borrowing my socks. I hope he had a double-glazed window which afforded him some warmth. Now I'm sorry I never went to see him.

More shocking news.

Nurse in hit-and-run on Warren Road now in coma…

I turn to another station.

…what does Zane Osborne's rumoured love affair mean to his fans.

Holloway takes this opportunity to whisper in my ear during the cricket scores.

Why the long face? Actors frequently feign salacious stories to elevate their ratings. The public love flawed people. They resonate.

The only thing I resonate with is the nurse I almost hit with Nic's car. It's no use trying to erase that terrible night from my mind, I'll be reliving it for years.

Although there's no way she can give a statement now…

My scalp tightens, a feeling of pure dread. Emma, my publicist, emailed the questions to me this morning. Talk about last minute. The meeting is to promote Season 2 of *Play Him, Play Her,* but these questions predictably bleed into rumour. Amanda Yeboah insisted we tape the interview at a discreet location to prevent reporters from flooding the place. Yet I have a niggling feeling they will dribble in from somewhere.

I park close to the back door and check the glove box for my spare phone. I toss out the owner's manual, pen and paper, tissues, insurance papers. As far as I recall, it's in my desk drawer, although it's more likely to be down the side of the couch.

Shit, I've really done it now. I call the number and there's no sound of it in the car.

Emma knocks on my window. Flame-coloured hair and a blunt fringe give her a distinctive look. She wears an emerald green dress and tennis shoes. Strange combination, but it somehow works.

A kid sits on the steps, holding a small leatherbound book. He reminds me of a Botticelli angel, curly dark hair and large eyes. The only difference is a small chip in his front tooth.

'Hey Milo. Great to meet you.'

'And you.' He jumps up and shakes my hand. I realise he only comes up to my chest.

'What have you got there?' I ask.

'Just a book. I wondered if… if you'd sign it?'

'Of course.'

I open the little book at the first page and leave a special message for my number one fan. 'You're dedicated, I'll give you that.'

He nods and smiles. 'Been here since 7.00 am.'

I look around but I don't see a parent. 'Are you on your own?'

'Dad was here.' He winces and looks down at his shoes. 'He had to go to work.'

'Need a ride somewhere? I can get you a car.'

'No. I'm fine thanks.'

Only I don't think he is, not if the hint of a bruise on the side of his cheek is anything to go by. 'Are you sure?'

'Quite sure.' His smile flickers on and off. 'I wanted to say… to tell you not to be discouraged. There's so much more if you know where to look. All the best… in there, I mean.'

He walks down the alleyway, hugging the book to his chest. He doesn't look back and he doesn't wave, and I feel a keen sense of hope.

Two men outside the studio entrance give me curious glances as I walk by, exchanging judgmental looks filled with gossip. *It's Zane Osborne. The one who plays the horny doctor on Netflix. He was screwing his assistant. What a man-whore.* This is the version they've read on *BarbedWire*, the one where the Grave Diggers have ripped my marriage apart. Shame seeps through me and I try to block it out.

We're ushered into a narrow room, mirrors and chairs on one side and barely enough room for a couch on the other. Emma curls up with a coffee and talks me through the questions. Hard-hitting and tough, but I'd agreed to all of it to put an end to the speculation.

Relax. Forget about Holloway, who I wish I'd never invited into my life, and who I'm admiring a little less. My attention must be pin-sharp. No distractions.

Is that a joke? Forgive the ET quote, but "I'm right here" …

Fine. But don't creep around the studio like a restless ghost.

Boo to you too.

I swat him away as if a cloud of midges is about to descend. Stacy, a former Fox News makeup artist, looks at the space above my head and then back at me with a frown. I tell her it was a mosquito, the no-see-um variety. Emma cackles.

Stacy applies a tanned glow to what she defines as my sallow and washed-out complexion – the au naturel me.

'You look fabulous,' she says.

Flatterer. As long as you don't look like an Oompa-Loompa.

Amanda pops her head in and shakes my hand. She tells me someone will be in soon to mic me and reminds me not to reference the camera.

Her head wrap matches the drop earrings that fall below her jawline, and her makeup is flawless. I'm guessing her hair is fashionably long now, the same mahogany waves I remember from school.

I'm sitting in the studio, staring around wildly, when director Nimrod Yung tells me I'm being cued. I barely hear the countdown before Amanda looks into the camera and begins her introduction.

'Cosmetic surgery isn't the only thing to be afraid of in Netflix's *Play Him, Play Her*. The series focuses on the upstanding Mr Holloway, a pillar of the local community. But, of course, nothing is quite as it seems. When burns victim Amaya Stone, played by Quiana Thompson, becomes his love interest, things get complicated for Britain's favourite doctor.

'Zane Osborne plays Ethan Holloway, the seemingly put-together cosmetic surgeon. Here, he discusses taking the role from *Play Him, Play Her* creators Andy and Simon Berne and how long hours of shadowing local doctors consumed his free time.'

She turns to me and says, 'What was it about the role of Mr Holloway that appealed to you?'

'Andy and Simon Berne asked me to come in and meet them and we spoke about the character for almost three hours. I liked the idea of a doctor doing pro bono work for children and war veterans, but I wasn't so happy about his fall from grace. But it's also about his family and exploring how his work affects that.'

Amanda pastes on another fake smile. 'You're a method actor. This, in layperson's terms, is someone who lives the life of the character. How do you prepare for scenes like these?'

'Prior to filming, I shadowed a Harley Street surgeon for three months to appreciate what commitment and dedication looked like. I'd maxed a little over three hours sleep and developed a tic in my left eye.'

'It certainly paid off,' she says. 'According to Marschōne Robinson, you're the creepiest Holloway he knows.'

There's a ripple of laughter and I feel myself flush. They don't know Marschōne shoots up heroin in his trailer and gives every new lay a designer watch.

Amanda stares at me, the crew following suit. I do what I do best, steer the subject from Marschōne back to me.

'For my role in *Lady Doddridge*, I played Thomas, the illegitimate son of Sir Amias Bampfylde. I slept in Exeter Cathedral, tramped around barefoot and ate restaurant left overs. For *Eidolon*, I slept in a makeshift tent on the beach and got hypothermia, which landed me in ICU.'

Amanda's mouth falls open. 'Do you think you're taking this too far?'

'Not at all. For Mr Holloway, it was vital to understand his motivation. I returned to a time where I felt the same emotions, to understand why it affected me. It means going into these dark places, locking myself away from family, so I can understand how his body moves, his passions, his drive. I live and breathe with him in the moment. It's a complete transition.'

'And Mr Holloway has a very dark secret.' Her teeth are clearly visible behind that smile. 'He's a serial cheater and a murderer. Do on-screen roles bleed into off hours?'

I'm seized with the irresistible urge to wrap my hands around her neck. Despite her popularity and ratings, which far outdo mine, I'm wondering if Amanda likes me. Or if she's doing this interview to destroy me.

'Sometimes,' I say, returning the grin. 'Interesting relationships come about. For instance, Stone and my character get the most airtime. There would be scenes in which Stone and I would talk in a car...'

'Or roll around on the bed.' The gold flecks in her brown eyes seem to glow. She had that singularity as a kid, too. 'Mr Holloway does that a lot!'

If this were a game, I'd pause and restart, steer the conversation away from sex and say something flippant. My mind cycles through my mental inventory for something sarcastically Holloway, but he didn't come into the studio with me today.

'Really, Amanda? If you think Holloway is more about sex than control, you failed to glean the finer details. To answer your irrelevant question, it's crucial the scene is authentic. If we, the actors, need more time to grow the chemistry – you know, longer takes – then that's what we do.'

'But what's it like being intimate with another actor on set?' Her eyes meet mine and it's like she's about to explode with childish curiosity. 'Does it make you nervous?'

'Not at all. There are guardrails in place dictated by contracts and, of course, consent. Intimacy coordinators meet with the show runner ahead of time to establish the arc and tone. They also meet with us to determine what's comfortable when choreographing a scene. It's not awkward, not with a closed set. Just talent and crew. You do what makes the most sense for the scene.'

Amanda blinks for a moment, then her expression clears. 'One reporter likened Mr Holloway to Daniel Day Lewis's character in *The Unbearable Lightness of Being*. For the audience, that would be a promiscuous and oversexed brain surgeon.'

'Both films strike an erotic balance, and both have doctors struggling with their free-spirited mistresses. Tomas may indulge in affairs, but he's no serial killer.'

Amanda keeps her voice bright and casual. 'Your fans think there's a similarity to your personal life. Your assistant, for instance. Is there any truth in the rumour that you chose her to "practice" on? Or was there more to it than that?'

Blimey. She's not messing around. I suddenly feel tense, as if she's dissecting everything I say, so she can twist it to suit her own narrative.

'Neither.' I pause. 'The reporters do an excellent job romanticising casual meetings. Coffee, lunch, walks on the beach. My assistant has a great sense of humour and enjoys teasing people on social media.'

'I'm sure your fans will be glad to hear it.' She smiles, but it's tight. 'Now she's missing. You must feel terrible.'

'Yes, it's been a frantic few weeks. We're all hoping she'll come home. Or at least contact her family.'

'I'm sorry this horror happened on your doorstep. I'm sure it wasn't what you expected.'

Silence is a language I'm fluent in and it's not my job to keep conversation flowing. She stares at me, as though waiting for me to tell her something memorable. What's memorable is that I ran with the acting crowd at school, always lying to cover our arses. Amanda knows, because she did too.

She unwinds with a smile. 'Tell us a little about Season 2.'

'All I can say is it will require me building stamina and using my survival skills.'

'We all know how successful you were in *Solo's* survival competition. Tell me, does the location play a vital role? Do you feel close to the place off camera?'

'The setting is a character in the story. On one hand, Exeter is historically beautiful, but on the other, there's something unsettling about the coast. Where Holloway is engineered tall and imposing, much like the cathedral, he is also harsh and windswept like the sea.'

'Nice analogy.' Her expression turns more curious than cordial. 'How does making a series like this differ from working on *The Ghost of Lady Doddridge* or *The Eidolon*?'

'My dream is to have a bit of everything, action, depth, complexities of characters and a great story. I enjoy anything physical, but I prefer to be challenged.'

I square my shoulders and stare at a woman I'd known since childhood, looking suddenly and utterly unfamiliar. While I listen to her wrap-up, I take a long sip of tepid water. I can't quite interpret the look on her face, but I fear it might be disappointment. After someone grabs the mic from my shirt, I'm suddenly legging it to the door, pushing my way past hot, sweaty bodies.

I head for the service entrance at the back of the studio, but it's locked. Using the front door instead, I burst out into a sea of shapes and voices.

'Over here, Zane; over here.'

There's a whirring and clicking and I'm running blindly into a gaggle of reporters with microphones and notepads. I don't speak, my fury boiling up inside. I try to step back from the jostling camera crews, but I can't escape the crush. Walking to my car is like wading through mud, their voices rising in pitch.

'How would you describe your relationship with Ms Gatlin?'

'Were you more than just friends?'

'How long was she working with you?'

'Will there be a divorce announcement?'

A face flickers past, an arm links mine. 'No more questions, guys.'

I'm ushered to my car and told to drive, but I fall against the seat, my hands shaking in my lap. Someone grips my hands and I look up and see Emma's face flushed, her eyes wide.

'You all right, love?' she says.

'Yes, I'm fine, thanks.'

'Now bugger off home. Fast as you can.'

She closes my door and motions for me to lock it. I pull out, reporters scurrying, flashes blinding through the windscreen. No doubt there will be some shite story splashed across the front pages of every newspaper and played out on TV.

Instead of returning to London, I race down the motorway, barely seeing signs to Exminster and South Town, my foot down all the way to Dawlish. I reckon if a police car wanted to pull me over, they wouldn't have been able to catch me.

Trending #InZane

@SherylAdams: Seriously? Did ZaneO have something to do with Nicola Gatlin's disappearance? Or is it the anti-Ozzie machinery in action, smoke and mirrors whataboutery.

@CirceAtNight: @SherylAdams It's a crock of shit. If he had, he'd already be in prison, not giving interviews and headlining fundraisers.

@Titmouse: This is a witch hunt. Anyone who thinks ZaneO would do such a thing is a hater. Let's do a sweepstakes.

@HeyWhatsUP: And yet here he is, sitting down for a 'nothing off limits' interview with Amanda Yeboah. The timing seems sus.

31

LILJA

The chorus of *Dirty Little Secret* brings me downstairs to Zane's study. At first, I think he must have left iTunes playing on his laptop, but the sound is coming from the desk drawer.

Zane's phone is sandwiched between a box of air pods and a rechargeable lighter, and I'm trying to understand why he left it behind. The screen is blank, even when I touch it, and something about it unsettles me. I haven't the foggiest why.

My brother-in-law is the only one who can hack a passcode, and today is his half day.

The Hotel Magdalene, my former workplace, is a blend of historic and modern, high ceilings and open fires, and well-kept terraces. Here, the head chef barks orders to the brigade de cuisine and there's a rhythm to the way they all work. The sauce sous chef begins his prep after the fish chef. The garnish sous chef starts after the fish prep, allowing one minute for plating and adding sauce. If all goes according to plan, it's less than ten minutes and several happy diners.

It's the first time I've been back since that awful day. I keep my head up, knowing I've nothing to be ashamed of.

I ask a server where the sauté chef is, and she points a thumb at the back door. Paul sits on a beer barrel, smoking a cigarette, the top buttons of his chef's jacket stylishly undone. He has a whiff of fried oil about him, and you know there's a lot happening in that head of his.

He puts a hand on my shoulder. 'You look like shit.'

'I'm touched. I didn't know you cared.'

'I don't.'

I shoot him a smile. 'Funny how life can explode in a matter of seconds. One minute everything's tickety-boo, the next your husband's affair is on display. If the press keeps hounding Zane all over England, it'll be the Pont de l'Alma tunnel all over again.'

'Don't you have some kind of security detail?'

'He's not Mick Jagger, for crying out loud.'

'You should probably think about it.'

I notice threads of muscle on the inside of his arms, and there's a new tattoo of a dandelion, seeds scattering all the way to his wrist. I see him follow my focus, consider making an explanation and deciding against it.

'Elin mentioned he might have done this before,' he says. 'When he was filming on the Isle of Wight.'

'I suspected he was. I couldn't prove it.'

'The point is you did nothing about it. That's why he's done it again. Fantasising things will get better and knowing they won't is the definition of madness.' Paul grinds the cigarette under his heel. 'Time to make a plan. Otherwise, you might find yourself living in a one-bedroom flat, sharing custody of your daughter with your ex-husband and his new wife.'

'It's not as easy as that, Paul. Ever since he started this series, he's been acting weird. Late nights are at an all-time high and he's been drinking more than usual. Get this. He took a whole pile of money from our bank account and stashed it in his wardrobe.'

'Blimey.'

'He's being a real arsehole.'

'Which for a man with a wildly overinflated ego, doesn't surprise me.' Pauls cracks his knuckles. 'Does he know what I'm capable of? Because I suddenly think he should.'

'That's why I'm here.' My shirt clings to my skin as I hand him the phone. 'I want you to unlock this.'

'Whose is it?'

'His, I think.'

Paul mutters something about some kind of firmware on his laptop, and I'm nodding and trying to take it all in. He asks for my phone too and tells me to wait, but waiting could mean ten minutes. One hour.

Left alone, I'm mesmerised by a bee bobbing over a clump of horsetail, undeterred by a strong breeze. Occasional laughter bursts from the gardens, glasses chink, alcohol wafts. I stand and roll my shoulders, filling my lungs with the scent of honeysuckle.

Zane can give his affair with Nic every excuse he wants, but it's a craving for intense pleasure, the secret, untraceable kind. He's cheated on me because I've failed to keep my attention focused on him – and yes, I've stopped building him up and telling him what he wants to hear.

I was sixteen when I first met him at a friend's party. Every head turned to stare at him, eyes sliding into a vertical scan. He was full of flattery, taking a genuine interest in everything they said – so effortlessly seductive. Even before his name became synonymous with Ethan Holloway, you could tell he was marked for stardom.

I get flashes of it sometimes, Zane's twenty-two-year-old face, his laughter, and a whirl of trees. Sometime later I was roofied. Two thirsty gulps. That's all it took. Not enough to put me under, but enough to return home with two bruises on my arms where someone had grabbed me.

'So,' Paul's voice makes me jump. 'Might be best to keep the sound off. Someone called Meggy has an assigned ring tone.'

'She called?'

'Yep.' He takes a deep breath and hands me both phones. 'I've reset the password and downloaded Auto Forward to your phone. You'll see everything from the target phone in real time, assuming you'll have to put this back where you found it. I've turned off the location services since you don't want him knowing you've taken it.'

'You've thought of everything.'

He smiles. 'You could also use one of these.'

I stare at the small disk in his hand.

'It's an AirTag. Provided it's within range of another Apple device, it will ping its location and you'll see it in your Find My app. What I'm saying is, if you put it in Zane's car, you can track him if he turns off his phone location. I took the liberty of setting it up for you.' He gives me a side hug. 'Call Elin. She misses working with you.'

'I will. And thanks.'

I sit in the carpark, studying the AirTag and checking its location via my phone. What if Zane doesn't drive his car but takes an Uber or a train? Wouldn't it be better to slip it into the lining of his wallet?

I turn the phone over and over in my hand. The case is some kind of hard carbon fibre, military grade, same as his regular one. It's smart when I think about it, getting the same colour and style so not to raise suspicion.

There are only two numbers listed in his contacts and two people he has been texting. Meggy Russell and Amaya Stone. The name would have set my pulse racing, until I read a flood of old text messages to get a snapshot of who she is. The one thing that stands out to me are Zane's responses, requesting her to bring any notes she might have on the script or offering dates and times to meet. The more I read, the more uneasy I feel.

Amaya is Nic.

She enjoyed Holloway's occasional flashes of arrogance, his playful jibes, his simmering sexual brutality – all the things I hate. But in all these texts, there's not one seedy response from Zane. Had Nic used Holloway's name in her contacts instead of Zane's real name?

I scroll through more work-relating messages, occasionally interrupted by a photo of a barely-there swimsuit, head thrown over one shoulder and hair tumbling down her back. Or a white tablecloth where a man's hand covers hers. No faces. No caption. Notably, my husband's hand and wedding ring. I clench my jaw so tight I can almost hear a filling crack.

The metadata tells me when the photo was taken. A memorable date. I'm trying to rack my brains where he told me he was.

Quaglinos with his publicist. He was clear about that.

As the texts continue, I see a change. But where and how this change occurred, I don't know. The messages stop abruptly on the day before his birthday party. There's nothing to lead me to Nic. Nothing to tell me where she is.

I tap on the information icon on her profile photo and wait for the map to load. But her details are blank. I check People Finder and she's not listed. His photo file is empty and his recently deleted photos, and I don't have the password to his cloud.

Where Meggy Russell is concerned, he is tracking her, making screen captures of every place she frequents. I'm amazed she gave him permission. Or did he take advantage of an unattended, unlocked phone seconds after she'd used it? Unlikely, unless her phone has a timed delay.

I follow the blue pulsing dot in real time, slipping along the Georgian terraces of Southernhay Road towards a stately house. Not only can I access Meggy's social media from his phone, but he's saved her address in Google Maps under SoHoEx.

I google the website, which shows a glowing front façade and the old timey feel of a townhouse. It's one I know well and only minutes from the Magdalene Hotel.

Zane's texts to her are spur-of-the-moment and many are during the early hours. Meggy doesn't always respond fast enough, which appears to bother him, but her responses when she does are efficient and unbiased.

For Zane, telling the truth is as terrifying as pulling back the curtain he hides behind and standing naked centre stage. In one text, he insists Holloway forced him into exploring infidelity and in the next, he swears the thought disgusts him, as if he's battling two personalities.

Playing Holloway has added a layer of complexity I wasn't expecting.

I read on.

He provokes me night and day, begging me to feel it skin to skin. He says I cannot feel hate without first feeling love, and now I'm filled with both.

What if Zane is using the pain of his past to fuel his anger? Would the sheer intensity of it be enough to drive him mad?

I can't process the words of his last text no matter how I try to reshape them.

I'm terrified Holloway will drive me to murder.

32

ZANE

Lilja and I may have divided the house into battleground territory, but it's still my home. I cancelled the removal company and apologised for jerking them around. I won't need bespoke suits where I'm going.

As I drive up the lane, I'm reminded of the grandeur of Barton Manor. Columns and pediments flicker between the trees, then the flash of white gravel along the sweeping drive. I park in front of the locked gate and let the car idle for a while.

In the good old days, Lilja would open the door and run down the steps as soon as she heard my car. She was always waiting for me. I remember the evening of the wedding like it was yesterday. A marquee on the lawn and an army of servers standing to attention like a row of liveried servants. There were hydrangeas on every table, their umbrella-shaped clusters an explosion of green and white.

I cupped her face in my hands and made her look at me. 'I don't know what I'd do without you.'

'You'll never be without me,' she insisted.

'Is this really forever?'

She nodded. 'Until one of us dies.'

Despite the heat of the lanterns, I felt a chill, as if someone had walked on my grave.

They say moving house is as painful as a divorce and as traumatic as a death. They're right. We've left our mark here, a tiny essence for the next generation, the residue of *us*. Yet here I am in unoccupied zone. Neither in nor out, just somewhere in between.

I take a spanner from the car's toolbox and walk to the gate. Loosening the bolt beneath the motor, I place it in neutral and open it manually. I'm only here to pick up my backpack and my spare phone.

Through the open window, I smell perfume – aromatic and lemony – and I know I've smelt it before. It's a beautiful evening and the front façade is aglow from the setting sun, and highlighted in all that glory stands a woman in a yellow daisy dress, her long, dark hair shimmering in the evening breeze.

'Zane! Over here!' she shouts, waving her hands wildly above her head.

A sick feeling rises in my throat and my pulse begins to race. I turn the wheel a little too sharply and the car mounts the lawn and whips under the boughs of the weeping willow. I brake to a stop at the corner of the house.

My brain is short-circuiting, and I can hear Nic's voice.

You should have stopped it. You could have.

I draw a ragged breath. She walks towards me, and instead of looking beautiful in that yellow dress, it is twisted around her thighs, and caked in mud.

But wait… The story was that she was swimming. Who swims fully clothed.

It should never have happened.

No. She's right, it shouldn't have happened. I should have taken that dress off and left it on the beach. But I didn't. I failed.

I'm breathing so fast; my vision is tunnelling. None of this seems right.

I glance back at the front door and there's no one in a yellow dress. It's simply a rose tree, one of a pair, shedding its yellow petals on the stone steps below.

I rest my head against the back of the seat, my hands gripping the wheel. Nic is everywhere. Her face stares back at me with every news notification, her eyes drilling into mine.

I open the car door and stumble around the back of the house.

No, I didn't kill her. I would never have killed her. I don't know what's wrong with me. But there's something broken inside, and I have the wild urge to pound my head against the wall, break my skull and bleed Holloway out.

A noise makes me jump.

Eee-oo-eep!

I spot the lapwing in the furthest corner of the terrace, teetering on its toes with its wings folded back. Snapping my fingers, I make a hissing noise, but it merely stamps its feet, lifting and lowering its wings as if trying on a jacket for size. I hate all that posturing and pouty display of dominance, and I don't like the way it's staring at me.

I slam the French doors and lock them. The lamp sheds a gentle light on the desk, and I fumble with the keys to the top drawer. Rummaging under notepads and pens for my spare phone I pause, one thought swirling around in my head.

Did it slip under the couch? Behind the curtain? Under the Persian rug?

There's zero chance that Lilja could have taken it from a locked drawer where I keep the only key. I hurl all the cushions off the chairs and run my hands between the back of every seat. When I'm sure it's not here, I open the study door and peer up the stairwell. Darkness doesn't tempt me beyond the first step. This is where my boundary ends.

I pour myself a whisky and for some perplexing reason, one of Holloway's final scenes comes to mind.


```
                        AMAYA

          (blinking rapidly, hand over her chest)

               I don't feel well.


                       HOLLOWAY

               No. I don't suppose you do.
```

                        AMAYA

        (drops the glass of wine she's holding)

             I can't breathe.

                       HOLLOWAY

        When presently through all thy veins
                    shall run

         A cold and drowsy humour.

        Shakespeare. A scene in Friar Lawrence's
        cell when he gives Juliet the vial. With
        propofol toxicity comes cardiac fail-
        ure. It doesn't mean your heart will
        stop beating. But without treatment it
        most certainly will. I think it's time
        to call it a night, don't you?

I hold my whisky up to the light, examining it for any cloudy residue, and then I take another sip. No one is trying to poison me.

To use a sartorial analogy, Holloway is the difference between merino wool and polyester on bare skin. Where one is smooth and sensual, the other rubs and chafes. There is so much to like about him, yet here he is, murdering his mistress.

Sound familiar? Holloway asks. *It wasn't some kind of homicidal episode. It was all part of my plan. Yet you… you pushed Nic and YOU were the one who covered it up. I bet you wake up every night to the sound of a woman's screams, caught short by bone hitting stone. Those same droplets produce an image from childhood which has lain dormant until now. It rises from the dregs of that scene, and you can't stop it rolling.*

I'm ten, sitting on a tree stump in my father's shed. It stinks of wood shavings, kerosene, and rust. The vents along the roof release most of it, but it takes a lot of getting used to. The door is ajar, and I hear pecking and scratching, and through the gap in the slats, I see blue and green feathers and the distinctive red wattle of a pheasant. Dad preferred to decapitate them. He said a jugular slice saved you from a mouthful of shot at dinner.

He holds a finger to his lips. 'Don't move, son.'

He stalks towards the door and presses himself against the wall. We wait and wait and I'm hoping it will never happen. When it does, the old man moves fast. As soon as the bird is over the threshold, he tackles it to the ground, shouting and scrabbling in the dirt. Sometimes he wrings their necks and sometimes he squeezes hard enough to crush a ribcage, compressing the lungs and stopping the heart. But this time, he brings it limp to the stump I've been sitting on and tells me to get the hatchet. The weapon feels cold and heavy in my hands, and I know what he wants me to do.

'Do it now!'

If I don't, he'll be whispering cruel things in my ear at bedtime. There are other words, but I don't know what they mean.

We'd been studying Sir Thomas Cromwell's life at school and how in 1540 it took three axe blows to remove his head. I'm thinking how incompetent the executioner was and my hands are shaking, and pee is rolling down my legs.

My hesitation is enough to tell Dad I can't do it. He looks up at me, his lips drawn back, using threats that stretch to ripping off my privates. I want to impress him, to be everything he wants me to be. Instead of him slicing off its head, the scene changes.

I lift the hatchet, and it comes down hard. There's only a trickle of blood on the stump and on my shoes. While Dad holds it up by its feet, cheering and whooping and patting my back, I'm healed of my worthlessness. I am a man at last.

But the scene always has a way of reverting to the truth. Back I go to that shed, the ground moving under me, Dad moving in and out of my vision. He steadies my elbow and I let him hang on long enough until I shake him off. This time I'm sobbing as he plucks the bird until it's half the size it was. Tail feathers first, then the wing. When it's naked, he tells me to take it to my mother, who chops off those long spindly legs at the joint, and dresses it.

After dinner, he gives me a sip of his beer as we watch the leaves sway in the evening breeze. He tells me tears are for sissies and I'm an ungrateful sod for not eating my food. He gets up off the step and takes his pocketknife, his rifle, and a sleeping bag, and disappears over the fields. Mum says he sleeps in a derelict house on the moors and lives on the land. He's hardy like that.

The residue of that memory is as sharp now as it was then. I remember blood dripping into the sink from my father's hands, his nails shredded and ingrained with it. Dad knew it made me sick. Even the soap on the kitchen draining board turned frothy and pink, and he made me clean it before my mother came in. Thing is, he left a sobbing child on the porch and never said goodbye. He's the only person I know who completely disappeared.

'Dad? What are you doing?'

The voice shakes me from the memory. Bizzy stands at the open door, her hair is clipped back with a nest of grips to hide an outgrowth of blue dye. I realise I've wasted more precious hours in la-la-land.

'I came back to collect a few things.'

I stare at the antique fork gripped in my fist; one I must have plucked from a collection on the shelf without any memory I'd done it. I realise her concern.

'Oh, this? It's an interpretive exercise. Imagination is at the core of everything I do, Bizz. What if this fork can feel me? What if it knows if I'm warm or cold? Happy or sad? When I move it, I can hear the air passing through the tines in the same way it can hear me breathe.'

She stares at me in that disconnected way of hers and I need to make a point.

'Imagine it's not inanimate like you'd expect, but able to do and think for itself. How dangerous would it be?'

'Depends.'

'On what?' I take a deep breath, rubbing a finger against the stubble on my jaw.

'Whether it can fly.'

For a few moments, the two of us are in sync. 'Let's say it can.'

'Then it would be like a weapon,' she says. 'A lance. An arrow.'

'See. Now you're using your imagination.'

I notice her eyes stray, the connection we had suddenly ripped away as she drops my old army boots on the mat.

'Thanks for letting me borrow them.'

I'm not sure if I'm happy that she has enormous feet, or I have small ones. Either way, she borrows my shoes, mostly without asking. Somehow, I'm focusing on her socks, which are askew, like everything about her. Even the limp, which she fakes every so often because of an illegal tackle, has disappeared. Does deceit spread? Am I the first to have carried the virus?

'You realise the forecast says rain next week?' she says. 'It'll be freezing out on the moors. Why don't you just sleep in the car? It's not like anyone would know.'

I realise Bizzy knows nothing of what has happened between her mother and me, and she thinks I'm still going to Bodmin. 'I'm not taking the car.'

'Seriously, it's not a competition. You can't just pitch a tent, light a fire and hunt rabbits. Wild animals could eat you.'

'Not sure that's a risk in Cornwall.'

She looks over her shoulder and then down at her phone and I wonder what's keeping her. 'There's a thing about you on Sky News.'

I give her my best frown, the one where my eyes go narrow like they're disappearing into my head. 'What thing?'

'Well, it's on now.'

I watch her profile as she turns, eyebrows knitted together. She hesitates for a moment and then walks upstairs.

I turn on the TV and flip through the channels until I find Sky News. Keeping the sound down, I read the closed captioning on the bottom of the screen.

> *... in a recent TikTok video with the words Play Me, Play You, Gatlin says, "It lasted a couple of months and, honestly, I felt exploited." Considering her disappearance, the rumour has taken the internet by storm and fans are losing their faith in Zane Osborne. More importantly, why is Nicola Gatlin in hiding?*

I scroll through Nic's TikTok and the weight of what I'm seeing threatens to crush me. For a moment, I'm shaking violently, I have to hold one hand down with the other. Nic must have scheduled the post to publish today and now Bizzy knows.

I realise how vulnerable this makes me, how things grab the rage of the public, and my face will be splashed across every newspaper. I intend to push the sexual harassment story. Nic isn't here to defend herself.

My publicist hasn't commented on my Twitter profile. But the troll, *HeyWhatsUP* claims I'm downplaying a lie, while others applaud me for my commitment. Over two-thousand retweets and five-thousand likes. I can't expect to wade through them all, but I can see the way the land lies. The fans are insisting I'm innocent.

Zane: one.

Troll: nil.

My mood shifts – something uncertain and exciting rising to the surface. There are advantages to gaining the public's sympathy. I could simply disappear. When they find me, I'll be covered in dirt and stricken with hypothermia. The public will soon wish they hadn't jumped to conclusions.

I open my study door. The girls are in the kitchen, eating cordon bleu food – a duo of gossipers. I stop short in the hall, Bizzy's voice a little shy of a whisper.

'He's downstairs. I'm not kidding.'

'How did he get in?'

'By unscrewing the gate motor, like he always does. Who are you texting?'

'Burgess. I'd rather he deals with this than the police.'

Deals with what? Me being in my own home or nearly throttling her?

I bolt upstairs to get my backpack and holdall before our gardener evicts me. As I creep through the hall to the front door, I hear my daughter's voice.

'Look at what it says about him in *The Guardian*. "Fame has exacted a high price on Zane Osborne and his turbulent stardom. Ozzie is famous for fame's sake rather than the result of any genuine talent. He has sacrificed his principles and stooped to degrading depths to continue his exposure. Nicola Gatlin was his assistant, and a few other things we're told." Did she really sleep with my dad?'

During the agonising silence that follows, I'm hoping my wife will contradict it.

'Yes. I believe she did.'

A ball of sweat rolls down my back. My daughter knowing I'd had an affair with Nic is much worse than *The Guardian* attacking my pursuit of fame. She will take her mother's side and hate me.

While I drive along the lane, my home shrinking in the rear-view mirror, I think of my daughter. Gone are the most important parts of me, the father parts. She'll forget she was a toddler on my shoulders as we raced along the beach. She'll forget about her tiny hand in mine, when she feared the Hogwoof, a creature I said lived in the deer park.

One day, she decided to seek her fortune and knotted a spotted hanky to a stick like Dick Whittington. She marched off across the lawn, over the ha-ha and into the park without knowing I was following her. When she got as far as Hogwoof's den, she began shaking and crying.

It wasn't her mother she called for, but me.

On her fifth birthday, she told me I was the best daddy in the *whoooole world*, hands drawing a large circle in the air. Sometimes, when she couldn't sleep, I'd lie beside her, and she'd press her cheek against my chest so she could hear my *heart beeps*. Now, the sordid truth is tattooed on her brain and all those precious memories are lost. I feel like I've already died.

Haven't you, though?

Not quite.

Then it's time to disappear. Go wild, live like an animal gloriously — hunting, killing, rutting — until the end comes.

What will my wife say when the police come to tell her the sad news? Which one of them will mention what happened to my father, and say, *it's history repeating itself?*

Trending #InZane

@CirceAtNight: The caricature of his no-talent Guardian exposé is comedy gold. Love the glasses and the beard.

@CumACropper: Who's Zane Osborne? Is he the hyena in *The Lion King*?

@Titmouse: How many of us have done even half as much philanthropy? Awful to suggest he did anything inappropriate with the Gatlin girl. Get your facts straight.

@HeyWhatsUP: @Titmouse Let's not forget the innocence he spouts ad nauseam. He DID sleep with her. Fact.

33

LILJA

Last night, Burgess patrolled the house and Bizzy and I camped out in front of the TV. None of us slept a wink.

Fortunately, before Zane left, I had enough time to cut a hole in the lining of his backpack and slip the Air Tag inside. But tracking him was sporadic.

Now I see he's returned to Holland Park.

On Twitter, the #FindNicola critical issue is, who was the last person she saw? Some are speculating it was Marschōne, ever since photos of him with Nic, rather than his live-in girlfriend, begin to emerge.

I check Zane's spare phone. He'd been calling the number all day yesterday, hoping to find it. With airplane mode turned on, it wouldn't have made a sound. There are no new texts from Nic – and without him blocking her, I can't help wondering why she hasn't called.

'Mum.' Bizzy's voice makes me jump. 'Can I help make breakfast?'

'You bet.'

We make boiled eggs and spread fish roe and cold cuts on toast. While she takes part in a group chat with her friends, I reluctantly answer a call from Zane.

'Hey,' he says. 'I just wanted you to know where I am.'

'Okay.'

'I'm in London. At the house. It's… it's very quiet without you.'

I change the subject. 'Did you see the news article about the police establishing a search perimeter? People keep reporting seeing a woman who fits Nic's description. That's good, isn't it?'

'Yes. I suppose it is. Do the police have a timeline?'

'It's still too vague. They're looking into her texts and emails. Now they're saying she'd scheduled her posts on social media.'

'Maybe she doesn't want to be found.'

'Too much time has passed for that, don't you think?' I walk out onto the terrace and close the door behind me.

'Look at Lord Lucan.'

'Why does everyone have to compare him with every missing person?'

'It's relevant.'

'No, it isn't. He's been dead since 2016.'

'Declared dead. Not found.'

'Well, there's something familiar.' We both know I'm talking about his dad. 'Zane let's not keep dancing around the truth. We both know who her mystery man is. It's only a matter of time before the police ask questions.'

He's quiet for a moment. 'How would you answer?'

'I'd say it's over between us.'

Then, as if a cloud passes in front of the sun, his voice changes. 'How can it be over? You've nowhere to go, unless you move in with that bohemian and dense mother of yours. What a life that would be, dredging up every penny to pay for a house with a sea view. No. You need me. You need my money.'

What I need is no longer his concern. 'Who says I'm going anywhere? The house belongs to my family and I'm not changing Bizzy's school.'

'Wow, you really know how to charm a man.'

'You have Holland Park.'

'And you live in the country with servants and a fancy car. How are you going to pay for all that?'

'With my cooking business.'

'Which makes, what? A few hundred pounds?'

It's been a hell of a lot less, but after everything I've done for him, all the shit he's put me through, I'll take my chances. 'Holland Park is yours. Take it or leave it.'

I can understand the appeal of getting even, but persuading Zane to leave me alone is the hard part.

I feel Bizzy's hand on my arm. 'Can I talk to Dad?'

Her question alone tells me she heard our conversation and I put the phone between us and listen to theirs.

'Have you heard from Nic?' she asks him.

'Nobody has. All I'm hearing is the police are getting nowhere.'

'She never said goodbye. It's not like her.'

'I'm sorry she left, but there were details I can't discuss.'

'What details?'

'Inappropriate photos on TikTok for one.'

'Of you and her?'

'It's what they implied,' he protests.

'Everyone at school thinks she's been abducted.'

'We don't know that, Bizz.'

'Everyone thinks it's you.'

There's a pause. 'Are they giving you a tough time? Because if they are—'

'It's fine, Dad. Anyway, I've got to get ready. Talk later.'

She hangs up. I feel the lump in my throat and grief wells up inside. How will Bizzy ever reconcile what her father has done?

On the way to school, I stare ahead through the wet blur of tears. The only person who can confirm any of this is true is Meggy. By loitering outside our property, she risks me seeing her via CCTV and by implication, opening the lines of communication.

I say goodbye to Bizzy and tell her she is the only solid, thoughtful thing in my life. It's easy to fake happiness in a gilded cage, not so easy to fly away.

With Zane's spare phone, I pull up Meggy's location. She's at Mol's coffee shop. I bunch up my hair inside a cap and decide on square reading glasses. The smell of freshly baked muffins and pastries permeates the place, and I see Meggy sitting between the window and a magazine rack, talking on the phone.

From my table in a dark corner, I take in her coat hanger

collarbone and a figure that falls into the skinny range. She wears jeans and a crossover cardigan, high-end labels mixed with affordable – Gap and Vera Wang. There's a gentle cluster of freckles across her nose and barely the hint of makeup. Although her eyes are narrow, they flicker with mischief, suggesting there's more going on than I know.

Since I have Zane's phone, it gives me a risky idea. I switch it to silent and dial my number, creating two open lines. Moving towards the magazine rack and ducking behind a child whose flailing fists threaten to cuff me, I slot Zane's phone between *Nat Geo* and the wall. Now I'm live mic'ing any conversation she might be having.

Taking a copy of *Amateur Gardening*, I return to my table and mute my phone. There's always that feeling she might look behind her and see me, but the grooves on her forehead are deeper today as if she's anxious and her mind is elsewhere. I put in my ear buds and pretend to be listening to a podcast.

A woman with dark glasses and a tight bun, the epitome of poise, enters the coffee shop. I recognise Nadia Siddiqui from *DevonLive*. She waves to Meggy and strides over to sit with her. Through Zane's phone, I hear them speak.

'Good to see you.'

'Thanks for coming.' Meggy's hands are shaking. 'It's a little crazy out there.'

'Telling me. What are you drinking?'

'Caramel latte.'

'I'll get you another.' Nadia drifts towards the counter and orders two coffees.

Even though Nic's disappearance has gone national, this reporter is covering a small part of it in Dawlish. While they're in their own bubble, they discuss the dark vintage feel of Lana Del Rey and the synth alternative of Banks. I realise this isn't a reporter meeting a source. They're friends.

Although Meggy speaks with a reserved tone, Nadia prattles about her daughter's grades. When she listens to Meggy, she scrolls through her phone, looking up occasionally to nod. I notice she doesn't respond to those texts, finger flicking them away as if they no longer matter.

'I always think you have the worst job, listening to abused people and trying to put the world to rights,' Nadia says.

'It's not necessarily about people who are abused, but about self-esteem and helplessness. I never assume someone will come out and tell me everything, but I make sure they know they're in a safe place.'

'Did you see that film *Disclosure*?' Nadia asks. 'The one based on Michael Crichton's thriller?'

'Yeah. The flip side of #MeToo.'

Nadia hesitates. 'Do you get many of those?'

'You mean women abusing their power over men? A low percentage, and that's only because men don't always report female bosses or partners.'

'You wonder what happened to the Gatlin girl. She suffered one volatile celebrity boss and then she had your client, emphasis on *had*. I reckon she was trouble, and nobody likes trouble.'

Meggy's downcast eyes tell me she's too cautious to divulge what she knows. She merely nods and continues drinking her coffee.

'I think one of those two celebrities knows exactly where Nicola Gatlin is.' Nadia digs deeper. 'I know who I'd bet on.'

Meggy looks around the room, and my eyes snap away. The adrenaline hits my bloodstream, inflaming the knot that has been growing in my belly.

'Have you ever had an affair?' Meggy asks.

Nadia's hesitation is enough for me to assume she'll fabricate something to keep Meggy talking. 'There is this guy at work. I don't know what it is about him. He's the exact opposite of my partner.'

Meggy's lips twitch. 'Do you think about him?'

'Sometimes.'

'But would you, if you could?'

'If my partner left me or died, maybe. But it's too close to home.'

Nadia's opinion is loud and clear. Boss/employee relationships rarely end well.

'Did you read my email?' Meggy asks.

'I skimmed it.' Nadia presses her fingertips to her temples. 'Not sure there's any truth to it. But I can ask around.'

'I'm worried, that's all. Worried for my client.'

'Well, okay, I buy some of it. Especially the part where Osborne's fans think he might know more about the Gatlin girl than he's letting on.'

'What if he doesn't?' Meggy leans forward a little.

'I don't believe it's Marschōne Robinson, if that's even his real name.'

My lungs feel tender as they're struggling to inflate. Only their voices seem to echo around my head, and I feel like I'm drowning. On and on they go, comparing Robinson to Osborne, but the meaning of what Meggy says about my husband sinks in.

'He's nothing like that,' she says. 'Not superficial in the least. Loses sight of the difference between script and reality but he's committed.'

Then Nadia's voice. 'Nicola was Marschōne's girlfriend, then Osborne swiped her from under his nose. There had to be male rutting because there always is. Marschōne got jealous and took it out on Nic. You see where I'm going with this.'

Meggy flinches, as if a fresh memory intrudes. 'No. I don't think so. Anway, my client won't talk about it.'

'Maybe he doesn't want to talk to you.'

The joke doesn't register, and Meggy continues. 'The press, the fans, everything is getting to him. He goes into what he calls "greyouts," where he says things, alarming things... I don't know if he's dreaming or having some kind of episode. Anyway, it scares me.'

Now it's Nadia's turn to look around the café before she lowers her voice. 'You mean he's admitted to something?'

'No. Nothing like that. He's a talented actor and has had a lifetime of pretending to be someone else. It's the character. Holloway isn't good for him.'

'That's putting it mildly. Holloway excels at the macabre. A serial everything.'

Meggy looks out of the window, her body suddenly stiff. 'I feel I should warn his wife.'

'You serious?'

'Dead serious.'

A phone call interrupts their coffee break. Meggy apologises to the caller and tells them to give her half an hour. While Nadia and Meggy go head-to-head with another revelation, I retrieve Zane's phone from the magazine rack and leave the restaurant.

Locking myself in my car, I turn on the heater, blasting my hands to stop me from shaking. Her voice seers into my brain.

I feel I should warn his wife…

I've been reading Meggy all wrong.

34

ZANE

Dammit. Meggy's in a therapy session and I need to talk to her.

My hands are curled into tight knobs and my voice sounds tight and strangled. There's one more account to empty and I try accessing the bank online. But the password has either been changed or I'm entering the number incorrectly. There's only one thing for it, wear a flat hat and a tatty jacket, and drive to the local branch.

I've noticed it's outside spaces that get to me, like the walk between the car and the front door of the bank. Suddenly I feel like a thief, hustling into the building and joining a three-man queue.

I try not to sweat or frown and casually glance at posters about mortgage rates and the sign of the rampant horse. When I get to the front of the line, the female teller looks as if she's fresh off a runway. Brown eyes, dark hair, a Chanel inspired suit.

'I'd like to make a withdrawal.' I slide my card through the machine and add my PIN.

I know there's several hundred thousand in this account and she'll call a manager. She keeps looking at me and the name on the card, and I realise she's too polite to blurt out who I am.

For goodness' sake, get on with it.

She clicks the mouse with a barely-there frown. 'Would you like the entire fifty pounds?'

'Sorry? There must be a mistake.'

She taps the keyboard again and nods. 'That's the balance as of today.'

I check my wallet and slide her another card. This time for a savings account, which is bulging at the seams. She taps on the keys for a little longer this time, her smile masking what's on the screen.

'Four hundred pounds,' she says. 'Does that sound about right?'

Four hundred. Is this some kind of joke? Have I been too complacent, too distracted, to notice my wife has been cleaning me out?

I nod and take the measly four hundred and return to Holland Park. Thank goodness I'd had the foresight to take the Hellman's trust funds. There'll be enough to keep me going for a while.

The room spins, and I curl up on the floor like a woodlouse. I feel abandoned, like my mother must have felt. I try to fend off memories of Mum when they pop up. Her last days struggling for breath in a hospital bed, and moments of consciousness shafting through. Then came the faraway gazes, eyelids fluttering. She spent her last days staring at a stark white ceiling and asking for Dad. After she died, there was no string quintet playing Vivaldi. I carried her ashes to Warren Beach and read a poem I'd written as a boy. The flowers I left were a mixture of hydrangeas, their colours so captivating I'd committed every shade to memory. Now I am the last of that tiny family and Bizzy is the last of mine. Here I am abandoning her, as Dad abandoned me.

Great Legacy, Zane. Meticulously performed.

I try to centre myself, but I feel like throwing up. Meggy's the only person to talk me down off this heart-breaking precipice.

I dial the number again and it rings and rings. *Come on, Meggs, pick up. A simple hello is all it takes.* She answers on the seventh ring, her voice hesitant and suspicious. She doesn't recognise this number.

'Thank you for answering, Meggs. It could have been anyone.'

'A nutter, you mean?'

'Yes. But this nutter is having a panic attack.'

'What's going on?'

'Everything. Dad. Mum. I feel like I'm losing it.' Then I sob. 'I'm okay.'

'You don't sound okay.'

'I'm learning to let go,' I say, somehow pulling myself together.

'I just wish the press would do the same. You know stories about celebs are fictitious. Nobody is on top of the world one minute or a freaky weirdo the next. I don't believe for a moment that I'm a freaky weirdo or on top of anything. Oh, God… my chest feels tight, and I can't stop shaking. Is it cold to you? I feel cold.'

'Zane. Slow down. You're going a million miles an hour.'

I gabble on about how Holloway has invaded my life and it's this dichotomy that has torn my marriage apart. Then the coup de grâce.

'She wants a divorce, Meggs. My wife. She's… she's taken all the money and now I'm reduced to begging in the streets.'

I can imagine she is thinking, *he's lost. I need to help him*. Already I can feel the strength returning, because a break is a break and she knows I need it.

'I'm worried about you, Zane.'

'You're not. Because if you were, you'd be here. I don't want to ruin the therapist/client dynamic, but you mean a lot to me.'

'Zane, listen, if this is going where I think it's going.'

'For what it's worth, it would be weird, even for me, to be flirting with my therapist, especially after screwing things up so spectacularly.'

'Oh, Zane, no. I never meant—'

'Why would you? Yes, I've been a complete shit. You can say it. But I want to make it up to you.'

I hope she says something positive to make my brain shift, because right now it's threatening to blow through the seam in my skull.

'We've talked about separating from yourself and inhabiting Holloway,' she says. 'We've discussed disassociation and psychosis. There are elements of these. But the character you play, rather than intense trauma, has triggered all this. I put your greyouts down to stress rather than any real symptoms of neurosis. Recently, you've been alluding to fragmented images of a drowning woman. Someone in your past you couldn't save. A relative, perhaps? If you were more open in our sessions, I could have helped you overcome these.'

For a moment, I don't move. I mentioned nothing about a drowning woman. It's not like Meggy followed me that night.

Did you check in the rear-view mirror? Did you check the beach?

No. I was busy disposing of a body and shitting myself.

With a sudden lurch of nausea, I remember Meggy does hypnotism. What if she'd used it during one of our last sessions? She couldn't simply be manipulating the topic just because she *suspects* me of murder. Could she?

'If I don't tell you now, I might not have the courage later. I've been having nightmares. Sometimes I lash out and hurt someone, and that's not like me.'

'Hurt how?'

'I don't know. I always wake up before the ending.'

*But it hasn't ended, has it? You still see Nic's face surrounded by a slick nimbus of blood. You can tell Meggy you've no idea how the argument started, but you sure as shit know how it ended. You made one hideous decision and now you're paying for it. It's no good pretending the house has shrunk and there's a rabbit in a waistcoat. It happened, Zane. All of it.'

'I'm sorry, Meggs. It's the shock, that's all. I don't know what do to.'

I'm losing sight of what she's trying to say, versus what I'm focusing on. I know she made progress notes during every session. But what if I had confessed? With a sudden lurch of nausea, I realise I've walked right into a trap. Whatever I'd said during a greyout has implicated me and, like a fool, I'd fallen for the bait.

All therapists are bound by confidentiality laws. She cannot go to the police.

I study my phone. Anyone could be listening to me through the mic and I wouldn't know they were doing it. What if there are wires in the walls of this house, listening to everything I say? The quality of the room is different now, as if the house is reading my mind.

'Zane, tell me about your dream.'

I'm a hundred miles away, staring at the clouds in a bubbling white sky.

Clouds…

If we were in a movie, this would be the climactic moment where she tells me I'm innocent and I have nothing to fear, and we both walk away as the credits roll. I'm about to tell her the dream wasn't a dream when I realise there is something I'd forgotten to do, something that needs my immediate attention.

The cloud.

My thumb hits END. I stare at the dead phone in my hand, wishing I had confessed, but the opportunity has passed. Far from making things better, I've just made them a lot worse.

Trending #InZane

@SherylAdams: Any hatred I had towards celebrity fans before all this kicked off has amplified 100%. All this shit-shamey nonsense is not okay.

@BantaBadger: @SherylAdams: Fans focusing all their hatred on Zane Osborne does nothing to harm his career. They'll still invite him to the MET Gala, cast him in movies and invite him to celeb events. It's his wife I feel sorry for.

@PinkRubberDucky: Does anyone think this "acting out" is just to improve his ratings? It bows to the Holloway cult.

@Titmouse: I am shocked to be honest. I thought Zane Osborne was more grounded, but as you say, if it's all about ratings, he doesn't care.

@HeyWhatsUP: Zane needs to chill his roll. He's an adult. He should have enough self-control to keep his dong in check.

35

LILJA

The following day, the rain has ceased under a heavy grey sky and sunlight slants across the patio. I cut some roses and arrange them in a vase on the hall table.

Bizzy was quiet on the way to school this morning and all my questions received short answers. She's processing it all. Sad about Nic and gutted about her dad. When my eyes slid over to her phone, she was tapping out a text to George.

It's an "if only" morning. If only I'd made three Prinsesstårtas instead of one. If only I'd used gelatine instead of whipped cream, the dome would be stronger under the weight of marzipan.

If only I didn't keep thinking of Zane, jumping out of the shadows with a jarring smack. Even when he was here, he lurked downstairs, his body coiled and alert, as if the slightest change in barometric pressure would set him off. I keep telling myself that the tag in his backpack is tracking his movements. I'll know the minute he comes back.

A thought flashes into my mind, unbidden. The first time I thought something was off was the night of Zane's birthday party. I don't remember how long I'd been asleep, but something woke me. On my way downstairs to the kitchen, I peered through the hall window. Droplets of rain sagged down the pane, and a bloat of light streamed in from outside. Red lights flickered through the drizzle, barely visible behind the dark tangle of trees, and dying to a trail of smoke.

At the time, I had assumed it was Zane leaving to go nightclubbing with friends. But there was something about those lights, a streak of blood red, grazing the drive. I can't think why it bothered me then in the same way it bothers me now.

The following day when I found him in the bathroom there were scratches on his chest, sealed with dried blood.

'What happened to you?' I said.

'It's nothing.' His anxious face still floats into my mind.

'Did you have a fight with someone?'

'There was a reporter outside Gary O'Malley's, nails like talons. He tried to grab hold of my shirt.'

'Does this reporter have a name?'

'I didn't wait to ask.'

I didn't buy the paparazzo story. Zane is the only person I know who can tell a lie convincingly and get away with it. I felt the interrogator in me brimming with questions, but any conversation would be a scramble of angry words.

I used to love Zane, from the belly laughs we had over a midnight snack to the way he told filthy jokes, as if reading the news on Radio 4. But when he betrayed me with Nic, I knew the marriage was over.

There is still proof I can give to the police. Retrieving his spare phone from my laundry basket (the last place he'd think to look) I open the message app.

My breath catches in my throat.

Nic is no longer listed as a contact. All her texts and the intimate photos she took of Zane have disappeared. He's deleted everything from his iCloud.

Meggy is now his only contact. My mind keeps returning to the email attachment she'd sent to Zane – that arty-farty picture of Nic, topless and smiling behind a rain-spattered window. Instead of being cryptic, it would have benefited her to have told Zane when she took the photo and why she was concerned, no matter how unprofessional it was.

I'm nosing through his draft email folder and there's one unsent message to Meggy, marked URGENT.

Meggs,

You were right about me and Nic. What started out as a consensual actor/reader relationship – rehearsing scenes and playing roles – became an affair. The constant fear of my wife finding out, the mental torture I was putting her through, drove me to fire Nic. But I couldn't stop seeing her. She was like an addiction...

My cheeks burn at the vivid descriptions of their sex life. How Nic longed for him in the same way as a woman who hasn't been touched in ages *longs*. I feel hopeless and ashamed for Zane, and for us.

On the evening of my birthday party, I was surprised to find Nic in my study. She asked me if I loved her, but I told her this wasn't what we'd agreed. I expected annoyance, or at least a discussion. Not outright rage.

What happened next is hard to write. She physically attacked me, all the while screaming that I'd made her feel dirty and demeaned. That I'd never given her the tenderness and warmth she deserved. I realise now I'd stripped her of her identity and everything she valued.

The next thing I was on the floor, and she was kicking me. All I could do was push her away. The greyout was short, a few seconds at most. But when I came to, she was gone. Now she's missing, you understand how frightened this makes me feel.

My stomach twists sharply. Looking back, there was nothing unusual or incriminating about catching Zane having a smoke in his study. It was his face. The stillness, the way he didn't take his eyes off me, as if he'd expected me to come through the door at that moment. People put their hands in their pockets for numerous reasons, but not old-school Zane. It's something he finds tacky. Of all the images looping in my head, that's the one I can't shake off.

When I told him to come upstairs to cut the cake, I picked up on the tension in his voice and I allowed myself to go along with it. But there's only one explanation – and my brain refuses to accept it.

If he had fought Nic off, it explains the scratches, those tell-tale marks he tried to hide behind a missing button. If I can't slot these last pieces into place, neither will the police.

But Meggy might.

The only thing I can think of is completing what Zane has started. If Meggy suspected him of having an affair, what more does she suspect him of?

Signing the email from Zane, I press SEND.

36

ZANE

**Police find body at Langstone Rock in
search for missing Exeter woman**

By Stan Marriott

Senior Reporter

11:22, 12 JULY 2022

Police searching for 32-year-old Nicola Gatlin have
found the remains of a body washed up in one of the
caves at Langstone Rock.

Formal identification is pending; however, her family
have been informed of the discovery, police say…

I feel the prickle of a presence and Nic materialises at my shoulder.

'Didn't think you'd get away with it, did you?'

Get away with it… Her words spider-walk down my back.

There were hundreds of fathoms and currents between us, yet
her body, which should have dissolved into particles, had survived
the ocean's pounding and found its way back to Langstone Rock.

The police are trying to improve the image quality of surveillance cameras on Warren Road. One of these cameras might have recorded the accident that night. For a moment, there is silence in both my worlds; the one that is Holloway's and the other that is mine.

Then the voice asks: *When did you last eat? No use trying to figure things out on an empty stomach.*

My voice or his? Holloway has no way of knowing if I'm hungry.

I microwave a leftover take-away and settle in an armchair. The sky has darkened, rain pinging off the puddles, and if I stare at the lawn long enough I can see a 3D rendering of Holloway's face. The only thing slamming me back to earth is Channel 4 news blaring from my computer speakers.

…One celebrity who has come under intense scrutiny due to allegations of cheating is Zane Osborne. Osborne, who has snagged the role of serial killer Ethan Holloway, has been having an on-again, off-again relationship with his assistant, Nicola Gatlin. Like we didn't see that coming. What if, like Rusty Sabich in Presumed Innocent, *there's an even nastier twist at the end?*

All at once, I feel like a man on a high ledge, studying a long drop. I should call the TV station and deny the allegations, saying it was a scummy reporter getting off on using my name.

I log off my computer and run through one of the last scenes in my mind.

```
INT. A BASEMENT IN HOLLOWAY'S CADOGAN
HOUSE - NIGHT


Holloway stands over Amaya's remains.


            HOLLOWAY (V.O.)

       After her shower, I told her
       to use the perfume I'd left
       out. The ancients used some-
       thing similar for embalming.
       Not Armani, of course, but many
```

> of the same ingredients. After
> she'd drunk one of my famous
> cocktails, I lay on the floor
> with her and counted until she
> stopped breathing...

Are those the exact words? I can't seem to remember my lines.

Even now, in the emptiness of the London house, the scene scares me. Everything scares me. Too many mixed reviews have forced me into the wings and now everyone is after my blood. What if the writers altered the ending and made it a happy ever after? Would it change the outcome of my own life?

There's no time to think about it. No time to think about what would happen if I went home. No time to do anything but save my marriage.

If you think your life is tied to the script, you're a bigger moron than I thought.

I'm reluctant to accept Holloway's judgement. He's been in charge ever since I accepted the part and I have a feeling things are about to change. On the four-hour journey home, the faint whisper of the car engine calms me, headlights filtering through a sea fog. As I approach the house, the high voltage terror of the unknown engulfs me.

I open the front gate manually, parking my car outside the garage. Sneaking in through the French doors, my eyes narrow at the eye-watering stink of lemon air freshener. The pillows on the couch have been plumped and neatly arranged, and the desk, polished to a shine, is no longer littered with my papers. I feel a sudden flash of anger.

The best way to deal with this is one step at a time. Step one, remedy the smell. Reaching into the drawer for my cigarettes, I find it empty. All of them are empty. Step two, pour myself a whisky. Only the bottle seems to have vanished, along with my stash of Waterford crystal. I sit down for a moment and try to make sense of the horror.

It's no good looking like a grumpy housecat. You've been thrown out.

It's one thing to want closure, but another to stare it in the face. It's not the quiet or the emptiness that scares me. It's more than that. It's that my wife has moved on.

The snick of the French doors makes me flinch. The sight of Meggy walking towards me should have been a relief. But it's the slow, painful realization that she's here at all.

'How the hell did you get in?'

'The gate was open.' She sits in the chair opposite me.

Coincidence? Or has she been following me?

She's wearing a grey dress, nipped at the waistline, and her hair is piled on her head to resemble a bow. Her face tells me to brace for impact.

'I have a question.'

'Fire away.'

'I'm trying to understand what you see in Holloway. It seems odd, you picking a serial killer.' She's wearing the psychoanalyst's hat again. Neutral, composed, detached.

'I felt as if I knew him. Understood what he was going through. Killing is not the sum of his role. He's charming and utterly brilliant—'

'And monstrously creepy. You'd never know how manipulative he is.'

'That's the thing. He's so composed.' Yet my hands are trembling.

'So the devil cleared his calendar and here you are, living with him twenty-four hours a day in his twisted and sociopathic world. I don't see the attraction.'

What's this devil stuff? Nic had mentioned the same thing. 'I went where my instincts took me.'

'Yet he lives his life through his own twisted narrative,' she says. 'Isn't that what you said? The narrative he creates to take control?'

'Yes.'

'I never thought of you as dark.' There's a menacing edge to her voice.

'That's how he's written.'

She pauses and then speaks. 'Holloway has a pattern of killing women when they threaten him. Something you seem enthralled by. On that basis, I wonder if Nic threatened you.'

'I'm sorry?'

Gone is the magnetic poise that usually tips into a lovely smile. She is rigid, her wrists perched on the armrest. It's not her scowl, it's the sadness etched deep into her face that makes me anxious. Meggy was the one who told me about the rumours on *BarbedWire* and showed me the photos. Only it wasn't the rumours she wanted to talk about. I would have found those out on my own. What I mistook for curiosity was a flimsy excuse to scope out my house. My mind is rewinding and whirring, a brainbox that can't shake off the question. What had she seen?

'You don't deny having an affair with her, but do you deny hurting her?'

'Of course, I deny it. It's obscene.'

The air holds a tropical damp that feels heavy on my skin. It reminds me of the same sweltering day Meggy came here for a party. I could see Nic didn't like Meggy. It would have coiled her jealousy a little tighter and Meggy would have sensed it.

'Look, Meggs, I don't know what you're alluding to.'

'You can help by being honest. At the very least, admit the attacks are from your own psyche and not Holloway's. Your email said you had a dream that you hurt someone. But it wasn't a dream, was it? She came here on the night of your party to ask if you ever loved her. Did it trigger you?'

The face opposite me is solemn and accusing, and she doesn't wait for a response.

'Then you said she attacked you. You had some kind of episode and when you came to, she was gone. But you didn't mean she got up and left. You meant *gone*, as in dead. I'm not here to judge you. I just want the truth.'

I frown, although it's not much of a frown, more a distorted grimace. I had written Meggy an email confession. Not exactly a confession, but enough for her to read the significance in my words if she chose. But I'd never sent it.

'An email, you say?'

'Yes.' She lifts her phone and shows me.

'That's impossible.'

She assumes I mean the part where I supposedly killed Nic. But I'm stuck on an email I'd no recollection of sending.

'She was trying to extort me. I'll admit we argued that night, but where the hell are you getting murder? I've been worried sick about her ever since they reported her missing.'

She senses my confusion. 'May I ask a direct question?'

'You've asked me quite a few.'

'Who are you right now?'

A chill skitters between my shoulders and my mouth falls open, but I can't seem to say my name. My brain goes on hiatus as she babbles on and on about what I'm doing to myself and others, and the damage I may have done to Nic.

Then she says, 'I can break confidentiality if I think you are a danger to yourself or others.'

The wheels in my mind turn frantically and then Holloway comes to the rescue.

She has nothing on you. Anyone could have written that mail. Insufficient evidence. Case dismissed.

Meggy's voice cuts through the sludge in my head. 'You've been in the habit of cancelling sessions, but recently, you've been demanding my attention. Calling at all hours and sending texts. Do you remember your last greyout?'

'I don't remember any.'

'You said you struggled with wanting to harm someone. Someone close to you. This classifies as something worthy of police involvement.'

'Meggs. I was speaking as Holloway who, as you know, kills his mistress.'

Her fingers toy with the crucifix around her neck. 'You know I'm bound by a code of ethics.'

'In my case, you can stretch the boundaries of that code. Where I'm a perfectly normal individual, Holloway suffers from an extensive list of personality disorders. It's obvious who was speaking.'

'Your assistant is called Nic, not *Amaya*, as you often say in your sessions.'

Terror makes my body tremble. I want to claw Holloway's face right off his skull. He's outmanoeuvred me again and I'm cornered like a sick animal.

'Like I said, I get confused sometimes.'

'Nicola Gatlin is dead, isn't she?'

All my thoughts scamper to a stop. 'What makes you say that?'

'Because if she were alive, you'd be out there looking for her.'

The room swims and sweat prickles along my hairline. In the distance, I hear the gentle crash of waves and the screech of a gull. But the wave sweeping through this room is not white-capped and briny. It is fear.

The tremor starts at the base of my neck as the noise in my head grows louder. The woman sitting opposite me has transformed. Her hair is black and she wears a daisy dress. Time has reversed far enough to give me a second chance. This time I won't screw up.

I know saying 'I love you' is dangerous, but not as dangerous as not saying it at all. One minute she's the big hole in my world and I want her so much it makes me ache. The next I'm itching all over, wanting to unburden myself and wipe the slate clean.

I pull her towards me, our faces only inches apart. I don't know if it's the perfume or her unequivocal daring, but something snaps inside. Her scent is strong now and she's yelling, and I don't know why.

Then time jolts. The room is full of whispers, and I try not to think about where they're coming from. Nic's eyes dance and flicker and she wrenches her arm away. I want her to loosen and settle into my rhythm. But she slaps me, and I slap her back, and hair screens her face. Her voice starts out composed and then plunges into a scream.

Stop it!

I'm gripping onto her, my nails digging into her flesh. I tell her she can't do this to me. Slink into my house as if to jump me and then change her mind. She may take pleasure in that victory, but she can't have forgotten the shit we're in. Then I realise she didn't jump me at all.

This isn't Nic. It's Meggy. I'm gripping onto *Meggy*.

She wriggles from my grip and pulls her arm back. I expect her to run, but not before a fist clips me in the mouth. Then she lurches down the side of the house to the drive and I follow her progress through every window.

I glance at the couch where she sat only moments ago. The emptiness bulges and strains and I try to recall those awful words. *She's dead, isn't she?* Maybe if I had been braver, I would have told her.

My impending exile from this house frightens me more. Why is Holloway always right? I will never recover my wife and child. Rather than chasing after Meggy, who is on her way to the police, I have two women to take care of. Two women who won't live long enough to incriminate me.

When I reach the landing, I hear my daughter's voice. Her bedroom door is ajar and a literature debate with best friend George booms from her laptop. She doesn't sense my hand withdrawing the key from the inside of her door and locking it from the outside.

One down. One to go.

Trending #InZane

@CirceAtNight: The fact that Zane is having a torrid affair, then selling his story to the tabloids so he can become a millionaire is disgusting.

@Titmouse: Zane Osborne isn't a monster. He's simply trying to make his way in an unimaginable situation. If sticking up for him makes me a horrible person, then I'm doomed too.

@HeyWhatsUP: @CirceAtNight He's not selling his story, dickwad. Someone else is. That's the whole point!

37

LILJA

What I had seen had the illusory clarity of a dream. The email I'd sent to Meggy was to reveal Zane's guilt, not to invite her to the house. Yet it took her less than twenty minutes to get here, like an angel guarding our perimeter fences.

A streak of brown hair and a grey dress wafted in through the open French doors. She took a seat, her legs bent at an angle, her hands neatly resting in her lap. All the time her voice was calm and soothing, hypnotic. A small part of me wanted to believe none of it was real, but as I peered through the crack in the study door, I knew it was.

Then everything in my world crumbled and the scene merged into a flurry of arms, slapping, shoving, blocking. Meggy must have been terrified. I wanted to run out after her, but if I had moved from my hiding place, Zane would have seen me.

A creeping sense of unease crawls along my arms. Why did he go upstairs?

The sound of his pounding feet stops me from lurching to the kitchen to retrieve my phone. Through the crack in the door, I watch him peeling off his shirt and scrunching it into a ball. I flatten myself against the wall as he rushes past.

I want to run upstairs to get Bizzy and then bolt for the front door. For whatever crazy reason, either curiosity or stupidity, I follow him downstairs.

When I reach the ground floor he is standing with his back

to me, half naked, and the washing machine trundles with a monotonous thud. I walk towards him on silent feet, but creaking baseboards give me away.

Before he turns to confront me, I ask, 'What are you doing?'

'Hey.' His hands go to his trouser pockets, his shoulders reaching his ears. 'Spilt some wine on my clothes.'

'What the heck happened to your lip? It's bleeding.'

'Look, what is this?' he asks, dabbing his lip with the back of his hand.

'It's a simple question, which you seem to be avoiding.'

'You didn't come down to ask me about my face.'

'No, I came ask why you were here. And then I saw Meggy.'

I stare at clothes doing cartwheels behind a porthole, pink suds shimmying on the glass. His spiteful words come as no surprise.

'Obviously, she was here for a session.' He leans forward and places two fists on the ironing board. 'You know what that means? She helps me study the psychology of my character, from paranoia to obsessive personality disorder. To you, that means whether Holloway's father was a bully and gambled all their life savings. If his mother simply ignored the abuse and how her abandonment affected him growing up.'

'It doesn't look like this session helped if she punched you in the face.'

'I need you to keep out of my business, do you understand? Because I'm having a tough time keeping it together.'

'I can see that.'

A vein bulges in his temple. 'You can't just take everything and throw me out!'

'Zane. Calm down. Or I'll call the police.'

He moves around the table so fast; my shirt is scrunched in his fist. 'Call the police? Are you nuts? You've taken my money – *my* money – and thrown my stuff out.' He points at his swollen mouth. 'Maybe you've forgotten, but it's me they'll believe, not you.'

I feel like I'm at the bottom of a deep well and he's up there, looking down. There's not a flicker of Zane behind that face. His forehead puckers as if he's battling inner turmoil. In those few seconds, I slam both my hands up into his chin and he loses his balance briefly, ramming into the edge of the open door.

It becomes a game to him, all this rocking from side to side as if he's dribbling a ball across his body from one hand to the other. The only way of escape is behind me, down the corridor and through the wine cellar. Rather than cringe and cower, I run.

Security code. Four digits. Please God, don't let me get it wrong.

Then he barrels down the corridor after me and time slows to a crawl. Somehow in those few vital seconds, I twist through the open cellar door and the temperature seal pops as it closes behind me. Shelf lights activate and I know he will access the code and be inside in less than a few seconds. I run sixteen feet to the hidden wine rack door, slip inside and slide the bolt.

A scraping sound tells me he's rolling something across the floor. I ram my shoulder against the door, but he's blocked my access back into the house. Getting a message to Bizzy is impossible without my phone.

I'm about to run through the butcher's station, past the wine barrels, and then out through the double oak doors to the drive, when everything goes dark. It's sudden, so unexpected, that without meaning to, I scream. Our power has never gone out before. Apart from a short glitch a year ago, we have been lucky. But today, my luck has run out.

Light from the transom vents isn't enough, it's almost darker outside than in. But a beam, slicing through the black, reveals a single lamp lit in the deer park enclosure. If the power isn't out in our area, then why is it isolated to our house?

My mind preys on its worst fears. Has Zane turned off the circuit breakers?

Except they're outside and he couldn't have timed it so accurately. Since all our keyless locks operate on battery, he can still access the cellar, but only from the inside. The double doors leading to the drive need keys.

The air is thick and black, and I feel like I'm falling. Twice I lose my bearings and slam against stools and walls and hard edges. Through the sounds I make, there is another noise loud enough to interpret as the clink and rattle of metal, and a light briefly arcs over the stone wall and then it goes dark again.

A torch? Headlights?

I start screaming as loudly as I can, fumbling for the wall and stopping to listen for any sounds, besides the patter in my chest.

Lightning slices everything in half, lighting up the outline of an antique cabinet. My fingers travel over a pattern of natural rock, the wooden edge of inbuilt shelves and the frame of the door. Numbness spreads through my body, and I can't make out any shapes, until another bolt of lightning sends a flare through a second transom. I jump, hand over heart.

The twist in my gut turns into a horse kick. The flash again, this time trailing the floor. There's someone there, a figure, coiling as if gathering his muscles to strike.

'Zane?' It goes dark again, and my body's alarm begins clanging. 'Zane!'

Moving forward would send me into him. Moving back would take me to the butcher's table, where I could hide underneath and wait it out. Surely, he can't see me any more than I can see him.

Unless…

No. Not even Zane would have night vision goggles. But he was the winner of a survivalist show, used to living out in the worst conditions, hearing the howl of wild animals at night and falling into depression from lack of human interaction. This unbroken darkness is nothing to him.

In a drawer behind the butcher's table is a cleaver, poultry shears, a meat tenderiser, weapons I can wield if I need them. Thunder cracks, and I count twenty seconds before the lightning.

Feeling my way back to the butcher's table, I reach the drawer to grab a barbeque fork and my hands feel nothing but wooden panels. Even the mallets and cleavers are missing from the rails above.

He couldn't have. He wouldn't…

But he has.

Fear flicks at the base of my throat. Is this payback for cleaning out his study and taking his phone? Or because he knows I'll use the meat mallet on him?

I hear a slam and the clanking of a bolt. He's locked the double doors to the drive.

My mind is a riot of ideas. He's taken all the cutting implements, but please God not the farrier nails. The workers found them in the barn which had been the site of an old forge.

I retrace my steps to the cabinet where there's a box of nails of varying sizes to match the horse's hoof wall. I grab what feels like a four-and-a-half-inch nail and head for the largest of the air vents.

The only way out is through the grating which is covered with chicken wire and large enough to crawl through. Chiselling away at packed mortar with the point of a nail will take hours. The best I can do is claw and pick, keeping a rhythm until I dredge enough mortar to pull out the wire. My fingers keep sliding across the surface of the nail, until I realise jiggling the spike is easier. It loosens minute amounts, and when I alternate between shovelling and digging, larger clods of mortar begin to work free. The effort takes stamina and determination. I have both. Bizzy's safety is my driving force.

What would I give for a screwdriver, a hammer, all the conveniences I've taken for granted? The temptation to cry for help is strong, but who would hear me over the patter of rain, mimicking my rapid heartbeats.

PART III

The Delusion

38

ZANE

The only thing worse than a crazy wife is a crazy wife armed with a meat mallet. Taking the utensils out of the drawer is simply a precaution. She's not been herself lately.

The haunting cry of the lapwing triggers an alarm inside my head. The sky is dark and ugly and full of July drizzle and if it weren't for the solar lamps on the terrace, my study would be in total darkness.

I keep telling myself marriage is like Snakes and Ladders, too many ups and downs and where every move is a matter of luck.

Now I'm out of luck. And out of time.

I sit at the desk and roll a joint, sprinkling pinches of weed mixed with tobacco. I check flights to Quebec and there's a seat on Air Canada leaving in two days at 10.50 am. I fill out the eTA visa application form with my passport information and email my submission. It could be days before I get a response.

As for the likelihood of me finding my spare phone, a scatter of images places me back in time and then scoots me forward as if I'm on a fast train to who knows where. Pinching the lighted end of my joint, I drop it in the top drawer. Selecting the torch app, I run upstairs to the bedroom and shine the light onto every corner, flinching from the glare in the dressing table mirror.

Balancing the phone on a chair, I dump every item of Lilja's clothing on the bed, dragging every dress from its hanger and every shoe from its shelf. When than doesn't yield what I'm looking for, I search the mattress and under her bedside table, for she could have taped it there.

A thought hits me as I slide to the floor, my back against the bed. What if Lilja had it on her and has already called the police? I never thought to search her. They could take twenty, thirty minutes to respond or they could be rolling up the drive right now.

It doesn't make me happy to leave Lilja in the cellar, but her cold vibes have disappointed me, and I can't read her like I used to.

The swish of an opening window breaks my thoughts, then a clatter, followed by the sound of splintering wood. Locking my resourceful daughter in her bedroom was useless.

I grab my phone and run downstairs and through the front door. She must have climbed out onto the flat roof and shimmied down the trellis, which I notice has separated from the outside wall. That must have been some fall.

The thing that concerns me the most is why she's not hobbling along the lawn on a busted ankle. The night air is chilly and the throbbing in my head is growing worse by the second. I can't see her, but I sense she's doubled-backed towards the house.

Is her love for her mother greater than her fear for me? A burst of anger warms my throat and I race back inside, cutting her off in the hall.

'Scare you?'

'A little.' She offers a tentative smile. 'Where's Mum?'

Locking her mother in the cellar doesn't sound very charitable, does it?

I could tell her the truth, or I could tell her a lie. Since both have become a little cloudy, I'm not sure which is which. I creep towards her, no sudden movements.

'I assume she's upstairs.'

'Stop lying, Dad. You always lie.'

I lift the torch to see her expression. The reflection worming in her pupils is me, but not me. It has split into two and I'm not positive how many people I've become.

'Dad! Where is she?'

I hold up a finger for silence. 'Did you hear that?'

She inclines her head slightly and I notice she doesn't look at me, doesn't match my stare.

'Rats,' I say. 'Tons of them under the house. One false move, one tiny droplet of sweat, and they will attack. Rats are very intuitive. They sense fear.'

'I've never seen one.'

'Doesn't mean they're not there.'

The thought that Bizzy could charge downstairs crosses my mind. I can't risk it. She watches my hand advance and sprints off on two unscathed feet towards the ground floor. If she'd been dribbling a ball, I'd say that flashy Maradona Spin was one I wasn't expecting.

Her voice is angry and urgent. 'Mum! MUM!'

For someone filled with so much parental love, she exhibits a stingy amount in return.

Discipline never works with Bizzy. Experience has taught me she shuns it, pig-headedness making her unmanageable. I've found it best to ignore her because punishing her wears me down.

The artery leading to the cellar is silent. Does she really think her mother is down here?

You are rather taken with locking people in rooms.

I stare, transfixed by the blazing light in her eyes. Looking at her is like watching a fly thrashing about in a web.

'The code,' she says. 'Give me the code.'

I shrug. 'Perhaps, she went outside.'

'Oh what, she just went for a walk in a storm?'

'Could have, yes. We have marvellous grounds.'

'You can stop playing the B movie in your head and get real.'

'Does this B movie have a name?'

She sighs loudly. 'I can't take you seriously, not when you're pretending to be something you're not.' She taps the keypad on the wall. 'Open it.'

The B movie is quickly turning into a horror show. 'She's not in there, Bizz.'

'Bullshit. You've locked her in like you did me.'

'Of course, I haven't.'

'So now you're saying my door locked itself? Come on, Dad. I'm not stupid.'

Her voice skewers its way into my brain, and then another voice is caught dead centre in the whirlwind. *She knows…* Her eyes glint as they track me, her body shifting and stirring as if it is reshaping itself. I can't get properly into the scene.

'You've been acting weird for weeks.'

Is she inferring I'm on drugs?

You take a bit of everything and suffer from a whole lot of nothing.

I haven't taken anything, yet she's looking at me as if I'm stoned.

While one voice tells me Holloway has accomplished his true mission, another begs me to separate. Suddenly I feel stripped of all the things I used to be, father, husband, actor. My therapist is doubtless spreading lies about me to the police – and worst of all, my daughter thinks I'm a killer.

Let's get one thing straight. You never asked me what type of fame you craved. All I did was add several feet to your pedestal. How's the weather up there?

My daughter's lips are moving but she isn't making any sense – and there I was thinking I'd had a great deal of practise with highly strung women.

'Nic told me everything. She said you made her do it… all that sex stuff.'

'I didn't *make* her do anything.'

'What are you? A rapist?'

'Bullshit, the little bitch was begging for it.'

'Oh God, I can't breathe.' One hand is flapping, the other, wrapped around her phone, indicates I'm to stay where I am. 'You killed her.'

The pale outline of Nic's face comes to mind. Where a thin layer of salt water separated me from her before she sank. I remember pushing through the wind, water whipping into a frenzy, its waves smashing against me. Out of my throat came a strangled sound, half sob, half laugh. Yet as the wind pummelled my water-soaked body I felt relief, as if I were finally free of everything.

My jaw works, but no words come out. A floating feeling comes over me, as if this weren't happening to me but to someone else. Her face appears grey, as if rendered in dots.

'I'm sorry,' I stutter. 'What did you say?'

'You're *possessed*. Whatever you did to Nic, you won't do to Mum. You're going to prison. Might as well get used to the idea.'

I tell myself prison time won't be that bad. A few months, tops, until my lawyer can convince a jury Holloway coerced me. My throat is suddenly dry, and I could do with a tumbler of water.

'No lectures, Bizz, okay? I've had wall-to-wall lectures from my therapist. I don't need them from you.'

'I'm sure the police know who's responsible. Why don't we ask them?'

She lowers her chin and throws her shoulders forward. I don't know if she's going to ram me or run right past me, and it worries me to think of where she might run. Only she's not running at all. She's tapping out a number on her phone.

She's calling the police.

I lunge at her, and her phone clatters to the floor, scooting towards the cloakroom. She spins under my arm and bolts upstairs in one fluid movement. For a second, I don't know whether to follow her or retrieve the phone. One I can come back for later, the other I need to restrain now.

By the time I reach the hall, she's sprinting through the open front door, and I run out after her. Halfway across the lawn, Bizzy slides through wet grass, and falls sprawling on her side with a scream of anger.

'Stay right there,' I shout.

She stares back at me with wide eyes, her mouth snarling. I fling myself at her, raising my fist and bringing it down just as Bizzy rolls away. My knuckles slam into wet grass as she scrambles to her knees. I grab one ankle and before I can seize the other, she kicks backwards, the bottom of her shoe meeting my mouth.

The pain is intense, but I'm flailing at her jeans, my fingertips skidding down her ankle, trying to clutch at her shoe, grabbing it, then losing my hold which would have pinned her down for good.

She gets up and bolts past me, her feet squelching through mud.

She takes off across the fields, shouting for her mother and leaving me with my tumbling thoughts.

I wipe my lips, warm blood seeping through my fingers. I let the realisation flood over me. Bizzy will accept that I tried to hurt her. She will think about it for weeks and weeks, and months and months, and wonder how far I might have gone.

The answer she wants to know is the same as everyone else. Did I kill Nic?

The answer is yes.

And no.

39

LILJA

Was that a scream? Or the wind?

Lightning flares and rain splatters against the vent. Terror crawls like a spider across my skin. The wind rouses the leaves from the gutters, and I can hear them scraping against the back of the house.

Zane's tomcatting is one thing, but the lead role in a series has made him crack. Holloway's poison is rotting him from the inside, and he doesn't know what's real any longer. The more I wallow in how Zane has ruined our lives, the more it feeds my anger. It's isolating when he's Zane, and destructive when he's Holloway.

I tilt my head to the vaulted ceiling every time the lightning breaks through. There's no other sound, except the tapping and scraping of the nail. Running the point along the mortar, large clumps begin to work free. I don't know why, but it makes me smile, as if someone has released a valve in my chest. One corner of the chicken wire is exposed and as I home in on the tiny gap, my heartbeat picks up, an animal instinct to fight my way out.

A humming sound, the purr of a car engine, gravel crunching under tyres. My chest tightens.

Are the police here? Or is it Zane leaving?

I call for Bizzy, but she can't hear me and I'm struggling to take a full breath in the silence. My throat is tight and dry from thirst, but the water bottles are in the fridge behind the hidden door.

Boom boom boom! The sound is both muffled and amplified, and I can't make out the voice. Has he come back to torment me?

The sound of my name, not my name exactly, but the words *Mum, Mum, Mum!* separates me from my task. I stagger through the meat locker, my hands slamming into shelves and my feet tripping up the steps to the wine aisles.

'I'm here. I'm here!' I shout.

I run between the barrels and along the aisle towards a splinter of light diffracting between the panels of the wooden doors.

'Mum, are you okay?'

'I'm fine. Are you?'

'Mum, where are the keys?'

'There's a spare inside the larder. Looks like a chapel key.'

'Okay.'

Then I hear the scrunch of gravel as she takes off towards the house. I'm counting the seconds. Ten, twenty, thirty. What's keeping her?

It's the purr of an engine outside, exhaust seeping into the cellar that confuses me. If it's not Zane's car, then whose car is it? Why was Bizzy outside with him? I cough from the fumes.

Then the click of the lock and warm hands clasp me. I cling to her; grateful she came for me.

'We've got to get out of here now,' she says.

She opens the Audi door, headlights steaming through the darkness. I'm looking at her muddy jeans and shoes, and then at the car. She senses my disorientation.

'Mum, get in!'

She must have driven the car out of the garage and then come for me. I'm trying to figure it all out when I hear the drawn-out sound of my name. 'Lily!'

I whip around to look behind me and glimpse his face. I feel like someone has dunked me in ice. He's too close, his hands reaching for my arm. My gut screams, run!

Bizzy is already in the passenger seat, and I scream at her to lock the car. It's me he wants. My legs feel heavy and slow, and my feet gain traction as I make headway along the drive with only one thought. I can't leave Bizzy behind.

An unfamiliar emotion prickles through my veins, not fear,

but outright rage. Even though guilt eats away at the thought, it's better to get help. I'm swearing and praying and straining my eyes for a car. But all I can see is trees and stars.

The gentle patter of rain tells me the storm has almost passed overhead. I glance at the dimpled surface of the duck pond, reflecting a starry sky. When Elin and I played hide and seek at night, I'm reminded of how I was the one who could see better in the dark, making out her shape before she found me. I'm hoping my eyes don't fail me now.

I hear a twig snap, followed by the hoot of an owl and my skin pops with goose bumps. My feet pound on the tarmac as a tentative bloom of fear ignites. Won't Zane take the tighter curve of the drive and cut me off at the gate?

There are no vans in the lane. No dark shapes rushing forward to save me. My pulse booms in my ears and my breath comes in rapid, shallow puffs.

I swerve to my right, gravel popping underfoot. I leave the drive for the shelter of the trees where wet grass muffles my footfalls. There is a pedestrian gate near the sunken wall to the deer park, which leads to the lane. Once I'm outside, I can run to the pub for help.

I can't leave Bizzy behind.

The breeze whispers through the trees and my skin crawls with panic. Where is he?

I slow down as a gust slithers through the grass, slapping loose twigs against my soggy jeans and sending a violent shiver down my back. Every few seconds I look back, but there's no sign of him.

I can make out the top bar on the pedestrian gate that stops the deer from jumping over. I see the pale strip of road through the rungs. Reaching up to open it, a hand claws at my arm, yanking at my hair and yelling at me to stop.

My body arches backwards, my hair caught in his grip. Before I can process what's happening, Zane's face looms out of the darkness and clocks my obvious shock.

None of the scenarios I'd imagined match this one. He'd been behind me all the time. I draw in a painful gulp of air and all that's going through my head is No, No, *No!*

This time, it's not adrenaline that cuts through the fear. It's red-hot anger. I twist and kick and punch, my hands and legs connecting with his chest and shins. My screams carry into the night, but he doesn't let go.

The only thing I know right now is that I need to talk him down, make him stop. He walks faster through the long grass to the lawn, dragging me and muttering about what a piece of shit I am. It's the name he keeps saying under his breath that gives me pause.

'Amaya… You ungrateful little bitch.'

Finally, he yanks me through the front door, the light from his phone scoring shadows into the wall. Suddenly, the lights snap on and our eyes narrow from the glare. With one hand, he shuts off his torch and slips the phone into his pocket.

His lip, where Meggy threw an accurate punch, has swollen to twice its size and blood glistens on his chin. As much as I want to run, he's gripping onto my arm, his nails biting into my flesh. He slams the front door with his foot and steers me into the kitchen. If I was hoping for a miracle, the twisted look on his face tells me otherwise.

'Where's my phone?' he asks.

I don't know what you mean, my face prompts.

'We're going to look for it, even if it takes all night.'

The frantic bickering in my head begins and a wave of fear overwhelms me. His mouth contorts and the unnatural light in his eyes rage like a black nova. He pulls me towards the nearest drawer and starts dumping cutlery on the floor and swiping jars off shelves. As we move closer to the kitchen table, my eyes are rooted to the vase of flowers, two baking tins and a cookery book. Somewhere behind them is my phone.

'Where is it, Lilja? In here? Or in here?'

I stand silent while he continues breaking plates and mugs, and then for dramatic emphasis, he heaves Mum's old Kenwood mixer off the counter with one arm. The bowl separates from the base, flips onto its handle, spilling the dough hook and the balloon whisk across the floor.

Then he studies the table. The sound of the vase and the baking tins smash-clanking to the floor makes me flinch. He looks exhausted and confused, but only for a moment.

'I don't have it.' Not a lie. It's simply not on me at present.

'My, you're full of surprises tonight.' He's stoops to look under the table now, bringing me down with him. 'You've been nothing but a stranger to me. Shoving me in the spare room and treating me like a second-class citizen. Now this.' He trails off with a pathetic shudder in his voice.

'You were the one shagging your way around Dawlish, not me.' Then the big one. 'For all I know, you're hiding Nic in some abandoned warehouse somewhere!'

The look on his face tells me that what I've said has affected him in ways it usually wouldn't, and his eyes are like two beads of hatred. He pours out words, blaming me for ruining his life, his name and his credibility.

I mutter something about calling the police, but it's an empty threat. There's no sign of my phone on the table. My last ember of hope has faded.

'What will you tell them? That I've done something terrible to my assistant and I'm about to do the same to you? They won't believe a neurotic mother with no bruises, no prior reports. But they will believe a celebrity with a bloody mouth. It'll be the worst public humiliation you've ever suffered. Something to think about.'

He's right. He could file a report for domestic violence and smear me as the monster, the same word the babysitter Irena once used.

Only I don't have blood under my fingernails like Meggy does.

I try to move towards the door, but he cuts me off and slams me against the wall. A chill rolls down my spine and my head feels like a thousand tiny hammers are pounding my skull. I struggle to look away from his piercing stare. I don't have the emotional energy to talk, and every inch of me wants to escape.

40

LILJA

As he hauls me through the bedroom, I'm shocked at the mess. Every drawer emptied, my clothes spilling off the bed. To distract him from focusing on his spare phone, I wrench my arm away and stand my ground.

'I want a divorce. I want out of this marriage and as far away from you as possible.'

'Pity you didn't think of that a month ago.'

'Get out!'

'Be my pleasure. Your story will be all over tabloids, how brave you were, how you put up with my affair with Nic for months without doing anything. You couldn't walk away like any other normal person, could you? You had to stay to see it out to the end like the strong, independent woman you are. You had to get enough proof to ruin me. Such a little strategist. It was the one thing you hated, wasn't it? My success.'

'Don't fool yourself, Zane. It was your choices I hated. Your selfish, psychotic choices. You never thought of Bizzy and how she might feel. You don't think she was hurt when people texted her clips of your sex scenes with throw-up emojis?'

A thought clatters in my brain. *What if he kills me?* I want to stop talking but the words gush out.

'You know it's true. She was grossed out and embarrassed and so were her friends. You're warped and damaged and trapped in your own twisted Holloway mind. You're a failure as father and a husband...'

I don't finish the sentence before his hands are around my neck as he pushes me to the floor, pressing tighter and tighter as I claw at his fingers. The last thing I see are his black eyes, unblinking and staring into mine.

***

When I come to, my breath comes in jagged rasps. I focus on the carpet where Zane is sprawled, his eyes are closed and his body limp, and it takes me a few seconds to realise what has happened.

'Mum!' Bizzy's face appears above me, her fingers wrapped around a cricket bat. 'Oh my God… oh my God. Are you okay?'

My voice crackles like dead leaves. 'I'm fine.'

She throws the bat on the bed and she's sobbing and staring at me, her hands grappling at my shirt. 'I… I hit him. I don't know if he's breathing. He's not moving.'

'Call the police.'

She shakes her head. 'He took my phone.'

I tell her he took mine too. She looks at his pockets as if deciding whether to go through them, but the moans he emits warns her to stay away.

There is only one thing on my mind and that's the spare phone. Dragging Bizzy into the bathroom, I rummage through dirty towels in the laundry basket until I find it. There's a low battery warning in the top right corner and I punch out 999. The line opens and I squeak out the word, "police."

But there's no reply. The line is dead.

I squeeze her hand and see the tears glistening in her eyes and it's hard not to cry too. I'm stunned Zane would be cruel as to frighten her. My nerves prickle, instinct and fear working hand in hand, and I steady myself against her.

Zane's whimpers and groans tell me we don't have much time. As we step over him, all I can think of is how useless it will be trying to track him without my phone.

As Bizzy helps me downstairs, I look out of the hall window

and glance down the drive, hoping to see the police. Meggy must have called them and the brief call I'd made will alert them. But all is dark, and beyond the gates the lane is deserted. The reporters have all moved on to another story, and a fresh pang of emotion rips through me. There's no one to help us.

I'm standing in the hall, one hand kneading my neck and trying to swallow, and Bizzy is behind me, fumbling for something on the hall table. I grab her arm and we run to the garage. But my car is no longer running.

I duck to look through the driver's window. 'My keys… They're not in the car.'

'Mum. Mum!' Bizzy shakes something jagged and familiar, and I stare at Zane's car keys in her hand, relief flooding through me.

'Where did you find them?'

'In their usual place.'

My brain goes briefly unto lockdown, and I can't understand how Zane overlooked them on the hall table. He must have been too preoccupied with finding his phone and taking ours to have noticed.

We lock ourselves in the Beemer and I press the starter in the console, hearing the chime as the video display lights up.

'Go, Mum! *GO!*

I accelerate into the drive while Bizzy grapples with the charger and plugs in Zane's spare phone. She presses OFFICE and then CONTACTS. Nothing.

Gravel crunches beneath the tyres as we lurch along the drive towards the trees.

I hear Bizzy screaming. 'Stop. STOP!'

I slam on the brakes. A pale face hovers above the windscreen, sliding around to the driver's side window. Zane grabs the door handle and shakes it, but it doesn't budge.

Bizzy's voice is mute above the buzzing in my ears and each movement feels syrupy slow. I slam my foot on the gas and the car roars forward, clearing a good portion of lawn before I straighten the wheel. We're flying down the drive and Bizzy presses the gate remote and nothing happens.

'He opened it. I know he opened it.' Bizzy opens the glove box. 'The spanner. He has a spanner for the motor.'

'What?'

'He unscrews something on the bottom. I've seen him do it through the CCTV.'

But the spanner isn't in the glove box. It isn't under her seat.

'Wait. It should be open. It should be unlocked.' She unsnaps her seat belt, her hand already on the door.

I slam on the brakes and she's out before I can stop her. In the rear-view mirror, Zane staggers towards us, one hand on the back of his head. I hear the squeal of the metal hinges and thank God the gate grinds open, the motor still in neutral as Zane had left it.

Bizzy jumps in and I pull out into the lane, praying that a car won't be coming the other way. We overshoot the verge, tyres squealing in mud and grass, and I glance up occasionally at the rear-view mirror as the house becomes a distant blur.

For a few moments, neither of us says anything. I draw in a ragged breath, my hands shaking on the wheel. I look at Bizzy, her face pale in the dim blue light. We've made it.

Her voice is a faint whisper. 'The phone's still dead.'

'But it's charging, right?'

'I think so.'

'Try it.'

'The screen's still black.'

I'm clocking 50 mph in a 25-mph zone, and I ease off the accelerator. Bizzy fiddles with every app on the display and Adrie Vander-Meulen's voice gusts through the speakers.

'*...his assistant who was jumping him in his own house. And now she's dead. Yesterday, we talked about all manner of injured parties interfering with their partners' lives through one deception or another. You might talk about regret, or how you'd love to turn back the clock and start all over again. But where do you fit in? Revenge or forgiveness?*'

Bizzy's changes the station and music fills the car, a sad girl song with bedroom lyrics. My thoughts fly back in time to Nic. I wanted her to say it was all a lie, that she never seduced my husband. I wanted her words to crack as if she was fighting back tears. I wanted to hear the desperation in her voice, the hysterical unravelling of a woman in pain.

When Zane said, 'She meant nothing to me. It's you I love.' I wanted to hurt him. Baseball bats, scissors, knifes. Awful things I wanted to do. The worst part was Bizzy sitting on the staircase with the cat, knees pulled up and holding them tight as if she were being held.

'Mum, go left here.'

Out here in the darkness something shifts inside me — a need. I need to get Bizzy to safety. There's a nervous fizz in my stomach, every second teetering on the brink of a horror movie.

We're listening to a club banger of a song about someone punching someone's lights out, running the streets, and doing well over a hundred on the highway. It's catchy, especially the chorus where the singer calls the other motorist *bitches*. Bizzy looks at me and I look at her and we're not quite smiling.

The sky is an oppressive band of black, moonlight barely filtering through. Just as I'm wondering why the roads are empty, headlights glare in my rear-view, floating to the middle like a low flying UFO. Familiar headlights. Audi headlights.

'It's him,' Bizzy says. 'It's Dad.'

It can't be him. He's injured, concussed. The lump on his head should be the size of a marble.

'Does that phone have a charge yet?' I ask.

'Yes.'

'Call the police. 999.'

'Okay, okay. I'm dialling three nines.'

She speaks so fast to the operator, there's no space between words, and then her voice sounds strange and distant. How far away is help? All I know is I need to keep moving.

'Mum, where are we?' She puts the phone on speaker and holds it between us.

'We're heading towards the roundabout and Dawlish Town Centre,' I say. 'This is Lilja Osborne. My husband is Zane Osborne. He's… he's chasing us.'

I don't mention he's out of his skull pretending to be a fictional character, or that Bizzy knocked him out with a baseball bat. Yes, he hurt us, and he hurt his therapist, but I can't have Zane blame this whole nightmare on us. I describe the car he's driving and rattle off the licence plate. Bizzy reaches into the glove box for Zane's insurance policy and relays the Beemer's licence to the police. The operator tells us to stay calm.

My eyes snap from the road to the mirror and my leg spasms on the accelerator. I gain a full car length in front before cutting into the middle of the road, forcing him to stay behind. He sounds the horn and flashes his lights, speeds up and for a second our bumpers are inches from touching.

Then he pushes for a second try, slides out into the other lane, and runs beside me. Blood roars in my skull as I keep up, ignoring the little voice in my head telling me to let him go.

We shoot through a tunnel of overhanging trees, driving along-side like boy racers, until a beam of light arcs over the road ahead. I know I should drop my speed and let him slot in front. In that moment, his face burns into mine, white and searching, as if he can't believe what's happening.

Will he speed up or slow down?

His hands are no doubt floundering on the gear stick, his feet hovering between both pedals. I slam on my brakes, watching the gap between us widen as the Audi races on. Hedgerows flash past and I want to stop. I need to stop. Turning into Kenbury Crescent, I slow down at the corner.

There must be something I can do, something that will shatter his world completely. As an idea hits me, a tremor starts up my arms, tears pricking my eyes. Apart from the trauma of this latest stunt, Zane will have a thought that rallies all thoughts, the worst of them all. No driver tries to squeeze another off the road, or brakes when they do. The thought of me, a normal person, becoming involved in this insanity makes me sick.

While he'll be hoping I rot in hell.

41

ZANE

After speeding away from two crazy women, I find a farm track, cut the engine and lights, and pause to get my bearings. What was a jagged hum in my head is now a full-on pounding and I rub my temples, hoping to relieve the pain.

Half the world is idiots and the other half take advantage of them. Which half am I?

I assumed imprisoning Lilja would undermine Bizzy. I was wrong. I've been flying blind for too long. There are no pain killers in the glove compartment or console and no stray water bottles under the seat. As luck would have it, my backpack and holdall are safe in London, and that's where I need to be.

I hear a rumble as something flashes past, moonlight on metal, and the distinctive outline of a familiar car. I gun it towards a pair of rear lights and brake before a police cordon at the turnoff to School Hill. Police cars are parked across the road, officers stooping to give directions. My vision blurs and the second outline of an approaching police officer overlaps the first. This is it. I'm about to be arrested.

I power down the window. 'What's going on?'

'Collision ahead, sir. Where are you heading?'

'Exeter.'

The word comes out as a question rather than a statement, but he doesn't appear deterred. He points in the general direction of the detour, and I follow my wife's lead.

That was close…

Blood roars in my ears, fusing with the sound of the car. I don't know if it's the smell or the mixture of nerves, but I'm feeling sick. Sea air and exhaust pour in through the open window and I'm about to hurl.

I recall a similar incident when Dad evaded the police on the M5 to Plymouth. He picked me up from school and told me we were going to spend the day at the aquarium by way of the pub. I don't know if it was the Dover sole, one glassy eye like a blob of mercury, staring up at me, or the way my father peeled away the flesh between the tines of his fork. But something made me queasy.

I kept staring at him: a brown-haired husk of a man, cheeks dipping slightly, and a grubby tie. He wore the same cracked leather jacket, like it was winter, the one with the suede elbow patches that stank of cigarettes. Only it was a muggy day.

My school tie was chafing my neck and my grey sweater was itchier than hell. After Dad had had a few pints we jumped in the car, heading to who knows where. Somehow, we ended up tearing through an industrial estate with the police officers on our tail. By now I was feeling sick. I mean – blowing massive chunks – sick.

'Just hold it in, lad. You can do it.'

I'd never thrown up on command and I tried to think of the big orange space hopper I'd seen in the toy shop, the one Dad promised to buy me at Christmas.

He gunned it all the way to the roundabout at the end of the road, tyres squealing. It had one exit – which was also the entrance – and positioned, Dad said, for the benefit of idiots too stupid to turn around in such a vast space. The police were closing in, and the sick was burbling up my throat. He must have understood the green tinge which surely covered my face and neck, and leaned over and opened the window.

'All yours, son.'

I leaned out as far as I could, and all hell broke loose. I couldn't stop heaving. It was like a trail of lumpy gravy, the door panel was covered in a brown glaze as well as the police car behind us. The screeching of brakes told me they had stopped as we sped on.

I learned a valuable lesson that day. Getting away with anything illegal might have given Dad a buzz, but if left unchecked he'd be doing time before my next birthday.

As I leave my past behind, the phone rings. Lilja must have come to her senses at last. Only it's not my wife, it's a private number.

'Hey, Zane.'

A southern American drawl under the guise of a faux upper crust British accent. My agent, whose voice sounds strangely as if it's underwater.

'Hi Alex. How's it going?'

'It's going. Awful about Nic. You must be upset.'

'Yes. Devastated.'

'I hope it isn't some ghastly serial killer. Zane, are you still there?'

'Yes. I can hardly hear you.'

There's something different about her. Disappointed. A little angry. Makes me feel like I'm standing outside my old headmaster's study door, waiting for a massive bollocking.

'All things aside, *People Magazine* was livid yesterday. Can't blame them. You really didn't have a good enough reason to miss that shoot.'

Shoot? What shoot?

'Although production knows you're pinned for September through December, it doesn't mean you'll be on hold for the dates those twelve episodes will shoot.'

I feel a surge of dread. 'Another change?'

'I get we thought this is a recurring role, but you need to understand there will be a major change in Episode 3. Something to do with the new writers adapting to the many faces of Holloway. Not to mention the idea of him killing Stone.'

New writers? The air stills, and for a split second, I imagine Simon marshalling a decision to write Stone out sooner than scheduled. My senses tell me it's much worse.

In those few seconds, a bone-aching tiredness wraps me in its velvety embrace. Here in my quiet space, I relive the last scene in Episode 2, immune to everything going on around me.

```
              ETHAN (V.O.)
    … I've got exactly ten seconds
    to get off the main road, and
    I'm speeding, sirens blaring
    behind me… telling me to pull
    over. The bastards know what
    I've done. They know … I turn
    off the headlights and swerve
    behind a white van and there
    it is, the turning to the
    lake. I'm gunning it along a
    country lane, rushing over a
    cattle grid… I'm thinking I've
    made it, I've made it, I've
    made it.
```

… major change in Episode 3. That's what she said. A change.

My chest fills with a searing pain and I'm pushing against it with the heel of one hand. 'Are you saying I'm no longer locked in?'

'The shooting schedule is firm, but I'll be brief. I've seen the script. You can discard the last revision I sent: the one where Holloway disappears to an unknown location. They've decided to cut it.'

Cut it? I run through the scene in my head; jagged fir trees shrouded in a grey mist and where a solid sheet of rain pours from the sky. The sound is hideous, like the rattle of ball-bearings against the tarp. I smell mud, barky and musty in the bobbing grass, and a breeze skitters across the water, making it ruffle and spread. Holloway has some kind of voice over where he says: *The wilderness doesn't like outsiders; the bogs will swallow you whole.*

He's trapped between two terrifying choices. Either he stays in his shelter until the storm dies down or he takes his own life.

```
    FADE IN:

    Out of the darkness, a light flickers. A
    man sits inside his shelter, warming his
    hands in front of a campfire.
```

                    HOLLOWAY (V.O.)

          They found the body. Before I
          say this, I'm not looking for
          any sympathy. I may be a mon-
          ster, but I'm still a husband
          and a father. The twins will
          be sorry to lose me. I hope
          their mother has reason to
          think of me kindly, a perfect
          woman whose life has been a
          nightmare, thanks to me. I'll
          never stop loving her. I know
          I can't just disappear to a
          remote house by the sea. Far
          away from everyone. A fresh
          start. There'll always be
          traces, fibres on clothes and
          skin. Blood under fingernails.
          They will find me.

WE SEE the wind extinguishing the flame,
sending hot ash across the moor.

WE SEE the man plunged into darkness.

CAMERA STEADILY MOVES IN ON the sparks,
which are doused by the approaching
deluge.

I press the phone closer to my ear. 'What happens to Holloway, then?'

'He's been cut.'

My knuckles whiten. This is it. One of those pin-sharp instants that will influence my entire career. 'Sorry? Say that again?'

'Holloway doesn't kill Amaya Stone. She kills him.'

Trending #InZane

@Titmouse: Did anyone see *Grain of Truth* this morning? Marschōne Robinson is getting more airtime. Woohoo!

@CirceAtNight: Not surprised. He's everyone's wet dream.

@SherylAdams: @CirceAtNight Nobody's asking you shithead. He's not everyone's wet dream. ZaneO is.

@HeyWhatsUP: @SherylAdams Really? You think ZaneO's fans are rooting for him? Did we watch the same *Grain of Truth*? Who's the shithead now?

42

LILJA

We pass more fences and hedgerows opening on both sides of the road. A camera flashes. I know I'm speeding, but that's the point, isn't it? Triggering cameras so a police car will pull me over. Then we'll be safe.

A car's high beams blaze into the rear-view mirror.

Bizzy turns in her seat and then shoots me a look. 'Can Dad track us? The car, I mean?'

The terrible thought that life can twist on us in a blink isn't something we need right now. Zane had never renewed his BMW Assist, which only transmits the car's location to emergency services should an impact occur. As for an inbuilt tracker, what would I know?

She motions at the back window. 'Because that's a dark grey Audi behind.'

Car lights flash off and on, as if warning me to pull over. I tap the brakes as we approach a bend and then speed up on a long stretch of open road. The car behind takes its cue and mimics my manoeuvre, then overtakes, cruising alongside us for three long seconds. The silhouette of a man's head, his face turned towards me, is clearly visible, his finger pointing at a row of houses. Then the Audi slips in front, its taillights glowing red.

I shriek as I slam on the brakes and lurch to a crawl. Bizzy head flies forward and back, her seat belt anchoring her in place.

'I'm sorry.' My hand reaches for her arm.

She utters three words. 'It's definitely Dad.'

My neck feels ice cold. I keep comforting myself that it's not Zane. It's a group of teenagers toying with us or a concerned driver pointing out a flat tyre. But I know the slope of those shoulders and the face. I'd already called the police to report a dangerous driver. Although Zane is neither drunk nor high, he's frightening a fourteen-year-old girl, *my* girl, and there's no excuse for that.

As he pulls into the turning, I hear Bizzy drawing fast, shallow breaths. She's gripping the seat with one hand and the door with the other.

Taking inventory of my options, I know the main road is ahead. One way leads to Elin and Paul's, the other will take us to Mum's. My foot twitches on the gas, my mind screaming to get out of here. My foot slams down and we're gunning it to the main road, turning toward a third option. Home.

The van ahead is the visual barrier I need. Hurtling to catch up, I overtake and tuck in front.

'Mum, slow down, you're scaring me.'

More houses, then a sign to Teignmouth and Dawlish. I keep straight. It's the safest thing to do.

'Mum. Slow down!'

I'm jolted by her words and despise myself for putting her life in danger. 'I'm doing everything I can, Bizz. Understand?'

'Yes.'

'And Bizz?' My eyes drill into hers. 'Thank you for calling the police. You're amazing.'

'Okay.'

I slow down at the carwash and tell her I'm sorry. But the fact is, she's right. I was careening along this road, paying no attention to how she must be feeling. As we pass, I realise it's closed. No people about. No police bike roaring towards us to help.

Then something I hadn't expected. The van behind us turns off down a residential street, exposing us to the Audi. Fear jolts beneath my skin and I feel shattered and wrung out from the chase. Ahead is a turning, where the words *narrow, no turnoffs*, fail to warn me.

'Mum. This is not a good idea.'

'It's fine.' My voice is tight and jagged. 'Everything's fine.'

Does a rapidly pumping heart mean I'm running on adrenaline overload? My vision is swimming and I'm worried I'll pass out. I'd watched too many crime shows to tell me we must keep going. There's no way I'm stopping on the side of the road to wait for help. Stupidity like that always ends with a predictable outcome – a hooded man rattling on the window and then smashing the glass with a thunderous crack.

The petrol gauge shows half a tank and the car's speed feels too fast at 55 mph. I draw in a ragged breath as the road curves and straightens again. My death grip on the steering wheel is causing shooting pains up my arms and I try not to transmit my panic to Bizzy. She's craning her neck at the rear window and grimacing as if every second is agony.

I scan the shadowy road for any sign of headlights. Two loom behind. The hard lump of fear is painful in my throat, and I can barely swallow. Before I can process what's happening, the head-lights close in and I can make out the silhouette of a driver. His bumper taps ours and the seatbelts catch as we jolt forward.

Bizzy shoots me a freaked-out look, her body rigid as if bracing for a second impact.

The car doesn't ram us again. This time, it mounts the grass verge and powers between us and the hedge, until the rear lights are two pinpricks in the distance.

As I slow down, Bizzy flicks her gaze from the windshield to the rear window.

'Turn around,' she says. 'Turn around!'

Judging by the width of the road and the car, there's just enough room to turn. A beam of light filters through the hedgerows ahead. It doesn't appear to be moving or getting any closer.

What's he doing? Is he waiting for us? Can he see us?

Instinctively, I turn off my headlights and reverse into a three-point turn. Shifting gears, we go forward and back, forward and back, now perpendicular to the road. Panic replaces accuracy as the car's back bumper hits the jagged hedge with a grating squeal. I realise turning in such a narrow space is a little optimistic. At each point, it feels as if we're hardly making any progress.

'Keep watching that car,' I tell Bizzy.

One more time and we clear the turn and the car surges forward. Bizzy twists herself towards the rear window.

'Anything?' I ask, keeping my lights off until I get back to the main road.

'Nothing.'

I imagine the rumble of an engine in the distance, but it's a squeal of wind through a crack in Bizzy's window. I pray a grateful prayer, until Bizzy's voice rushes at me again.

'Yep.'

'Yep, what?'

'He's coming.'

Shit!

I turn onto the main road and pick up speed. My mind imagines making a sharp turn before yielding to an oncoming car as the light approaching changes from red to green. It would be a move Zane wouldn't expect. Somehow, in this fake scenario, Zane gets caught in oncoming traffic and left behind.

Instead of headlights closing in and filling up our mirrors, they are two distant pinpricks of light, and I take a second to register why Zane has slowed down. A familiar car comes the other way, reflective checker pattern along its flanks and lights flashing. An overwhelming rush of relief floods over me.

I pull over on the kerb and rest my head against the seat. As an officer leaps out, I whip around to look for Zane, but there's no sign of his car.

43

ZANE

It's after nine in the morning, and in stark contrast to Holloway I'm shaking with nerves. You know what they say about concussion? It's best to stay awake for most of the night.

The back of my head feels raw and the pounding won't stop. I can't believe my daughter took a swing at me, knocking me out cold.

Like father, like daughter. The whispered words send a sliver of horror through me for she could be dangerous…

Light gushes through a trio of arched windows in the sitting room, rain spattering against the panes. I study the lawn that sweeps to a small summerhouse. Lilja filled it with miniature furniture and stencilled Bizzy's name above the front door. Suddenly, I'm rooted to views I won't see again.

Last night, I abandoned Lilja's car at the station and caught the 20.17 train to Paddington. I was grateful the carriage was empty, but it was the early hours when I reached Holland Park. The curved ceilings creating a sense of magnitude as my footsteps echoed on the hardwood floors.

I kept checking email for my eTA visa application, and there was nothing. Sleep was sporadic, alternating between dreams of high-speed chases and drowning women. How easy was it for Holloway to strip all layers of human decency from me? The fact I had terrorised my girls and hurt my therapist is unarguable, whether I choose to listen to reason.

How did I get so far away from myself?

I'm not a bad person, but I've done bad things. The lengths to which Holloway has forced me to go reinforces his power over me. The worst part was being blackmailed. It ate away at my soul. I couldn't let Nic continue to post blurry photos of us, letting her audience guess who her mystery man was. After her death, those posts kept emerging, every image getting sharper and sharper until my secret was out.

Moving around the immaculate house makes me feel like an interloper, and in many ways I am. The kitchen drawer still holds old letters, paid bills, and stacks of keys. Amongst all that junk is a credit card. It doesn't help that it belongs to my wife, but what else do I have?

Finally, an email from the IRCC for my eTA visa. I'm relieved they don't need more documents or an in-person interview at the nearest Canadian visa office. I know there will be a paper trail, but Quebec is a large city and that's not where I'm heading. Chartering a private plane with cash will enable me to go somewhere remote and I can camp out until the fuss dies down.

A fuss like this will never die down. Don't people still think of Ted Bundy and his ilk?

I'm nothing like him.

But I could be. Which brings me to the inevitable subject of plastic surgery since a life sentence is standard for murder. It'll be forty years before parole is possible, forty stifling years behind bars.

I unlock my phone, scrolling through the local headlines. Three arrested after a two-man brawl in Torquay. Eighteen-year jail sentence following rapist's trial at Plymouth Crown Court. Nothing about a car chase in Dawlish.

My wife used to love me – or rather, she loved who I used to be. I'm not the first to fall under a character's spell, all in the name of improving my performance. But I might be the first to have taken it too far. Would I do it all again?

In a heartbeat.

But I would do it differently, in a sensitive, collaborative way. I would take myself off for the duration, as Lilja had asked me to do, and then none of this would have happened.

I wanted to do the series and take centre stage. I have, in a manner of speaking, taken the "in" out of infamous and now I am legendary.

But I hadn't counted on Lilja's interference. After my first affair with the babysitter, she fell apart emotionally. My repeated denials pushed it still further and the fights, the slamming doors, drove a wedge between us. For years, we've hung on. But recently, her persistent needling has pushed me too far, tantrums inconsistent with my natural behaviour. Now, in my darkest moment, I know I'm still in Holloway's grip.

I add a shot of whisky to my coffee and then another, puckering when it burns the unsightly gash on my lip. When I hear the knock on the door, I freeze. Peering into the hall, I see two silhouettes through the glass in the door. Too late to duck and dive. They have also seen me.

Shoulders back, chin up. Keep my expression neutral.

'Can I help you,' I say, gripping my mug.

'Mr Osborne? I'm DCI Kylie Trivet. This is DS Sam Hussain. May we come in?'

I nod and scowl at their warrant cards. Their footsteps are heavy behind me until they stop and gawp at two original Stubbs paintings in the hall. While they do all that posturing, looking around as if they've never seen such impeccable taste, I kick a bag of weed under the couch.

Trivet sits on a chair, wiping a sprinkling of rain from her close-cropped hair. She's pale, as if she's been paper-pushing in a basement for too long. Hussain, who has a designer beard I would die for, stands by the window, admiring a crop of hydrangeas.

'Are those Pinky-winky?' he asks.

'Actually, no. They're Madame Emile Mouillère. Pure white in July and lime green in the autumn.'

He shoots a look at the ceiling. 'How many bedrooms?'

'Six, with an upstairs office.'

'Very nice.'

Kylie glares at him as if sliding a finger across her neck, then pulls out a notebook and pen. She studies my five o'clock shadow, which is closer to midnight, and my swollen lip.

'Bad night?'

'It's the press. I'm sure you understand.' I try not to fiddle with my cuffs or scratch my neck.

'I do, Mr Osborne. It can be crushing.'

Crushing. Interesting word choice and selected no doubt with brutal precision. Can the police sense my guilt? Does it come off me like a stink? Another gulp of my coffee and the tension thaws.

'Now that we're here, I'd like to ask a few questions about last night. I understand there was a hang up call to the police and a car chase.' After we debate the exact time of these two incidents, she says, 'Could you tell me what happened?'

'My wife and I were arguing over money. She withdrew a large sum and hid it in an account for which I don't have access. When I reminded her it was money I'd earned, she hit me.'

'Your lip.'

'Yes. I didn't call the police. She did.'

'I see. So, she hung up and didn't press charges?'

'There was no need. My wife… she has a temper. It can be quite explosive at times. Something to do with the Merlot. Anyway, I've learned the best thing to do is give her space. As I was driving away from the house, she started following me and I was terrified she'd do something irresponsible. You must understand my daughter was in the car with her. I stopped in a layby, hoping she'd stop and talk. But she drove past. I followed her for a few miles, only it was hard keeping up. She must have been going well over seventy. I'm sorry if I scared her, but she can't have been as scared as Bizzy.'

Kylie nods. 'The police confirmed she was a little hysterical, not over the limit. She did get a speeding ticket.'

Glad to hear it. Like everything, it's Lilja's word against mine. If I don't mention the lump on the back of my head, she won't mention my little outburst. What the police do with a reckless speeder with an underage child in the car is anyone's guess.

'About Miss Gatlin.' She opens her notebook.

Shit! Seriously? 'I've already given the police a statement.'

'And now you're giving one to me.' Seconds seem to rush by in a grey blur, and then she starts writing something. 'How would you sum up your relationship with her?'

I take a breath. 'Typical boss/employee. She was my PA.'

Questions fire one after another. Did she do a good job? If she did, then what was the reason for her dismissal? Kylie's impenetrable stare sends a chill down my spine.

'I asked Nic to leave because of…' I'm about to say sexual harassment and think better of it. 'She was taking painkillers and other stuff. It was getting out of control.'

She arches a thin brow and glances at my mug. 'Other stuff?'

'She engaged in recreational drugs occasionally. I don't know what she took.'

'When was the last time you saw her?'

'It was the night of my birthday party. I'd been doing an interview with Gary O'Malley that afternoon and when I arrived home, she was in my study.'

'Did she say why she'd come to see you?'

'She was angry I'd fired her and wanted another chance. I said no.'

There's a stretch of uneasy silence and I try not to fill it in with a smile. The cut on my lip will split open again and I'll be dabbing it with a hanky.

'The kitchen staff heard you arguing with a woman, which I assume was her. Could you elaborate?'

I take a sip of coffee and hope she doesn't notice my tremor. 'From what I understood, she was still devastated by her split from Marschōne Robinson. I think you can fill in the blanks. Anyway, I told her I couldn't discuss it with her.'

'So, she was seeing Mr Robinson?'

'I wasn't aware of the specifics.'

'Would you say you and Nic were close?'

'Professionally speaking, yes. She supported my work.'

'She never struck you as the type to leak your private life to the press?'

'Heavens, no.' I give my mug a half-spin on the side table. 'She was extremely loyal.'

'But there are photos. You and her on the beach, close-ups of your hand on hers. We know this because of your distinctive wedding ring.'

Not a trace of guilt, Zane. That's the key.

'I'm sure there are,' I say. 'She was never without her phone. She was proud of Marschōne and me, and protective.'

'You are quite a catch, Mr Osborne, from the standpoint of a young woman. A young woman who came to work for you and loved your movies. Perhaps she was in love with you.'

'I wouldn't go that far.'

'But she flirted and touched. It can be quite an exciting risk.'

My mind rehashes all kinds of visuals. Nic sitting on my desk, a slice of thigh peeking through a skirt. Slutty underwear, red glossy fingernails, the scent of Miss Dior. Nic could easily have told someone how many times we'd "flirted" and "touched." She'd certainly been in the headspace for revenge.

I don't hear the quiet footstep that sidles alongside me until I feel the hand squeezing my shoulder.

'Mr Osborne?' Sam leans down, worry lines scoring his brow. 'Are you okay?'

My mouth is scratchy and dry, and I'm lisping. 'Yes, I'm sorry. I'm finding all this a bit... you know.'

'Sad? Yes, it's very sad.'

I daren't wipe away the droplet running down the side of my face or the one on the other side that follows it. It won't be long now. Two more visits at most and they'll cuff me and send me to a category A men's prison.

Shit! I hope it's not Wakefield.

Sam gives my shoulder a friendly tap and whatever he says sounds as if it's underwater. Terror grips me and my ears ring. No, Holloway, not now. *Please*, not now.

'Would you like a break?' It's Sam again, looking after my welfare.

'No, no. I'm fine.'

Kylie slides a photograph from the back of her notebook and hands it to me. 'She looked like a nice person.'

I study a young woman wearing jeans and a blue tailored shirt with puff sleeves, hands scooping her hair on top of her head. She was posing in front of the hydrangeas, which hadn't bloomed yet.

'Yes. She was delightful.'

'Was this photo taken here or at your house in Dawlish Warren?'

I keep examining every inch of the picture, the way her hair lifts in a gust of wind, the silver heart necklace I bought glinting against her décolletage. I remember her cheeky smile and the way the third tooth from the left was slightly crooked. She was more sensual than my wife. Shorter, bigger busted. Legs like a sprinter.

Wait… would the police even think about checking where the necklace came from? Could they find evidence in our bank accounts? I don't remember if she was wearing it the night she died.

'Mr Osborne?' Kylie shifts in her chair.

'Dawlish. Definitely Dawlish.'

'When roughly?'

'Mid-March, I think.'

Scribble, scribble. Kylie looks as if she's about to say something and then stops and looks at the floor. I see why she's stopped. Sunlight puddles on the carpet, illuminating a stain near the foot of the coffee table where Nic had accidentally kicked over a glass of red wine.

'What were her responsibilities?'

'Social media, mainly.' I lean back on the couch and wonder why Sam is still standing. 'That means public appearances, press junkets, consulting with my agent. She was great at creating posts and managing my website. Then there were my appointments, which isn't easy when I'm called out at short notice.'

'Would you say she was someone you trusted with all your personal information?' Kylie flips over a page.

'Absolutely.'

'How many hours a week did she work?'

'She put in a tremendous number of hours. There were the occasional parties we had. She stayed late for those.'

'You spent a considerable amount of time together.'

I notice them both staring at me, but I don't take up the baton. 'She was well compensated, as her wage slips will show.'

Kylie passes me another photo. This time, there are bruises on Nic's face and one eye is swollen shut. Her dress is muddy and torn and twisted around her thighs.

I'm shaking my head and saying, 'No, no, no.' Not because I'm trying to take in what happened to Nic, but conflicted over why Kylie is showing it to me.

'They found her in one of the caves at Langstone Rock. She died from a head injury.'

'How? I mean, what was she doing there?' I hope the forlorn sound of my voice is convincing.

'She wasn't swimming, that's for sure. Not fully dressed.'

I hand the photo back, conscious of a twinge of fear. 'Did she fall and hit her head on the rocks?'

'Not the rocks, no. Her skull contained fragments of brick and mortar.'

Her eyes fall on my chest, and particularly my hands, as if assessing my strength. It makes me wonder if domestic disputes account for a large quantity of her caseload.

Stop-start images flash through my head and I can imagine the beach where they found the body, reflecting the lurid flashes of police cars. Then, in the corner of the room, I see Nic, her arms wrapped around a torn yellow dress and her eyes are misted with tears.

They know, a dead voice tells me.

Kylie and Sam are scouring my face as if a quiver of emotion has given away some secret. I remain perfectly still.

'Two teenagers, around your daughter's age, found her. They were too traumatised to make a statement.' Kylie tucks the photo into the notebook. 'I want to emphasise, Mr Osborne, how sorry I am. Losing an employee and a close friend to homicide is traumatic. If you like, I can put you in touch with counsellors.'

'Thank you.' I take the card she offers me but I've no intention of speaking to anyone.

'One more thing, I'm sure you're familiar with *BarbedWire*. Fans are baying for Mr Holloway's blood. They think he caused all this. Ridiculous, I know since he doesn't exist.'

A ball of dread forms in the pit of my stomach. I take no pleasure in knowing my one million followers are now handcuffed to my life and just as confused as I am. What am I supposed to say? Holloway is as real to them as he is to me.

Kylie eases herself sideways off the chair and gives me a long, hard look. As I show them to the door, I realise why.

When Kylie asked when the photo of Nic had been taken, I said mid-March because the hydrangeas hadn't bloomed yet. But it would have indicated to them that Nic had been to my house prior to being employed by me.

They knew I'd known her for longer.

Trending #InZane

@SherylAdams: ZaneO is being interviewed by the police. Did you see that photo of him blubbering in an upstairs window?

@BanterBadger: Blimey, how embarrassing.

@Titmouse: Do you think he did it? Def feel a sweep-stakes coming on.

@CirceAtNight: Holloway is messing with his head. It's like DiCaprio sleeping inside animal carcasses and eating raw liver in *The Revenant*.

@HeyWhatsUP @CirceAtNight It doesn't come close.

44

LILJA

I was grateful for Paul and Elin's company last night and a police car outside the front gate. We went through cameras, door locks and security alarms, removing anything Zane might have remote access to. By midnight, we were all too tired to do anything else.

Paul and Elin camped out in the spare room and Bizzy slept with me. I found her phone on the floor outside the wine cellar and mine was in Zane's desk drawer. I kept waking up in the dark to the sound of footsteps, then a stifling stillness, like the pause before a thunder crack. The heat was thick it smelt of baked earth and mildew, and my pyjamas were soaked through. The bathroom wasn't any cooler, but a damp flannel and fresh clothes made up for it.

I wore myself out, wondering if Zane had come back, until I settled into a strange acceptance that the footsteps I heard were Paul's. The sweep of his hand on the bannisters, the click of their bedroom door. Sounds I welcome.

I kept scrolling through my phone, feeling just as terrified about Zane's disappearance as I was with Nic's death. I checked his GPS repeatedly. No location found. His secrecy is inevitable, I suppose.

When I think of the old Zane, a grin splits my face. He could light up a room and hold everyone's attention with the stories he told. Was I in love with him? Or it was it a rescue romance?

I thought he was grown-up at twenty-two, and completely off-limits. Which was fine, because I could simply look at him and imagine what it would be like rather than go through the embarrassing motions.

Elin and I were invited to a party at the de Boinvilles. The house was enormous, with two balconies trapping views of putting greens and fairways. Just before midnight, a group of us ran onto the golf course, enticed by the promise of a fire pit, and the boys handed around a bottle of wine.

The girls acted silly around Zane, blushing and giggling, while jealousy chewed up my guts. When the flames were higher than us and sparks popped against the night sky, I was teetering between tipsy and drowsy. I told Elin I needed to pee. Instead of going back inside, I made for the tree line, undid my jeans and went in the long grass.

I kept thinking I could hear things; foxes yipping, twigs snapping. Droplets of sweat moistened my shirt one minute, and I was shivering the next. When trees began to bend inwards, I knew someone had spiked my drink.

Just as I was doing up my jeans, an arm wrapped around my chest, crushing the life out of me. It was Charlie de Boinville, whose breath reeked of weed. His sudden appearance was out of nowhere.

Something dark whispered. *He was following you.*

He pivoted me around, his hands pulling at my shirt. I kept saying, 'No,' but the words were distant and slurred. His thumbs dug deep into my cheeks, and he brought my face close to his. The drowsiness that threatened to envelop me earlier gave way to terror.

'Please, stop.'

He parted his lips in a vague smile, shoved me against the tree, his weight pressing me into the bark. None of it made sense. The words he used were humiliating and defiling, and I pushed and pushed, but his strength returned tenfold. The sense of invasion and entitlement shocked me.

Suddenly, Charlie's head arched backwards. Someone had hold of his hair. Zane showed him his fist and all that boyhood innocence, the soft, flouncy hair and the playful smile, was swallowed by rage. He pushed Charlie backwards, punching and kicking, and shouting obscenities I'll never forget.

Charlie's breath fogged from swollen lips; his words garbled. 'She asked me… she wanted…'

'I didn't!' I shouted.

Zane took my hand, and we walked back to the bonfire, not by the path I'd taken but through the long grass. The trees on both sides became walls, long grass tugging at my trainers, until we burst onto the green. I stopped for breath, hands on my knees, tears turning to sobs.

Even though nothing bad happened, Zane insisted we tell someone, and I said no. It would only implicate him. Charlie was so badly beaten, it's a secret we've always kept.

I was too young to date him back then, but I called him Studdo and he called me his Genevieve. It came from a poem about passions and delights, and sacred flames, and he said he'd write a few lines for me when I was older.

I saw him in a coffee shop when I was nineteen. Zane had energy that transferred to me and I could say anything to him and he never judged me. He wrote down the words he'd promised on the back of a coaster and gave them to me. I've kept them in my jewellery box ever since.

> *She listened with a flitting blush,*
> *With downcast eyes, and modest grace;*
> *And she forgave me, that I gazed*
> *Too fondly on her face!*

It was a year later before I saw him again. He'd begun a career in television, where he'd garnered a nomination for a Drama League Award. He was a different man, a sleeker version. When I reminded him of the party at the golf course, he was sorry – desperately sorry – and wanted to be the one to make it up to me.

Remembering all this now brings a follow-up question which can easily be answered with a simple *yes* or *no*.

Do I believe Zane did something to Nic? No.

Had I thought Holloway could instigate such a crime? A

character where lying is second nature and a murderer from the very beginning.

Yes.

* * *

I'm on my second coffee when I think of the CCTV. Recovering anything useful from our cameras is a dead loss. The system automatically overwrites old footage with new and I'd never thought to increase the capacity and reset period. Then I remember the backup file.

I check every image for anything that looked unusual. There are gaps in the dates and thin bands of static where Zane had turned off the CCTV.

Then I hit Zane's birthday party. The lantern over the front door throws a corona of light on the steps as guests spill into the house and valets armed with lamps escort late-comers up the drive. It was a beautiful evening.

I fast forward until Zane's car clears the bend towards the garage and disappears. Something catches my eye. Something in the foreground I hadn't noticed before. Where the weeping willow covers one side of the drive, a streak of white metal is clearly visible through the pendulant branches. The only person who ever parked in that little hidey-hole was Nic and by then she was no longer working for us. I rewind and see that she arrived around 6.15 pm, a small detail I never shared with Zane.

She came not only to collect the balance of money owed to her, but specifically to talk to me. I agreed to meet her in Zane's study, and it took every ounce of self-control not to pull her hair out by the roots until she was standing in a pile of pinfeathers. There was an enormous diamond on her finger and my mind was in revolt, unable to hold a rational thought.

'In love?' I said. 'That's a little cliché. If you run off into the sunset with my husband, remember this house is mine. I don't want to listen to your bleeding heart. You've got a nerve choosing tonight of all nights.'

'Wait. I want… I want to make it right. I know you think it's all my fault. But it isn't. Not entirely. You know how he… he wanted to make the role, to make it…'

'Authentic.' I thought I'd help her out.

'Yes. But then it went beyond what we agreed. He was gentle… and then he wasn't, and he became violent.'

'Two violent bosses in the space of a year? Do you realise how ridiculous that sounds? You entered this pitiful agreement of your own accord and from what I've seen and heard, you got what you wanted.'

Of course, Zane would vehemently defend his turf. He had no intention of leaving me to marry her. I advised her never to trespass on my property again or speak to Zane about this conversation. The last thing I saw were the oxeye daisies on her dress, bright yellow florets and white rays flickering along the terrace before fading to black.

But Nic had never left the property. She'd waited for Zane long after I'd gone upstairs to my guests. That was the part I hadn't expected.

Zane disappeared for a while, an hour, maybe less. Initially, I assumed he was showing the Bernes' the house and the grounds but then I found him in his study, smoking. After persuading him upstairs, he addressed his guests with his hands in his pockets. So trivial, yet so significant. Stacking everything I knew and not fully confronting him was a way of keeping a stock of mental ammunition. I thought that by keeping secrets I would catch him in a lie.

I'm startled by a pause of static. The time stamp on the CCTV jumps to 5.42 am the following morning. As expected, there's no sign of Nic's car but the thing I'm trying to make sense of is why? Why had Zane turned off the CCTV?

I remember getting up in the night and seeing red lights through the window. There was something familiar about them, the shape of them. At the time I thought it was Zane going out to meet his friends. But it wasn't Zane's car. It was Nic's. Had she stayed downstairs with my husband until the early hours and driven herself home?

I'd like to say I have the answers I'm looking for, but there's still a little more research to do. I sit alone with a secret I can never share. Life is full of opportunities, doors half open, others firmly locked, but this is one where I hold the only key. If Zane knew *Play Him Play Her* was made possible because of me, it would have been the end of us a year ago.

Like everything, it comes at a cost.

45

ZANE

Squinting against the biting wind, I walk behind the summerhouse to a twist of weeds. There, I dig a narrow trench and bury the last of Nic's things. Then I cover the narrow pocket of earth with grass and walk back inside; dizzy with nausea and an innate fear I can't shake.

Holland Park has never looked so solemn. There won't be time to have coffee and watch the sun rising between the horizon and the sky, my favourite part of the day.

I check *BarbedWire* for the last time. The only comment I focus on is Milo's, which has deeper implications than I'm able to understand. Instead of it being a relevant comment amongst a cluster of many, it appears like a message – a *personal* message – from Milo to me.

The Life-Light blazes out of the darkness and the darkness cannot put it out.

Darkness… why is he talking about darkness.

My mind goes back to that night. A yipping fox and darting shadows. I'm right there, as if it's happening all over again. I remember being too terrified to look at my face in the mirror afterwards and then looking because I couldn't stop myself. Dead eyes and an unfamiliar stare. Me, but not me.

A darker me.

Yes, I committed the crime, and if I get away with it, I'll do whatever I can to survive. It's no good blaming it on a greyout.

There are no such things. Panic attacks, yes, but not the type to give me amnesia.

What I can't get out of my head is the sound of Nic's shouts and the sheer hatred she felt at my rejection. She hadn't fallen in love with me from the standpoint of an obsessed fan. I would have forgiven her for that. She'd plotted and schemed, and I was the sucker she was going to blackmail.

She kept saying my wife knew. But Lilja never *knew*. She suspected enough to push me close to the edge, but I was smart enough not to engage.

Before I'd removed Nic's body, I was careful to disable the power source from the outside CCTV. Since CCTV is everywhere, including my own sodding home, there may be evidence of me parking Nic's Nissan at the beach. Not exactly me, but a person well disguised and carrying a sleeping bag.

They won't find any fingerprints on the body, not after I'd wiped every surface and by *every* I mean Nic's cheeks, her lips, her glossy fingernails – and under them. Although my wife can vouch for the scratches on my chest, she understood a crazed fan, or a reporter had done it.

Can the police prove I'd killed Nic beyond a reasonable doubt? Not if there is significant loss of DNA on a body that has been immersed in water for longer than seventy-two hours. I hope.

They know nothing of her personal effects. Her laptop doesn't exist, although the police may recover files through iCloud. They don't have her phone to extract data from its memory, but I suspect they will access her texts somehow. Mine to her were strictly professional, hers to me were not. How awful it is to be a fugitive with all the current technology to contend with.

The police were in my house and close enough to arrest me. They will determine the money I'd taken rightfully belongs to the Hellman's Trust. It might be a custodial sentence of ten years' imprisonment and a fine. Embezzlement is a serious crime. Now I need to lie low until everything goes back to normal.

I've written Lilja a letter which simply states that the bad press, the accusations, the sheer horror of what I've been through has caused me to withdraw. I've also told her that if anything happens to me, I've left everything to her.

I've also expressed regret over allowing Holloway into our lives. How sorry I was for signing the contract, even at the hint of how R-rated it was and the thought that Bizzy might see it. With acting, I'd told myself to live my lines. Feel them. Breathe them. Push them deep inside until I became them. I should have simply acted, just as Bizzy said.

I've also written to Bizzy, apologising for being such a messed-up father. I hope the tone of my plea carries weight. I'd hate for her to think I don't love her. I do.

I wrote to my agent, Alex Sinclair, telling her I'd rented a cottage in a remote part of Scotland to escape the press. It will throw everyone off my trail for a while. I also said how sorry I was for all the trouble I'd caused her, but being written out of the script was the last straw.

Had I done Holloway justice? Would he be proud of how far we'd come? It's sad that Holloway, the brilliant plastic surgeon who repairs injuries, did not know how to repair mine. He is the one who insisted I do everything for authenticity's sake. My casual encounters, my not so casual encounters, every wrongdoing meticulously planned down to the finest detail. When he congratulated me, it felt like empty flattery. Playing his character was supposed to be fulfilling, but it was much heavier than that.

Now Holloway will be tucked away in a drawer and forgotten. But will he allow it?

There's no more time to waste. I'd like to shower and shave, every whisker washed away, but growing my hair and a beard will keep someone from recognising me. Leaving my wallet, phone and wedding ring on the kitchen counter is a little dramatic, but they'll get the gist.

Taking a last look at Lilja's portrait over the mantelpiece, I realise she has a distinctive style, the uncanny ability to capture a man's attention. She's also a culinary genius – and for what it's worth, she'll stand the test of time better without me.

I take an assortment of pills, enough to down an elephant. If it comes to it, no one will find my remains, nor will they take horrific photographs that my daughter and wife will have to witness.

I shrug on my backpack and pick up my holdall. This is the last time I'll smell these smells, see these sights, and hear these sounds. I take deep breaths and map the images in my mind.

Posting my letters, I walk to the tube station. Pigeons peck at a splatter of rancid milk on the pavement, nascent signs that decay still lingers amongst the opulence of Holland Park. The weather has turned cold in the past few days and the woolly hat pulled down over my head is not unusual, although who needs dark glasses on a cloudy day?

I glance up and down the street and see a man unlocking his car. As if sensing my curiosity, he rotates slowly, failing to spot me behind the bus stop. For the next few seconds, I drop the holdall on the pavement and wait for his car to leave. When I stoop to pick it up again, it's the weight of it, a subtle redistribution of contents that makes me open it. The shirt is exactly as I left it but with one notable difference. There are sharp contours poking through the cotton fabric and larger than wads of cash.

I peel the shirt back and stare at a jumble of books – books on stage and theatre, acting and auditioning – my treasured college books.

The money is gone.

It's not the missing money – a sum that would take me to another country where I could lie low for a while – but the realisation that my wife has played me fairly. Fear tears through me and I nearly lose my balance.

When?

How?

Why hadn't I checked it before leaving the house?

I was in a hurry. I'm always in a hurry.

Every noise is soupy and thick, and the ground seems to ripple. Two pedestrians swinging a bag of shopping between them prevent me from yelling and punching a hole in the bus stop wall. I make no reply when they say good morning.

Then an idea wedges itself in my mind. I fully expect it to be gone, taken like the rest of my hoard, but £400 is still in the side pocket of my backpack and a further £15,000 hidden in a camping pot. I hear the staccato of my heart fading and I can breathe again.

The tube station across the street will give me a head start to Heathrow Airport via the Elizabeth line, stopping at Terminals 2 and 3. I hurl the books in the nearest skip and don't look back. A man carrying a leather holdall and purchasing a single ticket with cash is untraceable. Except for the plane ticket I bought with Lilja's card.

A high-pitched siren makes me jump and I stand on the platform, occasionally looking over my shoulder. As a fast train blows by on the other track, horn blaring, I search the nearest line for mine. It's still sitting at the points, waiting to be ushered in.

Come on, come on, come on. I'm dancing on my feet.

The screech of metal on metal, and it rolls in. I barely wait for the departing passengers before finding a seat inside. The train takes its sweet time to leave the station and the knot in my chest unwinds as the train cuts through the tunnels. The compartment is eerily cold. Only a handful of passengers this morning. Thirty-odd minutes of opening doors and closing doors and I can only hope the police don't stop and search this train.

Finally, the announcement for Heathrow.

I take out my phone in case Meggy is trying to call. But the infernal buzzing isn't a text from her. It's from my wife.

The police are here again. They've got a search warrant; the house is a crime scene. I understand they interviewed you in London. I expect that's where you are.

A bouncing ellipsis says she's still typing.

I know you're reading this.

A thick silence creeps through the air. It's all too easy to settle into the sunlit carriage, its curved walls shutting out the elements and smothering any fear. Not when I've overlooked the one means police have to track me.

My sodding phone.

A familiar frisson of panic sizzles in my stomach. Time to make myself invisible. As the doors open, I drop it between the step and the platform, leaving my past behind.

Trending: #InZane

@HeyWhatsUP: Lookee here. ZaneO's missing now.
I'm already singing the theme tune to *Jaws*.

@HackedOff: ZaneO is too arrogant and stuck up his
own arse. Profoundly incapable of functioning in the
real world. Unfollowing.

@Titmouse: Someone needs to regulate this kind of
press abuse. This is a new low. ZaneO doesn't need
to apologise for going missing. Poor guy needs a
break.

@CirceAtNight: All you armchair detectives com-
menting on the Nicola Gatlin case. This is a woman's
LIFE! Not a sodding Netflix show.

@HeyWhatsUP: @CirceAtNight To be fair, it will
become a Netflix show.

46

LILJA

For days, the police investigation focuses on Zane's study. Forensic teams have removed carpets and floorboards, scouring every inch of the corridors and wine cellar. They have dug up sections of the lawn and used ground penetrating radar for reasons they won't divulge.

Bizzy and I pack to go to Mum's, trying not to flinch over the crashing of boxes and dollies. We can't return until the police have cleared it.

Their rigorous interrogation charting my movements after Zane's birthday party is normal procedure. But it will leave us all scarred. Detective Symonds is happy to learn how I'd recovered most of the money from the Hellman's Trust. Our business manager, who oversees the taxes and payroll, knows how I struggled with a slowly haemorrhaging bank account. If it weren't for her advice to move the remainder to another account, I'd be penniless now.

It took Meggy two days to file a police report. Two precious days which would have prevented Zane from leaving the country. I expect she was afraid she'd struck a client and caused him to bleed. But her wounds were just as deep. Apparently, she'd seen Zane and Nic at Mol's Coffee shop a few times but as a therapist she was bound to discretion. I never divulged I'd stalked her, or that I knew she wanted to warn me. But I do think of her as a friend.

Adrie Vander-Meulen weighs in on the gossip. The same tribe of accusers who have defined how Zane's fans think have created new memes. Fans latch onto every post, cranking out comment after shouty comment, desperate for a piece of the Osborne pie.

But the drama isn't confined to *BarbedWire*. The news is rife with sympathy for me. Statements about what I must be thinking, published by everyone other than me. I am surprised to learn that a large majority of the public are still sympathetic to Zane and refuse to believe he's a fugitive. The police will comment soon, I'm sure.

I've left a message with the principal at Bizzy's school saying she won't be back next week, although I know she'll have to face a barrage of questions when she returns.

It's just the four of us at Mum's cottage today. Mum and Frank are cooking bangers and mash, while Bizzy and I play Scrabble. I notice she keeps checking her phone and I wonder if it's a love interest. Lucky for me, she leaves it on the table when Mum tells her to wash her hands.

The screen lights up with incoming notifications and swivelling the phone around, I see they're coming from *BarbedWire*. Eighteen replies to a regular commenter on the #InZane thread. There I was, worried about exposing Bizzy to her father's sexploits and yet here she is, my impish, ingenious daughter, offering vulgar and mocking comments under the handle, HeyWhatsUP.

The overriding urge is to give her a standing ovation. As she walks back in with clean hands, I say, 'Hey what's up?'

Her eyes go wide and then flick to her phone. 'Mum, you didn't.'

'I did and I can. You're underage.'

We laugh over a cup of tea as Mum and Frank try to put the world to rights. This time I don't shield Bizzy from anything.

Mum's shaking head tells me what's coming next. 'I suppose he thought he could get laid. Never mind the consequences.'

'It wasn't just the once,' I say.

'It's a win for you. Publicly you're the model wife.'

'Privately, I've behaved rather badly.'

'You survived. You both have.'

'You know what I regret the most?' I say. 'Stella scrubbed and cleaned every room. She could have inadvertently covered his arse.'

'The police can still find DNA,' Frank says. 'Somehow blood sticks to things, and it's hard to wash out.'

Frank puts his hand over Bizzy's. 'As strong as you are defending people's rights and making sure no one gets excluded at school, how will you get through this?'

'Maybe I'll write a memoir.'

Frank's smile widens as Mum pours him a Baileys. 'You'll both grow stronger every day, even when the pain splits your heart open. There will be no issue getting primary custody. You can cite him for abandonment and neglect. Let's not forget emotional, psychological, and mental abuse. I can attest to all of it.'

For now, I haven't processed what life will feel like without Zane. But I know this. I won't feel my throat tighten every time I hear footsteps. When the evil he's set in motion finally registers, there'll be no warm, elegant study to relax in, and no plush rug on which to walk barefoot. There will only be a thin layer of nylon to screen him from extreme temperatures and feral creatures. He will go hungry. He will not survive.

Berne Brothers have fired him, his agent no longer represents him, and I intend to make a statement to the press urging Zane to come home. If only to serve him with divorce papers. As for Bizzy, his frightening behaviour has hurt her, and for that I'm sorry.

The phone rings. It's DC Symonds. She tells me the police recovered Zane's phone at Gloucester Road station, where he changed trains for Heathrow. Unfortunately, CCTV footage hadn't identified him. The Sûreté du *Québec* in Canada confirmed he had passed through immigration minutes before the detainer came through. The paper trail then fizzles out. She's sorry Zane put me through all this, especially using coercive control through his character. I appreciate her phone calls and her willingness to keep me updated.

It's evening when my phone rings again. Maybe it's the blocked number or the static that makes me feel Zane is trying to reach me. I say nothing. Then the line goes dead.

I miss the old him and I make peace with the fact that Bizzy does, too. Phone silence is a reminder that he's no longer part of our family, but it is also a reminder of how great silence is.

The rest of the week is a series of highs and lows. Mum and I make Heta Nötter, a snack of toasted almonds, cashews and sun-flower seeds tossed in chili balsamic and served with Västerbotten cheese. I'm half laughing and crying and completely wrung out by the weekend. Bizzy and Mum look concerned at my outbursts, but they let me vent.

When Stan's name lights up on my phone, I sit on the front steps and gaze out to sea. He sighs, hollowed out by whatever he has to say.

'Nic's body was badly decomposed and trace evidence couldn't link Zane to her. Fibres are still being analysed and I'm hoping for better news. After police found Marschōne Robinson's watch on her body, they brought him in for more questioning. He fired Nic for destructive behaviour and wouldn't elaborate further. He also added that she never drank inappropriately or took drugs. The press will publish this today.'

Looking back, when I'd called Marschōne for Nic's references, his answers lacked passion. I should have known.

Stan continues, 'Since Nic parked her car near Langston cliffs, there is reason to believe she went there after the party. Police have matched scrapes along the side of her car with those of the nurse's car, which swerved off the road and crashed into a guardrail.'

'It just seems odd to me,' I say, 'that nobody found her body until the article came out in *DevonLive*.'

'Bodies have washed up days later, sometimes after months have passed and sometimes not at all. I'm sorry two teenagers found her remains, half clothed and without dignity.'

Car park CCTV would have proved Zane's innocence or guilt had the camera not been pointing at the ground. Rusty hinges and a broken bracket were to blame, and Stan believes weathering caused it. There is not enough evidence to prove Zane did anything and the frustration will stay with me for years. He promises to use his contacts in Canada and will keep me updated. The call ends with the usual, "I'll keep in touch."

With only a few more days before summer break, Bizzy will recover at home. I've invited George and Saneh to stay and I intend to make it fun.

47

LILJA

Three months later.

It's an early November morning and there's frost on the lawn. As sea air blows in with a gale, a vision of Zane's face comes to me, the crushing press of his hands, my back pinned against the wall. Each time I walk around the house, the silence is unsettling. It's what a fox must feel, as it creeps from its burrow at night, never knowing whether a predator might be outside.

The buzzer to the front gate jolts me out of my thoughts. CCTV tells me it's DC Symonds, alone this time.

She sits in the kitchen, a mug of freshly made hot chocolate in her lap.

'The Royal Newfoundland Constabulary interviewed locals in Northern Labrador. No one remembered him. But a tracker found his camp somewhere south of Makkovik. He brought back a few personal belongings, including a ripped sleeping bag stained with a large quantity of blood. DNA matched it to Zane's and concluded he must have died from a bear attack. They are still hoping to find his remains. I'm sorry.'

I can't seem to summon any tears and I'm thankful she keeps talking.

'We received a diary. It was waterlogged and impossible to decipher, but we salvaged a few pages. Would you be able to tell if it's your husband's writing?'

I feel the churn of nerves. She hands me a copy and the angular scrawl leaves me with no doubt.

> *Day 14*
> *Temp: 2°C*
> *Another full stack of firewood*
> *2 litres of water*
>
> *The wind is pounding, and I'll have to reinforce the tent. Sleet is coming down in sheets and I keep hearing snapping twigs. There's something out there. I'm questioning myself. Questioning why I'm here. I must live with what I've done.*
>
> *Today is the first day I'm feeling weak from lack of protein. I'm sleeping more. There are signs of animals everywhere. Scat, footprints, snapped twigs, fresh burrows. There are no rabbits in my traps. The landscape has shifted, water and mud puddle the grass and the horizon seems to move with the light.*
>
> *Day 15*
> *Temp: 1°C*
> *Half stack of firewood*
> *1 litre of water*
>
> *No more rain. Clouds and snow. Another tent day preserving body heat in my sleeping bag. I've had the first good cry in days, asking God for food. Whether God's up there or not, I don't know. My pleas must be going through to voicemail.*
>
> *The ice has driven the fish from the shallows and wading in icy water is not an option. I came here to get away from all the noise, the media accusations. Now I feel alone.*

There was too much pressure to be something great and now I'm insignificant. There are things out here that make my heart pound. Wild animals large and small. I'm feeling things I've never felt. Cut off from the world, I know how it feels to be a victim. It's so cold.

Day 16
Temp: 0°C
Quarter stack of firewood
Half a litre of water

Clouds and snow. I think of you and how I've let you down. I took away all your hopes and dreams and I had no right.

It gets tougher and tougher as the days go by. All I want to do is go home. Back to you, to my little girl and my old life. Then I realise how far away it is.

Day 17
Temp: -1°C
3 pieces of firewood
Quarter litre of water

I'm not usually this sentimental. I try to be as upbeat as possible but there's something about this place that pulls it out of you. I try not to think about you, but I can't stop thinking about what I did to you and it's tearing me up.

Weather, weather, weather. Just as you get a tiny slice of sunshine and you pin your hopes to it, down comes the snow. The cold permeates everything, and you must struggle to keep warm and dry.

It's your face I see in the clouds. There. Your chin. Your nose. Then it all breaks away because you're gone.

Day 18
Temp: -2°C
No more firewood
Tipped water over. Collecting snow.

I'm cold, wet, and scared. It gets to me psychologically and mentally. Sometimes I see a man between the trees. His face is craggy and old and the slant of his eyes and smile is familiar. He's looking out for me, making sure I eat. I think he's the one who keeps leaving fox and mice outside my shelter. I wish I could talk to him.

I know what you're thinking. I'm seeing things. I'm already mad, but I don't think I've peaked yet. There's still sanity in me. A few ounces, at least. My life isn't over yet.

Everything is damp. One sweater is mouldy. I can't go on. Tent feels like a tomb.

Don't know what day it is.
Thermometer blurred.
Freezing cold. No food. No water.
I don't want to die. Thinking of you.

Then a postscript:

I know you did it. I don't know how. When I come home, you won't see me. But you'll know I'm there.

I feel like there's a ticking time bomb in my chest, an unnatural glitch. Detective Nora asks me what Zane is talking about. I tell her I don't know. We both agree the postscript seems out of place with his state of mind. Were the previous paragraphs fabricated to make us think he's dying? I'm not the first to have witnessed the demon hiding beneath the veneer, and I won't be the last.

'You don't think he could have found help?' I ask.

'It's possible.'

I know what she's thinking and doesn't say. There was too much blood to say he could have walked anywhere.

After Nora leaves, I put on a puffy jacket and sit on the terrace. I'm in that strange limbo of a marriage I haven't parted with yet. It's easy to feel him in the garden, circling the hydrangeas, worried if the frost and snow this year will finally destroy them. Sometimes his ghost saunters towards the edge of the pond and lingers there, roaming through the reeds.

He looks at me, his eyes dark and wild. 'Why? Why did you do it?'

I bite back a swell of tears. 'I hated what you became.'

Again, that brittle laugh, his mouth smoothed into a chilly smile. The feel of his fingers biting into my flesh, leaving half-moon punctures with his nails. Every time I hear his voice, it's like a breath exhaled.

Then a sunray streams through the trees, turning the garden a blood orange. A flagstone catches my eye. The imprint of a dragon, once traced in wet concrete, its tail smudged by a child's hand. The words, *For my daddy* are as distinct now as they were then.

I rewind to an earlier time, when a coffee pot gurgled on the stove and Bizzy, six years old, sat at her miniature table with a wonky leg. Crayon crooked in her left hand and tongue pinking on her lip. Zane put on one of my hats and did a scene from *My Fair Lady,* where Eliza is having tea with the *Eynsford-Hill*s and recounting how her aunt was 'done in.' I hear a childish giggle and sag, tears streaming.

Then a voice. 'Ssh.'

The sight of Burgess causes a tug in my chest. He sits beside me and bumps my shoulder with his as if I'm a fragile thing.

I feel my cheeks flushing and clear the choke in my throat. 'You never think it's all going to come crashing down, do you?' For a mad moment, I feel an urgent need for him to hold me.

'You shouldn't be alone,' he whispers, his massive shoulder warm against mine. 'I'll make you a cup of coffee.'

'I'm caffeined out.'

'Baileys then.'

His face puckers an apology and the gentleness in his manner undoes something in me. I let him pull me into his arms and we sit in a tangled huddle.

'I know you're scared,' he says. 'But they'll find his remains next year when the snow melts.'

There's a creeping unease in my bones. No one knows what it's like waking up in the night and reaching out for him. Not because I miss him. Or still love him.

But an unfathomable twinge that he might come home.

48

LILJA

I jog upstairs to the bathroom and turn on the shower. We're going out for a celebratory dinner with Mum and Frank. I feel drained but calmer than I have been in days.

Nic's death still haunts me. In unexpected moments, the sound of her voice, the pleading, the tears, brings a tendril of panic. Why had I recoiled from her? Why had I treated her with contempt? I remind myself it was because she was my husband's mistress.

After dressing in a cream cotton twill dress and pearls, I hesitate on the landing to compose myself. One thing in particular sets my mind on edge. Zane's erratic moods, especially in relation to me. His near-violent response — the way he looked at me as if I was a lower species. I wondered then if demons could take the shape of men.

My phone rings. It's Stan Marriott and I don't answer. I'm too busy admiring Bizzy's hair which is tamed into submission, swept back like Mum's and the blue tips are gone. She's swaddled in a blue cable V-neck dress and biker boots and Saneh wears a sequin top and satin trouser set, her long dark hair swinging to her waist. George runs across the hall floor dressed in a suit; his blond curls even wilder after a combing.

'How do we look?' Bizzy asks, arms around her best friends.

'You all look gorgeous.'

Bizzy doesn't have to tell me Nic helped her pick out her outfit at Next. She doesn't have to tell me how much she misses her. Nic was the elder sister she never had.

If Zane is still alive, his narcissistic tendencies won't allow him to stay off social media for long. Let him see how far I've come. Let him see the old me he once fell in love with and the new Lilja he can't have.

I ask Bizzy to take pictures of me and I post them on TikTok. I want to show everyone why I'm celebrating.

'You look stunning,' Mum says as I join them downstairs.

Frank gives me a kiss on both cheeks and tells me he's getting his jacket.

'What are the police saying about the driver?' Bizzy's hand loops through mine, anchoring me in place.

Then I realise what Bizzy just said. *What are the police saying about the driver?* It's like all the bird sounds and cars rushing past in the street have receded into the background and only her voice is pounding in my ears.

Bizzy hands me her phone and I read the headlines.

**Police hunt male driver in
connection with hit-and-run**

By Stan Marriott
Senior Reporter

15:22, 20 NOVEMBER 2022

The driver of a white Nissan that collided with a nurse in a hit-and-run in June has been identified as a man in his early forties.

Victoria Wojcik, a nurse at Dawlish Community Hospital, sustained a fractured skull as a result and later died.

Ms Wojcik stated that a car deliberately swerved into her during the early hours although she wasn't able to confirm the date. Officers confirmed via CCTV that the oncoming car was going well over the speed limit and was weaving. The driver involved left the scene without stopping.

The driver was originally thought to be female, but a spokesperson for Devon and Cornwall Police have revealed that CCTV identified him as male. He was wearing a hoodie, which Wojcik likely mistook as long hair.

Officers have released an image from the CCTV and are keen to locate the driver of the vehicle involved. Anyone with any information is asked to call 101 or email 101@dc.police.UK quoting CR/036821/23.

No doubt, this is what Stan wanted to talk about. The accompanying photos show a happy twenty-nine-year-old in a navy-blue blazer and jeans, and a smile that made you want to know her. The second picture is too grainy to process, but the face with the drawn back lips and fingers curled over the steering wheel are all too familiar to me. I realise I'm leaning against Bizzy and she's holding me. A beat passes.

'Do you think it's Dad?'

I reach for her hand. 'No, he couldn't have done this. It was an accident. That's what they're saying. A terrible accident.'

When I think back to that night, was it a mix of rage and concern that drove Zane on? Had my husband killed Nic in our house? Had he — and this is the part I can't stomach — hidden her in the boot of her own car and driven to Langstone Rock? Then dumped her in the sea, left her car in the car park, and somehow walked the four miles back home?

Before all this happened, he'd hit a car coming the other way. I try to find excuses for what my husband had done. It all ties in now with what Stan Marriot had told me.

I wish I could believe Zane had simply dropped his phone,

leaned down to retrieve it and then almost collided with the nurse. A stupid, reckless thing to do. One of them had to get out of the lane to make way for the other, and Zane made the fatal decision.

Or had he simply given way to road rage?

Perhaps he never heard a screech of metal and brakes over the music he might have been playing. Somehow, I picture a flash in his rearview mirror, and imagine a driver staggering onto the kerb. Superficial injuries. Nothing more. Until my mind absorbs the sheer power of a headlong collision with a barrier.

He should have pulled over; he should have called for help. He could have. But he didn't. Two souls took leave of the earth that night because of Zane.

As we drive to the restaurant, my mind wanders again. The police may never know how Zane became entangled with Holloway or that he was the true perpetrator of these terrible crimes. The serious collisions investigators will piece together their report and whose door will be they knocking on?

Will they sue me for my husband's wrongdoing? Is this how Zane will strip me of my newfound peace? I trust the police and lawyers to determine that outcome if it ever becomes known. It's never too late to turn the day around. But it's too late for Nic and the nurse.

I know you did it. I don't know how.

I sit with my family as we raise our glasses to celebrate turning the house into a restaurant. Elin and Paul have decided to come and work for me full-time and Mum and Frank will help in the office. It should be a joyous occasion, but inside, I'm in a trancelike state.

I remember receiving the invitation to Marschōne's dinner party only yesterday. I made an excuse and said I had the stomach flu. At least, that's what I told Zane. I don't know what made me put this plan in motion, but I was angry he'd had one-night stands with servers, publicists, agents, and director's assistants. I could never prove it, but I knew it wouldn't take a watch on a chain to hypnotise Zane into an affair this time, not when he was already using the front door like a cat flap.

I devised a scheme to uncover the details of his infidelity.

Zane was always happiest in his study with his characters, burrowing deep inside their minds until he couldn't find a way back. He had no idea of the months I spent doing classes on my laptop, studying dialogue and dabbling at screenplays. Writing a saleable story with a guaranteed audience draw was the hard part.

Using "James English" as a pen name, I wrote a script on spec, knowing a team of writers would change the screenplay for the better. There was no need to shop it around or find a producer who was a good match for the overall vibe, not when I overheard Simon Berne on the phone telling Zane exactly what he was looking for.

His agent never sent him Episode 2. The copy I left on the stairs outside his study was written by me. A more threatening version which had Holloway hell-bent on not only drugging and killing Amaya but other patients as well. Zane never discussed it with Simon, but he certainly discussed it with Nic.

A brilliant doctor healing burn victims is now a serial killer. Don't you think it cheapens the whole thing?

Perhaps. But it drove Zane to do the honours – getting rid of the woman who had double-crossed both of us. Better him than me.

Did Simon invite James English to meet with him? Yes. Many times, but James refused, citing intense mental trauma after writing Holloway. He borrowed Burgess' voice on the few occasions Simon's writers needed to unwrap Holloway by phone.

There was draft after draft, rewrite after rewrite, all requested by either Simon or Zane. You could say I was a method writer, disappearing into Holloway for as many hours as I could secretly invest. Unlike Zane, I could switch him off.

Once the series was optioned, lead actors chosen and production funds were available, it was green lit. They paid "James English" a fee for the rights to a bank account under the business name Impasta, which if anyone cared to dig deeper, is mine.

Zane signed the contract for an erotic thriller to improve his ratings. He assured me there no nudity, no lurid sex scenes, no gratuitous violence, but I knew *Play Him, Play Her* had all of these.

There was no way to dilute Holloway's power, not once Zane had mapped and committed the script to memory. My poor, unsuspecting husband was sent on the ride of his life. He may have got all the recognition for playing Holloway, but Holloway was mine first and so were his words.

The red dress I wrote in the script originated from the dress Zane's father's mistress wore at the beach. It was something Zane often referred to in his sadder moments. You could say I used it as a psychology hack to mess with his mind.

I'd met Nic at one of Simon Berne's dinner parties last year, a lively girl in a sweet yellow dress and a mouth made for kissing. Everything Zane craved. It took £10,000 to persuade an out of work actor to play a part without cameras for which I was the director. She was brilliant. Amaya Stone could have been written for her.

I wanted to believe Zane would never betray me. I wanted to. But I knew in my heart he would fail the test. I've memorised all the emails between them, the photos, and the time I saw her kissing him in his study. But I'd underestimated her. You could say Nic was a seduction well played. She played me as much as she played him. Now she's *gone* forever, her light smothered for good. That's the part I could never have anticipated.

But she wasn't the only one who wanted to be his wife. Women loved Zane and he knew it. He'd always have someone – a hot server, a lonely widow, a closeted screenwriter, a producer. He proved beyond a reasonable doubt that he was a serial cheater.

The icing on the cake was impersonating Zane's agent while he was pursuing Bizzy and me in the car that night. I thought he would fall to pieces and give up the chase, and we'd be home free. Although writing him out of the script was a stroke of genius, the tragedy was how tormented he became. It uncovered a rage in him I could never have imagined.

There are secrets in every family, and this will always be mine. I wonder if my heart has a dark streak, an untapped fragment I've never known about. If so, Zane and I aren't that different after all.

He may have disappeared, but I know he's out there somewhere. I can *feel* him.

49

ZANE

**30-year mystery solved – partial remains
found on Newfoundland riverbank identified
as missing Dawlish doctor**

By Stan Marriott
Senior Reporter

13:22, 27 NOVEMBER 2022

Human remains found on the shores of the Big River
in Nunatsiavut, Newfoundland have been identified
as belonging to a 59-year-old Dr Braylon Osborne
who disappeared from Devon over thirty years ago.

Dr Osborne, from Dawlish, went missing on 11 April
1992 during a camping trip. Officials have ruled the
death accidental. He was the father of actor Zane Osborne, star of the hit Netflix show *Play Him, Play Her*.

In a bizarre twist, Zane Osborne went missing in
Labrador, Newfoundland, earlier this month and is
thought to have died in a bear attack. The actor made
headlines earlier this year when the body of his personal assistant Nicola Gatlin was found at Langstone

Rock. Police are keen to speak to Zane Osborne about the death of Gatlin, 19.

Newfoundland Police are appealing to anyone who may have seen Zane Osborne and would like to hear from anyone who had been camping or hiking along the lower reaches of the Big River.

In 1992, Dr Osborne's tent was found empty, with small animal bones littered near the remains of a campfire. It was thought that a 36-hour deluge and high winds on the week of his disappearance may have contributed to the accident. His remains were identified based on DNA analysis and old police reports of the incident.

The family expressed gratitude over the identification and recovery of Dr Braylon Osborne and remain hopeful that his son's remains will also be found. Specialist trained officers continue to support the family, and police enquiries into Zane Osborne's disappearance are ongoing.

* * *

If Stan were to write an article about me, he'd say I chartered a helicopter to an undisclosed location, somewhere beside a river and a dense boreal forest of spruce and fir. He'd say I dug a hole in the ground with a jawbone found near my camp and fashioned an A-framed cabin with bark shingles, the base of which was made from rock to retain the heat. He'd say I was remarkably resourceful — like father like son.

When I first arrived, I imagined Dad leaning against a tree, his accent Canadian and with a beard as long as Gandalf's. He had never been one of those weekend backpackers, he was a survivalist and he'd go camping for days if he could find the time. He'd have backup upon backup plan, and his stamina was unmatched.

Me? Not so much. I had to use my radio to alert an Inuit seafarer, Atanarjuat, who was willing to bring food from the mainland. He never asked my name, and I never gave it.

Over the next few weeks, my shelter evolved with more tools I bought from a hardware store in Goose Bay. At night grizzlies and wolverines trampled a path around my tent, smelling the fish I'd caught in my gillnet which was drying on a frame above the fire. When the snow came, foxes robbed my snares and fish was scarce. I needed Atanarjuat more than ever.

If anyone should come searching, they won't find the ground outside my shelter strewn with chocolate wrappers and an empty bottle of triple malt. Scout motto: *Be Prepared.* I buried those weeks ago.

They will find a diary. Of course, by then I will be long gone. My remains nibbled by the local wildlife, my skeleton stripped clean.

Or you might see an elegant man standing next to you at the station or eating a croissant in a bistro. You'll wonder why you're drawn to his dark eyes, the tilt of his head, the angle of his jaw, but you won't be able to put your finger on why.

Then you'll say, 'It's that man… you know the one…' Fingers snapping, hands waving, as you try to think of his name. But by the time you remember, he'll have disappeared into the crowds. Even then, it could have been a lookalike. There are so many of them about.

It's too late to remedy the damage, but it's not too late to set Holloway alight. I take three long breaths, strike that mental match and his face chars at the cheeks. It's like a series of fizzes before the light goes off, a burnt-out element in my head.

Is he really gone? Only time will tell.

Holloway had become a living thing, diverting me from decency and dropping me full pelt into depravity. He infected all of us with his cancer. But you, my darling wife, knew the evil that lived inside him. You knew what he was.

I feel strangely calm now as each day tumbles into the next. Wind no longer stirs the water. Milky ice has sculpted it into sheets. I hear the singular call of a little auk, driven inland by the storm, climbing higher and higher until it is a tiny silhouette in the grey drifting clouds.

Trending: #InZane

@HeyWhatsUP: He's not dead. He'll resurface in a month or two and write a no holds barred book under an assumed name.

@SherylAdams: @HeyWhatsUP I'm not going to dignify that with a response.

@HeyWhatsUP: @SherylAdams You already have.

@SherylAdams: @HeyWhatsUP The way you desperately cling to rumours is laughable given the vile crap that spews from your mouth. You should apologise for this rubbish take.

@HeyWhatsUP: @SherylAdams Not a rumour. Not apologising. This story isn't over yet.

NOTE FROM THE AUTHOR

Like other small-presses and independent authors, I rely heavily on word-of-mouth recommendations to reach new readers. A positive review would mean the world to me. All you readers are the champions of our industry and if you loved the book, then you are the one I wrote it for!

Preordering from your favourite author helps build buzz and is so important to the success of a novel. It sends a message to the publisher that readers are excited for an author's work, characters, and that series. I want to thank you for your support, and I hope you love *Play Him Play Her* as much as I do.

You can leave a review on my Amazon book page.

ACKNOWLEDGEMENTS

As always, I owe an enormous debt to so many people, without whom this book would not have been possible. My sincere gratitude to everyone who gave their time, talents, and support.

Thank you to my developmental and structural editor, David Imrie, for being astute and ambitious, and always pushing me a little harder with each book. Many thanks, too, to my eagle-eyed copy editor Sandra Mangan, for sharing your experiences as a reporter, and your journalistic expertise over Stan Marriott. He would have been a reporter without borders in the worst possible way if you hadn't reigned him in a little. Thank you to Meggy for showing me how good therapy works. To proofreaders Babs Morton and Kristin Gleeson for all your helpful suggestions and encouragement. Your passion and responsiveness have been amazing. Thank you for your faith in me.

I owe a special debt to Jane Dixon-Smith for the amazing cover and for her incredible work on the book's behalf. You really are a life saver! There isn't enough space to acknowledge every actor I have met, interviewed, or simply watched in awe from the sidelines. Thank you for everything you've taught me. I'm sure you are all keen to tell me what I got wrong about The Method. I respectfully refer you to the (fictional) Zane Osborne for his advice and expertise, thereby saving me from abject humiliation. Special gratitude to film producers and directors Charlie Lepper and John Schlesinger CBE for making me a better writer.

To Kelly Lacey at Love Books Tours for organising the book tour and so many heartfelt thanks to all the fabulous bloggers and reviewers who participated. betweenkirstyscovers, readingonthebrink, cosykindler, book_a_holic_17, bek.is.reading, martinkm_reads, the.b00kreader, reading.runes, emma_bookaholic, cherumanalil, fiction_vixen18, id_ratherbereading_247, bluefairybugsbooks, amorina.cartlon, lauren.bookstagram3, lozzieloves, afelton6212, bookaddict.twylie68, roxyrecommends, katieluvstoread, ericas_bookreviews, book_mouse2020, pagesand_pieces, bookdrunk, librarybooks_vs_ebooks, catreader18, onewriterswords, Sue.wallace1974, marbooks88, leebookadventures, twilight_reader. You guys rock!

Most of all thank you to my readers. Whether you've been with me from the start or whether this is the first of my books you've read, you are the reason I can make a small living doing what I love. Please keep leaving reviews, keep supporting independent books shops and indie authors, and most of all keep reading! Three cheers for putting up with Zane's #inzanity. I hope you know how grateful I am. All mistakes are mine, made mostly for the benefit of the story.

Last but not least, thank you to Jeff for telling me not to sweat the small stuff and for loving me the way I am. For Jamie, my coffee and walking buddy, for always making me howl with laughter. To my twin brother, Mark, for just being there. Our hilarious convos back and forth across the pond have made me feel less isolated and alone. To big bruv Giles for telling me not to let the bastards grind me down. And to Edward, my darling boss, who provides hourly interruptions in the hope I will serve and buttle for him as if my life depended on it. Meow to you too!

www.ingramcontent.com/pod-product-compliance
Lightning Source LLC
Chambersburg PA
CBHW011410310726
48972CB00011B/2912

9 798990 487116

ABOUT THE AUTHOR

Claire worked in hotel and catering, and as an Executive Assistant for companies in the UK, US and Hong Kong. She loves doing writing courses with Curtis Brown and her award-winning novels owe much to her years as a member of the Albuquerque Police Citizen's Academy where her main focus was the impact of violence towards women.

Originally from Bradfield, UK, Claire worked in London before moving to Utah, where she now lives with her family and her cat, Edward.